The End of New York

Booze, Broads and Brazilian Jiu-Jitsu

Zach Danesh

Archway Publishing books may be ordered through booksellers or by contacting:

Archway Publishing
1663 Liberty Drive
Bloomington, IN 47403
www.archwaypublishing.com
1 (888) 242-5904

ISBN: 978-1-4808-7302-5 (sc)
ISBN: 978-1-4808-7303-2 (e)

Library of Congress Control Number: 2018914714

Print information available on the last page.

Archway Publishing rev. date: 08/19/2019

Contents

In the Beginning There Was SoHo

2 009 was a good year; 2009 was the beginning. I graduated from a small art school in downtown Miami. I had studied printmaking; I was naive, a romantic, enamored with the past: surely, the world would give up on computers and go back to print media.

I moved on from Miami, pushing away paradise and reaching out for a land beyond. I left my home of five years and didn't give it a second thought. I a week with my folks in Massachusetts then took off on a bus for New York City.

New York City was the height of hip. This was where it was all happening. This was where every liberal arts kid with ambition was meant to be.

A friend of mine had left for New York the year before. He offered me one of his two bedrooms for very little money. He could easily have gotten way more money for the room, but he knew I was broke. He was seven years older than I and a day trader. He did me the favor of giving me the room for peanuts. I was a fortunate mooch.

I moved in with only a duffle bag of essentials. I needed a job right away, though I had saved a nest egg working at Jones Street Lounge in Miami. I scoured the city for a job with my Miami experience, which nobody in New York took seriously. I thought Jones Street Lounge in the East Village would be a guarantee, seeing as I had worked for the same establishment in Miami. Bad timing, they didn't have space for me.

I was only slightly panicked. I wouldn't let my nest egg get depleted. I was determined to get a job, any job. I knew it wouldn't be permanent; I just needed money. Jobs in the food and beverage game are never long-term. You always either quit or get fired.

I dropped off my lackluster resumes around the City, and got a call back for a spot in SoHo right across the street from my apartment. It was an Irish pub, at the same location as Skip and Aidan's in *Sex and the City*. This would prove to be a repeating theme: I had no idea the effect that show had had on the world until I moved to the City.

That restaurant wasn't half bad, as restaurants go. The staff was mainly female, hired for their beauty. I was a barback and busboy. We held *Sex and the City* tours. A bartender would line up rows of cosmopolitans and have them ready for horny housewives to imbibe with their girlfriends. My job was to collect the empty glasses . . . and flirt. I immediately had a cold war going with the other barback. He was like a Mexican Quasimodo and feared I would encroach on his job. That never happened. I was getting paid peanuts and couldn't support myself on it. I eventually quit, probably a week before I would have gotten fired.

The city was sublime. I had always loved it; it had always been a thrill to be in the Big Apple. Now was different. New York City was to be my new home. It was a totally different experience now, absorbing its milieu with razor intention. The textures of buildings, the smells of alleyways, and sounds of bustling streets flooded my senses. Miami was already a dimming memory. New York City was my now. And now was a feast for my younger self to gorge on.

The city encouraged your ego. It felt acceptable to be totally self-absorbed, and strange to think of others for very long. There was one common denominator among young people in the city: we were out for number one. We were here to be rock stars, not groupies. You could be a star in a variety of ways: actor, musician, chef, bartender, banker, driver, plumber, whatever. It didn't matter what the endeavor was. It only mattered that you were the best at it.

My friend who had hooked me up with his second bedroom was getting tired of me and wanted me to leave. I think it was partly due to me cramping his bachelor style: I walked in on him once watching a gay Israeli film on a large projector. I caught an overhead shot of two young men copulating missionary style; I hadn't realized that was possible.

"Hi, man." I said as I walked into the living room.

"Hey, bro," he said, only glancing at me.

"What are you watching?" I tried to show I was mature enough not to wince.

"It's a gay Israeli film."

"Oh, cool. I haven't seen that one."

"It's all right."

"Do dudes usually do it like that?"

"Yes, that happens a lot of the time."

"Oh, well, you learn something new every day."

"Yep."

"All right then, goodnight, bro."

"Night, bro."

Soon after that he asked me to pack my bags and scram. I was nervous about the sudden move. I had never gone searching for an apartment before and felt ill equipped. For all the things they teach in high school and college, they don't prepare you at all for real life. I had had a friend growing up who was blessed with money. We had lost touch over the years. He felt bad about that and wanted to make amends, so he offered me a place to stay.

Daniel had an illegal apartment off "Murder Avenue" (what people used to call Myrtle Avenue, which runs from Brooklyn to Queens). The neighborhood was getting better, but people still knew it by that name. It was a barebones flophouse next to a laundromat and across from a Hasidic middle school. We did have a view of the East River, though. There was no stove, oven, refrigerator or freezer. I didn't have much, so Daniel gave me some blankets to sleep on. The shower was just a spout from the ceiling that would spray freezing cold water into a drain in the floor. Daniel would do woodworking in the middle of the living space. Saw dust acted as a carpet. This kind of arrangement really only seemed feasible when you were a twenty-something.

Daniel had a job; he would drive his truck down to Red Hook to work with a Norwegian painter. I was envious. I didn't have the skills to work in an artistic environment. I had studied printmaking, but it was 2009, so there were barely any printing studios around. Also, the money in printing was lousy.

I took a stroll by myself one night down Murder Avenue. It was quiet midweek. I only saw a few Pratt Institute kids riding bicycles, some black men smoking cigarettes, and an old Hispanic man shuffling by with a brown bag covering what I assumed was a Corona. I was not earning money. I was thrilled to be in the City but had not predicted how difficult it would be. Yes, I was a member of the dread satellite parenting, snowflake, and self-esteem generation. We had MTV though (when MTV was still cool). *Liquid Television* blew my eight-year-old mind, and I was created whole because of it.

I spied a small, rundown bar only a couple of blocks away from the apartment. I went straight in, immediately feeling a lot of eyes on me. I knew what the initial thought was, "Who the hell is this white boy?" I agreed with that sentiment. Who the hell was I? I looked around and felt immediately out of place. Black men were shooting pool in the center of the room. Black strippers were strutting around in neon bikinis. The lighting was dull, which made their bikinis pop off their skin. The men in the bar paid me no mind, after gawking at me, and continued with their shots. One black stripper came up to me. She had on a neon green bikini, wore her hair straight and had on hoop earrings. Her breasts were small, but her nipples were alert. She touched my shoulder and offered her services. I didn't know if she was offering a lap dance, blowjob, or sex. I declined, made an about-face and went back to the apartment.

There was a lot of tension between blacks and whites at this time in Bed Stuy. Many blacks were angry. White youth had come piling in, driving up rents. Cute coffee shops would pop up, and then it was time for them to ship out. I understood their anger, but I also wanted them to see my end of it. I was broke. I was from a good family, from a good town, but I was making it on my own. I would have gone back to SoHo if I had had the cash flow and hadn't alienated my former roommate.

Daniel was a skinny, bohemian pseudo-intellectual, possibly dyslexic. He had a solid foundation in drawing and painting. He wasn't into athleticism; his skateboarding days were far behind him at this point, and he suffered from recurrent ulcers. I would take Daniel to a small park about eight blocks away to work out. It had pull-up bars, dip bars, and rubber mats. I had tucked my old boxing gloves, jump rope, and forearm grips away in my duffle bag. He would cough, wheeze and occasionally vomit, but he loved it. I also saw how it reengaged him in the weight of our reality.

A middle-aged black man came up to us in between boxing combinations, wearing a trench coat and big glasses. He was meaty.

"That's good. Get that good money," he said to us.

"What's good?" I asked.

"Good day for a workout," he answered.

"It sure is," I said.

"This man looks like he's gonna pass out," the black man chuckled.

"Nah, he's just taking a round off," I told him.

"My fighting days are over. Well, I thought they were. A couple months ago this nigga comes up to me in this here park. I beat his mother-fucking ass. That nigga got his clock cleaned. You got to be careful though. Niggas don't like to lose; they might come back for round two with a gun. Awright, young men, get back to it."

"Awright, peace," I said.

Daniel and I were able to make friends in the area, where the biggest boundaries were ones of class. The more we were seen eating low-end Chinese food, shopping at the dollar store, and working out in the park for free, the more we were seen as the same as them. Color became less of an issue. It wasn't erased, but it wasn't the focal point.

For dinner, Daniel and I would throw potatoes, bok choy, and onions into a pot on a hot plate and cook it up. Olive oil, pepper, and salt were the only things we had to flavor it. Daniel was ashamed of his wealth and dressed like a ne'er-do-well. He read the first chapter of every major philosophy book and was fully indoctrinated into critical theory. He had received his master's from Yale. When he was able to forget that he took himself seriously, he was fun. I knew this wasn't a permanent fix to my housing situation, but it was where I was for now. I fully committed to living the vagabond experience. Things were good for a while.

Daniel eventually got annoyed having me around. Who could blame him, really? I wasn't paying a dime to stay. Daniel had repaid his debt to me, and now I had to man up. Adulthood boils down to bill-paying and losing hair: now I had to start paying.

It was time again for me to migrate. I looked through Craigslist posts and came upon a spot in Bushwick. I didn't know anything about that part of Brooklyn, but the price was right, so Daniel and I parted ways. I was having a difficult time putting money in my wallet, but I had an answer. I would moonlight as a chauffeur! I had no experience, was a lousy driver, and didn't have a strong knowledge of the geography of the city. That was of no consequence. Fake it until you make it, goes the old saying.

Driving Mr. Panther

Paul hired me as his personal chauffeur. This was problematic, since I could barely drive, though I did have my license. I didn't know New York well enough yet, and I didn't have a GPS. All I knew was I needed income . . . and fast. I had met Paul in my days as an art student in Miami, at the time of year that the Art Basel Fair happens. I was working on a heavy bag at Crunch gym. I wasn't any good yet but I fancied myself a pugilist. Out of the corner of my eye, I saw a man approach. He was tall, older, skinny and looked like a rubber-faced Peter Fonda. He was smiling a big goofy grin and galloped over to me. Puttering with his hands as though he were doggy-paddling (I believe to emulate boxing), he engaged me in conversation halfway through my bag workout.

"Hey, that's pretty good! You're a dangerous man," he said with a big smile.

"Yeah, not really," I said demurely.

"You have to show me some moves."

"I don't know much."

"I'm sure you know a lot more than you let on."

"Nope," I said, as my eyes started to dart back to the bag.

"What else do you do?"

"I draw and paint."

"Oh, well, I'm going to go to Art Basel."

"That's cool."

"We could have dinner!"

"I am supposed to have dinner with my girlfriend."

"Oh, girlfriend . . . well, great. We'll see each other at the fair, then." He galloped away.

A New Yorker who made frequent trips to Miami, Paul would cross my path every couple of years, always seeming to forget that we had met before. Before I took off for the Big Rotten Apple, he asked me to train him. I agreed to it. We would run on the beach, always past the gay portion of it because he said it improved his running. I would run ahead of him, and he said it was "like a carrot on a stick." I hit him up before moving to New York, asking him if he needed a trainer there. He did not, but he did need a driver for the time being. I took the job with complete naiveté.

...

I crossed the street to the garage by his apartment, north of Columbus Circle. These cars were not Honda Civics; it was all high-end. If you were going to pay another mortgage to house your vehicle, it had better be a classy ride. The valet was prepared for me; within five minutes, he brought me a Maserati Quattroporte. It was slate-colored and had an interior that felt like an after-hours lounge. I held my breath as I eased the car out through the narrow entrance and onto Central Park West. My left side was clear, and I was grateful for the opening. I would have to hang a left and loop around to pick Paul up.

Normally, I would pick him up in the mornings and drop him off at work in midtown. I would pick him up at five or six. I realized that already I hated this job, at least partially due to my incompetence and the feeling of driving a car more expensive than everything I had ever owned. It was terrifying driving in New York without the experience that was needed. Yellow Cabs were chariots, steered by cabbies who behaved like gladiators. You didn't want to challenge a cabbie to a game of chicken.

I was to pick Paul up on a Friday night so he could bar hop with his pals. We hit the LES (Lower East Side) and picked up four young men. They were all gay and indebted to Paul for picking up the tabs this evening. We looped up on Delancey and got caught in traffic. It was difficult to tell how much room in the back or front I had. Paul sat shotgun but would turn around to engage the boys behind us. I was terrified I'd get us all into an accident. The humiliation would have been quadrupled because of the number of people in the car.

The boys in the back were getting loud. I imagine they had a few drinks before we got to them.

"Jeffrey, what's that I feel?"

"It's my wallet, dirty boy."

"Are you guys getting frisky already?" a voice called over from the right-hand side.

"Yeah, Matty! Come over here . . . it'll be a party."

"I wish I could Davis, but Jeffrey is blocking me."

"I ain't cock-blocking nobody, you queen!"

"Woof, this little cub needs to be led around with a leash!" Paul said from shotgun, as he turned his head over his left shoulder.

"You want to put a leash on me, Paul?" Davis said.

"Oh, don't tempt me!" Paul responded.

"Where are we going?" Matty asked.

"Let's go to G Bar first!" Davis said.

We passed Christie. Paul told me to take Lafayette Avenue up, cross over on 11th, and then come up on 9th Avenue. Then he asked, "Guys, what would I be? Women are cougars. What would you call me?"

"You're a big bad wolf. Maybe you could blow my house down!" Matty called out.

"Nah, I don't know about that. I want something sexier than that . . . a panther. I'm a panther . . .Grrr!" Paul exclaimed.

I found a spot but was barely able to get in when I parallel-parked. I felt the boys' eyes focus on me as I painstakingly maneuvered the car. They had barely seen me upon entering the Maserati. I wasn't quite in the spot, but that didn't matter. The boys and the panther exited the car and went across the street to G Bar. The coast was clear, so I maneuvered the car into a more proper parking job. The car beeped when it came within dangerous proximity to an object, and this protected me from damaging the Maserati.

I had the intense feeling of needing to pee. I had drunk a full Arizona tallboy tea can before this chauffeur gig. My bladder was pleading for me to relieve it. The streets weren't too busy, but I didn't want to leave the car. I started looking at my options. I saw an SUV I could duck behind and pee. But what if a cop grabbed me? I could go behind that dumpster. What if a disgruntled street urchin stabbed me in the dick, because I had pissed on his home? Dammit! I was running out of options. Paul and his friends would smell it, if I pissed my pants. I looked over the right-hand side of the street. I was only a few feet away from a dip down into a basement-level apartment's entrance, partly hidden in shadow. I could piss in a corner there and scrunch up to conceal my dirty, law-breaking ways. What if a tenant caught me and started punching me midstream? My bladder won the debate and forced me to hop out of the car to drain it. I looked all around and jumped down into the shadowy protection of this private property. I pissed long and hard, and my stream just kept going. I pleaded for it to stop, but it wouldn't. I saw four figures start walking down from the far end of the street. They started closing in, and my urine kept flowing. I started to make out their faces. The stream of piss turned to foam on the concrete. They were loud and proud gay men. They started to cross the street halfway to head into the bar. My stream weakened and finally cut off. I leapt out of the shadowy corner and into the safety of the six-cylinder luxury vehicle.

I waited in the driver's seat for half an hour, letting Paul's iPod play softly. I thought about Miami and how it had been to live there. I was in the city I had always wanted to be in, but nobody could have prepared me for how to make this work. I had learned things like algebra and geometry in high school. I wish they had taught me how to balance a checkbook and how to survive on peanut butter and jelly sandwiches.

The four young men and Paul reemerged from the G Bar. They crossed the street and approached the car, piling in more buzzed than 30 minutes prior. Paul suggested I take them to Splash next, so we drove further downtown. I was able to park four blocks up, near a Greek diner. I turned off Paul's iPod and switched to the radio. I heard the Rolling Stones and let it play. I felt the urge to piss again, immediate sharp pain, but I couldn't leave the car. I grabbed an empty water bottle from the cup-holder to my right. I looked around and matched my pee hole up to the bottle, taking a deep breath before releasing the stream. I was like a sniper slowing down his heart rate before pulling the trigger. I started pissing, but my penis flopped left. I realigned my pee hole with the bottle. I finished pissing and put the bottle in the cup-holder. I had a patch on my left leg of damp denim and spatter marks on the right. I started rubbing my pants vigorously, trying to heat them up so they would dry faster. I looked all around, and when the coast was clear, I opened the door, and dumped the frothy piss into the gutter.

I knew very little of New York City and realized that with no map or smart phone and an inoperative GPS on the Maserati, I was in deep shit. I didn't know what to do. It was close to ten. I decided to call my 16-year-old brother in Massachusetts.

"Jake, this is Dustin."

"What's up?"

"I'm lost in the City. I need you to lead me around. Use Google Maps!"

"Dude, I have school tomorrow."

"Hey, I need this! I need this job."

Then I heard my mom in the background. Her room was right next to my brother's room.

"Who are you talking to?"

"Dustin!" my brother answered back.

"Tell him you have school tomorrow."

"I did!" Jake answered.

"Jake, just tell me how to turn back to this gay club!" I yelled.

"What?" Jake asked.

"What does he want?" my mom called out from the next room.

"He wants to know how to find a gay club."

"Tell him you have school tomorrow!"

"I did."

Jake let me know how to loop around. It was just the information I needed to be able to be back in proximity to Splash to wait for Paul and his friends. I was sweating a bit and had to talk myself back down to a balanced level.

The boys got out of Splash close to an hour later. Paul seemed different. He was more amped up. I assumed he had taken a bump or two of high-grade cocaine. The boys were giggling in the back. I was to drive them back to Paul's apartment, so I went uptown where traffic wasn't so bad. Timmy and Jeffrey were making out behind me. I couldn't see anything, but Davis was scolding them to knock it off. Then Matty started to mock Davis. He was teasing him for being a prude. I wasn't sure what was going on, but I knew I had to get them all to Paul's apartment near Columbus Circle. Matty went to grab Davis's penis, and Davis yelped. Paul looked over his shoulder to straighten the boys out. I was not focusing on the streetlights and blew through a red light. Jeffrey commented on it; I was outed. Every one of these guys knew the truth: Dustin couldn't drive. I panicked, and my face went red. Paul asked me to pull over. We switched places, and he drove us the five blocks back to the apartment.

I was then tasked to bring the car back to the garage, though I felt mortified. Timmy, Jeffrey, Davis, Matty, and Paul left to continue whatever was going down at the apartment. I took the subway back to Bushwick. I felt like an unskilled, worthless marshmallow. I had no idea what else I could do with my little-to-no-skills. It looked like driving was out, because I sucked at that too.

...

Paul gave me one last chance to do my job. Since the GPS was broken in the Maserati, I had to drive the car to the dealership on Long Island. I had never been to Long Island, but I needed to prove my salt. I needed to show I wasn't an unskilled, worthless marshmallow. I would do this. I had notes written down on how to get to the dealership. When I arrived at Paul's apartment, he presented me with another set of printouts. I silently panicked, not knowing if I should follow Paul's printouts or my own. I decided to concede to Paul's.

I went to the garage where the valet brought me the Maserati. I took a deep breath and climbed into the driver's seat. I looked to my left and had to wait for my chance to take it uptown.

The drive onto 495 wasn't too stressful. I began gaining a slight confidence. I felt like maybe I could drive. Maybe I could be a man. Maybe, just maybe, I would be a professional driver. I used Paul's printed directions but realized that they seemed off. I made three loops back to see if I could spot the dealership but I couldn't. My heart raced. I decided it had to have been further down on 495. I kept driving. I saw my gas gauge tilt left. I felt my skin itch; I cursed myself for taking the job. I knew I was a fraud; I knew I was doomed to be barely a man. I hit Route 111. I don't know why I kept going onward. I felt like I would hit some kind of magic fog, and it would send me back to whence I came. Or it would be like Popeye on Nintendo, and I would be back on the other side of the screen again.

I got onto Sunrise Highway. My face was panic-stricken. I cursed myself aloud and realized just how ill-equipped I was to deal with real life. The roads were backed up, so I slowed down. A young man on my right side was calling out to me. He looked like Bill from *Bill and Ted's Excellent Adventure.*

"Hey, buddy. Are you lost?" he asked.

"Yep, yes, I am," I tried to remove the fear from my face.

"Where are you going?"

"I don't know."

"Well, you're pretty much in Montauk now."

"I guess I should turn back." I didn't stomp on the brake. I talked and rolled ahead, smashing into a minivan in front of me. The man on my right drove off. I reversed the car. I was about to cry like a sleep-deprived child but went numb instead. I got out of the car. The minivan driver got out. He was a bearded, foreign man. I looked at his bumper, which had a small puncture. My front grill looked almost perfect.

"I'm sorry. I don't know what happened."

"You got insurance?"

"I don't know."

"What you mean?"

"It's not my car."

"My car is banged up."

"Please, I'll give you money."

"No, we need insurance."

"Please, this'll cost me my job."

The man wouldn't take no for an answer. I had to trade info, which involved me calling Paul at work. I felt like the biggest loser in the world, no one bigger. I was the Ghostbusters' giant marshmallow man equivalent of loser. I had a rusted crown and cardboard throne in loserdom.

Paul would not meet me face-to-face. I had to drop the keys off with his doorman. There was no solace in the doorman's eyes. All he saw was a punk white kid who couldn't handle man work. Paul and I didn't speak for four years. I assumed I would never see him again.

I did end up seeing him, though. I became a bartender at hot spots. I connected with the Stan Ward Hotel and got to work at all the good spots. The first couple of times I saw Paul, he pretended we had never met. By the third time, he demonstrated that we had met, but wouldn't talk about the car. By the following year, we would talk about it and have a good chuckle. I may have merely scuffed his Maserati but he knew, and I knew, that my pride was forever dented.

Shut Up, White Belt

"How the hell do you tie this belt?" I thought.

I looked around in the locker room, and saw the other guys throwing on their uniforms. Everyone sported traditional white gis, and belts of either blue or purple. I felt my blood grow cold as I realized that I was about to test myself. I was back at it for the third time. The first two times were dreadful for different reasons. I couldn't run away from it this time, though. I had tried but found myself back in this white woven suit of misery. I felt the weight of it and looked down at my body. I dreaded even the notion that I felt any dread at all. I hated the idea that I couldn't control my emotions. They ran wild like a horse in a burning barn, and that was partly the reason I had to come back. I ran away but couldn't run far enough. I would have to confront myself. I would have to confront the bitch I was.

Yes, I would have to be broken, submitted, shit on, and spit back out (only to be repeated ad infinitum). This meant that I needed to embrace the suck. There was no other choice. I was going to try this damn Jiu-Jitsu again, goddammit, and I was going to like it. I was struggling with the newly unpacked white belt. It signified my virginal status, and made it known that I was fresh for the slaughter. A guy on my right covered from head to toe in fluorescent tattoos secured it for me. I happened to remember that folks get buried in rags like these and put in the dirt; there was something momentarily comforting about that thought. We exited the changing room and bowed as we walked onto the mats.

Class began, and we bowed to the professor as he stepped onto the mats in front of us. I looked to another older guy in the lineup wearing a purple belt.

"Nice white gi, guy," he said.

So it began; I was to be reborn in the molten metal soup of grappling.

The professor had us watch him perform the basic bump sweep in closed guard. Now, all of this looked ridiculous to me. I didn't really watch Ultimate Fighting Championship or any other MMA promotion. I had seen some wrestling, boxing, and Muay Thai. I hadn't seen this system of fighting before Jiu-Jitsu. It was strange and foreign. It couldn't make sense of it. I had been exposed to it twice before, but it seemed just as strange as the first two times. It was counter to everything humans did in violence. Striking made sense to me. Scrunching your hand up in a fist, sending it soaring through the air and smashing some idiot's jaw was all too human. If it was good enough for the cavemen, it was good enough for me. Jiu-Jitsu had been created by aliens light years away.

We practiced the bump sweep with our partner, and I felt the existential frustration of ignorance. I was like a screaming newborn but kept it all inside. I looked around the room to see the other guys execute the same move. I heard the bodies of these men being hurled onto the mats. I too landed on my back time and time again as my partner swept me over. Again, and again, and again, we'd use our hips to twist our partner up and over. We drilled the move back and forth with our partner. We repeated it like someone would continue to utter a mantra. It was then that I began to see the light.

I was really just an art nerd who had some physical chops. Art was so amorphous, and in the postmodern era, everything was art. So, where did that leave us youth? If I were to wager, I'd say it left us between a hard place and no place to take a shit. There was no truth left in art.

The bump sweep was truth; it was art, and it confirmed I was here. Yes, it was one simple move. Yes, this was only a small sliver of the light breaking through. I yearned for some more damn answers. Teachers had told me what was right and wrong. Before that, it was my parents, then my friends. Still I wandered aimless in the urban hell.

The next move the professor showed us was the triangle choke, and even more light broke through. . .

We went back to drilling the moves. My partner threw on the triangle choke, and it was immediate: I saw the white light befitting me as a white belt. I felt my body slump over, and I tapped my partner to let him know that it had worked, I submitted. If he had held on, it would have been lights out for me. Instead, I came back to the land of the living in a room with my fellow sojourners, all of us dressed in foreign garb. It was humbling to have been so quickly at death's door. My partner had simply clamped his legs together, bisecting my head and arm. He cut off the carotid arteries, and my brain began to shut down within seconds. This was the first submission I learned.

I was exposed. I was now aware of my staggering inadequacy. It tapped into something I couldn't imagine I had lived this long without: an objective truth.

As an artist, I was looked at as a dreamer, and dreamers often ignore limitations. I lived with little regard of real barriers, and it made me stupid. I know cutting off blood to my brain wasn't an ideal way to get smarter, but it worked. I got to see cause and effect in a way that pen and paper could never show.

Dreams are illusory, though they may contain the echoes of what can be. Dreams, like art, are gifts from another realm, but the physical realm we live in isn't a dream. The planet is an objective blue marble. It's harsh by default: if you don't respect its laws for even a moment, then good luck to you. Jiu-Jitsu had come to me on my third and final try. When the blood began to flow back into the soft gray matter in my skull, I saw a path. I would need to come back to the mat to find out more of this truth. I wasn't abandoning pen and paper but adding the sweep and the choke.

The professor pulled out a timer and we began to spar. I was paired up with the older purple belt that had made the comment about my white gi. We bumped our fists together signifying the start of chaos. He engaged me like only an act of nature could. I endured through the lashings of forces I could not oppose. I used everything but Jiu-Jitsu to keep him at bay. He snatched my collar and spun me around. He tried to cut to my back, but I slunk down to the shoulders. He cut over and mounted me. He was heavier than I had thought. I felt my breath leave me and did everything I could to squirm out of there. I pushed up on his chest and tried to bench press him off. He snatched one of my arms and spun up and over with it. I felt the pressure in my arm and knew that this wasn't good. I was able to get my arm (most of it) back. He threw me back down and climbed to the mount. He isolated my head and dug his knuckles into my neck. It was painful, and I felt a lightness that had become familiar. I tapped; he sat back triumphant; I promised that one day I'd be better than that caveman. I would evolve past him. I would do my utmost to go deeper down the path. I would climb to greater heights. I just needed to do the work.

The men lined up and proceeded to shake hands down the line. The battle of the day was over, and now we stood as an army united. All the guys in white gis looked visibly different after the training session. All was right with the world, because we had confronted it. We had confronted its cold objectivity with humility and swallowed its physical truths like medicine. The theoretical could be saved for the coffee shop where I made little ink drawings.

Nobody looked like Superman in their Japanese pajamas. Hell, I walked around with a good amount of muscle, but alas I was far from Superman. I was almost lowest on the totem pole, though I did see a couple of other white belts without my physical abilities and took some pride in that. I had a chip on my shoulder and couldn't have told you why. I found it strange I somehow expected to be "the one," but I think all men must believe that, maybe there's a reason. We need that fire, but the fire can burn you to a crisp.

Nobody is born knowing how to fight, or do much else, for that matter. It's a skill like any other. Some are made stronger; some are made quicker; some are made meaner. All men are born into the world as formless mud, and then they take shape. I planned to shape up to be a formidable hellion. I knew that it would be a long road. I also understood that I had a hunger for it and couldn't pinpoint where it came from. Most guys seem to have a similar story. We are bullied, beaten, or broken by forces beyond our control. Some men take it more personally, though. Call me sensitive, but I couldn't stomach being a loser. I hated it like I hated an enemy in a blood feud.

I went back to the changing room and removed my damp white clothing. I rolled up the white belt and stuffed it into my duffle bag. The men in the room were jovial, and cracking jokes. I had a smile on my face. I couldn't remember the last time I was this happy. It was an energy that permeated my being. I was filled with a divine spirit. I had confronted the force of reality. It was greater than me, and even the other guys paled in comparison to it.

Nobody is greater than objective truth. Nobody can stand taller than it is, and this permitted me to experience something that can't be transcribed.

Suffice it to say that a white belt like myself had better just shut up. I can't tackle the meaning I confronted that day. I just knew in my sore bones that there was much to learn. I had to shut up, open my eyes, use my body, and learn from the greatest teacher of all… truth.

I Was Bushwhacked

B ushwick was another word for "rude awakening." I wasn't in Kansas
    anymore. In reality, I wasn't in Miami or Boston any longer. I once
had a Manhattan friend who told me upon arriving to this new land
that I had been "Bushwhacked!" I lived off the Kosciuszko J train stop
on Greene Street, inhabited by mainly Mexican, working-class families.
My Spanish was decent, but that didn't matter. They were polite, kind,
and hard-working. I lived in a three-family building on the second floor.
I had three roommates. My room was the cheapest and had no windows.
I slept on a gym mat on the floor. At the foot of the mat, I had a pile
of clothes. There was no particular reason for this other than that I was
lazy and dirty. My drawings were scattered about, and my suitcases were
lined up against the yellow walls.

My roommates were an eclectic bunch. One roommate was 35 years
old. He had an ex-wife and a 13-year-old daughter back in Seattle. He
hoped to make it big in New York City as a DJ. We moved boxes upon
boxes of vinyl up three flights of stairs for him, along with turntables
and other audio equipment. His name was Jared. Another roommate was
26 years old. She was a model, singer, and actress. She didn't really get
work in that vein. The other roommate was a Hollister model three years
running. A Jersey girl, she worked modeling events and other odd jobs
that required her beauty. She was tall, blonde, blue-eyed, and athletic.
This was my temporary tribe.

Jared and I would walk five blocks to work out at a black body
building gym. This was before I discovered Brazilian Jiu-Jitsu. I had been
power lifting in Miami before I moved to New York; I enjoyed hoisting
metal plates and getting "swoll." Jared was not much of an athlete. He
was a big guy and carried most of the weight in his stomach. He could
shoot hoops, though, and hustle when he needed to. The blacks that
worked out at the gym were massive. They all looked like prizefighters
or football players. It felt rough, but nobody seemed to start fights.
It was like church, and at church everyone behaves. We all prayed to
the Mr. Olympia gods. We would do our rituals and connect to our
higher power. The communal grunting, shrugging and pacing were our
congregation. In New York, everyone hated each other in the abstract,

on general principle. When we got to relate in a concrete way though, the differences became muted.

After the gym, Jared and I would stop by a Dominican spot for a five-dollar plate of rice, beans and plantains. They even threw in a free bottle of water. This helped to rebuild the body. It was important to refuel after vigorously hoisting metal.

That part of Brooklyn was decent enough. It was changing, and police presence was noticeable. An influx of whites in their early twenties were moving into these parts. As a white boy, you knew not to go down to the Halsey stop. It was only six blocks away, but it wasn't friendly. It was tribalism at its purest. The influx of poor whites meant more whites to follow, which meant richer whites after, which meant coffee shops, higher rents and people getting the boot. This was the arc about to take place. In the meantime, more crime would occur. The whites didn't realize they were like game birds released onto a hunting ground. You would see young hipsters walk around with headphones playing the Killers, the Strokes or obscure Norwegian death metal bands rendering them deaf. You would hope, as a hunted animal, to have your senses about you. You would want every advantage of your sight, sound, and touch to inform you of the potential threats. Occasionally, I saw a tall, black, transvestite hooker walk the streets. I asked my neighbor about him. I didn't understand how this guy could walk around without getting beaten up or worse. He told me that this guy was no one to fuck with. He was able to do this because he was a furious street fighter even in heels and lip gloss. Nobody dared get in a fight with him lest he be known as the guy who got the shit kicked out of him by a dude in a dress.

In the early days of living in Bushwick, circa 2009, life was exciting. I had always wanted to live in New York City, but the dichotomy coming from Miami was staggering. I had moved from a tropical wasteland to an industrial slum. In Miami, I was an art student and worked shitty jobs. In New York City, I was a broke artist and worked shitty jobs. I had gone from fun and sun to hustle and bustle. I thought I knew New York when as an art student, I had had an internship in Chelsea. I didn't know then that people like young people (specifically students). As you grow older, nobody gives a shit about you—you are off their radar.

That internship: I had not realized how blessed I was. I treated it like my personal clubhouse. Like I said: we were the self-esteem generation. We all got trophies, and thought we deserved them. The only true competition, we were taught, was with yourself…talk about a way to propagate clueless brats.

My internship resulted from a connection with a world-famous New York architect I made while working the counter at the Equinox Gym in Miami. He hooked me up with this internship, one of the shining star galleries of the New York City art machine. Artists such as Kerry James Marshall, El Anatsui, Anton Kannemeyer and Lynette Yiadom-Boakye showed there. The gallery was in every major art fair of note, including the mega fair, Art Basel Miami.

This could have been a great start for me! I was linked up with a powerhouse selling expensive objects to rich people. Hell, I could have attended all the openings. I could have pushed my drawings and other works on paper. I could have become an art handler and learned the trade, but I did no such thing. I didn't understand that this would not be handed to me.

I was special. I was talented. I had a little hard body. What more did I have to do? I spent most of the time hanging out with the gallery cleaner in the basement drinking yerba mate and speaking Spanish. I had a blast bullshitting with Ricardo and being overly caffeinated, but it wasn't gaining me a career. I was the office boy, and I was a shitty office boy at that. They put me to work on artists' books. I can't tell you what they wanted me to do with them. I would take them to the couch downstairs. I would then flip through them and end up drifting off to sleep. I found office work terribly boring. I understood the art handler's gig; it seemed like real work, but I didn't have an in on that. When December came around, I was told my internship was over. They were very nice about it. I was totally unaware until about five years later that I was, in effect, fired. Yes, I was that stupid.

...

I didn't have a job again. I didn't have an unpaid internship at an art gallery. I had money saved from slaving away at a nice lounge in Miami, but New York was expensive. It wouldn't be long before I would start bleeding funds.

Getting a job at this particular time was impossible, or so it seemed. I had dropped off resumes throughout lower Manhattan. I had received no callbacks. My resume consisted mainly of businesses in Miami. Nothing counted unless it was New York City experience. It was demoralizing. I never went over the two-year mark on any job in the City. It was like playing musical chairs: someone wouldn't pay the electric bill, the music would stop, and then you hustled to find a seat so you wouldn't be out on your ass. Apartments were like that too. Hell, bars were too. Union Pool was the spot, and then the music would stop. Everything was momentary. I wondered if there was some kind of equation to figure out these migrations before they would happen.

My folks would tell me to come back home. I called my mom once to discuss my circumstances.

"I tried looking for work, but nobody is calling me back."

"Well, maybe you should just come back here. Maybe it won't work there," my mom said hopefully.

"No. It can work. I just need to figure it out," I assured her.

"Well, maybe it's just too difficult. What happens if you run out of money?"

"I'll be homeless, I guess," I answered

"You should really just come back home. It's too difficult there."

"What am I going to do at home? There's nothing for me there. I'll die there!" I exclaimed.

"Just think about it. It isn't too shabby. We have a new burrito place that opened."

"That sounds delightful. You sold me. I'll be back tomorrow."

I knew I had to spare my parents the travails and pitfalls of figuring out adulthood. They only wanted the best for me and to spare me from the ass- kicking life had in store. That was a futile endeavor. It was excess stress to invite them onto the rocky path I was walking. I was terrified of being out on the street. I knew I was too soft for that shit. I was a good Jewish boy from a good family from a good New England town. I would have been mincemeat. I decided to call my childhood art teacher.

"Hey, Jack."

"Hey, Dustin. What's happening, man?"

"Jack, I think I need to come back home. I am bleeding money, and this may be the wrong move."

"Oh yeah? You just got there. How can you be bleeding money?"

"I don't know. It just seems to vanish."

"So, buy a loaf of bread. Buy some peanut butter. You don't need the jelly. Make sure the bread is dark. It will have more nutritional value."

"I don't know if I can do this. I think I'm not cut out for this," I whimpered.

"You can't say that after only a couple of months."

"Maybe I can."

"Dustin, and I mean this with all due respect, don't be a pussy, man! Figure it out. Buy a loaf of dark bread, and some peanut butter. Get it together. You'll die here in this small town! Ya hear?

"Okay. Okay. Thanks, Jack. Thanks for calling me out."

"No worries, Dustin. Go buy a loaf. This'll make a man outta you."

"Thanks, Jack."

"Talk soon, kid."

That was that. Jack set me straight. Our generation sure seemed to be a sorry group of babies. I thought about my mom and how tough she was. She had had her spine fused because of scoliosis, living in a back brace for years. She grew up in a home with Holocaust survivor parents who held refugee drunken benders. She worked at Filene's Basement to put herself through college and a master's program. She forcibly made life work. My dad couldn't get into an American med school. He had to go across the border to Mexico to get his education. He made side money by smuggling flavored douche across the border . . . yes, flavored douche.

I don't know how such tough adults raised such insubstantial children. I knew to follow their lead but not necessarily their command. I was lucky, in a way. I had people there to scoop me off the pavement, in case it got really bad. I promised myself that it would have to be fire and brimstone bad before I asked them for a hand.

I discovered a small French-style bistro in SoHo. The place was quaint. It had quite a bit of money poured in to rehab it. Originally, it had been a shithole to shoot pool in. As a boy, Bobby De Niro would come in and hang out. I wondered how often he would leave Tribeca now and visit the old hood.

The pastry chef was a diminutive, second-generation, gay Chinese man who spoke quickly and with malice. There were two owners. One was a large Trinidadian man who owned other businesses and real estate; the other was a Korean-American woman. She was pretty and nerdy. Her day job was in tech. How these people got together to form a half-baked idea of a French bistro in SoHo was beyond me. (The place died within a year, and I only lasted five months before needing another job.)

I figured I wasn't getting jobs because I looked desperate. I needed to feign confidence in order to secure a job. I stood outside the place and worked up the nerve to go in. I plastered a frenzied smile on my face, walked into the establishment with purpose. I eyed a man behind the counter, a little shorter than me. He had dark hair, glasses, and dressed like a preppy. He didn't look like he was from the City. He looked like me, a newbie. I asked him if they needed more staff. He almost invisibly rolled his eyes and grabbed his manager, an Asian guy dressed in a suit with a soft face. He seemed gentle and engaged. I assumed he was gay, so I played ambiguous.

"Hi, sir. My name is Dustin. I was curious to know if you needed help."

"We could be looking for someone. Do you have a resume?" he asked.

"Yes, I do." I fumbled through my backpack. I pulled out a slightly crinkled resume, silently cursing myself for not using a better folder. I stayed in character as confident young man. I needed this job.

"Okay. Oh, I see here you mainly have Miami experience. That shouldn't be a problem."

"You have a really beautiful space here. It's a wonderful spot. I would love the opportunity to work for you here at this place."

"Okay, let me show this to the GM. I'll let you know."

"Yes, absolutely. That sounds great! I'm available to start right away."

I left the bistro and starting walking toward Chinatown, only a few blocks away. I was able to drop my guard. I felt low. I hated the feeling of being on the bottom of the totem pole. I knew one day I would need to work for myself.

As a restaurant worker, you're a nomad. You travel from business to business with wine key and lighter in hand. You stick around for a while, and then when the landscape starts to gray, you leave for the next one. You just hope this next one is bountiful, and you won't starve.

I went into a Vietnamese restaurant. I ordered a bowl of vegetable *pho*. It arrived within minutes. The place was right by the courthouse and crowded with lawyers. I added hoisin sauce and Sriracha. I placed the basil leaves, lemon wedge, and sprouts from a side plate on top of the soup. I took a few sips with the white porcelain spoon.

My Nokia buzzed in my pocket from a number I didn't recognize. I answered it to hear the Asian guy's voice from the bistro. He offered me the job! He asked me to come back in 30 minutes. I was elated. My visions of homelessness were dissipating. I felt reborn. I was to be a counter boy. I was thrilled. My daydreaming began, consisting of painting, drawing, making coffee, and flirting with the hot corporate girls of SoHo.

I walked back to the bistro, saw the same guy behind the counter steaming milk. He gave me the slightest glance of recognition. The Asian guy came in and handed me a W2 form. I sat at one of the marble- top tables and filled it out, handing it back to him. Then I was allowed behind the counter, where the coffee guy introduced himself.

"Hi, man. My name is John."

"Hi, man! My name is Dustin! I'm thrilled to work here with you!" I said, over- enthusiastically. I could tell John was a little apprehensive, and probably wondering whether the managers just hired a meth-head. Hooray.

"Okay, man. So, Dan (the Asian guy in the suit, who was the owner's brother) wants me to show you the ropes."

"That sounds great!"

"The kitchen is located in the basement. We keep all the granola, croissants, sweets, and what have you up here."

"It looks great!"

"They said you're gonna be our counter guy, right?"

"Yep, I think that's what they said."

"Okay, I don't need to show you much about the espresso machine then."

"Where are you from, man?"

"Chicago. You?"

"Boston." (I always meant north of Boston, but nobody there would know where Marblehead was.)

"How long have you been here for?"

"A couple of months. What about you?"

"The same. Let me take you downstairs to see the kitchen."

We went down into the basement. It didn't look health-department legal. It felt like a wet dungeon, with archaic metal machines scattered about, more like a Victorian torture chamber than a well-functioning kitchen. We encountered the pastry chef Pichong, who stood about five feet four inches tall. He was dressed in kitchen whites and had his hair in a combover. John was about to introduce me when Pichong spoke first.

"Hey, what are you doing down here? I am working, can't you see that?" His English was broken. He blurted the sentences in diarrheic bursts.

"Yes, I see that, but Dan told me to show Dustin the facilities," John explained.

"Okay. Okay. Show over. Thank you," Pichong blurted.

John looked over at me and smiled. We went back upstairs. John and I went over the operating system for ordering, then the logistics of opening and closing shifts. I started working shifts a couple of days later, after a day or two of training.

Our general manager was a borderline personality, though I am not a psychologist and cannot definitively say this. I can say, though, that based on WebMD, this GM was a fucking loon. His name was Nathan, and he was big. He was half white and half Asian and from the Napa Valley. Like so many restaurant workers before him, he was also a pill-popper. He had a girlfriend ten years younger than he. I assumed she was with him because she was too inexperienced to know that she could do better. I assumed he knew she could do better too, which was why he put her down, so she wouldn't high-tail it out of there.

My second day started with a pre-shift meeting. Nathan gave us a talk on proper restaurant etiquette. We were pretty much all newbies to this world. Most of us were under 25. One of the baristas was an older guy with a French background. He looked like Christopher Lambert circa *Highlander*. He even talked like Christopher Lambert, with a strange accent that was neither here nor there. We had two girls who worked with us, students from the New School. Every conversation with them seemed to steer back to the elusive Patriarchy. It was good fun, like playing six degrees of Kevin Bacon, but replacing Kevin with "The Man."

The shift was slow. We had successful SoHo types come in for dinner. It was then that I noticed directly that Nathan was strange. He would rub his nose compulsively and dart his eyes around. He was frenzied. He would bark orders at all of us one minute and be jovial the next. It was like dealing with Dr. Jekyll and Mr. Hyde. He picked on all of us for different things. He had to best everyone at his or her specific talent or perceived talent. John was a big sports fan; he loved the 49ers and the Bears. Nathan knew more about the teams than John. The Christopher Lambert barista Charles was a part-time actor. Nathan would brag about how he used to model and get commercial work, having never taken an acting class. I used to box in Miami, but Nathan was the better fighter. Nathan would get into drunken brawls and best whoever the opponent was. The girls were up-to-date on the latest feminist theory, but Nathan was hip to it before them because he had lived in San Francisco.

Allowed a shift drink or two at the end of the night, we would have our drinks at the restaurant first then meander out into the neighborhood. John, Charles, and I went to a trendy bar a couple of blocks away. We had a buzz on from not eating and gulping down two big Bordeaux glasses of Cabernet Sauvignon each.

The bar was too rich for our blood, but you only lived once. We ordered up three glasses of red. I was going to order soda water, but Charles and John bought me a glass anyway. We sat at the bar off of Lafayette Street. The bartenders had cool hair and tattoos; the waitresses were beautiful and young. I could make out the faces of some vaguely famous people. Here we were, three young gentlemen fulfilling their New York City dream. None of us came here to be mediocre.

I pulled out my sketchbook filled with rubbery cartoons.

"Hey, mate, can I see that?" Charles asked.

"Sure, man." I handed over the sketchbook. Charles flipped open to a page with a cartoon of a skeleton having intercourse with a bubbly woman.

"Dammit, man. These are great! This should be in a gallery. Is this what you do?" John looked over the page as well and nodded approvingly.

"Thanks, man. Maybe one day. I love drawing."

"Yes, mate. I can see it. I'm an actor in trade. I do the barista work in-between gigs."

"I make short films. I act in them too," John added.

"That's great. My brother acts too," I said.

"The three of us are going to rise to the top. You hear me? Let's toast to our future victories!" Charles exclaimed.

The three of us held up our glasses and gave cheers to New York City. We had arrived. The three of us would be written about in *Interview*, *The Village Voice*, and *Juxtapose*. It was destiny. Sure, we were in a city of eight million. That was of no consequence. We were shoo-ins for artistic glory. It would take several years for me to learn that New York City is a harsh mistress on her period.

The money I was earning at this bistro was pretty lousy. You couldn't expect much in terms of financial gains from this line of work. We were just lucky that our neighborhoods in Brooklyn hadn't blown up yet. Bed Stuy and Bushwick were havens for bohemians. It was possible to make 400 bucks a week and live a decent lifestyle.

The weeks passed by, and things became routine. Pichong would chastise us for not knowing all of the ingredients in his *palmiers.* The owners would sit by the bar and stare despondently at their computer screens. Nathan would go from our best friend to worst nightmare—several times a night.

One day, Nathan was moving around more frantically than usual. He was pestering me, but I refused to engage him. I tried to make myself busy by wiping the counter, repeatedly. He came over to me with a big knife. He claimed my boxing wouldn't help me against an opponent with a knife. He even held it near my face. I didn't budge. He had a big smile on his face. He put down the knife and went over to John to pester him. This was irritating. I rarely had a manager who wasn't off. They all seemed to be riddled by some kind of mental malady. I always regressed to playing the dumb blond, so I could go about my business in order to earn my keep.

The end of the shift was approaching. I wasn't much of a drinker at this point but felt very much like I needed a shift drink. Nathan had been carrying on throughout the night with his outbursts. Charles, John, and I were gulping down some Prosecco that had been popped open earlier. It was raining and chilly. Nathan was throwing back some whiskey. He talked to us about his past. None of us wanted to hear it. He was wearing on us, and we were looking forward to talking about our own endeavors.

"I used to manage the hottest cocktail bar in San Francisco," Nathan declared.

"Go 49ers!" John said.

"You guys can't imagine what that was like. This place is a cakewalk. That place was elite."

"Yes, mate. I'm sure it was," Charles placated.

"I haven't been to San Francisco," I said.

"You know, this one time . . . well, this one time. . . ." Nathan started to peter out. "There was this football player dude who showed up with his girlfriend. We were all getting along. We were closing up. I had some seriously righteous crippy. They knew of an after-hours spot in Mission Bay, so we went there. It was a house party. Cool as fuck, and we were tripping. He kept giving me side-glances. I was like, is this dude for real? So then he asks me to go into a bathroom in the basement. He had some high-grade coke. He asked me if I had ever made it with a dude before. I said nah. We were really high. Anyway, we started fooling around . . . and it was going a little far for me. He held me down over the sink and raped me." Nathan poured another shot of whiskey.

We were frozen, but someone had to say something.

"Did you press charges?" I blurted out.

"Yeah, numbnuts, like I was gonna go to the police to say I was raped."

"Damn, bro. That's fucked up," John said and chugged the rest of his Prosecco.

"Well, mates. I guess I'm off. I have an audition in the morning," Charles said.

"Yeah, I think the rain let up. I'm lifting in the morning before work," I said.

We all exited the bistro, and Nathan locked the gate. We all scattered for different trains to different places. It was wild that he had confessed this to us. He wanted us to see him one way and switched it on its heels. I had to assume he was telling the truth. It would make sense. There was no punch line. There was no "I got you." He revealed this horrible thing to us. We never spoke of it again, but it gave us some insight into him. I can't say it made me like him anymore; I just understood him better.

. . .

John, Charles, and I became a unit. My roommate Jared would swing by the spot too and joined the team we created. It felt like we were this generation's rat pack. We didn't have the money, fame, or glory.

We did have the swagger, though. Women were easily obtained. Third-wave feminism had prevailed in aiding the man and not necessarily the woman. You simply invited a woman to a bar within a three-block radius of your apartment, got two rounds, and offered to pop in a copy of *The Big Lebowski*. It was as simple as that. Jared was 35, divorced, broke, and looked like Quentin Tarantino after losing all self-control, but he could have any woman he wanted. Half the time they paid for the drinks. We would gather around and talk about our recent conquests. It was devoid of decency. No detail was insignificant. Grooming of pubic hair, smells of heretofore mentioned regions, duration of any given session, were all discussed at length. We validated each other's indecency. This was normal. It was New York City, and this was how New York City functioned. It was a playground.

We didn't just fixate on modern-day hook-up culture. We did go see art shows, theater, and all New York had to offer. Jared would DJ occasionally in small venues, so we'd hit up the shows. Jared had a show off of Nostrand and Vernon. I went alone. It was a specific demographic, almost completely comprised of middle-aged African American couples, speckled with a few Puerto Rican couples. Jungle Juice was being served in a giant punch bowl in the kitchen. I was the only white boy, aside from Jared. Nobody really talked to me, and I was annoyed Jared had invited me. I went back home after only an hour. The next day I ran into Jared in our kitchen. He told me it was an orgy. There was a room upstairs, where everyone went to fornicate. There was a reason nobody was talking to me, and it wasn't a "white boy" thing. It was a "Who is this creepy young dude by himself?" thing. Jared had just thought I would enjoy his music. (I did enjoy the music he was spinning.)

We had another big night that same week. Charles invited us to a Gallery show in SoHo not too far away from the Bistro. I worked the day shift with John, and we cut in time to grab a bite before meeting up with the rest of the pack. There was a small hole-in-the-wall to grab a falafel sandwich. John and I went there to eat and drink mint tea.

"Did you hear some of the checks are bouncing over at the bistro?" I asked.

"Yeah, man. I heard," John responded.

"I think we need to find new jobs. I don't want to work without pay."

"I hear you. Where do you think you would look?"

"I'm not sure. Maybe we could go look on the West Side."

"Yeah, I like the West Side. Do you know of any spots?"

"Nah, not really. I hear there's a new hotel, though, built over the High Line."

"It sounds promising."

"Sure does."

"Let's chill in the park before the show starts. We still have some time."

John and I walked over to the park in front of La Esquina. The park was barren. There were only a few benches to speak of, and the greenery was just adequate. We sat down. Natives of this neighborhood were hanging out. Their gray hair and basic attire referenced a time past. This was where the artists had lived, and now it was where the artists worked. Billy Joel had immortalized the old dynamic in the song "Uptown Girl." Now it would have been about a SoHo girl knocking boots with a Bushwick guy.

John and I discussed our plans. He talked about making another short film. He believed he had the opportunity to get it to Sundance and then be a real filmmaker. I discussed making graphic novels and parlaying that success into a weird cartoon show on late night television. We validated each other, a constant need, given the highs and lows of our particular lifestyle. There was no promise of a stable future, only the promise of the odds not being in our favor. We checked the time and realized we needed to head over to the gallery. The light was fading, and the city took on a new setting.

On these bustling streets, people tended to dress well, and by "well," I mean expensively. John and I wore cheap jeans and busted sneakers. We hadn't learned how to pull it together yet. New York City had some implicit rules of dress. One was not to wear ugly athletic shoes without doing athletic activity. We looked like obvious non-natives. It would us take some time before we became part of the fabric.

We arrived at the gallery, where there were people spilling outside the entrance. Some people were wearing knitted jumpsuits that covered their faces. A group in their twenties were on the steps in front, off to the side of the entrance, smoking. They looked cool. They wore beanies, and torn Levis, and had edgy haircuts. Charles came outside as we were going in. He was at least ten years older than we were and European. He knew how to pull it together. He wore a fedora, nice dress shoes, and an Army jacket.

"Hey, mates!"

"Hi, Charles!" John and I greeted him.

"Hey, mates. I'm here with some other friends. I'll introduce you later. We're all hitting the Randolph later for cocktails."

"Okay, we'll see you there."

John and I went into the gallery up the stairs. There was a collection of figurative 2-D and 3-D works, all created by multicolored knitted loops. I realized then that the people we had seen out front in the jumpsuits were part of the show, like kinetic or live sculpture. It was a little like Gilbert and George.

We saw Jared flirting with a small Asian girl. She was dressed like a schoolgirl and wore a black leather backpack that had rows of plush black horns sticking up from it. He nodded to us, but we got the sense he was in work mode. We continued through the show. These opening nights were more about people-watching and less about the show. It was about schmoozing, boozing, and pretending you were somehow a member of the glitterati.

We tried to get decent looks at the work, though the place was overrun. People had Dixie cups of red wine and placed themselves inconveniently in front of the works. If they saw us trying to look past them, they would shuffle a few feet away. I couldn't help but dart my eyes around the room. Many of the girls here were gorgeous. They exuded a sort of upscale, bohemian, yogi mastery of tantra. Any time I was able to receive a glimpse back from one of these girls, I felt a small thrill. It was an affirmation of being in the grand mecca of urban cool.

The work reminded me of Joseph Beuys's "Felt Suit." Beuys was a member of the Nazi youth movement and had even volunteered for the Luftwaffe. He created hundreds of these suits modeled after his own *Hitlerjugend* suit. They were stark, bleak pieces that rang with the doom of the time. Many in suits like those made decisions controlling life and death on a daily basis.

On the other hand, when I looked at the colorful, whimsical pieces, I also saw something on the other side of the coin. These pieces, made with colorful yarn, celebrated life. They were inventive and altruistic. Both were valid, just like night and day are both important. This night was about adventure. The day was about work and patience. The night was about now.

It was close to nine, but the exhibition was still open. It appeared they were continuing on in the space with an afterparty. Charles came over and told us that some people were heading over to the Randolph now. John and I told him we would meet them over there. We exited the gallery, because we needed a head start. I knew that they would cab it and get there before us. John and I had little money, didn't want to spend it on a cab, and needed to hoof it. It was a good thing we were wearing sensible New Balance. We walked uptown and over East.

The Randolph was a beautiful space. It felt like an old man's bar, but not one that had been left to decay. The bar and woodwork were stained dark. Booths and stools at the bar were upholstered in red leather. We spotted Charles and people at the bar near the center of the room —only two other guys in their thirties and four girls. Jared wasn't with them. Charles made introductions. I immediately locked eyes with a brunette in the middle. She had a nose ring and wore a leather jacket over a white floral dress. Charles was drinking white wine, but everybody else had a cocktail. John and I ordered two Yuenglings and moved toward the bar, since there was no room at the table. Charles joined us up at the bar, too.

"Hey, mates. That was a great show, ya?" Charles asked.

"Yeah, absolutely. It was great," I said.

"Yeah, there were too many douches though. They think their shit doesn't stink!" John rolled his eyes.

"Dude, what do you mean? Did you see the girls there?" I asked.

"Yeah, they look like hippie gold diggers!" John said.

"Hippie gold diggers! How can you be a hippie and a gold digger, mate?" Charles asked.

"Well, you take a trust fund chick and give her an art school education. Then you give her an apartment in the Village and send her on her way. Some hedge fund dude will snatch her up, and they'll have a pretentious little family and move to Williamsburg."

The brunette in the leather jacket and dress came up to us and joined in the conversation.

"Yeah, you just wish you had that," she said to John.

"Yes, I do!" John said.

"Well, at least you're honest about it," she said.

"Hey, mates, let's do another round." Charles bought a round for the four of us.

"The ones you really have to be annoyed with are the DACs," the brunette said.

"What's that?" John asked.

"DAC stands for Dysfunctional Art Chicks. Those are the ones."

"Well, I went to art school. I'm down with them, unless they're militant man- haters," I said.

"All women are the same, mates. They just want to be dominated," Charles declared.

"Oh, really? You sure that's true?" the brunette asked.

"Yes, it's in the genes. When they fight nature is when they become miserable and plagued with multiplying cats…"

"Sometimes, I like the control," she retorted.

"No, you only think you do," Charles snapped back.

"You wouldn't know," she smiled.

"I'd like to find out," I said and smiled at her.

"Oh, would you?" she asked.

"Yes, yes, I would."

I looked over and noticed a man in a motorized wheelchair. He rolled into the back of the bar with an entourage of mainly attractive, exotic women. He wore round-rimmed glasses and was bald with a white goatee. I was in awe. This was one of the most famous contemporary artists alive today. He had originally worked in photorealism but then got sick. He was confined to a wheelchair, and his work became pattern oriented. He was a force. It was obvious to everyone in the room, whether they knew of him or not, that he was a big deal. He looked thrilled to be him. Sure, he was condemned to a chair, but these women were all over him, and they were hot.

It was nearing 11:30. We all made our way out of the bar. The brunette stopped me.

"Where are you going?"

"Home with you," I responded.

"Yeah? You think so?"

"Yes, I think so."

She hailed a cab, and I got in with her. She told the cab driver to go to 16th Street and Seventh Avenue. We were in the back of the cab sucking face. The sounds of the world outside the back seat of the cab became dimmed. The present was about wet smacking sounds, busy hands and tugging of garments.

We arrived at her large, sprawling building that seemed to take up half the block. She warned me her apartment would be dirty. I didn't care. We went up a flight of stairs. She opened up the big, heavy metal door to her apartment. It was a studio; the bed took up most of the room. Clothes were strewn about. She seemed embarrassed and started throwing the clothes into a pile on a chair in the corner. I picked her up and dropped her on the bed. We started taking off our clothes. I took off her bra. She had her nipples pierced with silver bars. I rubbed my erection against her. She told me to use my hand. I took off her white panties and put a couple of fingers in her. They felt wet and hot.

She began writhing on the bed. She told me to make a come-hither gesture with those fingers. I did as I was told, and felt my whole hand get wet. Then ribbons of cum sprayed out of her. It looked as though a sprinkler system had been activated. She lay there breathing heavily. I grabbed my pants that were only three feet away. I went into the left back pocket and pulled out a Durex extra-sensitive, ripping open the purple packet, and rolling it on. I pumped away inside her. She scratched my back, and I came. I grunted and slid out of her, breathing heavily myself, lying with my head next to her pierced nipples.

We readjusted ourselves. She told me to stay. She said she had to be up early in the morning for work, she had a job at Sotheby's. I didn't know what she did and was too tired to ask. When she asked if I could bring her keys to Sotheby's in the morning because she preferred the deadbolt locked, I told her I could, because I didn't work until later.

In the morning, I heard her take a shower, then rustle around, pulling together her outfit. She leaned over and kissed me on the cheek. I pretended to be in a deep sleep.

I got up 15 minutes after she left. I went to the bathroom and got cleaned up. I put on my clothes, which she'd placed on a chair in the corner. I left and locked the deadbolt like she told me. I got a bagel and orange juice before jumping on the 6 train.

I got off at 59ᵗʰ and Lexington. It was very busy at ten a.m. Almost everyone was dressed in formal business attire. I went into Sotheby's, where a middle-aged black lady asked me whom I was here with. I said I was looking for a particular brunette. The brunette came down the stairs. She was wearing different clothes from the ones the night before, jeans and a black cardigan. She took me onto the second level.

I saw freestanding aluminum wardrobe racks with clothes hanging in black bags. Everything was labeled. There must have been at least 25 of them. I asked what her job at Sotheby's was.

"I don't actually work for Sotheby's. I do wardrobe department work."

"Oh. What is this shoot for?" I asked.

"Madonna is shooting a film here," she stated.

"Madonna makes movies?" I asked.

"Yes, she makes movies now."

"Wow, Madonna makes movies."

"Did you bring my keys?"

"Yes, I have them."

I handed her the keys. We exchanged numbers and then kissed. I went back out onto the street. I found the Green line.

I jumped on the 4, and transferred at the Canal stop to get back home on the J. As I rode it back, I looked below and saw Peter Luger's Steakhouse. It was closed, and only a few trucks were driving down the roads. Pigeons were hanging out on the rooftops. I continued on into Bushwick. Later, I would come back into the city to work at the bistro. Soon after that I would quit.

Coke Is Usually a Bad Idea

I was out of work, having quit in fine romantic fashion. I had no other job waiting for me; I let the chips fall where they would. I was 23 without a wife or kids. So, if there was a time to quit that way, now was it. I quit because I was angry, and then got angry with myself, yet again, because I did not have another job.

My lease was still good for a couple of months. Jared had dropped out of the lease early. He hated his accommodations in Bushwick. He moved in with a middle-aged white guy and his Korean girlfriend in Bed Stuy. I was left with the two models and a third, more recent, roommate. She was a Pratt student, not quite a dysfunctional art chick, but she was definitely strange.

I had been used to my life with Jared and the models. It had felt adequate, and I had assumed it would go on until I was 30. Now, it felt like a tiny betrayal that Jared was unhappy and needed to change his locale. It proved constant that when Jared felt the pressure of life, he grabbed his shit and left. He left Seattle, and now he was leaving Bushwick. I couldn't figure out what I was going to do.

I racked my brain, thinking about the possibilities of employment. I found restaurant work a drain. Granted, I was on the bottom of the totem pole. All work sucks when you're on the bottom rung, but I didn't know how I would climb to bartender. It felt like I wouldn't be given the chance. Also, I could barely count to begin with and had horrible short-term memory. You need to be able to count to tend bar, so your bank at the end of the night is correct. And you need decent short-term memory so you can remember multiple drink orders. I felt the only thing I knew how to do was make dirty cartoons, but I couldn't monetize it. Who knew that the mass majority doesn't appreciate cartoons of skeletons boning doll women?

John, Charles, and I all left the bistro the same month. Charles took a break from working to act in a NYU student's film. John jumped over to a position as a busboy at the Stan Ward Hotel on the High Line in the Meatpacking District. He had worked at one of the finest steakhouses in Chicago before coming to New York and was the youngest server they'd had. But he was tired of the job and wanted something that used very little of his cognitive abilities, so he took a position as busboy captain at the Stan Ward.

I had only worked low-level positions in Miami. I had only been a counter boy and busboy in New York. I had shitty bosses, low pay and no way to ascend the restaurant ladder.

There is a process. You need a representative to appeal to the manager, who has to okay it with the owner. So, you need to be competent. You need to be likable. You need to shut up, keep your head down, and do whatever you are told. Once you climb the ladder, you have more room to speak up. I hadn't worked with bartenders yet who would rep me. And I had an innate disgust of restaurant management. This would prove to be difficult.

It was a Friday night, and I was alone. The girl I was hooking up with had left me. She didn't so much leave me, as stop showing up. She was a very sexy Polish girl. I enjoyed having sex with her a lot. I realized that I had to stop showing it; if I was too into girls, it scared them away. It made you seem like a crazed wolf who hadn't taken down an elk in a while. I felt lonely with Jared in Bed Stuy now. I had never really hung out outside of the apartment with the models, and I barely spoke to the Pratt student.

It was bleak. It was nine p.m.; I was unemployed, bored, and lying down on my gym mat. My yellow walls were draining my optimism. I wanted a girl for the night. It would distract me from the futility of my situation. I thought about where I would go. I didn't want to make a major effort. Jared and I hadn't gone out much in Bushwick. We only had two bars nearby. The one closer to us looked like a remnant of a bar after a nuclear holocaust, a hipster shithole; the other was slightly more upscale. I figured my chances of meeting an easy, tattoo-speckled girl would be better there. I put on my finest flannel shirt, and less dirty jeans, and walked over to the bar.

The bar was fairly busy. I was surprised, but this part of Brooklyn was more developed. People wanted to go out to party when they weren't working their restaurant jobs. I eyeballed the room. I noticed pretty girls of all colors. I went to the bar and ordered a PBR. Flannel shirt: check;

beard: check; PBR tallboy: check: I met the criteria of a young hipster looking for loose women.

I realized that I had only taken the Polish girl to the shitty bar. I never took her to this bar or, in fact, any other bar. I couldn't help but think there was a reason she stopped showing up. I didn't make too much of an effort. My thoughts about her began swirling in my head. She looked like a Bond girl. The first time I undressed her on my gym mat and pushed aside the pile of clothes, she was wearing black lace stockings. She was platinum blond who smelled floral with hints of menthol.

I felt lonely. I felt like the only living boy in New York. Now, I wanted to regain that lust for life. I stood at the edge of the bar and drank my PBR fairly quickly. A middle-aged Puerto Rican man took notice of me and engaged me in conversation.

"Hey, man! What's up?" he asked enthusiastically.

"Nothing much, man."

"Cool man, nice beard! I was thinking of growing one. The ladies like it, no?"

"Yeah, sometimes, I guess."

"What you want for a drink, papa? I got you."

"I guess I'll have a whiskey soda."

"Okay, papa. I got you!"

He ordered a whiskey soda for me, and a tequila Sprite for him. The bartender got the drinks quickly. I felt good, as I sipped it with a straw. I didn't like PBR much, but it was three bucks for a can. I was unemployed. So that was the drink of choice. Now that this friendly gentleman was buying me a drink, whiskey it was.

He was warm, and I felt happy to have a decent drink in my hand. My eyes kept darting around to the ladies in the room to see if I got any glances back, a swing and a miss. Sometimes, it doesn't bode well for a man to go in for the solo hunt. It makes you seem like a dog with rabies. I relinquished my desire to make small talk. I felt deflated from the Polish girl ditching me. This gentleman was friendly, and it was nice to talk to another human being.

"So, papa. You live here?" he asked.

"Yeah, I do."

"That's cool. Brooklyn is the shit, dog. This is the place dreams are made."

"Yeah, that's what they tell me."

"You want some of this?" He pulled out a small plastic bag from his pocket filled halfway with white powder.

"No. No, I'm good."

"Okay, papa. I'll be right back. I'm gonna hit the bathroom."

"Okay, I'll keep an eye on your tequila."

He went over to the bathroom, while I hung out at the bar. I never touched cocaine. I had lived in Miami, and I saw a lot of cocaine there. I was offered a lot of cocaine, but the fact was, I was a square. I enjoyed alcohol, and that was that. I hadn't even smoked weed at that point. My body was my temple, but I didn't mind flooding my temple with rivers of booze now and again.

He came back jittery but in good spirits. He offered me some of his bag again, but I declined. He ordered us another round of drinks. I was feeling groovy. I felt good in my body. In the moment, I was able to let go of the feeling of abandonment. I released the hopes and dreams I had. I forgot about my past. It was just now. I was warm and had brown distilled spirits thinning my blood.

The bar took on a new mood. It felt hazier. It felt darker. Had they turned the lights down? The Puerto Rican man was fidgeting more than before. He wasn't in a bad mood. His body was twitching in an arrhythmic manner. He went into his pocket and pulled out the bag half way. He took his index finger licked it and let the white powder collect on it. Then he took his finger to his teeth, and rubbed it in.

"Hey, papa. You want to make some money? I want to get out of here for a bit. We'll drive around, and I'll pay you to hang out," he said.

"I don't know man. That's kind of weird. We just met."

"No, man. What you think I'm asking you? I just don't want to be alone, and I need some air. I did a little too much yay-o!"

"Well, that makes sense."

"I'll give you three hundred dollars."

"Sure, then."

This was obviously a very stupid decision. At the time, three hundred dollars was close to what I made in a week busing. I thought this would be easy money, and it would help me out with my draining funds. Sure, this jittery Puerto Rican man was a perfect stranger to me, but he seemed nice enough. He had bought me some whiskey sodas. How bad could he be? Also, I was far more sober than he was. I imagined I could punch him square in the face and run.

We left the bar and walked down the block to his car. It was an old Lincoln. We got in and started driving. He put on his stereo and had Gypsy Kings playing. It brought back fond memories from my youth when my dad had played them.

"This is fun, son. You hear that? That's the Kings playing. The night is nice. I'm feeling like a goddamned Superman!"

"Yeah, me too."

"Damn, I need more yay-o! You know what I mean."

"I think maybe you had enough."

"No, man. I'm just getting started!"

"So, what about the $300. Can I have that now?"

"What?"

"You said you'd pay me $300 to take the drive with you."

"I don't got that on me. I got that at my crib, son! I don't roll with that on me."

"You said you had it!" I said, irritated and now sobering up to the idea that this car ride might be my last. I cursed myself for my stupidity in trusting a junkie.

"I can get it to you. We just got to go to my house."

"Fine." I began to regain some hope that I would get this money, and that he was mellow and on the level. We drove onto the highway. I didn't know where I was going. I pulled out my Nokia and saw it was almost dead. I noticed a sign. It read "King's Highway." I hadn't heard of this part of Brooklyn. We drove into a neighborhood of small homes. It looked like undeveloped parts of Queens. He parked in a driveway, and we got out of the car.

"Hey, we got to enter through the back. My old lady is sleeping, and she'll be pissed if I wake her up."

"Fine, whatever." I hoped this wasn't a deadly decision I just made.

We went back behind the house, where his yard was very dark. I saw a few tires strewn about. We entered through the back door. His first floor looked like a crash pad for one of Scarface's henchmen. It was gaudy and cheap. He told me to take a seat, while he went to the bathroom. I sat on a long, tan couch with my hands clenched. I felt sweat beads forming on my brow. Had I made a final decision?

He came into the room shirtless and without pants. Only off-white boxers covered him. His belly was hanging over his underwear. He had a long scar along his abdomen. I was horrified.

"Man, what the fuck? Put on your pants. What the fuck is this?" I barked.

"No, man! Don't be like this. I was hot. Don't be like that," he responded.

"How do you expect me to be? Put on your fucking pants!" I raised my voice.

"Keep your voice down, dog. My lady's sleeping," he pleaded.

I stood up. My shoulders were tense. I had no idea where I was. It was around midnight. I didn't know which train to take to get back. I thought I might need to make a run for it. And if I did, there was no guarantee I wouldn't get mugged by somebody else.

He went over to his cabinet and opened the drawer. He was searching around inside, then turned around to face me.

"Yo, dog. Did you take my coke? I can't find it."

"No, I don't do coke."

"Where the hell is it?" He went back to searching.

He started looking behind the bureau and into his cupboards. He turned around, to face me again.

"Yo, give it back."

"I didn't take your coke. You promised me money. Where's my money?"

"What money?"

"You promised me money!"

"What? When did I do that?"

"You have to be joking."

"I need that coke."

"I don't have your coke."

I felt the profundity of the situation at hand. I saw flashes of my parents crying over my grave. I saw my two younger brothers in therapy for the rest of their lives. I imagined the headlines: "YOUNG, DUMB, ART KID'S REMAINS FOUND IN THE EAST RIVER." I felt my internal organs and a pulse emanating from them. I then felt my muscles and my skin. The weight of this situation electrified me. It was fight, flight, or freeze. I knew I couldn't afford to freeze.

"All right, enough of this shit. I didn't take your shit. I'm out of here!" I said.

"No, we got to find the blow first!"

"I don't have to do anything."

"You wait right there."

He went into the next room. I felt intense panic. Did he have a gun? Did he have a machete? I didn't want to find out. I watched the horrific scene play out in the auditorium of my skull.

I imagined him coming out with a small aluminum bat. I pictured him using it to intimidate me. Then I pictured him swinging at me. He'd miss as I wrestled him down to the tile floor. What would happen then? Would I have to beat him unconscious with my fists? Maybe he would swing and break my hand (or worse, crack me in the face). Then I would kick him in the groin, but he'd be too coked up. He'd begin to strangle me, and I'd poke at his eyes. I would have some room to execute a double leg takedown on him. Then I'd smash him in the head repeatedly. I figured I could put him to sleep with six or seven hard shots my elbow. What if he had friends nearby with guns? What if he came out with a gun and not a bat? Calculating all of the permutations and how to handle them, I cleared my mind to figure out the best possible response to this very real moment.

I had a clear shot to the door. I needed to take this opportunity to flee. It could be my last chance. I felt my carotid arteries pulse. My muscles tensed. My hands formed into tightly balled fists. I darted to the door. I turned the lock and felt him come back toward the couch. I heard his bare feet stumbling on the tile. I sprinted down the block. Three young, black teens watched me sprint and just stood there, staring. I ran until my legs started to wobble. I pushed myself until I started to wheeze. I ran to a bus stop. I saw an MTA bus following, not far behind me. I pulled my wallet out of my pocket. I immediately searched the contents to see if I had my MTA card. I had it, and a calm washed over me. The bus driver looked at me with disbelief. He hadn't expected to see the likes of me in this neighborhood at this time of night.

"Where are you trying to go, son?"

"J . . . J Kosciusko, sir . . . J whatever," I huffed, still catching my breath. I felt sweat running down my pits.

"Okay, you'll get off at Gates, then."

"Thank you . . . Thanks."

I sat in the seat behind the driver, so he could let me know when the stop came up. I took deep breaths and calmed down. I turned my head to the right straight ahead. It was quiet out. There weren't many cars; the streets were almost empty. I wiped the sweat from my forehead and felt my shirt cling to my skin. I breathed easy. I felt tired. I felt relaxed. I felt stupid and grateful.

I got home safely and stripped down. I rolled over on my gym mat and lay there with my eyes open. I was safe. I was tucked away in my windowless room. Tomorrow was a new day. The sun would rise, and I would have a new opportunity laid out before me. I needed a new job. I needed a legitimate job that didn't include socializing with drug dealers. Tomorrow was a new day.

I cut my lease early. I wanted out of Brooklyn for a bit. I had friends in France. I decided to drop my stuff off with Jared in Bed Stuy for safekeeping and booked a ticket. I would come back, find a new place to live, find a new job, and avoid anybody I suspected of peddling drugs. Yes, sir. Tomorrow was a new day!

And Then God Created Chat Roulette

...

send (ent)

Afterward, the world was forever different. It came into existence during the latter part of the first decade of the 21st century, and it was like the second coming of Jesus or the Big Bang. It was better than any adult site that had come before. It was the creation of Chat Roulette.

Chat Roulette was created for the sole purpose of allowing strangers to meet from around the globe. A truly magnificent thing, Can you imagine the byproduct? People from different cultures and backgrounds could meet who would not otherwise meet. It would break down all prejudices. It would create a world where we were all neighbors. Nobody would be lonely ever again. Nobody would ever be isolated. We would all be citizens of the world!

This would have been splendid if men weren't horny, slobbering pigs. Yes, world peace would have to wait. We just had to see tits first. We'd get to the world peace thing another time.

Like other men, when I stumbled upon this godsend (or maybe a gift from Lucifer), I traveled into full-blown, revolting self-destruction. The site was simple. You clicked "ok" on a popup screen allowed Chat Roulette access to the camera on your computer. Once you clicked "ok," you began the search for girls. I don't know what those girls were thinking, but I knew what these men were thinking.

As the screen would pop up with a new woman, you began your search. You had the option to skip her with a click if you wanted to move on, and she could do the same. Those were the rules. Other rules included not displaying private parts. This was commonly overlooked.

People got flagged for displaying their genitals. But this didn't happen all the time. Mostly, people just clicked "skip" in order to move on. Some girls would flash the camera. I found it exciting. It was like a virtual orgy. Occasionally, women would linger. This would more often than not lead to mutual masturbation. Something about this was almost more exciting than real live women. It was an anonymous realm, where the rules of society did not apply.

I quickly became obsessed. I would run home from work in order to log in. I would spend hours into the late night searching. It was as though I were a caveman on the hunt. It took dedication. You might only have moments to hook a girl into staying connected. I practiced my boyish charm. I had my big innocent smile ready for when the new connection was established. I got swiped over, but once in a while I'd rope one in. I met the first on a random night. Her strawberry blond hair alerted me immediately to perk up. She gave me a coy smile. I felt a sudden sense of dread and excitement. She was truly beautiful. I typed to her, "Hello."

She reciprocated with a wave. The display let me know she was from Maryland. I inquired through my keyboard if she liked living in Maryland. She nodded. I told her I thought she was very pretty. She smiled again and told me she thought I was handsome.

We looked at each other for a moment. I could see she had beautiful breasts. I didn't want to be a creepy dude. I wanted to be a gentleman. I just didn't know how to do it. Real life was one thing. In real life, we have social cues. These cues allow us to read each other. It's a nuanced dance we do in mating.

Men lost these skills with the advent of technology. We lost the connection with the physical. I wanted to hook up with this girl, but I didn't know how to go about it. I couldn't put a hand on her knee. I couldn't brush her hair back. I couldn't lean in for the kiss. It was the end of romance. I decided the only move was to ask.

"I don't mean to be rude, but I find you very beautiful. Could I please see your boobs?" I typed out to her.

I sent the message over to her and watched her read it. The action had a weightiness to it. I felt ill at ease in that quiet moment. It wasn't unlike the feeling of floundering in front of a real girl.

She smiled at me and pulled her shirt over her head. I was breathless. I was in awe. I was high. She asked me to take off my shirt, and I did as I was told. Now we stood before our cameras presenting ourselves to one another. Now what? Again, she wasn't in front of me so I couldn't smell her, taste her, or pull her in. I stood before her virtual presence in virtual godly awe.

"Would you mind if I touched myself?" I typed out and sent.

I felt my stomach hollow out. Did I ruin the moment? Was this taking it too far? I knew the rules in the real world. I didn't know them here. I wasn't sure what was okay. I only knew I was lost in the electric wave of her strawberry blond locks.

"Yes, please," she typed and sent back.

I pulled off my briefs, as she started to play with her breasts. I played with myself and displayed myself to her. I knew in the back of my mind it was possible that she or somebody was taping it. I didn't care, though. I was entranced.

I was excited but kept my breathing steady. I was afraid to make a sound. She then pointed the camera down toward her loins. I saw her perfect pink cavern and was transported there. She touched herself, and I could hear her subtle moans. I shut off the output on my sound, but she hadn't. I could hear more than just soft moaning. She then pointed the camera back to her bust. Her mouth opened ever so slightly. I was overcome with excitement and caught my byproduct onto my briefs. I was sweating and dizzy. I held up my briefs to her with my ejaculate. She smiled.

"Very good," she typed.

"Thank you," I typed back.

She gestured a kiss through the monitor. I sent one back. I clicked out of Chat Roulette. I rolled over onto my back. I was hooked. I had taken my first hit, and it was over. I would progressively become more entrenched in this virtual orgy. I was in a downward pink spiral of no return.

I went about my routine of work, training in mixed martial arts, drawing and biking. It all became filler until I could get back to Chat Roulette. I was obsessed. The rush trumped everything. I lived solely to get back online to meet a new one. I began to daydream at work about the past encounters. I was exhausted throughout the week. I couldn't get enough sleep. I was up most of the night, searching online. The rest of the day was spent dreaming about the night. I couldn't help myself. I mostly kept this dark obsession to myself. I told John about it, but no one else. John even went on a couple of times, enamored with my tales of gold. He was quickly disillusioned and moved on. I stayed behind in the great virtual expansion. I kept looking for gold. The greed and lust were a drug for which I had no antidote.

I descended into the darkness. I think I stopped even flirting with girls in the physical world. Unless they were on my screen, they weren't real to me. John told me to get off the site and get out there. I couldn't, though. I would find at least one girl a night who would strip for me. It wouldn't always continue like strawberry blond first did, but it was still satisfying. I knew this wasn't healthy. I knew this was affecting everything in my life for the worse. I knew this needed to stop. I would just go on once more. Surely, one more time would be enough.

I tried once more. Once more led to once more again. Once more again led to after this final time. After this final time led to a final farewell that never came.

I was fucked. This was now taking more from me than I was getting. The climax wasn't a fair trade for my life. I saw all things I held dear slipping away. I wasn't drawing nearly as much. I was stagnating in my Jiu-Jitsu. I barely hung out with friends and became a hermit, basking in the glow of my screen. I was also always tired from staying up all night searching. It was as though I were the first Cro-Magnon and living for the hunt. I needed to satisfy my biological imperative, and this felt like the only way to quench it.

I was back online searching, and wasting my life force. I kept clicking through new connections. I saw people from all over the globe. I saw groups of people gathered around one screen. I saw lonely sickos, just like me. I felt I was looking in a mirror and not at strangers. I saw the flashes of females skipping me and moving onto the next sad loser. I saw practical jokers, masturbators, and loonies. I saw the creatures of the night and the living dead roam through. I looked upon the end of romance, and humanity--and it was chilling. Then she stopped my scrolling.

She was an older woman from Switzerland. She had brown, medium-length hair, glasses, and a green blouse. I had contorted my face quickly into a charming (desperate) smile. She smiled back. We stared at each other for a moment. I wondered what she was thinking. I had my mike turned off, as usual. I typed "Hello." She waved and typed back, "Hello."

I began to type, "Do you go to this site often?" I felt stupid writing that and backtracked. I typed, "What time is it there right now?"

She typed back, "around two p.m."

It was close to two a.m. in New York. We were separated by land and time. I would never have encountered this woman in any other space than right here in cyberspace. We were in another dimension of sight, sound and mind. It was like dating in the Twilight Zone.

I was less nervous about propositioning a woman through this site. I had spent hours of time in this realm. I had squandered so many hours hunting, obsessing, and obtaining online. It was getting to be my whole reality.

"Can I see your breasts?" I typed to her.

"Sure," she typed back.

I was as excited a child is unwrapping a birthday present. She undid her blouse. I saw a pale pink bra under the blouse. She reached behind her to undo the clasp. Her bra fell gently off her pale, ample breasts.

"They're great," I typed.

"Thanks," she typed and smiled.

"Can you stand up and spin around slowly?" I typed.

She did as I asked. She had a green tribal tattoo around her belly button and a green tramp stamp behind. She wasn't wearing any bottoms. I knew that she had been searching too. I knew she was just as sad and lonely as I was. We weren't lonely any more (in the moment anyway). We were together, separate from the whole world. It was just the two of us, separate from the banal planet.

"Can I touch myself?" I typed to her.

"Yes, please," she typed back.

I had my underwear ready to catch my elation. I began to work myself. She did the same, and it was satisfying. I got my fill. I had spent countless hours on this one moment. Nothing else went through my mind. No one else was in my mind; it was just the cyber woman and me. It was just two WIFI-crossed lovers (lusters?) jacking off on opposite sides of the globe. I was getting close and aimed right onto my briefs. I released and went blind for a moment.

When I came to, I had the contents of my work neatly displayed on my Calvin Klein's. I raised it to the camera for her to see.

"Very good," she typed.

I caught my breath.

"It would be nice to do this again," I typed.

"I would like that," she typed back.

"Do you have Skype?" I asked.

"Yes, I do," she said.

Thus began a pseudo-relationship. We would meet at two a.m. my time, two p.m. hers. The moment was reserved for our encounter. Skype was our cheap motel. The immediate benefit of this was that it got me off Chat Roulette and out of the vast electronic chasm. She was methadone for my sexual heroin addiction.

After our third encounter via Skype, we chatted. She took me around her house, which was beautiful. It was everything you'd expect from Scandinavian design—clean, minimalist, and efficient. She showed me her view. It was extraordinary— lush, green, paradisiacal. All I knew about her was that she was like me (in the worst ways). I didn't know anything about her life.

"That's a beautiful home," I typed.

"Thank you," she said.

"So, what do you do for work, if you don't mind me asking?"

"I don't work that much. I work nights at a home for the elderly."

"That's cool. Do you live alone?"

"No."

"Who do you live with?"

"My husband."

Shit, I thought. This counted as infidelity, didn't it? Was cyber cheating real cheating? We had never met. Was this more akin to interactive porn? Was interactive porn cheating? Was I a homewrecker? Maybe her husband knew. Maybe it wasn't such a big deal. Maybe I was a digital sidepiece. I was the virtual pool-boy. I was an innocent bystander, looking for love on all the wrong websites.

"Does he know what you do at two p.m.?" I typed.

"No." She typed back.

Dammit, I thought. I was a piece of shit. Well, I wasn't a piece of shit yet. I hadn't known. I hadn't noticed a ring. I had been lied to, per se. Also, was this really cheating? I never met this woman in the flesh. I doubted I would ever meet her. This would be a non-issue, if it stopped here and now. It didn't stop though. Weeks went on, and we continued to meet at two. It was our dream world. Dreams don't hurt people. I was hallucinating this whole thing, and it lacked any bearing on anyone's life.

My schedule changed. Now I was closer at the service bar in the Stan Ward Hotel lobby, a job John had gotten me after he started work there. My shift wouldn't end till three or four in the morning. I was used to not getting much sleep anyway. I let her know my schedule change and that I wouldn't be able to meet as often but that I really wanted to continue our Skype liaisons.

She seemed to understand. Now, we met once every two weeks or so, irregularly. Our initial hot and heavy typing sessions were slacking off. Then they froze over, and I lost her. She stopped picking up my Skype calls. That two-timing bitch was probably Skyping someone else! Was she tired of me? That selfish bitch was probably tired of me!

I finally caught her online after the third night of attempts. She looked detached, not excited to see me.

"Hey, where have you been?" I typed to her.

"I've been working a lot."

"Oh, that's cool."

"Yes, and my husband and I are planning a trip," she typed.

"Oh, that's good."

"How are you?" she asked.

"I'm good."

"That's good."

"See me in Paris. I'll come to Paris, and we can see each other. That would be good, right?"

"I don't think that's a good idea," she typed.

I knew what this was. This was the brush-off. It was sad and good; it was what was coming; it was what needed to be; it was over for us. I was old enough. There would be no traces of her hair on my sheets. There would be no stray socks under the bed. No landmarks that made me think her name (which I still didn't know), and no favorite café we shared. Our affair was a mist erased by the power of the sun. Now I was dark, cold and lonely.

Back in the chasm of isolation, cured of addiction by biblical guilt, I was hollow. I needed to remake myself into a man. I gathered my blue belt, gi and mouth guard in my green duffle bag and went down to my dojo. I rolled with beasts of men and got my ass kicked. Eric, the purple belt bully, buried knuckles into my neck. He twisted my arms and sent me to Marc, who proceeded to pummel me. I was then passed along to the champion, Dantae. He triangle-choked me, and the veins throbbed from my temples. Then the Professor sat on my chest, until I could not take any more punishment from the utter, crushing dominance.

I was humbled, broken, and a mess on the mats. Then I was rebuilt whole. I was resurrected into the physical world, released from the dimly lit cyber cell. The physical punishment served as penance for walking in the shadows. . I could only vaguely see her in my mind, in a theoretical Switzerland. Of course, I would find new ways to sink into depravity.

Cracker Devil Faggot

I moved to "Bed Stuy, Do or Die," in 2010. It wasn't the Bed Stuy of Spike Lee's *Do the Right Thing,* but it still had its rough patches. I moved into an apartment with my new best friend, John. My roommates at my last Bed Stuy apartment two blocks away were sad old guys and that had taken its toll on me; John and I were as close as brothers now after working together at the bistro. He'd gotten me a job with him at the Stan Ward Hotel. In this quadrant of Brooklyn, we were teammates in the gridiron of the Big Apple, an immediate and apparent sensation, undesirables now. . We were two of a total of four whites in our immediate neighborhood, which was predominantly black and Puerto Rican. The looks shot our way included speculation, annoyance, and possible violence. We had made this choice out of necessity. We had a two- bedroom on the third floor for $1,100, unheard-of. Our building was no gem; it was partly a Section 8 that had been beaten to hell. In its heyday, it had been an elegant prewar hotel. It still had beautiful molding on the outside, but all five floors had been left to rot on the inside. A Hasidic man, Walter, owned the building. He was a hip Hasid who swore and talked about girls. I felt the *payes* were a kind of camouflage; he needed them to blend in with the other Hasidic real estate moguls.

John and I both worked a variety of shit jobs. We barely pulled in four hundred bucks a week each. There was little sexy or glamorous about the Stan Ward. It was built on the old High Line railroad, now a New York City greenway. It lurched over the abandoned, aboveground railyard that had once connected the northern and southern parts of the West Side. Its facade was glass. Hotel guests staying on the facade-side would frequently fuck close to the glass, so they could put on a show for the peepers below. Old-school, hard-ass New Yorkers ran it, and hired naive, inexperienced bohemians, sassy gays, and drug abusers. The only reason to stick it out was to have it on your resume. That was a golden key to any other hotel or restaurant in the city for employment. That's all it took: one year of quarterly employee evaluations, unrelenting hours of manual labor, keeping your head down, clocking in, clocking out, and taking it on the chin. John worked mainly during the day as a barista (having been promoted from captain of the busboys prior). I had also climbed the ladder like John, and I was thrilled to be on the service bar slinging drinks.

We saw all kinds at the hotel. There was a lot of foreign money, A-list celebrities (and some C-list), Chelsea art glitterati, lawyers, corporate climbers, and sometimes Lou Reed. There were three venues on the ground floor: the Biergarten, which was huge and partly seated outside; the Grill, which housed the main dining room along with a private dining room; and the hotel lobby service bar.

When John and I both had a morning open, we would go to the park nearby at Tompkins and Greene. It was unremarkable at first sight, but had the echoes from a thousand mini-gang wars. At the western edge of the park were a basketball court, handball court, and monkey bars. One set of monkey bars was for children; they included a slide. The other set was purely utilitarian. They were meant for exercise. John and I would "get that good money" and "build that body." We were the only white guys who would. It was usually a little tense, so we tried to stay out of the way and show our respect. Our neighbors didn't seem to understand that we were just as broke as they were. Yes, our folks had money (from busting their asses), but we were making it on our own. If I could have afforded to live in Greenpoint, I would have. Greenpoint was north of Bed Stuy by a couple of train stops. It had been Polish; the girls were gorgeous, and there seemed to be a void of violence. You could breathe easy but you paid through the nose.

John and I pushed our bodies and "got that good money." We worked hard to show that we weren't pussies and that we valued work. After a couple of weeks, we were accepted. We were honorary hood now.

One of our regular workout buddies was named Marvin. He was a construction worker about 15 years older than we were, of medium height, strong, with a tattoo of a bull on his arm. His ear was adorned with a diamond stud. He had a John Wayne kind of energy about him; he talked a little slower and moved with confidence. He was kind to John and me from the beginning. We would share my jump rope and trade exercises we had learned. It's safe to say it was Marvin who decreed that we were to be accepted at the monkey bars. I could picture him saying in our absence to the other gentlemen, "These boys is alright, ya hear? Ain't nobody gonna do nothing to them. So sayeth Marvin!" And they obeyed.

One morning, John and I walked over to the park. Marvin had gotten my number the last time we had worked out together. He told us he would meet up with us. The three of us started doing jumping jacks on the rubber mats below the bars. We took a moment to stretch and complain about the aches and pains we had from work.

"You know what? I got this pain in my left knee. I was working a tile job, and my knee is all busted," Marvin said.

"Yeah, man. I smashed my hand into the espresso machine as I went to shut off the steamers. My knuckles are all banged up," John said.

"You know what, guys? I was bringing a bus tub back from the bar and slipped on a wet floor. My back is pretty sore," I said.

"We three is all beaten up. We'll take it easy then," Marvin instructed.

"All right, let's get some pull-ups in."

We started cranking out pull-ups. Descending from the bars one by one, we each started our own sets of exercises. John was doing crunches; Marvin switched over to the dip bar; I dropped to the ground and started doing pushups. I looked over as I got up off the ground at the nearest entrance to the park. Two black men were heading our way. One was about six foot five. The other guy was smaller but very built and about my height. I hadn't seen them in the neighborhood before, though John and I had only been in the neighborhood a short time. The smaller guy jumped on one set of bars to do pull-ups. I stretched out and got on the bars closest to me, as the big guy grabbed the bars in front of him to do pulls. Here we were, both doing pulls-ups only a few feet from each other. I only glanced at him, as I was hoisting my chest up to the bar. He looked like Michael Clark Duncan--big, muscled, and powerful. Even under his oversized white t-shirt, you could see how strong he was. He lowered himself from the bar to take a break. I cranked out a few more pull-ups and then lowered myself back down to the rubber mats. I heard him breathing heavy; he turned his back away from us. I went over to my jump rope and started working my lungs. The big guy began pacing. His smaller friend went over to him. I overheard them speak, and I tried to avert my eyes.

"Cracker, devil, faggot! This is Bed Stuy," the big guy said.

"Lenny, it ain't worth it!"

"Yo, can you believe this shit, Deshawn?"

"Yo, man. I'm telling you. We all just here to get that good money."

"Cracker, devil, faggot! This is motherfucking Bed Stuy."

"Yo truth, man. He ain't doing nothing."

"This is motherfucking Bed Stuy. . . that cracker devil faggot thinks he can come up in here and be here. He gonna go!"

My heart rate skyrocketed. I whipped my rope around faster; I needed time to figure this situation out. Who was this guy? Was he an actual gangster? Was he just a ruffian? Did he have a weapon? I used to box in Miami, but I wasn't that good. If I were able to kick him in his horse dick and punch him in the throat, would I have enough time to run away? Did I have to get violent? If you don't fight back in prison, you are destined to be a punk ass bitch. How bad a beating would I take? Would I be hospitalized after this?

Lenny began to make his way over to me. Deshawn tried to get in the way. John tried to smile to break the tension, but Lenny wasn't having it.

"Don't smile at me, faggot! You're next," Lenny shouted.

Then Marvin got in the way. He put his hands out. Lenny towered over Marvin, but Marvin stood his ground. He looked straight into Lenny's eyes and didn't divert them.

"You ain't gonna do shit. You hear me, son? You are going to back away," Marvin commanded without any wavering in his voice.

Lenny stood there quietly. He looked over at me, and I looked straight back at him. Deshawn looked at John, and John looked back at him. We all stood silently there for a moment.

"Aight, Lenny. Let's get out of here," Deshawn said.

Lenny and Deshawn walked back through to the gate. I breathed a sigh of relief, as John looked at me and chuckled. Marvin turned to us and patted me on the back.

"I hate that racist shit. Those guys are stupid. Sorry about it. I got you guys, no matter what," Marvin reassured us.

"Wow, Marvin. Thank you so much, man. That was intense. I thought I was going to have to throw down. I didn't want to have to do that," I said.

"What? He would have beaten you into a paste!" John laughed.

"I would have gotten some shots in! I boxed!" I said, halfheartedly defending my manhood.

"Dude, did you see the size of him?" John asked.

"Look, it's all over now. You boys should get home. It's all good. We wouldn't let that go down. Go on now, ya hear? We'll get another workout in this week," Marvin told us.

"Okay, thanks so much! We owe you one. You rock, Marvin," I said.

I gave Marvin a hug. John and I went back to the apartment, cooked up some rice and beans, and enjoyed the meal as though it were our last.

I tried to group my work days together. I preferred to have an uninterrupted two to three full days off. This ensured I could gain momentum making art. I would work on a big red table, a gift from prior roommates that had weed residue on it. I imagined it had belonged to a weed dealer, and he'd had no more use for it, so he left it on the street. Sometimes, I would bring my pages or sketchbooks to a local coffee shop to work there. I received a text from Marvin a day after the incident in the park, asking me if I wanted to get a workout in. I texted him back that I was busy with some sketching and that we could train soon.

I went about my day. I was working on some recent pages, penciling out a comic. It was about my ex-girlfriend. I had only had three serious relationships at this point. She was by far the worst. "Why would I stay with her?" one might ask. The simple biological answer was that we fucked a lot. The more nuanced answer might have involved emotional dependency and/or chemical addiction. I was penciling out this particular comic and sipping on a heavily soy-laden coffee. The comic was about a run-in with her I had had at a bar in Williamsburg. I had tried to avoid her. She refused to take no for an answer when I told her

I wouldn't go home with her. I was penciling in the part of the comic where she was waiting for me at the rear exit of the bar. She's naked and shaved. She won't let me go; she imprisons me. Her vagina grows into a gigantic Venus flytrap and swallows me whole. I was using non-photo blue drafting lead. No one in the cafe could tell what I was sketching, unless they looked conspicuously. It was their own nosy fault if they got an eyeful of pulsating pink pussy!

I got another text from Marvin. He asked if I wanted to get a drink later. I had never gone for a drink with Marvin before; I didn't know he drank. We had only met at the park to work out. I texted him that I'd let him know later. I went back home, so I could ink the pussy pages I had started. It was getting late, and John wasn't home. I remembered that he had a date with a ballet girl in Greenpoint. He would probably be staying at her place or returning around one a.m. I looked in my fridge; it was barely stocked. I had some cooked pasta in a plastic tub, so I ate that cold sitting on the couch. My table was in the living room because my room was a shoebox. John was annoyed about it, but I mostly worked on my stuff when he wasn't around.

I received another text from Marvin, and by this time, it was . He was again asking if I wanted to go out for a drink. I texted him back that I was about to ink some pages. I told him John wasn't around, so I had a chance to get some work in. He insisted I should come out for a drink. I apologized and said we would another time. I went back to work on the pages, drawing over the lines with my Micron pens. The paper was absorbing the ink well, so it was exciting to see the image start to take hold. The room was silent, but I didn't notice.

Marvin texted me again. I went over to the couch to check the message, which read:

"You been lookin' good."

I was not sure what he meant. Was he reassuring me of my progress at the park? It seemed like an odd, random text. I didn't know what to say, so I typed back:

"Thanks, broski. I've been working hard."

A moment passed, and he sent another text:

"You a sexy white boi."

I froze. I wasn't sure if what I thought was happening was happening. Was this happening? I didn't know what to type. I said:

"Thanks, I'm aight."

He texted me back:

"You are a sexy white boi. Do you think I'm sexy?"

I was flabbergasted. This man who had defended me at the park was defending his bitch. He was manning up to protect his lady boy. I can't say I minded the protection, but I was shocked by the come-on. I had never given him any indication that I would be into this. John and I always talked about girls at the park. Maybe he thought I was lying. I didn't know what to say, so I didn't respond. My phone started buzzing, and it was Marvin, so I answered the phone.

"Hey, Dustin."

"Um, hey Marvin."

"I could see you was a little nervous."

"Nah, man. We cool."

"Yeah, you know I just wanting to let you know that you's a sexy white boy," Marvin said, slurring his words a little.

"Ah, ya. Thanks, Marvin. I appreciate that."

"So, what do you think of me?"

"Well, you know Marvin . . . you're cool and all. It's just that, you know, I'm into girls. I got no problem with any of it though. You know my brother's gay. It's cool."

"Yeah, but you never know. I was just thinking that maybe it was a possibility. We like hanging out. I don't mean no offense."

"No way, Marvin. We boys. Not a problem. We can get a workout in. John is off tomorrow."

"Okay, Dustin. That sounds good. I don't work until later, so that be good."

"Okay, Marvin. We'll get it in. I got to get back to my work now. Aight?"

"Yeah, sexy white boy. Tomorrow. Cool."

We hung up, and I sat dumbfounded. Wow. Thank god he wanted

to be more than just friends, or he might not have protected me from Lenny. This landscape was strange. I was not used to this culture. I grew up in the suburbs of Boston and moved to Miami as a young man. It was different there. People were loud and proud. There was no hiding one's persona. It was on the surface. People would fly their flags high. Here, in Brooklyn, one had to be careful. You wanted to be able to navigate all social circumstances.

In the morning, I set up the teakettle with water and put the burner on. I grabbed a green tea bag and looped the string around the handle. I put some granola into a bowl and poured almond milk over it and added a scoop of organic peanut butter to the mix. John woke up from the noise I was making. He sauntered out of his room, grabbed a mug and put a tea bag in it. He made a peanut butter and jelly sandwich. We sat on the couch and ate breakfast. I told him about Marvin's texts and his call. He thought it was funny. I told him we were going to be working out with him at the park soon and not to talk about it. We put on our sneakers, gym shorts, and hoodies, and made our way over to the park.

Marvin was on time. I almost had to forget about 10 hours earlier to look him in the face. We shook hands and brought it in for a quarter hug. John did the same. We went back to our routine. We all started doing our warmups, then moved to our bar exercises. The initial feeling of discomfort was replaced with normality. By the end of the workout, it was as though the thing had never happened. It was understood, and we were all just boys who had each other's backs. I was grateful to have Marvin watch my back, even if he wanted more than to just watch it.

I had to work at the Stan Ward later. It was midweek but busy, because it had become a destination spot. After I got dressed and threw my bike lock into my backpack, I carried my bike downstairs and rode along Bedford Avenue toward Manhattan. It was a little chilly. I flipped the lining of my helmet upside down to meet my sweatshirt, so it covered my ears. It was about 3:30 in the afternoon, and Williamsburg was pretty quiet. I ascended the Williamsburg Bridge on my bike. It was also quiet. For once, more people were going into Manhattan than leaving it. I descended the bridge. Nobody was in my way; it felt exhilarating to speed on this straightaway. I stopped at a red light and sat perched on my bike until the light turned green. I had to hustle. If you were late, it could very well cost you a job. I was beginning to pick up speed when I saw my green light fade to yellow. I looked both ways on one-way Christie Street. No cars. It was that odd time in the city, when it almost feels like a village. (For the city that doesn't sleep, it sure enjoys its mid-afternoon naps.) I blew through what was now a red light. I got to a second red farther down, but this was a two-way street with cars on either end; I had to stop.

An officer on his bicycle rode up next to me.

"Do you know that you just ran through a red light?"

"Um . . . no."

"Riding through a light is a traffic violation."

"The street was clear."

"License, please."

I felt angry and alarmed. This fat bicycle cop was ticketing me for no good reason. I had put no one at risk. I just needed to get to work to keep the New York City economy going. I guess he was just playing cashier for the city. So here we were: two cogs in the machinery of the metropolis. He wrote me the ticket and told me I could protest it in court, then he rode off. I wondered if I could have gotten away from him. Was I faster? Would he have tried to shoot me as he chased me through the LES?

I got to work and locked my bike to a pole out front. I ran down to the service quarters to dress. My uniform was hanging up for me. I put on my slim Dickies work pants, white dress shirt, black tie and black apron. I put a wine key in my pocket, found my hiding place for my penny loafers, and put them on. I ran up to the floor and checked in with my bartenders. I went back to the walk-in to check for garnishes. Then I pulled out my traffic ticket and read it over.

The ticket stated I owed $180 for the violation. I was angry. If I had been on one of those Chinese delivery bikes with a motor, it would have been $260, so I guess I was lucky. Still, it pissed me off. Any time I felt like I was starting to build my savings, something like this happened. This was one of those learning moments about adulthood. Much of life is constant disappointment; part of being an adult is accepting that and moving on.

I rode back home after my shift and obeyed every traffic light. My bike was legally a vehicle, and I couldn't afford another ticket at the moment. In fact, I did continue to get tickets. The tickets would increase in cost. The next ticket cost me $240. One of my Jiu-Jitsu buddies took pity on me. He knew I would keep getting stopped, so he made me a Police Benevolent Association card. This was like being protected by the mafia. The card probably saved me more than a thousand dollars and more than a few migraines.

The next morning, I went downstairs holding the creased yellow ticket in my hand and spent a good 15 minutes muttering to myself. A group of five black men were hanging out at the bodega on the corner. They called over to me.

"Traffic ticket?" one of the guys asked.

"Ya. Traffic ticket," I responded insecurely.

"What'd you do?"

"I ran through a red light." I got up off the stoop and walked over to the guys.

"That's it? You gotta be kidding me?"

"Nah. Apparently, it's a violation."

"Motherfucking NYPD."

"Ya . . . motherfucking NYPD."

"How much they got ya for?"

"One hundred and eighty bucks."

"Damn. Really? For a bicycle?" The group of guys started chiming in with their misgivings about the New York City Police Department. I felt immediately more comfortable with them. I felt like I belonged. Here, we were all just men griping about "The Man." It felt good.

I noticed another guy approach our group. I had to look up. He was six feet five inches tall and wearing an oversized white t-shirt. Then I saw his face. It was Lenny. I thought to myself, "Fuck." It was big, fucking Lenny. It was big, fucking Lenny who wanted to beat me senseless, whom I hadn't seen since the incident at the park, and who was unable to kick my ass only because Marvin got in the way. It was that big, fucking Lenny. Lenny towered over all of us and began fist-bumping. I took a moment to notice the knuckles on his fist. They were blunt, deadened knobs. He went from left to right in our circle. He fist-bumped the first guy, then the second. He went to the third guy, and I was next to him. He looked at me, and I looked at him. The moment was still. He nodded with approval at me and presented his skull-flattening fist. I fist-bumped him, and he continued on until all fists were bumped. I tried to hide my sigh of relief. Lenny got into the conversation with us about how "The Man" is out to keep us down. I expressed that paying this ticket was gonna be hard for me. I explained that I was not making much money. One of the guys consoled me.

"Nah, man. You just go to court. They'll throw it away. Just make sure to make the court date. And remember, dog, you white!"

"Oh, ya! I guess that's true. Thanks, man."

"No worries, dog. Don't let the NYPD fuck up your day."

"I won't!"

"That's what's up."

"Word!"

I went back to my apartment and felt one with the community and not as bad about the $180 I would potentially have to pay. I was also relieved that it appeared that Lenny and I were cool now. I later found out that he lived at the end of my street. He was notorious as a street fighter. He was said to have the ability to make large men break down and cry with the punishment delivered by his fists! He had done time but was back in our wonderful neighborhood. Yes, sir, all was right with the world. I wasn't going to be beaten to death, I could have the ticket dismissed, and I was white!

Hood Life

Like I said, I was living in a downtrodden, prewar building in Bed
     Stuy with my homeboy John. . After it had been a hotel in the
1940's, and then a barracks for the drug wars fought in the streets of
Bed Stuy in the seventies and eighties, it was a fleabag flophouse. It was
befitting for two young men with no direction.

Bed Stuy had been slowly changing. We had more police presence,
and things were calming down. For a time, there were two cops patrolling
every two blocks or so. Once they had stabilized the neighborhood, they
weren't out in twos anymore. Things reverted a bit when they left. You
had to look over your shoulder. I made friends quickly on the block, ones
who looked out for me.

I got a good deal on the apartment. Our landlord Walter was Hasidic
only on the outside. In his payes and black gabardine, he cursed like a
sailor. All I had to do was tell him I was Jewish to get a decent price. He
told me I couldn't hide my Jewish face. I knew I had a Jew nose and Jew
lips, so I put them to good use by getting a deal.

The building manager lived in an illegal unit on the side of the
building. His name was Dino. He looked like a cross between James
Brown and RuPaul. He was a tall, gay, black man who used to be a
dancer. What kind of dancer, I'm not sure. He was a jack-of-all-trades
and would pitch himself to anybody. John and I were nobodies, but he
felt the need to sell himself to us. He would claim he was a "dancer,
singer, writer, and designer. I got my own line of curtains and plans to
start my own brand. Yes, sir! You are going to be reading about me. I'm
Dino, and I'm gonna take the media by storm."

Many of our neighbors refused to pay their rent. John and I always
paid, and on time. Many tenants refused to shell out. Occasionally,
we had a "guest" who would hang out in the stairwell to smoke crack.
Known in the community, he was a twin. Nobody had heard from his
twin in a while. This crackhead had just been released from Rikers and
was hanging out in our hallway to get high. This was Brooklyn before
the developers turned the building into a luxury property.

Four generations of a Puerto Rican family lived in separate units
in the building, the Pascals. The grandmother was 60, the mother was

45, the grandson was 30, and he had four children with his wife. Each of the four children was named after a character in a comic book. The grandmother went by Mama Bee or Bee. She was the matriarch and oversaw the building alongside Dino. Her grandson Tito didn't work regularly. He sold weed and did freelance gigs involving cars.

Tito would look out for me on my bike rides home from the city. I would get out of work late and ride through the projects to get to my apartment. Tito would be up all night pacing in his black hoodie. I was grateful to see him. It meant I had someone to watch my back as I was coming in with my bike flung over my shoulder. Tito and I would talk before I'd head upstairs. We learned a lot about each other, and we couldn't have been more different. At first, his family thought I was a gigolo, because of the hours I kept (and the fact that I kept in shape).

On certain nights, I would see the building owner's car parked out front. I thought it was weird that Walter was around at these hours, since I knew he had at least five kids. He seemed to be around at random times though.

Mama Bee told me about her brother. He was no longer. Apparently, he had been shot in the hallway during a bad deal. She also told me about a trans-woman friend of hers. The trans-woman took a ride with a gangster looking for a good time. Unfortunately, the "good time" was far from good; it wasn't even lackluster. He didn't realize that she had been a man, and, when he found out, he cut her throat open. Mama Bee had seen a lot of murders in her day. She had even fought grown men when she had had to. She had been a gymnast when she was young and then a body builder. We had a good amount to talk about surprisingly.

John and I were adopted into the Pascal family, though our backgrounds couldn't have been more different from theirs. John came from a good middleclass family in the Chicago suburbs, and I had a similar upbringing in the Boston suburbs. The Pascals had lived in the building over 20 years. They had lived through gang wars. They had lived through riots. We all shared the same dilapidated roof though, and that made us kin.

One evening, I asked Tito why he didn't want to work. He was a genius with cars. The guy had wired his own Honda Civic with a camera out the back to a monitor in the dash. He retrofitted John's seventies Peugeot bicycle with a new derailleur. I imagined what it would be like to have Tito's mastery of mechanics. I thought working with machines must be superior to working with people.

"Hey, Tito. What's up, man? You have so much mechanical skill. Why not use it to make money?"

"I don't want to be a slave, son."

"It's a job, though. You get paid, right? It ain't slavery."

"It is. I ain't a part of that system."

That was that. I couldn't push further. I loved the family, but we had different outlooks on life. I was the outsider. In essence, I was a guest, and a guest around these parts best "shut the fuck up."

I had my drawing table in the living room and would work for hours on my graphic novel and standalone drawings. This was the bohemian way: there are two strategies you can choose from to be a working artist. You can take a job that has nothing to do with your art: Julian Schnabel was a line cook at a restaurant; Charles Bukowski was a postman. Or you can take a job in the art field. Seth MacFarlane was a writer and storyboard artist before getting his own show and Gary Panter did album covers and set design for *Pee-wee's Playhouse*.

I chose the "nothing to do with your art" path. This was partly due to my having studied an archaic commercial art. Printmaking was from some other time. I went into restaurant work, because I had made that decision in art school. Had I known how the art world functioned, I might have decided to study computer art. Well, live and learn. Mine was the romantic, bohemian life, living in squalor, working around alcohol, and making art in the wee hours.

One night, I heard yelling from below my window. This wasn't unusual. I had gotten used to falling asleep to the far-off sounds of gunfire. But this night was different, because I recognized the voices. Dino and Walter were fighting. I couldn't make out what they were fighting about, but I didn't think it was about the building. I pressed my ear to the screen. Walter got into his car and drove off.

I ran into Tito the next night. I asked him what the two had been fighting about. Tito told me they were having a lovers' quarrel. I laughed, but he insisted they were lovers. Tito's judgment wasn't always on the money. He had thought I was a gigolo when he met me and had been known to be wrong about other people's lives. I dropped it and went on my way.

The building was vile. John and I would find rat poop all over the apartment. We washed our dishes before *and* after cooking. John was a bit of a hypochondriac and thought we were going to get cancer from living around hundreds of pellets of rat shit. Maybe he was right. But we weren't making the big bucks, and I wanted financial freedom. I wanted to be able to buy a property, maybe start a business. I was committed to the squalor; it was tough and rough. But I wasn't like the Pascals. I needed to fill in the missing pieces.

Tito was a toughie and declared it often. He grew up fighting. He didn't go to a martial arts school or boxing gym; he learned from fighting on the streets. Some would say there isn't a better teacher. I grew up totally differently from Tito, in a nice suburb. I fought a little in my youth, but not like Tito. I learned how to handle myself from studying with learned toughies. I was training in mixed martial arts at a spot in Williamsburg. I didn't care whether I kicked ass or had my ass kicked. In the eyes of our patron warrior gods, we were all created equal. Tito would remind me that the stuff I was learning wouldn't stop someone from busting a cap into my brain. I knew that. But it felt good to at least be able to handle myself in some situations.

John told me that Dino and Walter had had another fight, louder than the last one. Dino had packed his bags and left the building. I was shocked. Dino--jack-of-all-trades, dancer, singer, writer and designer--was no longer with us. He split for New Jersey.

I ran into Mama Bee in the hallway to the front entrance.

"Hey, Mama Bee, what happened between those two?"

"I don't know."

"Mama Bee, you know what's up. I need answers."

"They had a fight, and Dino split," she said and turned away from me.

"That's crazy. Come on, you know more than that." I pushed further. I needed to know what had happened to cause this rift between them.

"I can't say."

"Your son Tito said that they were lovers. Is that true?"

"Yes, but you didn't hear it from me." She turned away and went out the front door.

Dino and Walter had been lovers. A gay black man and a Hasidic family man had been having an affair. This was a shock to me before I realized how common it was. As I rode my bike, I sometimes saw young Hasidic men ascending the Williamsburg Bridge. More often than not, these pious men were looking for lady-boy hookers in the LES, or so I was told. In the Big Apple, nothing was what it seemed. The big, beautiful apple had a chubby worm crawling around inside of it.

I was learning every day, with hood life teaching me more than school ever had. I was beginning to lose my leftist leanings. It had been easy to be a liberal when separated from the real world. I started to see welfare being taken advantage of firsthand. Even my good friend John milked unemployment. One week, I worked an extra shift to help out my manager. I had a third of my paycheck pulled for taxes as a result of earning so much. Life was a challenging proposition; I hadn't really been confronted with its realities before. I had been able to keep my liberal views without being confronted about them. Now that I was working my ass off, I started to see behind the curtain. When you hit a man in his wallet, it's personal.

Diehard liberal friends were living in Cobble Hill and other nice, whitewashed areas. It was difficult to argue with them, since we now lived in two different worlds. I was living the hood life, and they were living the good life. I loved my community but saw that the system hurt the people in it rather than helping them.

I also acknowledged that I won the parent lottery. My parents were hardworking, smart, and valued education above all else. Nobody is perfect, my folks made their mistakes, and lord knows I made mine. They didn't make the big mistakes though. I was spanked once; they never cursed me and had my back. If I had a nickel for every time I heard a mother curse their kid on the Brooklyn streets, I'd be rich.

I was reborn in Bed Stuy. My eyes were opened to the world. I didn't become Pat Buchanan; I just got reeled in from the deep waters of the liberal left. I started swimming to the right of center, though occasionally still on the left. I had known nothing of the left dominating academia; I just thought there was only one way to think, speak, and be. After Brooklyn, I felt like Neo taking the red pill and waking up to the way the world truly was.

When we lived there, John and I read the *New York Times* every morning. It didn't sync with our reality. Over time, it became obvious their narrative was awry. They weren't living what we were living.

I never regretted living in Bed Stuy. I don't have a tattoo, but if I did, it would read, "Bed Stuy, Do or Die" across my back for all to see. The real world was not what it had once seemed or what you saw on TV. In the real world, Hasidic men and gay black men had secret love affairs. In the real world, four living generations of Puerto Ricans and two naïve white boys were family. All of us were subject to the challenges life had to offer, regardless of background.

The Stan Ward Hotel and Me

I got back from Europe. I had seen Big Ben, the Eiffel Tower, and the Mediterranean. I was almost beaten to death by strippers in Paris. It was an exciting trip, but I was ready to get back to New York City in order to bend it to my will. I was grateful that Jared had held onto my stuff in Bed Stuy.

While I was away, Jared said there would be a room for me opening up in his apartment. It didn't have a window, but I was used to that.

The other thing I needed was a job, right away. I was burning up my savings. I reached out to all of my contacts, and only John had a lead for me joining him and his merry band of busboys at the Stan Ward Hotel. Why not? It was September. Fashion Week would be starting. The city would again enjoy the influx of its money-spending patrons. Now was the time to strike that minimum-wage-plus-tips gold!

John had set up an interview for me with a floor manager. She was a Type A black woman, dressed in heels and fake spectacles. It was a short interview. She was from Boston and had graduated from Harvard. She knew Marblehead, so she thought I was well-to-do. It helped. They were looking for clean-cut college boys to give that Brooklyn vibe to the place. My orientation took place the next day.

I arrived in the Meatpacking District early on a beautiful Indian summer day. The hotel was on Little West 12th Street. John was lending a hand with the orientation, so I went for a walk nearby to kill some time until he could come out to show me in. I walked around the block and saw scaffolding in an alleyway behind the hotel. Thinking this could be a good place to get some pull-ups in, I popped off my shirt and began hoisting myself up and down. I was cranking out reps! I worked up a sweat after two sets of pull-ups and a set of push-ups. I got my "swoll" on. John found me shirtless, drinking from a water bottle with my backpack at my feet.

"Dustin, what the hell, man?" John said in disbelief.

"What'd I do?" I asked, only half-unaware.

"I'm the guy who got you the job! You are gonna be late for the orientation, and you are sweating like a rabbi near bacon!" John responded.

"Oh, sorry. I saw the scaffolding, and wanted to work my body, broski."

"We don't have time for this."

I put on my shirt. I felt my t-shirt absorb the sweat from my back. John took me through the south-facing end of the building, through the Biergarten. It was swarming with Brooklynites in their twenties, fresh from college. They were all the same as I was, new disciples of the restaurant workforce. We were led into a private room of the Biergarten used for weddings and other celebrations. I saw a few different managers there but only recognized the black lady in her heels and fake eyeglasses.

A handsome Asian man stood up in front of the crowd of new staff. He was about six and a half feet tall. He wore a gray suit with Puma sneakers and had a thick New York accent.

"Hey, guys, my name is Neil, and I'm the GM. I'm thrilled to have all of you here with us. It's a great opportunity to work here. I don't mean to showboat, but we are the hottest game in town. I know, I know, none of you want to do this forever. I get it. I got a chance to talk to many of you. You're artists, writers, actors, and musicians. I think you'll come to find that this place will help you pay the bills while you go about your art."

The crowd seemed both excited and insulted. Here we were, artists, writers, actors and musicians; and we hated being labeled to our very core. He both called us out and welcomed us in. He had savvy. He was old school NYC. In fact, as I've mentioned, the Stan Ward Hotel only hired old-school New York hard-asses for management. It was a great strategy. Those men and women were known. They had reputations. The Hotel had a ton of money on the line; who better to handle it than the veterans who had shoveled in that eighties money?

John left after his part of the orientation was over. I had no one to talk to, so I sat there in my head, not able to share the micro-thoughts spinning in my brain. I examined the other faces in the crowd. They all faced forward, so I couldn't read them. Did they feel as I did? I wasn't sure.

A couple of gentlemen in blue work pants and lighter blue, half-sleeve shirts came into the room, carrying a flat screen TV. They set up as Neil continued on with his spiel.

"I've been working in restaurants for a long time, guys. I did everything. I washed dishes, bussed tables, waited tables, bartended, and, of course, managed. I was the GM of Nobu. My cohort here, Liam, worked with me," Neil pointed at a plain thin man in a suit to his left.

It seemed apparent that we were meant to drink this Kool-Aid. We were here to be indoctrinated into the culture of New York City food and beverage. I felt a sense of fight or flight. This didn't fit into my New York City fantasy. I had imagined myself working for Cartoon Network or Nickelodeon. I hadn't thought of this as my career as some thing that would feed me as I went about my life.

"Guys, this a great opportunity for you. After working here, you'll be able to work anywhere. We will train you to be the best you can be. We'll have fun. We work, but we party too!" Neil smiled.

We watched a video on the flat screen. We first saw the face of the owner of the hotel. It was as though Big Brother were speaking to us. The owner was a handsome, middle-aged globetrotter. He was ungodly rich, with a slew of famous girlfriends. He had made his money in Big Pharma before switching to the hotel business.

"I am pleased and delighted to invite you to this opportunity to become part of this fantastic team. We here at this group are special. We have the most exciting staff. You were chosen based on your charisma, savvy, and fortitude. Together, we will create a culture."

The video then showed a montage of the hotel being built. Photos of the owner in a white seersucker suit and construction helmet filled the screen, then we saw the other properties under the same umbrella. After presenting the kitchen staff, concierge, and laundry services women, the video stopped, *sans* credits.

Liam now addressed the crowd. His Irish accent was strong.

"Hello, ladies and gentlemen. It is a delight to meet you. I am looking forward to getting to know all of you more during our time here together. We are a corporation and need to abide by certain rules. We can still have fun."

A new video appeared on the screen, of much poorer quality. A red title appeared on the screen and then faded away. It read, "Sexual Harassment is Serious!" The video went on to show terrible actors going through various scenarios that could be deemed sexual harassment. It caused us all to chuckle. But the Stan Ward Hotel took this seriously. Lawsuits were a very real thing in the corporate world. Whether many of these cases were legitimate was of no consequence. The fact was that lawsuits cost the company revenue. This lame video helped ensure they held up their end of the law, which could possibly save them a couple of million dollars.

The meeting came to a close, and people started to mingle. I went straight out through the Biergarten and into the muggy streets of the Meatpacking District. I walked over to the L train to transfer to the G to Bed Stuy. I would start work that week at the Stan Ward Hotel with a merry gang of busboy pranksters.

Stutterers, Bussers, and Sluts

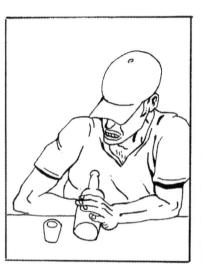
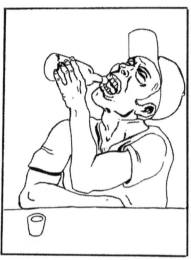
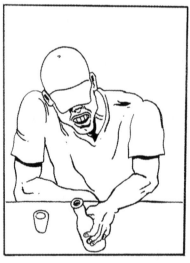

I had been in bussing, lifting, eating, drawing (repeat) mode for a couple of months. It was good for me. I was 23 with a whole life ahead of me. My busboy brethren were in my corner, so although New Year's Eve was coming up, I was spared the night shift. I had a date with a Colombian firecracker. We had barely spoken at Barnes & Noble before she'd had to go back to the West Coast. She was in town again, so we met up at Union Pool. We made out at the bar for two hours and then went back to my shithole in Bed Stuy. We had sex until the wee hours, and then I left for work at 7 a.m. I went about my shift a brainless corpse. My body was operating at a geriatric pace, but my mind was replaying the night on repeat. I tried to recall every detail, as I cleaned tables and dealt with hungover patrons. I thought about her areolas, her curly hair, and deep brown eyes . . . was she shaved? I couldn't quite recall.

My bosses didn't bother me; they were grateful I had shown up. I took a moment to look toward the outdoor lobby where the year before, the hotel had built an ice-skating rink. It was a way to bring in families, who in return would spend six dollars for a hot chocolate, among other things—such as skate rentals. We had cute young ladies instructing the children how to skate, and a young model running the skate shack. The Stan Ward Hotel knew what it was doing; it cast a wide net to haul in that beautiful green currency.

That night, I took my usual break when John happened to be working the barista station. His night had not been as successful as mine. He was still fried from imbibing too much Maker's Mark and laced marijuana. Recounting my play-by-play with the Colombian firecracker was like having another round of first-time sex. John enjoyed being a voyeur, a witness to our Olympic sexual event. This kiss and tell was common among the men and almost equally common among the women. If somebody claimed they didn't talk about their exploits, they were either fibbing or hadn't had any.

My shift was coming to a close. January first was here, and it was slow. Business tended to freeze up at that time of year. Even the great city succumbed to the elements. I went into the basement toward the laundry services area. My locker was in the lobby, which meant I had to change in full view of anybody who walked by. I pulled off my black Dickies and black apron, removed my soiled oversized white dress shirt, loosened my black tie and left it tied as I removed it from my neck. I threw on gray chinos and a white tee with brown beaten boots and my Levi's sherpa jacket and baseball cap. I saw John around the corner. He had also changed into his winter garb. We munched on some banana bread left in the employee cafeteria and escaped to the upstairs lobby. We dropped our bags off with our good friend Annie, the lobby host in. She would keep an eye on them for us.

John had played hockey and was good on skates. I was a danger to others and myself. We climbed into the small ice rink in front of the hotel and glided on the ice. I should say John glided; I inched along muttering, "Shit! Balls!" quietly, hoping not to fall.

Out of the corner of my eye I spotted her. She was with a girlfriend and looked like a mess. Her skin was cracked and dry. Her hair looked as though it had been whirled around in a tornado. She was small, quiet, and kept her attention on the rink. She happened to be friends with one of the room service guys and was meeting up to see the rink. I just happened to be there. It would be either serendipitous or ill-fated; only time would tell.

The room service guy called over to me. We were friendly from our encounters throughout the hotel. He introduced me to the small, disheveled girl and her redheaded friend.

"Hey, Dustin. These are my friends, Molly and Felicity."

"Hi, ladies," I said.

"Are you having fun skating with the children?" redheaded Molly asked.

"I sure am. I'm actually afraid of having an accident around them. These skates are very sharp!" I said, as I steadied myself on the railing.

"You don't want to make a bloody mess on the ice. It'll take them a whole day to clean it, and then nobody gets to skate," the disheveled Felicity said.

"Nobody wants that. I better get off the ice. I have a bad feeling about this now." I looked over to John, who was rounding the corner.

I exited the rink and returned the skates to the pretty girl in the shack. I wanted to head back to my apartment in Bed Stuy and sleep. I was starting to feel the sex, booze, and lack of sleep catch up to me. Annie handed me my bag. I was passing by everyone at the rink on my way toward the street when Felicity stopped me.

"Hey, Brian Boitano, where are you going?" she called out to me.

"I'm pretty burnt out. I need to get back to the Stuy."

"I live off the L in Williamsburg. We could take the train together," she said.

"Yeah, that works."

We walked up two blocks to 14th street. We passed the Apple Store on our way to the 8th Avenue L line. The train came quickly and was surprisingly not packed. Normally, 5:30 would have been rush hour, but it was January first, and the city was recovering from its collective hangover. Felicity and I descended the snow-powdered stairs into the subterranean world of New York. The train arrived promptly. We sat next to each other and spoke about New York City and all its glory, two young people who were going to climb to the top of the Big Apple and turn it into our slice of apple pie. We exchanged numbers as she got out at Bedford Avenue. I transferred to the southbound G as my fatigue turned my brain to cold gray slush. I didn't compute that she was into me, but when I messaged her within a day or two, we arranged a hangout.

We agreed to meet up in the city, where I would be getting out of work at seven. I had a friend, Kat, originally from the Czech Republic, who was beautiful, artistic, bohemian, and not for me. She was married to some malcontent who merely looked at her but never engaged her. Kat mentioned a bar that a group of her friends were going to, so I mentioned to Felicity that there was a sort of hullabaloo at Tom & Jerry's in NoHo. Felicity would bring her roommate and good friend from college Erin. I was the common denominator. I was bringing people together. I was the harbinger of good will. I was a nice young man and thought I might get to second base with Felicity if all went well.

I met the girls at Think Coffee, where they were chatting and sipping Americanos. We walked ten minutes and entered Tom & Jerry's. It was a Wednesday--hump day. The place was fairly full of young people and had an air of cool. The music was good: the Specials, the Clash, and Violent Femmes. I eyed Kat from the bar. She looked gorgeous. She was there without her husband. I had met her friends but couldn't recall any names. I introduced Felicity, Erin, and Kat. It was jovial at first.

The music was good. Kat and I started dancing. We would play this way when I worked with her at Skip and Aiden's. It was natural; it was what was needed. I saw Felicity and Erin slink away toward the bar. I went over to Felicity to pull her toward the floor. She smiled and said she needed a drink first. The dancing died down, and we all ended up sipping cheap beer. I could feel Felicity's mind race. I tried to read her but couldn't get specifics. I assumed she thought that I had either been with Kat before or wanted to be with her. I assumed she thought I was an asshole for bringing her here. I stopped trying to read her mood and kept the party rolling. Kat left with her friends first. Erin, Felicity, and I shared a cab back. We got dropped off in Williamsburg. From there, I would take the G train back to my apartment. I didn't have money to burn on a cab. I knew I had pissed off Felicity and thought this would be the last of it. I was wrong.

We met two nights later. She knew of a cool bar off of Union called Barcade. It was an arcade with beers on draft. This time it would be just us--no Kat, no Erin, nobody but us. I was to meet her inside the bar. I found her sitting on a stool in the corner. She looked smaller than I remembered her. I went up to her with a wry smile.

"Hello, lady," I said.

"You think you're hot shit, yeah?"

"Pardon me?"

"You think you can get any girl?"

"No."

"All right."

"So. . . ."

"I got this round. You can get the next."

She ordered us two Deliriums. I was put off by her greeting and immediately tried to suppress the feeling. I had forgotten my dancing with Kat and saw Felicity as irrational. But I might as well have a beer. We went to the Dig Dug arcade machine. I played and she watched. The mood became lighter, and we started talking about the games at hand. I lost all three lives at stage nine, and we moved over to the Frogger arcade machine so she could play. She was doing well. She mentioned she practiced this one. I jumped in and lost at stage two. It had been a while since I had played these machines. They were clumsy heaps of technological history. For us, born in the mid-eighties, they harkened to a day before iPhones, interconnected loneliness, and mass disinformation. In fact, many movies of this time were a reformulation of eighties creations, like the reboots of Transformers, Teenage Mutant Ninja Turtles, Evil Dead, Robocop, Total Recall, and so many more.

I got a second round, and we moved over to play Galactica. I loved this game. It reminded me of when my brother and I had downloaded a cheap knockoff and played it for hours on end. It was nearing ten, and the place was packed. Felicity offered to have one more beer at her place.

We walked about fifteen minutes and got to her apartment. Young Dominican men hung out in front of her stoop, some with neck tattoos. All had fades with proper lining. They looked us up and down. We went up two flights of stairs into a building that was ill-kept. We hung a left, and she pushed open a heavy metal door to her kitchen. It was nicely decorated. In the living room, she had a cowhide carpet and an old flag on the wall. The walls were painted white but left raw. She had a minimalist dark wood coffee table, with coffee table books all about architecture. It turned out she was getting her masters in architecture. She popped open two Abita Purple Haze beers and put on the Talking Heads. She poured us a shot of low-end tequila, and I became buzzed. I went to take a piss. The bathroom was small, and the toilet was low. I sat so I wouldn't take the risk of pissing on the seat or forgetting to put the seat back down. I got back, and then she went to piss. I sat on the couch and felt my body sink into it. I felt relaxed; I was content.

She got back and poured another shot of the tequila. I felt my cheeks warm. She sat closer to me. She started talking about school, but I was calculating my move. I wasn't sure if she could tell I was losing my focus on what she had to say. I noticed her shirt seemed to lose a button, and I could make out the ridge of her bra. She took a moment's pause, and I leaned in. She reciprocated, and we started making out. She hopped onto my lap. I slid my hand into her red flannel shirt and grabbed her breast. For a tiny girl, she sure had a perky set. I lifted her up and took her into her room, only a few steps away from the living room. I pulled off her flannel; her tits sat upright in her black bra. She pulled off my t-shirt. I pulled her pants down and moved my mouth toward her pussy. She stopped me. She had trouble undoing my Army issue belt, so I helped her. She pulled my pants down, and I was half-erect. She put my penis in her mouth, and I felt my penis soften. I wasn't sure there was a connection. It felt like we were faking the moment. I pulled away from her. I felt only slightly embarrassed and laid down next to her. She rolled over to face me and rested her head on my chest. We didn't talk about anything. We just existed for a moment. I started playing with her nipples and could hear her breathing get heavier. I started kissing her neck and then moved down toward her pussy. She did not stop me this time. I licked her clitoris softly and, with my left hand, started stroking my penis. She was becoming wetter, and I grew hard. I knew I would have to act quickly, once I got the condom on. I removed my mouth from her pussy and looked to the floor for my pants. I grabbed a condom, but I had started to lose my rigor in the search. I went back to eating her out and started again to stroke myself. I became hard again and quickly put on the condom. I worked my way up to her. She looked tiny under me; I didn't think I had ever had a girl this small before. I worked my way into her and started pumping. Our rhythm was off, but I went at it. We fucked for a while, but she would not climax. I, too, would not climax. We called it quits and laid there.

We enjoyed a little pillow talk and didn't speak of the mediocre sex we had just had. The more we talked, the more I realized that I thought she was not worth my time. I had hooked up with her because she liked me. That was the most compelling thing about her. My low self-esteem had been elevated merely because a girl pursued me but she was pretentious, curt, and lacked feminine grace. I remembered not being attracted to her when I had first seen her at the ice rink. This interlude was not just lackluster; it was a letdown. I got dressed and kissed her on the cheek. I told her I had to be up early for work.

I woke up the next morning in my small rectangular room. It was bright—the blinds did nothing to keep out the eastern morning light. I was flooded with the fresh memory of last night's events. When I arrived at work, I noticed she had texted me an emoji of a smiley face. I sent her one back. She asked what my week looked like. I removed a bus tub of dirty plates to the dish pit and looked around to see if a manager was nearby. I then texted I was free on Friday, so we agreed we would meet.

I immediately had regrets. I felt like it was a waste of time, but I also felt compelled to see her. I was embarrassed to admit to myself that I had a reason to see her. I wanted to prove my sexual prowess; I wanted to give her multiple orgasms and show that I was a formidable lover. I don't know why I cared. I don't know why I didn't take a step back and heed the signs I had received from her, revealing to me that she had more than a few problems.

...

I was getting tired of bussing tables. It had been a couple of months since I had taken on the position for lousy pay, so it was to be expected, but I knew that I needed to climb the ranks. I needed more money. I knew that they valued me greatly as a busboy and would hate to lose me. That, unfortunately, wouldn't motivate them to move me up; they would rather have me bust ass hauling dirty plates. I decided to slow down my productivity, so they could see me in a new light. I needed them to see that I was only merely adequate at bussing tables.

I worked at a 30 percent reduction in my output for a couple of weeks. Then they called me in for a meeting to discuss my future at the company. It looked like a promotion was in order. It had worked! When you wanted to succeed in the corporate restaurant realm, you apparently needed to do less. The big, money-guzzling hot spots need good soldiers. If you work really hard and bust ass in your job, they'll love you, but it is not a tender love. It is more like a man's love of his hunting dog. The hunter will be pleased to have you fetch his rabbit but not invite you to the table; you'll be lucky to get a few bones and maybe some innards. You need to show your discontent with the job ever so slightly. You do need to show up on time and bang it out, but you don't need to do it with a smile. The more you show your malaise, the more the upper management thinks that this here worker bee isn't challenged enough. What should we do for him? Should we fire him? No, because then we'd need to find a new rube. Should we demote him? No, because he'll end up quitting, and then we'd need to find a new rube. Should we promote him? Yes, that's the ticket. We'll promote the little shit-kicker. I spent a month being sour. I cut down on my jovial output and tried to just trudge along. Finally, I had a manager come up to me and offer me a transfer to the bar back team. The manager put through the paper work, and by the next shift, I had a new job.

My uniform stayed the same, but my title changed. Hauling bus tubs filled with dirty plates was in the past. Now, it was pulling booze, grabbing buckets of Kold Draft ice cubes, and flirting with the cocktail waitresses. I was thrilled. I worked with two guys in particular who were world class bros. Max and AJ were from Arizona and were beefy frat guys. They spent their off time working out and smoking weed. They were refreshing. Everyone else was an artist of some sort. These guys were unapologetically cavemen. I was a hybrid—not quite a hipster and not quite a caveman. I could navigate through the tribes of the city with ease. Sometimes, my speech even changed, depending on the demographics.

The one thing that united us bar boys together was our fear of the bar manager . . . Cain. Cain, simply put, was evil. He had a raspy voice, and his face looked like Skeletor's with the addition of a nose. He was stocky with long, muscular, gorilla arms. He barked orders and threatened certain death if we couldn't do the job. He was responsible for millions of dollars' worth of stock. Everything went by him: all of the ordering was his doing, and all of the numbers were by his calculation. He had studied computer science and was far from stupid. For us, he was akin to the super villain Lex Luthor. If we forgot a mason jar filled with a garnish, we were reamed out. I knew of a bar back who had been

15 minutes late due to a case of diarrhea and was caught by Cain and immediately fired after horrific barking. No one was safe. If you had a stomach bug, you were better off shitting your pants.

We, the bar boys, ran the show from behind. Sometimes, we were lucky enough to work with the angel of all barmen, known as Gates. He was sweet, handsome and half-Japanese. He would pull us aside and teach us how to make cocktails, when it was slow. This would become our preparation for assuming the mantle of barkeep. We all wanted it. It became a competition of who could get it first. Whoever played the political game the best would win the spoils. The frat boys Max and AJ won the job first. They were transferred to the service bar at the back of the hotel. This spot was known as "The Box." It was a prison cell-sized room with a bar fully equipped with liquor and a barista station.

I had another bar boy brother named Winston. He was English, pretentious, and the writer in our crew. He wore Doc Marten's boots, bowler hats, and Fred Perry shirts. For a young man who had fled Great Britain for the New World, he sure had an affinity for the old one. We worked hard to impress Cain. None of us ever had Cain's approval; nothing was ever good enough. If we carried four buckets of ice, we should have hauled six. If we brought up three cases of beer, we could have brought up four. We would hoist three racks of glassware over our heads and maneuver through the dining room across a floor tiled with pennies. It was work befitting 23-year-olds, whose bodies could handle it. Now, only eight years older, I was not so sure.

Every day was seemingly the same as the one before, but every once in a while, someone would get fired or be crying in a corner. We found ways to keep our spirits up. Usually, this involved Gates or another bartender feeding us a shot of whiskey here and there. Every now and then, someone would get fired. One of our bar brethren was caught chugging a can of Porkslap in the walk-in fridge. He was fired on the spot. We all were on our best behavior for a couple weeks after that. We still snuck shots, but we made sure to turn our backs to the cameras.

This time of my life was when I learned what the term "Eskimo brother" meant. One server was a major party kid. He did everything:

uppers, downers, red pills, blue pills, liquor, and chronic. I was a total square compared to him. He stopped me in the hallway during my shift, when I was bringing dirty glasses back to the dish pit at the back of the hotel.

"Hey, Dustin!" Duncan said.

"Hey, bro."

"Dude, I didn't know you hung out with Emily."

"Who?"

"Emily, the hostess."

"Oh, yeah, Emily. Yeah, I hung out with her for a bit."

"Yeah, dude. I just hung out with her too."

"Oh, yeah?"

"Yeah, we're Eskimo brothers!"

"What's that?"

"I banged her on Saturday night! We both banged her. We're Eskimo brothers, get it?"

"Oh, yeah. That's swell, man."

"Did she talk through the whole thing with you, too?"

"I don't know, man."

"All right, bro. Catch ya later!"

"Yep."

I felt a sense of disgust. The restaurant world is incestuous. Not only had Duncan informed me that he had shared the most intimate of encounters with the same girl, but he described her idiosyncrasies. She *had* talked through the whole thing. She had had a whole conversation as we were in the middle of having sex, as though the sex was something happening in the background. It was like trying to watch a movie on the big screen with someone chatting during the climax.

It was then that I decided to limit my afterwork hours to just a few fellow workers. I occasionally met up with AJ, Max, Winston, and a few others on the bar team. I didn't want to become everyone's Eskimo brother. I would be happy just being a bro: singular and independent, with a life outside the hotel walls.

...

Staff had their own entrance on the Hudson River side of the hotel. Hotel workers would smoke butts out back by the water, their view cut off by the traffic on the West Side Highway. The security desk (all retired NYPD) scanned staff in at first, using our IDs. After a while of getting to know us, they would just wave us through.

Then we would go down to the bowels of the hotel, where a team of Chinese ladies tended to our wardrobe. They dressed us, all in different uniforms. As a busboy, I wore those slim black Dickie's, with white shirt with the sleeves rolled up as high as I could get them, a black tie, and an apron. All of these articles of clothing had my name ironed on in patchwork. The staff even had our own dining hall, across the main dining room with that floor tiled with pennies, thousands of dollars' worth of pennies.

My job consisted of physical labor speckled with the use of minor parts of my brain. I had to pull liquor from the basement and bring it to the main bar to restock the shelves. We had four wells upstairs, so this was cumbersome. I'd load a cart with bottles upon bottles of cordials, liquors and liqueurs. To get them, I'd have to present my requisition to a young man downstairs, and he'd make me suffer. I would wait, and then I would panic. My eyes would dart to my watch, because if I wasn't back in 15 minutes, I would get chewed out by Cain, the raspy-voiced New York hard-ass who was our boss. It wouldn't be my fault; this lazy sack of shit would be responsible, but I would never rat anyone out. If you lived in Bed Stuy long enough, you learned the sacred rule well: "snitches get stitches."

This stuttering, stammering mama's boy would always make me wait. I would sweat bullets as he crept along, still stoned from his morning toke. His name was Jasper, and he was an old-school Bed Stuy boy. I liked him enough, but if this had been a war, I would have shot him myself. He was lazy, and he was going to cost me my livelihood. I left my cart to run back upstairs to tidy up the bar a bit. They wouldn't be able to say I had abandoned my post for too long. I ran back downstairs.

Jasper was finally getting it together. He wouldn't load the bottles onto my cart; he'd just leave them on the floor for me. I mentioned he was lazy, right? I would push the cart to the service elevator and bring it up to the main floor, hustling to make up a few minutes. I had to pull this bar together fast, so my bartenders could start generating the money we all relied on. I set them up with a full well of ice, liquor, syrups, and garnishes. I'd make sure they also had menus, plates, and flatware. Then they could work their magic and be masters of their domain.

Max and AJ were working the box near the lobby bar of the hotel. People could lounge there, have a bite to eat, and enjoy a real cocktail. The rest of us didn't mind that Max and AJ were the first of the bar backs to graduate to service bartenders. We were happy. These two bros were class acts. They could hold their liquor and talk a good game. I snuck over to say hello and snag a shot of espresso from the baristas behind them. Max told me everyone would be meeting up at the Funky Monkey later, a dilapidated three-story dive that was open after hours for all of us industry people. It was the place to talk shit, drink piss, and meet a chick.

My shift dragged along. Felicity was not texting me back. We had had a minor disagreement, something about how I didn't listen to her. I wish I could have remembered more of it. She finally texted me back, but I chose not to respond. It wasn't a very nice text, something to do with me being a misogynist or some such thing.

John, Jasper, Max, AJ, and I went over to the Funky Monkey. The Arizona bros had stolen a bottle of Ketel One out of the stock room. Jasper must have assisted them, but I asked no questions. I was happy to supplement my drinking with a stolen bottle of vodka. We all bought beers from the downstairs bar. None of us was going out to the rooftop bar. We would have frozen our buns off there, unless we were already drunk.

"Yo, this is the shit! Fuck the hotel," John said.

"Yeah, that Cain is a piece of shit," AJ said.

"Well, he's not that bad. We talk mad sports," Max said.

"He hates me. That Skeletor-looking motherfucker hates me," I said.

"Yo-you know th-that g-guy is the w-worst!" Jasper stuttered.

"I don't know how we can afford to stay in this city, if we don't make more money," John said.

"Yeah, seriously. John and I live in a crap apartment in Bed Stuy. We're lucky though. We only pay one thousand or so," I said.

"Damn, really! AJ and I pay a hell of a lot more than that," Max cried.

"What about you, Jasper?" AJ asked.

"I I-live with my m-moms," Jasper said.

"Yo, say what? You live with your moms? Dude, you're like 23. Isn't it time you move out?" John asked. He was visibly drunk now. John was known to be a mean, wild drunk; I had reined him in from time to time, once stopping him from screaming "Race Wars!!" on the streets of Bed Stuy in a drunken state.

"Y-yeah, man. I-I-I'm saving that dough. You know, s-so I c-c-can take those ladies out!"

There was a pause. John's face turned from harmless to harmful. His brow furled, and he let out a laugh.

"Yo, Jasper. You're a virgin," John continued chuckling.

We were all quiet. I felt Jasper's embarrassment. We all did. AJ looked away, Max looked at me, and I shrugged my shoulders.

"N-nah. I-I-I h-have had mad b-bitches in my day . . . shit, what are you talking?"

"No, you haven't. You've been at your mama's house. Shit," John said with a big grin.

"I'm feeling pretty tired, John. Let's head back. It's late," I said.

John suddenly snapped out of his mean trance. He went over to Jasper to shake his hand. Jasper obliged, so he wouldn't lose face or reveal that he was, in fact, a virgin. Max and AJ also left but since they had decided to hit another spot, Jasper went with them.

John and I sat in an almost empty L train to Brooklyn.

"John, what the fuck was that, man?"

"What?"

"You know what. You were so fucking mean to Jasper. I mean seriously, "virgin"?

"What, he didn't mind. I was just fucking with him."

"No, he minded. He was just hiding it. You embarrassed him."

"I don't think so."

"Dude, I am not as drunk as you. You really hurt his feelings."

"Oh, really?" John sobered up in that moment.

"Yes, you did. His feelings were hurt."

"Oh, should I apologize?"

"No, you'll only remind him of his failure with women."

"Oh, well . . . what do I do then?"

"Nothing. Just be very sweet to him the next time you see him around."

"Okay . . . I didn't mean to be a dick."

"I know that, John."

"I love ya, man," he said, his eyes dull and gray from vodka and beer.

"I love you too, man."

. . .

Felicity was a vindictive bitch. We had been dating without the label for many months. But I couldn't bring myself to call her my "girlfriend." I wasn't seeing any other girls but couldn't picture myself being with her forever. It was funny to me that the sex had become stellar because in the beginning, it had been lousy. We had more in common than just smashing our genitals together, though. Goya was our favorite artist; in fact, "Saturn Devouring his Child" was our favorite painting. We both seemed to gravitate toward the macabre. She was working on getting her master's in architectural preservation. She would point out details on old buildings, as we went for walks in Williamsburg.

She assumed that I had ladies on the side. No amount of reassurance could have satisfied her. She would counteract her paranoia by talking about which guy had hit on her. This wasn't a marvel to me. Men do that; it's quite normal to me.

One night we were at her place, in bed. She had to study and was reading a textbook. I didn't have a book with me, so she pulled one off a shelf. She assured me I would love it. I flipped to the first page, which had an inscription written in it.

"You are a vision and a remarkable woman. Love, Pierre."

I thought, "You have to be fucking kidding me." I was hit with a low-boiling anger, so I breathed deeply and engaged the diminutive lady tucked neatly in bed with her textbook.

"Why would you give me a book that was a gift from an admirer?"

"Whoops, I totally forgot."

"No, you didn't. Don't bullshit a bullshitter."

"I'm sorry. It isn't a big deal."

"So, was this a guy you fucked?"

"No, I met him at my store in Nolita. He's harmless."

"Why did you give me this book?"

"No reason. It was a mistake."

"No, it wasn't."

"Why are you angry?"

"Because it's fucking disrespectful. You know what? I'm outta here. Have a good night."

I got up to put my clothes on, and she threw herself at the door. I was tired but wanted out. I thought about moving her out of the way. It wouldn't have been hard; she was barely 90 pounds. But I didn't want to get accused of "assault." Her eyes were glazed over, and she was getting visibly upset. She might have been small, but she was bending me to her will. It didn't matter that I was double her size; I was broken down. She backed me up into a pink lounge chair in the far corner of her room. She sat on my lap and cried. She pleaded with me to stay, saying she was sorry. I knew I was a sucker. I folded, and we went to bed. She clung to me, and I sneered in the dark until we went to sleep.

...

Quarterly reports were out. It was the time of the month managers experienced cramps caused by corporate and took it out on us worker bees. There was a buzz on the floor. Waiters were talking to busboys, who were talking to bar backs, and word got back to us in the box. I was between bar-backing a shift or two in the Biergarten and bartending in the box. Word was going around that management was kicking everyone's ass. Corporate was hammering them, and it was their task to hammer us.

One of our bartenders came back upset from a talking-to in low spirits, his mood deflated. I was in the middle of pouring a specialty cocktail—a half-ounce of grapefruit juice, a half-ounce of simple syrup, three-quarters of an ounce of lime juice, and a little under two ounces of Silver tequila. I shook it up and poured it into a glass filled with Kold-Draft ice cubes. I put it on the service mat for the cocktail server to garnish it with a grapefruit wedge and deliver it to a guest.

"What's wrong, Winston?" I asked. The baristas behind me in our cramped space looked over.

"I work so hard for them, and you'd think they'd appreciate it. No. No, they don't. I need a new job."

"You're just upset. It's fine. They have to go about this nonsense."

"Those wankers had the gall to say my cocktail knowledge was weak."

"I'm sure. . . ."

"I'm bloody well English! I know how to make a perfect cocktail! We birthed the cocktail! While Americans were drinking moonshine and fucking their cousins, we were mastering the cocktail. You know what? These daft monkeys can piss off. Good luck to them finding anyone half as good as me!"

"They're not firing you. It's fine. Have a shot."

"You're up. They wanted me to send you to them."

"Pardon?"

"You're getting evaluated now."

"Damn it!"

I went through the main dining room. It was mostly empty. Dinner service would be starting, and the lunch crowd had long since petered out. I made my way out the side door into the Biergarten, where two managers greeted me. Usually, you only had to deal with one. Two of them—that already seemed off. I sat down across from the two New York hard-asses. Cain was on my right. His Skeletor face wore its ever-present grimace. The other had permanently squinted eyes, like he had seen too many Clint Eastwood flicks. They both had folders out in front of them. I almost felt honored—folders about me.

"So, it seems you aren't cutting the mustard," Cain rasped.

"Yeah, it seems that way," said Squinty Eyes.

"What do you mean?" I asked.

"Do you want to ask him, Mitch?" Cain asked.

"Sure, Cain. So, do you even like being here?"

That rattled me. I hadn't expected that. I thought it was apparent that nobody really wanted to be here. I wouldn't have chosen it had I not been motivated by money. Were we supposed to *want* to be there? I was confused.

"Yes, yes, I do."

"Well, it looks like you've called out a bunch. It also looks like you're often not around when you are needed."

"I bring the garbage around back. Nobody else does it, so I do that job."

"These reports are pretty lackluster," Mitch said.

"Yes, pretty lackluster. I would say they suck, Mitch," Cain rasped.

I was facing the windows that faced into the main dining room and feeling like a loser. I was a grown man by now but felt ill-equipped to handle this. I shut down and couldn't speak. I could have cried in that very moment. I felt like a total and utter bitch. How pathetic was I?

"You think that you don't have to work as hard as everyone else?" Mitch asked.

"No," I said.

"Do you like being the weakest link?" Cain asked.

"No," I said.

"Are you sure you even want to work here?" Mitch asked.

"Yes." I was embarrassed that I was holding back tears. I couldn't speak more than one syllable. I sensed a few of my co-workers looking at me through the windows, and I felt tremendous shame. I had no balls. A eunuch, that's me.

"Well, I guess that's that. We'll move you out to the box full time, then."

"Thanks."

I was dismissed. Essentially, I had been promoted to full-time service bartender, because I hadn't done a good enough job in the Biergarten. Promoted after a tongue-lashing. This was the corporate way. It would have been more costly to hire and train some newbie. It was more cost-effective to put me into another venue. My performance there wasn't in question, so they made the best move for the company.

I went back to my post at the service bar. Winston had already had one shot of tequila. The box was quiet. The espresso machine wasn't in use.

"How'd it go, mate?" Winston asked.

"Fuck those guys. Stupid, talentless hacks."

"Ah, that bad."

"I don't know if I can work here anymore. They just promoted me to full-time in the box. I'll do this for a while, put it on my resume, and then get the hell out of here."

"That sounds like a call for a cheers, mate."

Winston poured us two shots of Don Julio, and down our gullets they went.

. . .

My twenties were burning away, and I was a master at the box. We had taped up our names behind the window looking out to the cocktail servers. It was the wall of fame and commemorated our bar brethren. We were the ones responsible for slinging drinks, pitchers, sodas, wine and beer, our tasks bestowed upon us by the bar king known as Cain. He was a harsh ruler. He and Vlad the Impaler would have had a lot to talk about over martinis. My life was routine. It boiled down to biking, fighting, drawing, drinking, fucking, and sleeping. It was the life of a young barman. I had just broken up with Felicity for the second time., but she lured me back with the promise of peach cobbler. She didn't really know how to cook, but she could make a hell of a cobbler. Winston referred to her to solely as "Peach Cobbler."

I was still drawing every day and working on my graphic novel before shifts. Sometimes I alternated that with drawings and gouache paintings. I was determined; I had the dream etched in my mind of being a successful cartoonist. There was no Plan B; the only thing I had my sights set on was to be legitimized as an artist.

I worked with more than a few people I would later see in commercials, on television, and in film. It always felt like a kick in my balls; I resented them. I wanted to get where I thought I ought to be going, but it wasn't happening. Rejection letters were no longer painful. They felt like nothing after a while. The world was telling me that I wasn't good enough, but I knew I was. It was more likely I would die before I was recognized, and they'd find thousands of my drawings (like Henry Darger). Too bad I wouldn't be alive to see it.

The box was our domain. We were prisoner, dweller, captain, and steward of that fine place. We weren't kind to strangers stepping into our realm. We had our own rituals; we performed our own sketches, traded product, and boxed. We would wrap our hands with rags and take turns trading combinations. Sometimes, we would work on the big steel fridge. We all felt like Supermen after pounding the doors with our fists. We were half-in-the-bag noble savages.

One kid there, Jack, used to work in the ice-skating rink, teaching children to glide like he could; he looked like James Dean. I didn't like him from the start. He wore tights and spent his workday gliding around on the ice and flirting with rich moms. He had connections with celebrities. He had graduated from NYU and was sure to succeed; there was no other path for him.

He wasn't making enough money dancing on ice, so he asked to be moved to our realm. He was to be our bar back for a time and take orders from me. Winston and I were both equally tough taskmasters. I resented Jack's gifts, and I envied his potential. He also hadn't earned a spot in our domain, since the box was reserved for those who were beaten down by life.

I had changed. When I was younger, I was never like this. Not that I was old, but I could feel an old-man mindset setting in. I was pissed that this guy had it so good. I made brash assumptions, because I really didn't know much about him other than he was destined to do great things. I had also heard he used to date a gorgeous actress and resented him even more for that. I was filled with fear, because I had no idea what life had in store for me.

It was a busy evening at the hotel. Winston, and I were in a frenzy making pitchers of alcohol. We couldn't work fast enough and were barking orders at Jack. He kept his head down and ran back and forth from the box. He was pulling bottles of liquor, getting us ice, bringing clean glasses, and taking orders without questions.

Management alerted us that a humongous party was to be seated momentarily. Our manager came up to us at the service window with bloodshot eyes and red nostrils. I knew Winston and I were about to enter a mad frenzy of slinging drinks, pitchers, and bottles. It would be a lot of work, and we were about to demand a lot from Jack. We were going to feel the pressure from our manager, and we were going to send the shit downhill to Jack. This was known as the chain of command. The Army had it. The corporate world had it. Even restaurants had it.

Within a few minutes, the cocktail waitress brought our first order. It was cumbersome, including five different pitchers of specialty drinks. We were short on pitchers and the alcohol we would need. We needed to start banging. Winston and I divided the ticket; Jack stood behind us, and I spun around to him.

"Jack, we need two more pitchers now!"

"We also need five bottles of Ketel, now!" Winston chimed in.

"Okay," Jack responded.

"Not okay! We're about to get our assholes kicked in! Ya hear. Not okay!"

"Yes! I'll go!"

Winston and I were working in a cramped corner. We poured our juices and alcohol rapidly; we made sure not to splash all over the countertop. We would have to build these pitchers of drinks in three stages. We were advised that this party included hotel corporate. This meant that we couldn't bullshit. We needed to get the recipes right. If Cain found out we were winging it, we were doomed to wallow in the service bar ad infinitum. Jack was taking some time to gather the supplies. I knew that he had to deal with the stockroom guy. Those guys were the laziest of the bunch, but Jack needed to muscle them; he needed to make things move for us. We needed to make things move for our manager. The manager had to answer to corporate.

Jack ran back, dropping off the pitchers, and exited through the swinging door. He came right back in with the bottles of vodka. Our ice was low—we should have sent him for ice first. He was too new to know the priorities.

"Hey, mate, what are we going to cool down these drinks with? Am I supposed to use my cold, dead heart to freeze this pint?"

"Come on, bro. We're in the weeds. This is going to turn into a real shit show, unless we make this happen."

"Yes!" Jack looked dazed.

I believe he had begun to feel the regret of leaving the ice-skating rink and those rich moms. Now, he was under the thumb of two disgruntled barmen. He disappeared through the swinging doors and reappeared minutes later with a bucket of ice.

"Seriously, bro! We need more than that!"

"Yes. I just thought that this. . . ." Jack replied

"Don't think, mate! Do what we say. It works if you just listen." Winston sent Jack back out to grab cucumbers.

We had the first round of drinks up. Jack came back with cucumbers, but they weren't sliced. We needed to help the cocktail waitress prep glasses with garnishes. We didn't have enough prepped ingredients, so Jack would need to start cutting.

"Jack, why aren't these cut already?" I asked.

"I wasn't told," Jack began to answer.

"Mate, it's your bloody job. We need to clear out our sinks now, before the next round. Get cutting!" Winston demanded.

Jack started cutting behind us, next to the baristas. Winston and I cleared out our sinks and our stations for the next round. The ticket began to print. We had multiple tickets that had printed, since other tables needed service too. It would take a lot of organizing to move this product out. Jack came back with the cucumbers and began to load them into our caddy next to the lemons. I pulled one out and shook my head. Winston grabbed one too.

"Mate, are you serious? What's this?" Winston asked.

"What do you mean?" Jack asked.

"These are too damn fat! Also, there's no courtesy cut . . . what the fuck?"

"Nobody showed me," Jack answered.

"There's no time for this. We just got to move with them. It'll cost us time to slice and go. Whatever . . . get more ice!" I ordered.

Jack left again to snatch two buckets. He was visibly sweaty, and his optimistic aura dimmed. We were crushing him—two higher-ups ripping into him. It was all too familiar. I had become what I had hated, a cruel ruler. I had become Genghis Khan… worse, I had become Cain. Winston was madly swinging his shakers around. We were in the heat of it, keeping our heads down and pushing through. The espresso machine hissed behind us at a regular rate: the people outside were moving toward the end of their meals. Our printer spat out fewer tickets, and our pace slowed. It started to die down. Our purple cabana shirts were sweat-stained.

After hours of busy service, I had a moment to relax. Winston and I told Jack to take a break. He excused himself to hit the employee dining room downstairs. As calm began to set in. I felt utter shame. I was disgusted with myself for becoming Cain, the horrible thing I never thought I would become. I had delighted in beating Jack down and now felt remorse.

"Jack kicked some ass for us, didn't he?" I asked.

"Sure did, mate," Winston said.

"We really bossed him around, eh?"

"Yes, well that's how it goes. We did it for Cain."

"I know."

"You think we were too hard on the lad?"

"Maybe."

"Alcohol solves all problems, mate."

Jack came back into the box. We had three tequilas poured to shoot. Winston looked through the window as I looked up at the security camera, but I knew the ex-cops who were watching didn't care one way or the other. We clinked glasses and gulped the harsh spirits.

"You did a great job, Jack."

"Yes, mate. You sure did."

"I was happy to help," Jack said.

"I'm sorry if we were harsh."

"No, not at all," he said earnestly.

Jack had worked hard for us, and we were grateful. His hair was all over the place, and he had stains all over his uniform. We had gotten the job done together. It wasn't much longer before Jack switched to another post in the hotel. He was focused on fulfilling his dream; this was merely a short stop on his personal journey. He quit a couple of months later. He would pop in to say hello once in a while. After that, he seemed to disappear.

I saw him once more months later, in summer in Williamsburg. He was going to LA to try out for a pilot, so this was his last hurrah in the Big Apple. He came up to me and gave me a big hug. Our relationship had grown to one of respect and brotherhood. We shared some kind words, and that was the last I saw of him in the flesh.

About a year later, I heard about him, however. A friend from the hotel mentioned he had made it. I was visiting my folks in Boston. We were eating dinner and watching TV. My folks loved the show *Extra*, so it was on at a time I could see Jack with two other actors being interviewed about their new show on a major network. He had gone from a bar back to a Hollywood star. Jack had made it! He was a player now; he had realized his dream and left the past of the Stan Ward Hotel like a nightmare.

I still see his face occasionally by the luminous glow of mass media. He's one of the few living the life that so many of my compatriots have been trying for. I'm not surprised anymore to see familiar faces in entertainment. I have seen old managers in pharmaceutical commercials, an old girlfriend in a Netflix show. I even saw a cardboard cutout of a former hostess as an Amazonian in a movie theatre. I have lived in major metropolitan areas for most of my adult life. The flickering of other people's success had become my mirage as I lay dying in a desert with no oases.

...

I was coming to the end of my rope with the Stan Ward. I was back with Felicity and actually ready for it all to come crumbling down. My gym in Brooklyn kept me sane. A couple of nights a week, I trained in Mixed Martial Arts under my professor, a seasoned beast. Monday nights were sacred. A few of us spent from six o'clock on drilling Brazilian Jiu-Jitsu and kick boxing and working strength and conditioning. The last part of the night, we sparred. It was glorious. The outside world melted away, and we lived life fully. After beating the shit out of each other, we would get falafels. Again, Monday nights were sacred.

Felicity was unstable. She assumed I was sleeping with all of my cocktail waitresses. I loved the waitresses but never pursued them, though any of them would have been worth it. I avoided them because they were perfect and would need no excuse to walk away. But one day, Felicity sealed our fate as we took a walk on the Williamsburg Bridge toward the LES. We walked and talked about Massachusetts. She was from there too and most definitely a "Mass-hole." In talking about the different demographics in NYC, most of us were equal opportunity haters. Every group had annoyed us in some manner. That was the trademark of a New Yorker. If you spent enough time there, you couldn't help but notice patterns. We segued into the demographics of our hometowns. She began to talk about how many Jews there were in her town. I was going with it; I wasn't acutely sensitive but couldn't tolerate what she said next. It came out of left field.

"I hate Jews," she said.

I was dumbfounded. I tried to gather my thoughts to be able to tell her what was going on in my head. I made an obscene comment filled with anger. But I said it calmly; I didn't have it in me to scream at her. "You know the man you're fucking, the man you're with, is Jewish and the grandson of Holocaust survivors. What you just said was terribly offensive."

"Oh, don't be so sensitive."

I was silent. We continued walking. It was awful for me to realize that we couldn't go on. The relationship itself was already decaying in a plain pine box, and no rabbi would grant the burial rights. Our relationship would be buried without the proper shiva.

But I didn't end it immediately because I was addicted to her. We had what professionals refer to as a toxic relationship. I needed to quit cold turkey and couldn't. But Felicity was acting out, and it was making me crazy; she was five feet of terror. I told her I needed a couple of days to be by myself.

I had been close friends with a woman I had met when I was twenty. She was twice my age, but we had dated on and off for years. I went into Manhattan to visit her. We weren't sleeping with each other anymore; I had come over to hang out, have some wine, and talk. Felicity texted me wanting to know where I was. I could have lied, but I chose not to. I think my subconscious knew what I needed to do. I texted her back, telling her that I was with my friend. Felicity knew of this woman's importance in my life and was enraged.

I got back to Felicity's place by 10 p.m. She demanded we speak, so I obliged. She got in my face and barked at me, while I stood there quietly. I pulled out the key she had given me to the apartment and dropped it on the kitchen floor. I had to leave. I felt a swell of unprecedented violence and didn't want to make a mistake. She screamed at me.

"Run away, you fucking pussy!"

"You need professional help, bitch!" I yelled back as I descended the stairs.

That's when it finally stopped. We were done for the last and final time. It felt somehow like we had been in a succession of horror films, each even more gruesome than the one before. The budget had gone up each time, so the stakes had gone up with it. In the final installment, there was almost a bloodbath.

I was elated with it finally being over. I would no longer be dating that diminutive Irish succubus. This five-foot-nothing hellion was the worst, a "Nightmare on Union Street." Did I mention that she was an alcoholic? She tried to get back together, texting me at two or three in the morning drunk. I refused to respond. I was off that junk and didn't want to go back. I was a new man, past the point of counseling. I had earned my badges, and I wouldn't succumb to a hit of the hellion. One random day, my phone rang with her number showing. This was new. I hesitated but picked up.

"Hello?"

"Hi, it's me . . . Felicity."

"Yup, I know."

"So, how're you?"

"Great."

"Good . . . good. So, I was thinking we could meet up for a drink."

"I'm going to train some Brazilian Jiu-Jitsu but can meet at seven for tea."

"That sounds good."

We met at the West Cafe. I had my bike locked out front, and I was still sweaty and scratched up. She was wearing an open blouse, revealing her black bra. I knew what she was after when I saw her. I had wanted to think she had changed. I knew better. Nobody changes. It's a lesson I should have understood already.

We sat down. I had ordered up two cups of herbal tea. We spoke nonsense for a bit. Then I realized why I was there; she had brought me there to punish me.

"Yeah, so you been dating anyone lately?" Felicity asked.

"Not really," I answered.

"Oh, well, I dated a bit. I dated one of my co-workers. He was kind of boring, and then it was awkward. I dated a cop. . . that was fun. I dated a musician guy. He lives right by here. I was hooking up with a lawyer. . . we went out for nice dinners. There was Brian. You remember Brian. You used to work with him at the hotel."

She kept going, rattling off a list of men who had been inside her since we broke up. It was vicious, gross, and cruel; she wanted to go for the jugular. She wanted me to know that she was desirable. Even if I didn't think so now, other men wanted her. (She didn't realize that it takes almost no effort for a woman to get laid.) She also wanted to activate my caveman mode. If I let instinct take over, then I would mark my territory and go where so many men had gone before (into her gaping hole).

I didn't want to sink to her level, but I felt like letting off one jab before this massacre was over. I brought up one girl I had dated.

"I actually did date this one girl from my French class. She was a master's student and a marathon runner with very long legs," I told her calmly.

I could see her hide her grimace. She was tiny, and so I had let her have it; it was a little jab for a little girl. I knew "long legs" would be a punch right to her nose.

The stakes were raised. She invited me to her apartment. She assured me it was fine, because her roommate was home. I had to agree. If I declined, she would know she had succeeded in fucking with me. I would go, hang out, and leave without giving her anything. It was only a five-minute walk away. On the walk, I had to keep the conversation up. I felt my mind veer off but had to focus. I would not give her the satisfaction of hurting me. We got to her place, and I brought my bicycle upstairs. She brought out a bowl of cherries and changed into a pair of Daisy Dukes. I ate her cherries and put her words out of my mind.

We listened to music, while I feigned laughter and kept a smile plastered on my face. She moved closer to me on the couch, as I sunk back into the armrest. We talked more nonsense. I wanted out of there.

I had done my part; I had learned a lesson; it was time to walk away. I pulled out my phone, pretending to read a text message. I told her I had to go and headed for the door to grab my bike and ride back to my apartment. She saw me out. It had been about a year since I had exited that apartment in a fit of rage. We had screamed at each other in the stairwell. This was the end of a battle with mortars launched and no casualties. Our relationship had been cold and dead for a year. The smoke was clearing, and the rubble of what we once had was clear to me.

"That was a lot of fun. We should do that again sometime," she said.

"Sure, that sounds nice."

We never saw each other again.

On to the Next Bar

The Stan Ward Hotel was planning on doing away with the box. They were going to move us outside with the patrons. I wasn't having it. I didn't want to help this corporate hellhole make any more money. I had put in my time and seen many folks come and go. I wrote up my resignation. They didn't care. That's how it goes in the Big Apple. There's always a Megabus arriving with new blond-haired boys to replace the moldy ones.

Over the next five years, everyone was replaced. They either left willingly or kicking and screaming. The original owner of the hotel sold it. He was still a figurehead and consultant, but times were changing. The rents in New York City and its boroughs were exploding. By the end of my time in NYC, I was Paul Revere riding through town, warning all the 20-year-olds to run. It was getting harder to live there. Every low-end neighborhood had cute coffee shops. No place was safe. You either had to live in Sunnyside or Jersey, and even those places would blow up.

John and I had moved into another apartment, right above the Classon G line. We got it for a fair price. John's bedroom was facing the street. I had a feeling that his wall and the exterior wall were one and the same (and made of fiber board). His room was like an igloo. After we moved in, he became so terribly ill that I thought he might not make it, but I was still thrilled we had secured the apartment. John's parents shipped him an electric blanket, and he miraculously recovered.

I was off the schedule at the Stan Ward two weeks after I resigned. I would not set foot in the building until about a year later. I was disgruntled, but I was also blessed. I had put two years into that place, and it had a big name in the city. If you had put in your time there, you could work just about anywhere. They hadn't been lying at that orientation. It was the golden ticket to any spot you wanted.

I got my resume together, but there was no need. I had another bartender reach out to me. She had left the hotel a couple months before me and secured a bar manager position at a Mexican speakeasy in Chinatown. I was a big fan of tequila and mescal and was excited to get to it.

The team embraced me, and it was glorious. I didn't have much experience dealing with cash or guests. I had spent most of my time in the box, so I was scared. I didn't want to embarrass myself. Shauna, the bar manager, took me under her wing and got me going. I was not only flying; I was soaring. The money I was making was like nothing I had ever known. I didn't realize how little I had been earning before. I had another friend who tended bar at all the hipster spots in Williamsburg. He was wealthy by our standards. He had been one of the first of the Stan Ward barkeeps to jump ship and discover the world outside of the hotel. He became rich. Now I, too, was experiencing the benefits of making real money. I left with cash in my pocket, and my paychecks were substantial. It was a tequila-soaked dream. The only downside was that the GM was off. She was abusive and inconsistent, but Shauna would deal with her, so we were spared.

We drank in plain view of the guests and bosses. It wasn't frowned upon. I usually confined myself to sipping Modelo Especial on tap. Our clientele was very cool. You could assess their status by posture alone. Many of them were old-school LES. Most of NYC was in major flux at this time, too many kids from Ohio, Orange County, China, and Europe were taking over. The real New Yorkers were going away, but I didn't know where. They just seemed to evaporate like rain on the grimy streets.

I would ride over the Manhattan Bridge to get to work, passing "Murder Avenue," which had been cleaned up, and was just Myrtle Avenue again. When I had moved to that neighborhood, it was rough. Now rents were high. Later on, it would also boast a Starbucks and Chipotle. The city was losing its identity. It wouldn't be long before New York became a strip mall.

I had spent enough time in New York to have memories all over the city. I could look down a certain street and remember the date I had had with an African waitress from a Fort Greene spot. I could look down another street and remember almost getting hit by a drunk driver in a Mini Cooper. The interactions, too many to count, culminated in the product I had become. I was shaped by the city. I came in as soft, pale dough, then got baked to a golden brown.

Now, I was no longer mixing, shaking and pouring drinks from a hidden lair. I was a barman, out front and center. I was not a master of the craft, but I was getting there. From this point on, I would carry on the tradition of libation and chitchat. I felt a swell of pride.

Shauna tried to protect us from the irrational GM, who had explosive episodes coupled with a drinking problem. This was quite normal in the industry. Everyone had a vice. Liquor was available and acceptable. I was not a serious drinker. It was a part of my life, but I kept it separate. I always had MMA on my mind. If I had been drinking too much, I found it would cost me on the mat. The GM was originally from Jamaica and had also worked at the Stan Ward. I had many connections from that place. We all put our time in and then split. The ones that split earlier lit the way to greener pastures. Most of the jobs I ever got in NYC were from ex-Stan Ward employees. Once a place became dry, we left like locusts to the next locale.

On her last night, Shauna had protected us for her final time from the GM, ended up getting fired, and resented that none of us had spoken up for her. Thanks to Shauna, I had barely spoken one word to the GM; I only poured her Jameson's and smiled timidly. But the GM ended up getting fired too. Her mother was sick, so she looked forward to going back to Jamaica to see her. Before leaving, she allegedly stole $10,000. I don't believe any charges were pressed. But I had left before she did. I felt the winds changing and knew the place would be coming down, particularly with Shauna out of the picture.

A year later, a bartender buddy who had also abandoned ship was walking through Fort Greene with his fiancé, strolling through early in the morning with coffees in hand. They came upon our old GM. Nobody had laid eyes on her since her grab and run. He told me she was barefoot and wearing a crusty black dress. Her hair was matted, and she was in a daze. She came up to him and seemed to recognize him. She asked if he had seen her raven, and he replied that he had not. Then he and his fiancé walked briskly away. The stress of the city, her mother's death, bi-polar disorder, drinking, and substance abuse had broken that woman.

I switched to yet another bar. Jones Street still wasn't hiring, but the owner of the chain had teamed up with another man to open an Asian restaurant in the Sunset Hotel. I was back to work in the Meatpacking District. Many of my Stan Ward associates were also there. The Jones Street chain owner was a guy I had worked for in Miami. He was a callous, calculating, fat, gay, Israeli guy named Jonah. On a good day, he resembled Alfred Hitchcock. He enjoyed parading around with boys to show off his status. The other owner of this joint venture was an Asian man whose parents owned a bank. He was a Muay Thai boxing bro who had a different girl picked out for every night of the week.

Jonah was a tough cookie. I showed up for my interview at the new restaurant knowing he would bust my balls. He dealt only in high-end spots and demanded the best. He expected excellence because he had millions of dollars on the line.

I went into the interview with a strategy. I had researched sake and whiskey, so I would try to vomit out all of the information I had and not let him question me. I needed to exude complete confidence, because his bullshit detector was not to be trifled with. I was not a seasoned barman but had to fake it. I would not let him pass on me due to my inexperience. He remembered me from the Miami days but that didn't win me any favor.

My strategy worked; he brought me onto the team. This place was where I became a fully seasoned professional who identified truly as a bartender. I took it seriously. My regulars were wealthy and came in to see *me*. I held court, ran a tight ship, and stashed as much money away as I could. I felt it in my bones that my time in NYC was coming to an end. I didn't know when or how, but I knew why. It was getting too damn expensive. I didn't know how long John and I could hold out. I only knew that I would live this moment with vigor. It wasn't the end yet, so I was going to make it count.

...

I had a tough go in my first six months at the new spot, Nashi. It was a rough ride. My bar manager wanted me fired; other people got fired and replaced in rapid succession, and the place attracted every trashy Meatpacking glitterati. It was hellish and fun all at once.

Our first GM was a middle-aged Asian woman. She was decidedly single, with dead ovaries, and mood swings. In other words, she was an utter bitch. I had to keep my mouth shut and bust my ass.

But my bar manager Warren grew to like me over the months. He was a smart, capable mixologist. He had a master's in jazz composition and knew a good bit about visual art, too. He had read everything from Henry Miller to a biography of Charles Mingus. He was an out-of-control party animal, typically balancing at least four different women, in a loop. He also enjoyed mixing Vicodin and Adderall. He had a dual nature—a hellion on service bar and a charmer with guests. He would step outside the bar to demonstrate lesbian scissoring for particular guests, one of his many parlor tricks. Our upscale bar crowd loved it. He was a "legit" bartender in the Big Apple with a big following; everyone adored him. This made him a celebrity. This was only possible in the city, where everyone exceptional in their realm develops a celebrity following: chefs, barmen, singers, cabbies, even dentists, depending on whether or not they are that ephemeral thing, "legit." Warren's regulars came to the bar because they knew him from our sister restaurant—made famous by, you guessed it, *Sex and the City*.

One night, one particular regular of Warren's came in for a drink. In her early forties, blonde, wealthy, and attractive, she sought him out, but he had that night off. She told me that he was the best bartender she knew. She adored his special technique of drink-making. I felt left out; Warren had never mentioned this secret technique.

I had to ask a friend of his for the inside scoop. Apparently, Warren used to stir a martini with his penis (for special guests, of course). Times had changed, and compared to him, I was a huge square. At the *Sex and the City* lounge in the early 2000's, they used to party during shift. I knew a bunch of these folks, all in their mid-thirties to early forties now, all glamorous and beautiful with rent-controlled apartments. These guys used to hide cocaine in empty matchbooks and pass them around like Tic-tacs.

I was the youngest bartender at Nashi. I had slowly earned Warren's trust. The Asian female GM quit, and I was left with decent managers. Jonah was no fun, but I knew to smile and nod when he was near. Our bar team was solid. I was the most reliable but far from the fastest.

Mostly, the whole staff was beautiful. I think that's partly why they were hired. I felt inadequate at times, and at others, like I was playing into the New York City dream. Here at the Sunset Hotel, the help were participants in an illusion. Guests were taken into the bowels of the hotel where red velvet carpet, chairs, black lacquer furniture, and sharply dressed young people were the stage play. In essence, it was a kind of dinner theater. It was always alarming when the shift ended, and we turned the lights on. The dings and dents, the blemishes, and syrup blotches showed the truth. We were in the business of putting on a show, and once the house lights came on, the show was over.

I knew this ride wouldn't last forever. For the first six months, it was war. We were a new restaurant with tremendous overhead, major competition, and staff with party habits. I saw the owners fight on numerous occasions, and three chefs replaced. I saw my buddy get bumped up to a GM position without the title (or pay). I knew it was only a matter of time. My sights were set on earning as much money as I could, learning as much as I could from Warren, and experiencing life with intention. I had my eyes on a particular prize, the prize of being a master of the city.

I Was at The Height of My Bar Craft

Money gets cold in the winter too. I was set up and ready to sling drinks and sushi but knew it would not be a lucrative night. The streets were covered in dirty, gray city snow. I went over to the computer and looked to see how many covers we expected for the evening . . . 13. I felt a sense of futility in. I would be lucky to make 30 bucks. That's like three burritos, three meals for me out in the Village. My bar was set up ahead of schedule. I had closed the previous night and put things away with exactitude. My Hawthorne strainers, double strainers, julep strainers, shaking tins, stirring glass, stirring spoon, muddler, garnish jars, syrups, citrus, and bank were all in place. I went to check the beer fridge and noticed that we were down to a half case of Sapporo in bottles. It wouldn't matter tonight anyway.

Most of the servers had been called off. Heather and Jeremy were already dressed in their black garb. Their Chinese busboy showed up late, still sporting his track pants and fitted baseball cap. I went to the office and changed out of my sweaty, gray v-neck and beaten up chinos. I donned my black garb, purchased entirely from the Salvation Army. The clothes wouldn't hold up to the scrutiny of daylight, but under the dim lights, they changed. The clothes that would look just right on a zombie in a horror flick took on a new life in the muted light. I looked in the mirror behind the bar and saw that my face, slightly scuffed from Jiu-Jitsu two nights prior, seemed miraculously clear in this red velvet, Asian, basement bar restaurant. I took a sip from my heavily soy-filled coffee. Just moments earlier, I had been sipping it at Starbucks and sketching the corporate girls.

You didn't see corporate girls in Brooklyn. You saw Bohemian rich girls, all dressed in a pricey education uniform that still somehow spelled "stuck in the service industry." They were mainly hot. The tats sported by these nouveau beatniks typically consisted of feathers, cages, birds (in or out of the cages, depending on your outlook on life), and Sanskrit. They would pick a side of their heads and shave it, letting the rest of their hair grow to shoulder length. It looked as though they had had brain surgery and were waiting for the hair to grow back. They all dressed in torn black jeans, thrift shop t-shirts, and motorcycle jackets. They had grown up with slut walk pride and liberal views on giving their bodies to the Brooklyn hipsters. Mostly, the men had never worked around lumber but dressed like lumberjacks and enjoyed playing the part. If you were bearded and/or tattooed in Brooklyn, you were guaranteed a continuous diet of young, reckless ladies.

So before work, I loved going to the Starbucks right by Google corporate headquarters. The girls would cycle down from the offices to get their lattes. They were in stark contrast to their Brooklyn counterparts. Their hair was perfect; they wore heels, and little outfits that brought to mind hot teachers in times past. They seemed sane, smart, and even pleasant. They lived for Soul Cycle, Juice Press and SoHo hotspots. They appeared masters of their adulthood whereas the Brooklyn crew of young artists lived in malaise.

When one of these Google girls got in the Starbucks line, I'd consume them with my eyes. I would pick them over as I sketched, as if I were at a buffet. I would grab a little leg, a clavicle here and there, and a little gastrocnemius (calf muscle) undulating from the balancing act on their heels. This was my joy, treat, and meditation every workday at three. I considered it an exchange: eight to nine hours of bar work for one hour of caffeine- and libido-fueled discovery.

Yes, I was a cliché too. I was the artist/bartender, the Brooklyn guy working in the service industry. Yes, I had come from an upper middle-class background. Like Julian Schnabel (a line cook and Jewish), I worked at night and made art during the day. On the occasional night of drinking too much with my compatriots, I would hang around the house and do very little. Most of the time, I would reject the invitations of my cohorts. I would wrap up the cleaning of my bar, cash out with my manager, and hop on my bicycle for the ride back to Brooklyn.

Most mornings, I would wake up, have my tea and oatmeal, and read the *Times*. I'd emerge, more often than not, to find an empty apartment. My roommate John worked art production in the daytime, and I worked at night. I'd sip, eat, read and think, and after that, review my drawings. I would have either finished a set of pencil drawings or finished inking some. I would take notes and put them aside. Then I'd go into my tomb of a room and pack my rash guard, shorts, mouthguard, and tape in a green canvas duffle bag. I'd hop on my bike and head over to my MMA school. Dantae was our main instructor, appointed by our professor Robert. Dantae was a solid purple belt; he had competed in the cage five times and won every single time. He was listed as a champion in Dead Serious MMA. He was driven, moody, lean, and occasionally mean. He was like me, a cliché, covered in tattoos with a shaved head and cauliflower ear, dressed in athletic gear. Day classes were typically less attended. I would train with handymen, chefs, service industry folks, and the unemployed. Morning class was for blue-collars. We'd work technique, and focus on the details. We'd go over wrestling, Judo, and Greco. We'd go over a guard position, a submission and defense; then we would grapple. We would get to roll on the mats and fight to choke our opponent or hyperextend one of his limbs.

Night classes were more intense. Everyone would show up ready to take out their aggression from the day onto the partner at hand.

This was my way of life, my routine. I didn't have a career path in mind. I had dreams, but knew dreams were often illusory. I didn't have any idea of how to increase my income and didn't think I had any way out. It was work, make art, bike, fight, and fuck, repeat.

I experienced life differently from so many men in generations before mine. Even most Generation Xers would have settled down with a family by this point. My generation got waylaid by academic promises, *Sex and The City,* and social media. We paid out the ass to study the arts or take courses that brainwashed us with a victimhood complex. We communicated in 140characters plus images, our most popular being a small poop with eyes and a mouth. The future was now, and we were living it, and experimenting with it.

That's why I gravitated toward the physical: I liked riding my bike. Even when it was cold and miserable, I enjoyed the hardship. I would ride in and out of Bed Stuy and see black men meandering around the parks smoking menthols. I would ride through south Williamsburg and see the Hasidim with their dented minivans and droves of offspring. I would ride through Williamsburg and see rich people of all colors and creeds sipping lattes and shopping. I would ride along the Williamsburg Bridge and see the East River, then exit the bridge into the LES and see Dominicans, New York City natives, and transvestites. I would ride up through the East Village and see students who didn't seem to realize how lucky they were. Then I would take a left on 11th Street and go west. The houses were gorgeous, old, and European in style; the people seemed to be living in another dimension. To enter these small side streets with gorgeous homes was to penetrate a membrane and drive through it. Once on the other side, you felt present. The anxiety from the traffic, pedestrians, cops, ambulances, and lights dimmed. Here, behind this membrane, was like entering Narnia.

I would make my way up to the Meatpacking District and the Sunset Hotel. Locking my bike outside the hotel, I'd venture down the ramp into the bowels of the building through the workers' quarters. Asian ladies would wander from their uniformed services room, West Africans would step out of the locker room to work the bathroom attendant positions, and young, pretty girls would don black dresses to work bottle service in the rooftop lounge.

As I said, on this night we had 13 reservations. John had cut our servers down to Heather and Jeremy. Xin, the Chinese busboy, was high and working solo. Then there was yours truly, the barman. Heather, a Korean beauty, came over and gave me a hug. Her body was designed for sex; it was divine. One of my co-workers, Ben, occasionally slept with her. At first, Ben had made me angry. It was nothing he did; it was who he was. Ben was the Texas model. Along with being annoyingly handsome, he happened to be very funny and smart. He was always dressed in slim-fitting pants, a perfectly ironed shirt and black suspenders. I felt like a Robert Crumb cartoon across from a Michelangelo. I would have deemed myself the ugly stepbrother except that I felt my status was secure: I was an artist, MMA practitioner and cyclist. Anyway, it was New York City, and everybody got laid. Tinder, OK Cupid, and Plenty of Fish had been around for years or, if you were old school, you could just hit a hipster dive bar. We were all well into our twenties and full of our own possibility, drive, and desires. Ben wasn't here that night, so my male attention sufficed Heather, who was a pro, looking over her tables to make sure the chopsticks were placed neatly on top of the small plate just so, an inch from the edge.

Jeremy came over to chat. He was tall, lanky, and charming. He had just moved to the city—at 22, about my age when I had first shown up on the shores of Manhattan. I had a younger brother his age, so I connected with him immediately. He was from rural Pennsylvania, a theatre student, and hungry to forge a future. I was beaten down, pessimistic, and hoping for any kind of future. I fed off his naïveté and goodness.

"So, Dustin, I met this girl at a party."

"Yeah, what'd she look like?"

"She's tall, nice tits, kind of plain, simple."

"Nice."

"Yeah, so anyway, we exchanged numbers."

"When are you going to see her?" I inquired.

"I don't know, man. I mean I think she's hot. I think she likes me. I think she may be DTF, but I'm not sure. I mean, you get laid— what do I do? I am so used to just having a girlfriend. How does one get a girl in New York City? What should I do?" he asked, dismayed.

"I don't know, man. I mean it isn't hard. Women outnumber men here. I see so many lame dudes with cute chicks. I know a lot of people use apps. That seems like a guarantee, because everybody on those things is on there to screw."

"Well, I met her in real life. So, I don't know what to do."

"Where does she live?"

"Queens."

"Where do you live again?"

"Washington Heights."

"Fuck, that's a far commute to make this thing happen."

"Well, what do you mean? If we both meet halfway in midtown. . ."

"No, that's not what you are going to do," I commanded.

"What am I going to do?"

"You'll invite her to your neck of the woods in Washington Heights."

"Yeah?"

"Yes, then you'll pick a bar no more than three blocks from your apartment. You will have beer stocked in the fridge, and a copy of *The Big Lebowski*."

"What?" he asked incredulously.

"Yeah, so you'll meet this tall lady at the bar within a three-block range of your apartment. Make sure your roommate is out. You'll have a round or two with her at the bar. You will start to talk about movies. You'll ask her what movies she likes. You will then mention you have beer at your place and a DVD of *The Big Lebowski*."

"Yeah, and then?" he waited with bated breath.

"And then . . . you'll be making out with her and possibly having sex with her within 15 minutes of the movie starting."

"No way!" he said exuberantly.

"Yes, way!"

"How do you know this'll work?"

"I've done it!"

"Really?"

"Yes."

"All right, thanks, man!"

"No worries, man."

Jeremy went back to circle the floor, waiting for a table to arrive. I went back to looking over some finer details of my bar. The bottle in the far-right side of my well was a Japanese whiskey infused with sesame. I gave it a swirl. It was filled only halfway, and I decided to leave it that way. I wanted to burn it out, so I could clean out the bottle; the fat from the sesame tended to coat the bottle with a film of oil. We had another whiskey infused with seaweed . . . that wasn't a hit. We barmen tasted it from time to time. At least we were putting it to good use.

Two parties came down the stairs. The manager gave one table to Heather and the other to Jeremy. I wished they had stopped by my bar; this was sure to be a night with little reward. My ticket machine buzzed within moments. Two orders for two tables printed out. I read the printouts . . . mainly wine. No way to put my shakers to use. I poured the glasses of wine and set them on the service bar with their tickets, then turned away to sketch on an order pad-- a skull, with a joint sticking out of its teeth.

Hearing steps, I turned around. A man in his forties in a gray suit, buzz cut, clean-shaven, and wearing glasses sat on the far-left side, away from the main dining room. I went over and greeted him, thrilled to have a guest. I might make two dollars tonight.

"Hello, sir. Would you care for a cocktail list?" I asked.

"No, I don't need one."

"Okay, sir. What would you like?"

"Do you have any orange vodka?"

I thought, "No, sir. This isn't New Jersey. We don't do that here," but I said,

"I apologize, sir. We don't have any flavored vodka. I could make you a vodka soda and put some orange bitters in it."

"Okay, that sounds good."

"Coming right up."

I went over to the other side of my bar. I put four Kold-Draft ice cubes into a Tom Collins glass. I did a six-count of Tito's and cracked a can of seltzer. I filled the glass the rest of the way with seltzer and put a lime wedge on it, and a black straw in it. Then I dropped in some orange bitters, set the drink in front of him, and continued our small talk.

"How are you liking the weather? It's pretty nippy out."

"Yes, but it seems colder in Greenwich."

"Oh, you came in from Connecticut."

"Well, I work in the city half the week."

"Oh, that's cool."

"Yes, my family is in Greenwich."

"Are you expecting someone to join you? We do have a full menu available at the bar, too, in case you're interested."

"Yes, she'll be here soon."

"Okay, cool."

Within a moment, I saw a figure coming toward the bar in heels: big lips, big breasts, hair pulled back, and a short skirt. In the lamplight overhead, I could see she was a Hispanic transgender woman. She gave the gentleman a kiss on the cheek and pressed her bubbling breast implants against his gray wool-clad chest.

"Oh my god, papa, I have not seen you in forever. Where have you been? You looking good, baby," she said

"Oh thanks, you're looking good too, Claudia," he said sheepishly.

"Hello, miss, can I get you a drink?" I asked.

"Oh, my god, mama needs a drink. It's cold out there. It was never this cold in Colombia! I mean, shit, nigga, you got to warm me up. I'm frozen!"

"Sure thing," he said quietly.

"So, what can I get for you to drink?" I asked, trying to not expose the shock I felt seeing this family man meeting up with a tranny hooker.

"Mama likes white wine, baby." She nearly fell over the man. Her breasts ballooned over his neck and shoulder. "Billy here, is gonna want me good and drunk. He likes to take advantage of me when I been drinking too much."

"Okay, we have Sauvignon Blanc, Chardonnay, Pinot Grigio, Riesling. . . ."

"Yeah, papa, I'll take a glass of Riesling. Billy, that's the one I like, right?"

"Yes, that's the one," Billy said, a little embarrassed, I thought.

. I held a wine glass up to the light to notice smudges; it was clean. I poured a taste from a previously opened bottle of Riesling into the glass in front of the lady and held the bottle with the label facing her as she tasted it.

"Oh, just pour the glass. I'm sure it's good. It'll be good enough to get me fucked up, and then this *pajero* will have his way."

I left Billy and Claudia to get reacquainted and went over to my service bar. I noticed a ticket pop up. It had "cherry bomb" and "bordello" printed on it, two specialty cocktails we made. I prepared the cherry bomb first. I put a scoop, with my stirring spoon, of cherry jam into a metal tin, then poured an ounce of lemon juice into it using my jigger and dumped that into the tin. After that, came syrup infused with black pepper; I put a little under an ounce into the tin. I flipped the jigger around so I could use its two-ounce side and filled that with tequila. The raw materials in place, I rinsed the jigger well and built the bordello in second metal tin. A coin of cucumber went into the glass. I muddled it lightly, then added an ounce of lime juice, an ounce of Nashi-infused simple syrup, and two ounces of bison grass-infused vodka. I put ice in each of the tins and about four Kold-Draft cubes into the cherry bomb. Sealing the tins, I shook them in a zigzag pattern, allowing the Kold-Draft cubes to smash against their metal insides and blend the raw ingredients into a cohesive, chilled mass. I cracked open the tins and double-strained the drinks into their respective glasses. I placed the two cocktails and their service ticket on the rubber mats of the service station and went back to check on Bill and Claudia.

She was sitting on his lap, and his red, clean-shaven face was lightly perspiring. Billy leaned slightly over the bar to ask me a question.

"Hey, pal. I was hoping Claudia and I could have a little more privacy."

"Oh. Would you like to dine at one of our lounge tables here behind you?"

"Well, I was hoping for somewhere a little more out of view."

"Well . . . we do have a private dining room behind that red velvet curtain over there. . .

"That would be nice."

"But we want you to take care of us, papa," Claudia added.

"Okay, let me go to my manager."

I stepped out from behind my bar and walked across the floor to talk to my manager.

"J.C., so here's the deal: I need to set up these guests in the private dining room. This is my only chance to make money tonight. I need this, Jonny. I need this chance. They want me and me only to attend to them. You cannot go in there. I will run the food, the booze, and bus. Only me. It's a one-man job."

"Sure, Dustin. Do what you gotta do."

"I love you, man!"

"I know."

I shuffled back to Bill and Claudia and led them to the private dining room. I pulled the curtain closed, put their menus down, pouring them water and letting them know I'd be back in five minutes.

Back at my bar, I opened their tab. I went back to my sketchpad for a minute to give them time, then into the private dining room. Claudia's blouse was open, her tan breasts flopping out on Bill, her nipples flat and dark. She was necking with him a bit and looked like she was playing with his junk under the table. His red face looked at mine, and I turned my eyes to a painting of a samurai three feet away from them.

"Oh, papa, you got to give us some warning! You could have walked in on me sucky sucky this nigga here!" Claudia said, as she giggled like a horny teenager.

"Sorry, folks! I just wanted to know what you would like to eat…"

"Just order whatever you think we would like," Bill said.

"Okay, I'll get on that. I'll be back in a little bit."

"Okay, papa. Don't be back too soon," Claudia giggled.

I put in an order for a tuna tart, then some sashimi. I didn't want them getting full too quickly. Within moments, the tart was up. I went into the kitchen to pick it up from Frankie, our jovial sous-chef. Back in the dim dining room and beyond the red velvet curtain. This time, I waved my hand beyond the curtain to let them know I was going to have to come in to serve them.

"Yes, papa. Enter. I put my tits away," Claudia called from behind the curtain.

"Here, we have a tuna tart."

"Damn, Billy. They be bringing us Mexican sushi. Look at that, fancy."

"Yes, I think you guys will love it. Would you like another drink?"

"Yes, bring us whatever you think we'll like," Bill said.

"Okay, maybe a glass of sake. That should be nice."

"Please do," Bill said.

I went back to my bar. I had a lot of sakes to choose from, but I was not good at pairing sake with our food. I loaded a tray with two glasses of *nigori* ("milky") sake and pushed my hand past the curtain as fair warning. They were making out; I studied the samurai painting. His face samurai showed stoic, battle-weary fatigue. I wondered what would happen if he were suddenly here in the room with us. Maybe he would cut off Bill's head and ravage Claudia; maybe he would kill them both. Maybe he wouldn't pay any attention and start practicing his katas.

Claudia and Bill stopped kissing and looked at me with feigned shyness. I presented the glasses of nigori.

"Damn, Papa, this looks like you know what!"

I blushed. Bill looked at me and chuckled.

"Does it taste like it too? Mmm, mmm, papa. This is getting me in the mood for sucky sucky. I hope you got a second glass for me after this one!"

"Okay, folks. Your sashimi should be ready soon. I'll go check on it."

I started to walk away. Claudia called out to me.

"Hey, papa."

"Yes."

"Is you gay?"

"No. Why do you ask?"

"Because you walk like you've been fucked."

"Oh."

"You should give a girl like me a try sometime. You ain't going back after you been here." Claudia pushed her breasts together and winked at me. Her collagen-injected lips puckered.

I laughed nervously. Masa was finishing up the sashimi, placing in quadrants on a slate slab. Ginger outlined the thinly sliced fish, landscaped with wasabi. Pickled radish gardens completed the scene of a ceremony. I thanked Masa and carried the plate to the curtain. I gave my hand warning again —Claudia had her breasts out again. Bill's face was red, looking up at the ceiling, with Claudia's shoulder moving wildly. I was happy I could not see under the table. Claudia locked eyes with me.

"Here are your sashimi," I said, vainly trying to focus on the task at hand.

"Do, you like these *tetas?* I got them done in Colombia," she asked me, pushing them together with both her hands. Bill turned his attention away from the ceiling and looked at them admiringly.

"Yes, they're nice," I said, as I realized that I meant it. I wished they weren't attached to a person with a penis, but they were pretty decent.

Claudia smiled. I put the sashimi plate in front of them and pointed out which fish were what.

"We need more sake, papa."

"I'll be right back."

I poured two glasses of *junmai ginjo* sake and brought them in without my hand signal Claudia was gone, and Bill still looking at the ceiling. Had I missed Claudia leaving to use the restroom? No, she was there on the couch, her body splayed, her buns up and down in Bill's lap. His red face glistened with sweat as her head popped up.

"Sorry, Papa. I didn't know you'd be back so fast. Just leave the drinks. We're almost done here."

"Yep," I put down the drinks and looked back at the samurai. I could swear he was crying now. I shuffled over to my bar.

After a good 15 minutes, I did my wave and entered the private dining room hoping not to witness anything new. Claudia's tits were packed away. Bill's tie was undone and his shirt unbuttoned a little, revealing his undershirt. I dropped the check; Bill handed me his card; I ran the card and printed the receipt and brought it back for him to sign. Claudia and Bill stood up, and I walked them to the exit. Bill shook my hand and smiled. I felt him palm me cash, which I tucked away in my pocket. Claudia touched my chest.

"You were wonderful, papa. I had a great time here, and I know Bill did too. I took care of that." The people at two tables in the restaurant looked over at us.

"Thanks, I appreciate the hospitality," Bill said.

"Yes, well, thanks so much for coming by tonight. I hope to see you again soon."

"We sure will be back," Bill said.

"Oh yes, papa. We will. I gotta get more of that white drink!" Claudia laughed.

I never saw them again.

I went back over to my bar. I put my hand into my pocket and pulled out the cash Bill had palmed me—two $100 bills. I had made $200 facilitating this debauchery

I bussed the private dining room. I pictured Bill, driving back to Connecticut, parking his BMW in the driveway, walking up the steps of his beautiful colonial mansion, greeted by his two perfect children and his blonde wife. The storybook ending to an Edward Gorey tale. Claudia was a shadow in a faraway place. I had played my part in the business of creating mirages, helping provide a playground for New York City dream-seekers. Bill was living his dream; Claudia was living hers; I was living mine.

I later hopped on my bike, $200 richer. The bike lane of the Williamsburg Bridge was empty going into Brooklyn. I could hear cabs and Ubers cruising below me. The square lights of the brick buildings were like a lighthouse, illuminating my return to the borough of reality. The air was cold and sobering. I breathed deeply and felt the burn in my legs as I pumped the pedals. Bill and Claudia slowly left my thoughts as I rode back to Bed Stuy, to my rundown apartment only a couple of blocks away from the Marcy Projects. I couldn't predict my future; I was just living in the present. I would wash up, go to bed, watch random clips on YouTube, and pass out and do it all over again tomorrow.

A Date or a Job Interview

I didn't notice her right away. She was sitting at the service end of the bar, with a group of women in their thirties. She was a brunette, plain but with a decent figure, and seemingly uncomfortable. I was in my zone. When bartending was good, I likened it to a rousing game of Tetris. I once took half an Adderall at the behest of my bar manager, Warren. It made me feel like the Terminator—emotionally unshakable, a tactical, drink-slinging killing machine. I had no Adderall on this particular night but was still in the zone, when I saw her. She avoided looking at me directly, but experience told me that she was admiring me. I used to be hapless with women but enough years in NYC had made me a virtuoso. Really, the game was rigged. To be a lady's man in New York was like being a pro fisherman camped out over an aquarium.

She and her girlfriends had had a few rounds before our other bartender dropped the check on them. Five credit cards were put down, as I expected. Women hardly ever picked up the tab for one another.

A blonde woman in the group approached me as the others, including the brunette, climbed back up the velvet stairs. Then she gave me the brunette's number. About the time I started to break down my bar for the night, I gave the brunette a second thought. Her name was Grace, but I couldn't remember exactly what she looked like. I just knew she was a brunette and had a decent figure. I was underwhelmed that she hadn't handed me her number directly. I pegged her as a beta, lacking the strength and spontaneity I found non-negotiable. Men and women both want strong partners. Wolves take down weak elks for sustenance but breed with alphas. Humans too are evolved to seek a strong partner (even if it's not for love and marriage).

I sent Grace a text about two days later, which read, "Greetings from your friendly neighborhood bartender. My name is Dustin, by the way."

She texted me back; we planned to meet up in Greenpoint after I got out of MMA training at my gym. Since I couldn't shoot back down to Bed Stuy to clean up before we met, she would have to take it or leave it.

She said Greenpoint was her neighborhood. If the "date" went well, there was a possibility of continuing it back at her apartment. I wondered if she'd consciously given me this signal.

The weather was lovely that night. Greenpoint was a gem in Brooklyn, originally predominantly Polish, until (yes, you guessed it) hipsters moved in. I wish I could have moved to Greenpoint instead of Bed Stuy. Greenpoint had the prettier girls. It was safer, and the cafes were like Parisian salons. I was early—wouldn't want to keep a lady waiting. I locked my bike on a rack across the street.

As I crossed the street to enter the bar, I witnessed a dispute. An older Polish man walking his Jack Russell down the street shoved a younger hipster male passing by. I waited a moment to see if I needed to break it up before it got more violent. When these things occur you can almost feel it in the air. Rage is like smoke, and I don't have the lungs for it. They shouted back and forth for a moment. Then the hipster went on his way, and the Polish man felt vindicated. I always shied away from conflict, and would have walked away as well. It's easier to be a third party. I hoped that if I ever got in a situation, somebody would jump in to help me. I continued on my way for romance.

In Bed Stuy, our problems were racially based; in Greenpoint, everyone was pretty much white. The problem there was gentrification. The more I thought about it, though, the more I realized that was the case for Bed Stuy as well. Race was just a convenient talking point. New York City is a jungle. We were all different species trying to carve out our own habitat. Things got ugly, National Geographic-style, when we began to encroach on new territory.

I made my way into the bar and looked around. Grace hadn't arrived yet. I nodded to the bartender, the classic breed of Brooklyn barman adorned with tattoos and a mustache. The space was beautiful, with high ceilings and a second floor up a long flight of stairs. The bar top was made of white marble, and they had an absinthe fountain, a throwback to the grand old days of bar culture. It was mostly populated with cool young drinkers. I had a preoccupation with the performance aspect of bartending. Personally, I never liked to reveal the man behind the show. I would go full Daniel Day Lewis in my bar craft. I didn't like the audience to know me too well, or it could ruin the show.

A young waitress told me I could grab any table I liked. I sat at a two-top, waited for Grace, and began to feel slightly nervous. I saw Grace before she saw me. She was prettier than I remembered. I stood up to greet her as she approached. She had on white shorts and a green, sleeveless top. I was wearing all black and looking disheveled, which was my normal look.

She was nervous, and this made me more nervous. I also partly reveled in the discomfort. I liked "bad dates" and even enjoyed the inner monologue and feeling of desperation. It was like a little vacation in quicksand.

We soon had drink menus, as we both needed a drink quickly. I asked her what she normally liked drinking, and she said she enjoyed everything but gin. We went through the list of specialty cocktails, an intriguing inventory. The list consisted of riffs on classic Prohibition-style drinks. I saw a variation of a Sazerac I might like, while she saw a riff on a sidecar. Our waitress came over and took our order, recognizing this as a first date, which made me feel somehow exposed. The music wasn't too loud, but I wished it had been, since loud music helps drown out awkward silences. We had glasses of water placed in front of us. I drank mine down, thirsty from MMA and riding my bike.

"So, was that your first time at Nashi?" I asked her.

"Yes, it was," she answered.

"Who were your friends?"

"The blonde woman was my friend from work. The other women were friends of hers from Soul Cycle."

"Oh, cool. Did you try our cocktails?"

"No, I had wine that night."

"Yeah, that's always a good move."

This was going nowhere quickly. It was a little weird; we had no bridge here. It seemed like there was nothing to talk about. We hadn't talked when she was at my bar; she hadn't even handed off her number in person. So, now, here we were, two complete strangers meeting for the first time. We now needed to start from ground zero and build up a rapport. This was going to be work, inorganic and strange.

The waitress brought us our cocktails. Mine was crafted beautifully. Grace and I switched cocktails to taste both; I savored the expert mixture and examined the glassware. I held equal parts of love and disdain for bar culture. We sat in silence now, and I almost couldn't look at her; it was growing more uncomfortable, and I wanted out. We took more sips from our drinks.

"So, you like living in Greenpoint?" I asked.

"Yes, I like it. I bought my place here two years ago, before it got too expensive."

"Congratulations. That was a good move."

"Yes, I'm fortunate."

"So, have you been living in New York a long time?"

"Yes, my family is on Long Island, but I've been in the city for ten years. What about you?"

"I've been here around six years."

"Do you like it?"

"Sure, I do. Where else is there, anyway?"

"How long have you been working at that spot?"

This was becoming increasingly boring. I knew I had to kick this in a different direction but didn't have a read on her. I didn't want to take it to places she didn't want to go. She seemed corporate, and the more we talked, I found out she was. She worked for a medical supply company and happened to be Jewish. I admitted to being Jewish as well. It was like there was blood in the water, and she was the shark.

"So, do you believe in God?" she asked me.

"No. I like the idea though. It's a nice idea."

"Do you celebrate the holidays?"

"Not since I've been here."

"Do you see yourself having kids?"

"I'm not sure. I guess maybe. I don't know. I don't think I do well enough to support a child."

"Oh, I want kids."

"Oh."

"Have you been to Israel?"

"Yes."

"What did you think about it?"

"I loved it. It's a special place."

"I go once a year. I have family there."

"I want to go back at some point."

"Do you want to be a bartender forever?"

"I enjoy it. It supports me as an artist. It keeps me free to train, fight and eat."

"That's great. Do you think you'll open your own bar?"

"I don't know. I haven't thought about it."

"Where do you see yourself in the next three years?"

I was astounded by this date, a full-on interview. I hadn't known I was applying for a job. The job I had unwittingly applied for was, apparently, "Partner for Life." It included being husband, father, moneymaker, love-giver, child supporter, as well as gritting my teeth, never punching out, keeping my mouth shut, growing gray, and ending up in a joint plot six feet under with a star of David marking my remains on a stone slab above me.

I signaled for the check. The waitress brought it over, and I put down cash. Grace asked me if I could walk her down the block, back to her place. I agreed. Chitchat ensued, and the mood lightened up. We were out in the fresh air, no longer cornering each other, which made us more open. And the booze might have been working its magic. We got to the outside of her condo—a nice building in a prime location. As we were saying our goodbyes, I pulled her close to me. We kissed, and I grabbed her ass firmly. I asked her if I could see her apartment, but she said no. I had suspected it wasn't going to go any further but had thought I'd give it a shot.

I grabbed my bike and cut over to Kent Avenue, riding south toward my apartment on top of the Classon G train stop. We never hung out again. The benefits package for the job she offered me was a shortcut to the dirt plot. Maybe in the near future I'd sign up for a job that made me happy. But is anyone ever happy in one of these gigs? I hoped so. Until then, I'd stick to bartending, drawing, fighting, and living.

Warren Made Me Do It

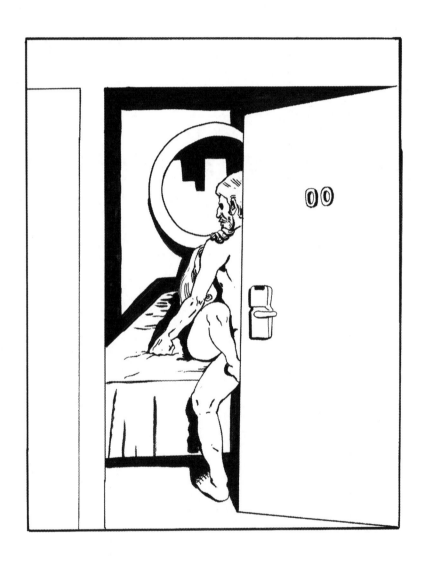

I t was a typical Saturday night behind the bar. Warren had started it off with 40 milligrams of Adderall, but I was fairly sober. It was just the two of us. Warren and I took a shot of his special whiskey, Rittenhouse with sesame seeds steeped in it. It tasted nutty and oily. Our barback, Pat, was as high as could be. Small of stature, his eyes were bloodshot, and he had refrained from getting a haircut for weeks, leaving him with an overgrown bowl cut.

Kay, one of our regulars, had come by. In his usual fashion, Warren jumped out from behind the bar to scissor with her. The other guests were delighted by the display. We were making money. All cash went on the back bar behind us in a wooden sake box. Pat was slow at fetching needed citrus. He moved like a snail, and his attitude was lousy. Warren began to get annoyed; it wouldn't be too long before he would bitch Pat out. Warren was nobody to mess with. He had wanted me fired during my first six months, and I was thrilled to have gotten past the rough patch.

Calvin, an old friend of mine from the Stan Ward Hotel, had just been promoted to manager. He was mainly on the floor, so I only saw him occasionally as he brought guests from the host stand to a free seat at the bar. I was happy about that, because he was the nervous type, and that nervous energy really killed my buzz. Plus I had to feed him shots throughout the night. Most of us rarely worked sober. I wasn't an abuser of alcohol at this point, and nights I worked as the sole barman I would abstain.

Chris, our sake sommelier pulled Warren and me aside. Over time, every wasted ounce of product could drop profit margins. It was annoying to be schooled in the minutiae of sake pours during the heat of service, but sometimes it had to be done. Ben, one of our servers, listened at the service bar as Chris discussed the pour.

"You see, guys, we pour up to the line here," Chris said, pointing to the part in the carafe that sucked in before opening up.

"That's where I poured!" Warren responded.

"No, you poured here," Chris retorted.

"Okay, fine," Warren said.

"Which one is this?" Ben asked.

"It's Three Dots," Chris said.

"What does it taste like?" Ben asked.

"You know what it tastes like," Chris said.

"I forgot," Ben said.

"Warren, pour him a taste," Chris demanded.

"I forgot too!" I chimed in. Chris gave me a look of disbelief.

Warren poured a big glass, and we passed it around, chugging the Three Dots. Chris darted back to the floor; Ben hung around.

"I have a woman at one-o-six who says you used to be quite the *cock-tailer*," Ben said to Warren.

"Who is it?" Warren looked over, squinting to see her from across the room.

"She said you used to stir quite the gin martini."

"Oh . . . her . . . that dirty rich girl."

"Who?"

"She was a regular at Jones. She loved it when I stirred her martini with my cock," Warren chuckled.

"Looks like she wants another one," I said.

"What are you gonna garnish it with? Your pubes?" Ben added.

"Only if she tips well," Warren answered.

Ben went back to the floor. It was getting packed. The well-to-dos were out and about. I felt like a schlub. I was dressed in my Salvation Army button-down gray shirt and oversized slacks. My hair was matted down on the side from my bike helmet. I hadn't had time to shave. In contrast, Ben looked like a model. In fact, he was a model. He looked like a dark-haired Brad Pitt. I was thankful I had a personality to boost my overall appeal.

I was shaking and double-straining a cherry bomb into a rocks glass for one of our regular boozehounds. I noticed a solitary guest descend the stairs, an unsuccessful actress who had once appeared on "Friends." My regular was pretty and looked loopy from ingesting a handful of anti-depressants. As I placed the drink in front of her, I noticed the solitary guest get closer, a pretty white woman in her mid-fifties, wearing a cream-colored dress. I greeted her with a smile and set a drink menu in front of her, but she turned it down and ordered a glass of chardonnay.

I went to Warren's side of the bar to pull a bottle.

"Dude, she's your type! She's like—what—70?"

"No, man. She's 54, tops."

"Dude, she's checking you out. You should flirt with her."

"Don't I always?"

I went back over with a wine glass and the bottle. I poured her a heavier glass than our sommelier would have liked. We locked eyes. I noticed the color of hers was almost gray. I tried to make small talk when I had an opening, but it was uncomfortable. Warren kept giving me looks that I hoped she wasn't picking up on. He was becoming like an older brother to me, so I didn't mind his teasing. He delighted in my weird, older-lady fetish, which made me feel exposed and embarrassed.

We had a steady flow because our reservationist did a good job pacing seating; Warren could easily handle the service bar. Not needing to pump out drinks gave him more time to encourage me to flirt with my older lady.

It was time to make the unsuccessful actress another cherry bomb, but I already had one tucked away I hadn't shaken yet. I checked the single lady's chardonnay. I saw she had sipped it down to the regular pour level, then darted my eyes to see if Chris had noticed I had overpoured her.

"Are you enjoying the chardonnay?"

"Yes, it's very good. I like it a lot."

"Have you tried sake?"

"No."

"Let me give you a taste of one."

I went over to Warren's side of the bar and got a taste of the Akitabare. It was a simple junmai and very cheap, so it wouldn't matter to Chris. Warren asked me if I had sealed the deal already. I turned away and went back to set the taste in front of her. She took a sip and seemed to like it.

"Are you hungry as well? The sashimi here is excellent."

"No, I'm just here for a drink."

"I'm Dustin, by the way. Don't hesitate to ask me for anything."

"I'm Lisa. Pleasure to meet you."

I shook her hand and immediately felt stupid. I don't normally shake hands at the bar, and I felt exposed, that it was obvious I had been looking at her with intention. I glanced at the actress who was ready for yet another drink. She usually had three cherry bombs before departing for another bar. I placed her third cocktail in front of her. She now sat with a younger girlfriend; I could hear them talking about how terrible New York City men were.

Warren pulled at my arm.

"Dude, please tell me you're going to roleplay that you're her nursing home attendant!"

"No, that's not going to happen."

"Dude, she's staring at you. She wants it. I'm telling you."

"I don't think so."

"She's sitting by herself, and nobody is showing. She wants a young stud to filthy her up."

"Goddammit, Warren."

I went back over and poured her another glass, while I made more small talk with her.

"So, are you visiting or…"

"I'm in the city. Upper East Side."

"Oh, that's cool. Do you make it down to Meatpacking that often?"

"No, not really."

"Yeah, it's a bit crazy. It is an easy trip to make it back uptown though."

"I'm staying in the hotel tonight."

"That makes it even easier."

"Yes, where do you recommend I go?"

Was I misreading her? Was she giving me an opening? I knew enough about women to know that they know. I know, and they know. If they didn't know, then the human race couldn't go on. I noticed she wasn't wearing a wedding ring and wondered what her deal was. I poured her another glass . . . on me.

Warren pulled me over to his side of the bar and demanded I

give her my number. He had overheard her say she was staying in the hotel, even with all the noise. I was nauseous. I had the potential to embarrass myself if she wasn't signaling to me after all. I wrote down three recommendations for her in the area on receipt paper, adding my number on it. I slid the paper to her and noticed nobody was paying attention to me. She looked at me as I explained the spots I'd listed and mentioned that if she had any questions, I had also thrown my number down. I turned away before she could say anything and brought the unsuccessful actress a check before I went back to Lisa.

"How long are you working tonight?" Lisa asked.

"I'll be here…"

"He'll be done in 20 or less," Warren interjected from the service bar. I tried to relax my shoulders.

"Oh, that's not too late."

"No, early night."

"Okay, I'll take the check."

"Okay."

She paid with a credit card and left, going back up the stairs. Warren had Pat begin breaking down the mid-bar and told me to break down my well; I did as I was told. Five minutes later, Lisa texted me, asking what I drank. I texted back, "Tequila," and showed Warren, who was thrilled. She invited me to the bar upstairs, a different venue. Warren sent me on my way and told me he would take care of the rest, as long as I gave him every detail.

I changed into my street clothes, exited the hotel, and went back through the main entrance. The bouncers knew me. Confused, since I never used the public entrance, I wasn't sure of where I was going, and cut past the host stand quickly, feeling exposed and ashamed. I wanted to get her up to her room as quickly as possible.

Then I saw her and an empty seat to her right, with a tequila on the rocks waiting.

"Hi, Lisa."

"Hi, Dustin."

"How do you like this spot?"

"It's nice. I like it."

"Great."

I drank my tequila quickly. If I hung around too long, I was bound to run into regulars, co-workers, and friends.

Lisa drank her wine slowly. Our small talk remained impersonal, but the bar was so loud it was almost impossible to hear each other anyway. That helped. I snuck my left hand onto her knee as she stared at me with her gray eyes. I finished the rest of my tequila and felt as though a warm wet cloth had been placed on my forehead. She asked me if I'd like to go to her room. Of course I would, so she paid the bill, and we made our way through the hotel lobby to the elevators.

I was acutely aware of inquiring eyes turning our way. It was like walking over hot coals, so I shuffled ahead of her in a brisk fashion and waited at the elevator. She caught up and used her key card to activate it, and we got into the elevator alone. I grabbed her and pulled her toward me, and we started to make out. We got off on the ninth floor and entered her room, where the bed took up most of the space. I unzipped her dress; she had nice breasts. I took off my shirt, and she undid my pants. She proceeded to blow me. I pushed her back on the bed. She had condoms in her nightstand drawer. We fucked aggressively, and I came fairly quickly, then rolled over back beside her. She didn't give me a moment to rest. She blew me again. It was sensitive but not painful, a leech sucking blood from a dying organ. She put another condom on me, and again we fucked, this time less aggressively. I turned her around and pounded her from behind, this time going longer, and slumped on top of her.

I was ready to relax, when I felt her crawl down to my loins. She was like a woman possessed. This time, when she put my penis in her mouth, it hurt. But she was a witch, charming my dead friend back to life. My zombie penis responded, and again we went at it. We finished, and I was done for. She tried to go down on me again, but I stopped her. I was done until the end of time. No more, I thought. No more.

"So, why are you staying at the hotel tonight?" I asked.

"I'm getting a divorce," she answered.

"Oh . . . well, sorry about that."

"No, it's for the best."

"Yes. This was fun."

"Yes, sure was. You can go now. You don't need to stick around."

"Okay. Sure. I can split."

I got dressed, then she saw me to the door, not five feet from her bed. We kissed, and I got back into the elevator. I hopped on my bike and cut east on 16th Street, then rode down 2nd Avenue. I would stop at a Punjabi on my way back to Brooklyn, before the Williamsburg Bridge. I was hungry and thirsty; she had drained me. My dick felt like a piece of driftwood floating around in my pants.

Battle at Blue

I was a passenger on the road to misery. We were all in our teammate Gerard's car, driving down to a part of Brooklyn unknown to most of us. South Brooklyn had remained untouched by the machinery of developmental progress, a throwback to a Brooklyn with Brooklynites living in it.

It was a lovely spring day in the city; could I enjoy it? No, I was shitting a brick, and a heavy one at that. We were going to test our mettle and I hoped to get a medal, gold preferred. We were going to a grappling tournament.

I dreaded competing as though I were standing before a firing squad. It was my "fight or flight" taking over; flight was impossible, and I feared the fight. There was always a chance you might freeze. A lot can go wrong when you freeze. And there were so many things that could go wrong. Why would anyone subject themselves to this voluntarily? Was it just for the possible glory?

Glory wouldn't have been enough. We signed up for this because we needed to know. We had spent countless hours perfecting skills. Drilling, sparring, repeating—they had become masturbatory. We couldn't go one more month without finding out where we stood in the world. Had we learned Jiu-Jitsu? Could we face our maker and accept what was to come? We willingly ran toward the chaos like demented lemmings.

We entered the great hall of grapplers. The matches had begun already, and we saw men forcing their will on one another. It was too late to opt out. We changed into our gis and tied our belts. My blue belt was adorned with two stripes showing that I was a Jiu-Jitsu guy.

I was no longer a white belt. The job of a white belt is to shut up, get beat up, listen up, and say "thank you." Now, I was blue. I was part of the culture. I had a say. I had responsibilities to the team.

I was a steward of objective reality now. I was no longer just taking but giving back—sometime in the form of smashing, sure. I was both mama and papa to white belts now. Sometimes, I gave nurture and other times I dished out punishment.

Yes, there were rules. Nobody was above them. The guys above me were my mama and papa; they would give to me and take away as they saw fit. This was the next part of the journey to illumination. None of my gains had been easy. It had been agony, but the payoff was divine; we journeyed on.

We stood in line to weigh in, edging closer to go-time. Why it was so daunting for me, I couldn't tell you. I had sparred regularly. I was a solid blue belt. I had a reputation for being a tough customer. But I wondered if I was an open book. That added to my anxiety. Was it obvious that my nature was showing? Was it obvious that I wasn't strong or heroic? I just wanted to get through whatever was to be my destiny.

Gerard got called first. Gerard was the biggest of us all and had to grapple with giants. We gathered at the sidelines as he stepped out onto the mats. His opponent stepped out. He was more muscled, slightly taller, and black. Gerard showed no visible signs of stress, but I knew they were there. The referee had them touch hands. His opponent rushed him and tackled him to the mat. We called some notes out, but Gerard was squashed. He was planted on his back for the duration of the match. That was it. It was over. Gerard left the mats and came toward us. He was disappointed, and I could only think of myself. The firing squad was lined up for me now.

I stepped out on the mats, and my opponent stepped out at the same time. I couldn't believe we were in the same weight class. He had a baby face, but the body of a defensive lineman. I had one more moment to rue my decision to do this damn thing. We shook hands, and then it was go-time.

He grabbed my collar, and I felt a grip like I had never felt before. This wouldn't end up being the first time I would experience an unbelievable strength. Sparring is different from competing. People conjure all of their force. It's not just about technique; it's about being tougher than the other guy.

This guy's arm was made from a stone pillar. It attached to me without any give. I fought the arm with everything. My teammates were calling out from the sidelines, but I couldn't hear much. We were in the battle now. There's a world of difference between watching and doing.

Everyone can see things so clearly outside of the action, but once you're inside it you see in bursts. I was in an alternate reality now.

I pushed with both hands on his elbow and popped my hips down. His grip loosened enough that I saw the moment in a burst of vision. I had a clear path to his hips, but only for a moment. I toppled him to the ground. He bucked like a bull, and I clung to him with everything I had in me. I wrapped up one of his arms. I began to twist it up toward the ceiling, but his strength was unimaginable. I couldn't use my two arms to control one of his. He was possessed by a demon it seemed. But I stayed on top long enough to end the match victoriously. The ref stood us up, and I was wrecked. It was only a couple of minutes of battling, but I had used my whole being to achieve the win.

I awaited the next opponent and knew that this match was going to be even more difficult. My opponent had won his match too, so he knew how to win. He was formidable. Who wanted it more? That's where we were at. It would be a contest of two men who found a way up the ranks.

We stepped out on the mats. He was bearded, older, and had a focus that I couldn't emulate. We shook hands and it was go-time again. He didn't hold on to grips like the first guy had. He was quicker. He was quicker to make adjustments. He was present enough to note what I was doing. He was figuring me out, and quick. I began, utilizing a boxing in and out to play with the distance. I knew I had to get the takedown. I wasn't good on my back, and if he got the better position I wouldn't have enough to escape.

I shot in from far away. He sprawled on top of me and made a cutover to my back. I adjusted by spinning to my back. I locked up my guard. Now, I was in a position I could finish guys from, but he was strong. Also, this wasn't sparring. It was a battle. The clock was running out. I hoisted myself up and grabbed his arm. I went for the kimura, one of the first arm-locks I had learned; it generally worked for me.

I wrapped my two arms around his right, and began to twist it up and over, hoping to dislocate it. He tucked his hand on his inner thigh. Now the arm was stabilized, and I had seconds to pry it from his body. I used my hips and legs to add more pull. My body was beginning to fail, and I was about to lose the match. I wanted it but wanting isn't enough. The cold objectivity of the contest indicated that I was lesser than he was. I exploded my hips again and again, but it was no use. The bell sounded. They stood us up, and he was victorious.

I later donned the silver medal. I had my photograph taken and saw in it a young man elated. In fact, my whole team was happy. We did it. We went through a nightmare and came out euphoric. I'd like to say that I conquered fear as yet another accolade of the day, but it wasn't so. I had just met the power of fear with a willingness to be tortured by it. I learned that I could not change the character of fear: it is a force eternal, and I'm just a passenger. I gained a new appreciation and reverence for fear.

We got in the car and drove back into the Brooklyn we knew. My body was depleted, and I needed sustenance. We recounted the day's journey and noted our findings. We were Jiu-Jitsu guys now, and that's what Jiu-Jitsu guys do. We meet with objective truth as a regular practice and worship it religiously.

Later I ate a much-needed burrito. I drank a cold beer with a lime wedge jammed into the bottle. I ate everything on my plate; I drank every last drop of beer. I felt the stings of scrapes and contusions. I saw the streetlights glow with the light of human ingenuity. I felt my human body exist outside myself and felt deeper than my muscle and sinew. I communed with the cosmos and slept a deep, dark, sleep for what could have been an eternity.

It All Came Crashing Down

Warren had been fighting with the two owners, so I was tense. I was protected and didn't have to engage, since I was just a barkeep. I didn't do manager meetings, create new cocktail recipes, or figure out schedules. At the same time business had started to slow; this had created a huge conflict between the two owners. The Israeli decided to stop setting foot in the restaurant after an explosive fight. So Gene, the other owner was lost because he was without experience and without help in making the big decisions.

As the months rolled on, we began to cut down our sake. We couldn't keep enough bottles in-house. It was clear the money from the investors was thinning out. It's why our inventory was shrinking (and the fact we weren't paying our distributors on time). Our staff began to leave one by one. New staff were brought on the team green.

We had made it to the two-year mark. Most restaurants die within the first year, but we had been teetering along. Warren was around 35, had a strong following and could work anywhere. I was just a hired hand and would continually need to find a new spot. But I wasn't as good as Warren and knew I had fewer options. A few of our bartenders had left but Warren and I were the mainstays.

We had about seven major investors. They were predominantly Asian and worked in finance. One came in once a month for a whiskey and to go over the numbers. He was normally jovial and didn't stay too long. I had even met his children and his wife.

His name was Ken, and one evening he came by. He wasn't jovial; he was stern. Our Asian owner sat talking with him at the bar. I poured them each a glass of sake, but they didn't touch it. I tried to leave them be and not eavesdrop. They were speaking rapidly, and their voices grew louder.

"Ken, I told you! It's a slow time of year."

"That's no excuse, Gene! You promised growth at this point. The claims you made were fraudulent."

"Hey, we're pulling our weight. I made a new structured deal with the hotel that will save us tens of thousands."

"That's not good enough. I have serious money in this. You aren't going to jeopardize my family."

"We are going to get past this bump in the ro—. . ."

"Bump in the road! Listen here, Gene. . . Next conversation we'll be having is with my lawyer present."

Ken got up off the bar stool and stormed off. Gene looked dazed, beaten up. It wasn't just the lumps he had on his face from training Muay Thai. He looked lost. He drank down his glass of sake and then drank Ken's too. I didn't approach him. I tried to pretend I hadn't heard any of it. The bar guests didn't seem to notice; they were having their own conversations. I heard tickets go off in my printer and moved over to the service bar. I started to pump out drinks. The younger servers didn't know exactly what was happening, but that was for the best. They would all get new jobs if need be, or Mom and Dad would help out.

A couple of weeks later, Warren pulled together a party, a small, corporate get-together. Things were getting dire, and we needed all the patronage we could get. Warren had reached out to the hosting group and taken the payment because he was their contact. The contract was transparent.

The party was fairly easy. It only lasted two hours, and some of the crowd lingered to drink more. The rest of the night was easy. We wrapped up on the early side. The bar was still making money, and I was grateful for that. But I didn't realize that this would be the last shift at Nashi I would work with Warren.

I came in the next day at four, my normal routine. I had gotten into the city an hour beforehand, so I could have a coffee and draw. My set up was easy. I pulled out my syrups and propped them up on the rail. I heard muffled noises coming from the back office. Suddenly, Warren stepped into the dining room. He looked me in the eye and then pulled out his phone. He started to text.

Gene came out of the office and went up the velvet stairs. I leaned over the bar and asked Warren what had just happened.

"I've just been fired," Warren told me.

"What the hell?" I responded.

"He thinks I was pocketing the money from the corporate party."

"That's a lie. You had the invoice and a check made out to the business."

"Yes. He just wants me gone and is using this as an excuse."

"I can't believe this. This is bullshit."

"Yeah, sure is."

"Maybe we can work this out. He's been stressed with money recently."

"I'm not staying. His business can tank. I don't care anymore."

"Please…"

"It's a done deal."

He exited out the back service entrance. Our unofficial GM J.C. came out of the office. J.C. was one of the few managers I could ever see as a person. He cared deeply for his staff. I could tell by J.C.'s body language that he felt defeated. Gene came back down the velvet stairs, wide-eyed and pacing. He called over to me.

"Okay, Dustin. You're point man now. Can you make up great drinks?"

"I'm not sure," I responded meekly.

"Okay, I'll have to pay a mixologist. We're going to be fine. We're going to push Nashi to the next level."

"Yup."

"I got to run. You're the king of the bar now. We don't need him anymore."

Gene exited up the velvet stairs. I leaned back over the bar staring down into the drain. I noticed a dried cherry that had been left there the day before.

"Are you okay, man?" J.C. asked me.

"No. Are you okay?" I asked J.C.

"No."

"Well, I guess I have to put in my two weeks."

"Are you sure?"

"Yes, J.C. I'm sure."

"I understand."

"That was some cold shit."

"Yes, it sure was."

"I got to pull this bar together now. How many on the books tonight?"

"Only sixty."

"Okay, I can handle it. No need to call in Tommy."

"All right, man."

Within a moment of J.C. walking away, I received a text from Warren. He wanted the stockroom down by the garage opened because there was product in there that wasn't Gene's. I vaguely remembered Warren got free cases of Grey Goose from corporate. I sent my barback to open the door so Warren could pillage. I didn't want to know the details. I hoped Warren wouldn't steal any of the bottles of Basil Hayden or Japanese whiskey, but I wouldn't have minded a lot either way.

Gene had taken his Porsche over to their second property in Williamsburg. I pulled the bar together and opened the lid to smell my citrus to make sure it hadn't turned. It dawned on me that I was on the home stretch of my gig here.

It had been a never-ending ride fueled by whiskey, sake, and party. Now, the house lights were coming up, and the final song of the evening was about to play. The next two weeks went by quickly. I wasn't worried about money; I had a nest egg, but I didn't want to tax my savings too much. I didn't have a job lined up. Sometimes your principles cost you nickels and dimes.

I went back home to Massachusetts for Thanksgiving. I thought I would stay a full week. I didn't let my parents know about quitting, but they started asking questions. They knew it wasn't normal for me to take this much time off during the holidays. I finally came out with it and assured them I'd bounce back, but I wasn't sure how long it was going to take. Bills don't ask if you are having a rough time. But for the holidays, I put them out of my mind and enjoyed the slower pace of my small town in Massachusetts.

I received a text from Warren during Thanksgiving dinner with my folks. He told me Jonah was offering me a bartending gig at Jones Street Lounge. I was elated. My noble move had not been ignored. I accepted and breathed easier.

When I later had time to consider this offer in more detail, I realized what it really was. Jonah was sticking it to Gene, pulling both of his bartenders out of the business. Jonah was a big deal in the dining scene in New York, and Gene was a johnny-come-lately. Gene had pissed Jonah off by not playing ball. My getting pulled into Jonah's restaurant was a "fuck you" of sorts, not a heartfelt move on Jonah's part. He was using me like a chess piece. One day, I would need to forgo business owners. I would need to be my own boss. I was tired of making these assholes money.

Playing the Part
of a Liberal

I t was no secret that I had come from a nice, upper middle-class town. It was that way for most of the young bohemian transplants to the city. This involved a game of posturing, where we all pretended to come from more blue-collar homes. I had friends from my hometown who had come to New York to achieve things too. We would all run into each other. New York was a small town in that way; we hit up the same spots. We all got falafels from Mamoun's. We all hit up the Bean for coffee. We all hung out at Washington Square Park to peoplewatch. You couldn't really dodge anybody. I think that's why I had gotten in the habit of wearing a baseball hat wherever I went. I would drop the hat down to become invisible. More often than not it seemed to work.

I ran into Ellen in Washington Square Park. She was years younger than me, and a student at NYU. I already had a bias against NYU kids, and this whippersnapper only added to it. Ellen was a cool bohemian girl. She came from a well-to-do, educated family. Her two brothers were veritable geniuses. She was a super leftist, but I didn't begrudge her that.

It was a pleasant encounter on a spring day though I always had an odd feeling when running into people from my hometown. I felt as though I immediately regressed to 16-year-old Dustin. Ellen greeted me warmly, and we began to hang out once every two weeks with her roommates. One of the roommates was a young student I knew from our hometown, a brilliant Russian studying engineering. The third roommate was the adopted daughter of academics. It was always a change of pace for me when I visited them. As soon as I would get to their Cobble Hill apartment from Bed Stuy, I felt like I had taken a mini-vacation and traveled to Greenwich, Connecticut.

We made vegan food, and I tried to keep up in the conversation when it turned to topics like feminism or gentrification. I showed my true colors when I spoke my mind because I certainly wasn't in their bubble. I didn't know the terms "heteronormative" or "cis-male." I had no idea that women were as physically strong as men. Society had labeled women weaker by pushing gender roles on them, but that was all bullshit. I tried to learn their ways and customs, like an anthropological investigation into the ways of young, rich, protected, brainwashed, intellectual elites.

I tried to hear what they were saying. I just couldn't agree with most of it. They gave me the nickname "Dusty D," and would tease me about my views as if I were a redneck who didn't know any better. Sometimes I'd be able to break some of their beliefs, but mainly I wouldn't. We remained friends, though. I was their token conservative. By the way, some of the views that made me a conservative in their eyes included that there are two sexes, white guilt shouldn't be subscribed to, and radical Islam is a threat to Western society. I was in support of gay marriage, was pro-choice, and fine with immigration (legal, of course). Basically, I was a moderate. So Dusty D, the truck driver, would come on by to be the butt of their jokes.

The kids also looked up to me in some ways. I was worldly compared to them. I worked nightlife as a bartender and always had a raunchy story to offer. I think they partly craved someone outside of their echo chamber. It seemed like they were bored by the same falsities. They knew deep down that most of what their professors were teaching was bullshit. It almost seemed like Dusty D was the real professor. He professed to know what was really going on. These poor kids didn't have an iota of a clue as to what being in the workforce was like. The simple answer was that it sucks. But it is also great, because it's sobering and gives one a solid foundation in reality. I became grateful that I had gone to school in Miami. Miami-Dade Community College never gave me any of the propaganda these overpaying, snot-nose kids were getting. Also, I had been a genius down there. The standards were so low that I felt like Albert Einstein. God bless Miami-Dade Community College.

The kids in Cobble Hill invited me to a party; I was certain to be one of the oldest there. It was to be a salon of sorts. All of the academic friends they had amassed at NYU would be there to discuss the inherent evils of whites, the subjugation of women in the Western world (forget about the women in Saudi Arabia), how gays are burned at the stake in Alabama, and how the nuclear family is all that's wrong with the country. It sounded about as much fun as getting drilled in the head. But I wanted to be accepted. I wanted to be liked. I wanted to be one of the smarty-pants *pishers*. I decided to curb my own opinions a bit to blend in. I would not mention my disappointment in Obama, whom I had voted for twice.

I arrived in Dusty D fashion, late and scratched up post-grappling, sweaty, and in classic men's casual wear. I stood out like a sore thumb. It was a large gathering for a three-bedroom apartment in Cobble Hill. Most of the men appeared feminine. Most of the women appeared masculine. Weirdly, many of the women were knitting, and many of the men were playing cards. It was as though the men and women were, in fact, different and behaving accordingly despite the superficial garb.

Ellen had made a nice spread of hummus, chips, veggies, homemade kale chips, and vegan chocolate chip cookies. Most of the guests had brought cheap beer or wine. I showed up with two large bottles of Corona and was introduced to everybody upon entering the living room. It was about as exciting a party as you could imagine with academics. I worked my way around the room to the cookies. Ellen handed me a glass, and I cracked open a bottle of Corona with a wine key I kept in my backpack. I poured the cool, clean beer into the glass she handed me and took a large gulp. I could overhear snippets of conversation from around the room, things like "middle America this" and "fucking Republicans that." The common denominator for everyone in the room, aside from political affiliation, was the uppity academic tone. I wanted to get along, so I decided to go with the grain. I was tired from training, and Dantae had choked the hell out of me with a triangle choke. I wasn't in proper shape to get shitty with NYU brats. Dusty D would be absent tonight. Instead, the one formerly known as Dusty D would take his place.

I drifted near the couches on the wall that led to the bedrooms. I heard talk of gay marriage, and I knew what the right answer was for the room. I didn't really have a strong opinion one way or another, but I have a gay brother with a serious boyfriend of many years. I consider his boyfriend family at this point. I wouldn't have cared if they had a civil union or gay marriage. I felt that gays should be able to get married, but it wasn't a top issue for me. I heard one of the girls in the group talk about how shitty George W. had been. I heard them lambaste John McCain.

I guess they had forgotten that Bill and Hillary hadn't been fans of gay marriage either. I played to the room and waved my liberal flag.

"I hope one day my brother can get married to his boyfriend. It's 2013, dammit. It's 2013!" I declared.

"Well, when you have middle-American whites shooting down any support for it, then it feels like it's the Stone Age!" a girl with half her head shaved exclaimed. I couldn't help but think about how 70% of black voters had supported the ban on gay marriage. Tonight, I was playing the part of a diehard liberal, so I chose to forget that interesting little tidbit.

"It's inevitable. Gays will be able to marry. The older generation is dying off. So help me God, my gay brother is gonna be married," I said passionately.

"Why are we going down this rabbit hole?" a blond, gay kid said.

"What do you mean?" I asked.

"Why is it we need to operate from the same cis-story that all of straight America runs by? I mean, seriously. It's like we want to domesticate the gay. Maybe gays shouldn't have to conform to heteronormative trends like the failed institution of marriage. Can we not allow gays to be subversive? Can two men who fuck not be condemned to walk off the cliff of despair with all of the other straight breeder lemmings?" he declared to the room.

"Gays deserve rights though, right?" I was clueless to his point of view.

I had never heard a gay argue against gay marriage. It was a huge knock to my perspective. I had thought I had a grasp on what the collective wanted. Apparently, the infighting was intricate. I didn't know what to do now. Should I denounce gay marriage on the spot? Could I do that as a straight white male? I could picture myself:

"Yeah, down with gay marriage! This is the one thing those evil Republicans and I can agree on." "Yeah, that's right. No gay marriage! No gay marriage!" The gay guy would respond. Then the whole room would get sucked up into the excitement of the group collective:" Hey, hey, ho, ho, this gay marriage really blows!"

"Yeah! That's right! No fucking gay marriage. Gays shouldn't be domesticated! Gays should be able to run free on the Great Plains! Gay marriage is for fags!" I'd imagine myself saying.

I came back from my reverie into the conversation, with the gay kid explaining the history of the Stonewall riots. It all seemed so complicated that I was partly impressed with the logic of it. I think I found conservative principles easier to understand and maybe that was why I believed them. The principle of less regulation by government made sense to me. Relying on Big Brother gets in the way of getting things done; people should earn their own keep. We evolved to chase down the deer, kill it and eat it. We evolved to expect reward for effort, another principle that is straightforward.

This new idea of being against gay marriage and pro-gay was a kick to my sensibility. I hadn't thought of it that way before. I wanted my gay friends to tie the knot because I didn't see them as in need of different standards. I believe building a family is good for a healthy society, so they should be able to follow suit. What the hell did I know? I hadn't stepped foot in a Queer Theory class in my life and was basically reading the Cliff Notes from these kids.

I went back over to the table with snacks, where I saw a tray with rice and beans. I took a plate and shoveled the remains onto it. I ate standing by the window, as I thought to myself that I felt too old to be in the room. I may have only been two to three years older than the oldest in the room, but I felt like a relic. One of Ellen's roommates was a heavyset girl named Charlotte. Her parents were academics, and she was following suit. I'll let you guess her field of study. She would cite convoluted statistics like, "1 in 5 girls are raped in college." I didn't believe that a girl had a 20 percent chance of getting raped in college. If that were true, why would parents send their girls to college? I've read stats that drop it down to about 10 percent, which is still terrible, but it's not as terrible as 20 percent. This girl also happened to be a virgin, but not for religious reasons. I think she enjoyed my tales of sexual escapades, because she knew nothing of them. She was awkward but sweet.

I had learned more out of school than I had learned in it. Entering the workforce was an education unto itself. Charlotte used me as an elective class. I was her professor in the school of hard knocks. I may have been "Dusty D," but it was "Dusty D, PhD" to her.

She came up to me by the window as I took the last bite from my plate. I picked up my room-temperature Corona and took a swig.

"Are you playing well with others?" she asked.

"Sure. I'm keeping my mouth shut and nodding a bunch," I said.

"I see that."

"Do you know mostly everybody here?"

"Yes, a few of them are in my gender studies program."

"I met one of them earlier, I think. Or maybe he was in queer theory."

"Did you have enough to eat?" she asked.

"Yes, I had cookies, beans, and rice," I answered.

"That's a winning combination."

"It's everything the body needs. Well, not quite everything."

"Yeah, I know what you mean. I'm needing other things too."

"Yeah, like what?" I asked.

"I met this guy at a kinks meetup. I don't know if he is into me or not. I don't know what he likes either."

"Oh. What do you mean? Like S&M?"

"Kind of . . . more like rope stuff."

"Oh. Well, did you get his contact?"

"Yes, but our schedules aren't lining up."

"So, what do you plan to do with him? Rope stuff? Not sex stuff?"

"We'll probably do rope stuff with heavy petting."

This sounded totally boring to me. Call me old-fashioned, but if I find a pretty girl that I like I want to have sex with her. I don't think about how good it would be if she were immobile. I don't think that would facilitate an orgasm. I want to go the way of the birds and bees, not the way of Harry Houdini!

"I'm sure he'll hit you back. If he doesn't, then it wasn't meant to be. I'm sure there'll be more suitors to come."

"Where are all the good men in this city?"

"They're probably all tied up."

I went back over to Ellen to say my goodbyes. She wanted me to stay longer, but I felt like a grandpa here. Grandpas are meant to go home early, remove their dentures and dream of their retirement property in Florida. I was getting bored and looked forward to getting back to my apartment. I wanted to ink a few more pages of a graphic novel I was piecing together. I made my way to the door, and immediately regretted playing the liberal. I should have been who I was. The party would have been more interesting. I couldn't ever express myself at work with complete honesty, so I should've said my piece and fought those ravenous radicals with everything I had. Who needs friends anyway?

Cops Be Chasing

I had a long Monday, but it was a glorious Monday, because I wasn't working my job. I had spent the day grinding out cartoons and scrapping with the guys at the dojo. Now, I needed one last thing to end the long day. I wanted to see the lady I had just started hanging out with. It gave me something to look forward to after I arrived home, but I hadn't seen her in a week, and she was getting restless. I knew I wouldn't be seeing her again if I didn't make the effort. Men and women cannot remain stagnant; they need to expand. If that doesn't happen, it ends, and I wasn't ready for that yet. I sprinted down Wyeth Avenue toward Bed Stuy. I needed to shower, quick change, and be at her apartment as soon as possible.

We had good sex. She was fuck buddy material, not girlfriend material. I think she read me the same way and understood that we weren't a pair. Maybe we could have been, but I knew (from her mouth as well as her friend's) that she was a walking, talking, blowup doll. As progressive as many men are, we still don't like the idea of making a harlot our bride-to-be. And as progressive as many women are, they don't like the idea of being the bride of a degenerate. So, alas, our relationship was fated to be in the bone zone.

I looked forward to the ride to Crown Heights, only 20 minutes, but that would help me relax before seeing her. I dried off from the shower and ate a peanut butter and jelly sandwich. It was unusual for me not to be hungry after my Monday night training session, but now I needed nourishment for another reason. I took my bike out the door, wearing a cap, shorts, t-shirt, and Vans. It was perfect outside. I leisurely pedaled down Nostrand Avenue as other cyclists passed by me. I normally cared about that, but I didn't that night. I was relaxing from an arduous training session, looking forward to seeing her, and getting that sexual healing. My body needed it.

The Crown Heights demographics were slightly different from Bed Stuy's. Crown Heights had blacks, Hasidim, Puerto Ricans and a smattering of whites, too. In Crown Heights, they seemed to have more people from the islands, but I don't know if that's true statistically or not. Crown Heights had the better restaurants; that much was true.

Cruising down, it was strangely quiet. The commonplace is that New York is the city that never sleeps, but it appeared that on Monday nights, New York was the city that had decided to stay in and watch Netflix. I cruised down Nostrand but knew I would have to cut over back to Bedford, where she lived, in about five minutes.

I had broken the bike-riding law about stopping at red lights in New York, so I knew that I had to stop at them. I also understood that the cops loved catching cyclists, because it was an easy ticket. The first time I had been caught running a red light, my first ticket wasn't cheap. The second had jumped to $400, and my third ticket would be $1,000. I didn't know if the fourth ticket would jump even higher. Maybe they'd amputate my toe (at my cost). I made sure to stop at all red lights.

I was taking my time anyway because I knew I would get there eventually, and my right ankle felt like someone had beaten it with a mallet. Peddling made my ankle feel better, so it was a win-win. I was surprised at how fast Brooklyn was changing. I had already noticed more white people here. It seemed that within a year's time, the whites were carving out more of a piece of the pie. I knew it wasn't necessarily a color thing; it was inevitably a dollar thing. I wondered how much longer I could stay in Bed Stuy.

I rode up to a solid red light and stopped. I noticed a mild-mannered, bearded white guy, around my age, looking to pass. He waved me along in a kind, midwestern manner. I declined and waved him over to cross the street. It was a pleasant exchange that didn't take place all that often. Mostly, people were not well-mannered.

I sat on my bike at the red light. It just wasn't turning green. I began to get impatient, so I looked around and saw no cars. I decided to cut through the light. In certain states they have what's called a "dead red" law. It allows cyclists to abide by the light as though it were a stop sign. I decided that this law would pertain to this situation at this given moment. It was a quiet Monday night after all, so I pedaled through the red light.

Before I could even get ten feet across, a police cruiser shot up next to me. Its siren went on, and the lights flickered red. I was both shocked and angry. They had been hiding on a side street like spiders who had just caught their fly. I had only moments to process, since I was caught and in plain view. I saw into the squad car with the two officers sitting in it. They looked me dead in the eye, and all I saw was hostility. I knew that they wouldn't consider letting me off. I knew I would have a $1,000 ticket waiting for me.

I didn't get along with the NYPD all that well. There were a few cops I trained MMA with, and I liked those guys, but more often than not, most cops seemed to be there only to bust balls. The upkeep of the city wasn't cheap, and tickets were a great source of revenue. I felt like I had I paid enough in taxes, though, and couldn't stomach forking out more funds. I had never disobeyed an officer before, but the money that I was about to fork over to the city was substantial. It motivated me to cut and run.

I picked up my bike and rotated around. I was on a one-way, after all, and knew they wouldn't speed against traffic—especially after a cyclist on a Monday night. I started racing down Nostrand Avenue. My heart was pounding. I darted over to a side street, which was also a one-way. I looked over to my right. I figured the cops would be there and saw the nose of their squad car peeking out onto Bedford Avenue. "Motherfuckers," I thought.

I went back down the side street against traffic but on the sidewalk. I knew it would be worse for me to get smashed by a car (especially without health insurance). I took a right on Nostrand Avenue, against traffic and up on the sidewalk. My adrenaline was pumping. It would end very badly for me if I were caught. Would it be within their rights to shoot me?

I saw a fenced-off lot. I wasn't sure if there were an opening, but when I turned the corner and saw the gate was open, I didn't know where else to ride. I didn't know how far they would follow me or if other cops would be aware and on my tail. I was incredibly paranoid and dreading my immediate future. I pictured the story making it to the morning news, and cops going door to door to find me. They would be damned if a cyclist ran from the cops. Hell, the whole force of the department would be levied against me!

Two older black gentlemen were in the lot. One had on a trucker's hat and suspenders, and the other wore a wife-beater and khakis. They looked kind, so I decided to ask them to help me out.

"Hey, fellas. I was curious to know if I could hang out in this here lot?"

"Hey, son, we saw the whole thing. You better come in here and take it easy," the one with the trucker hat and suspenders said.

"That's right, Leroy! We got him till the heat dies down."

"Those boys be happy to catch a boy like him, Bobby. Come on in, young man. We got you!"

"Thanks, guys." I was sweating profusely as I made my way in.

It was a lot filled with random vehicles, but it didn't look like a parking lot. It wasn't necessarily a mechanics' lot. It looked almost like a junk heap. I spotted a large van, and the guys led me there with my bike. It was dark behind the van, with the streetlights only illuminating one side. I began to take control of my breathing. Leroy and Bobby stood by the front of the van and looked over at me as I was concealed in shadow.

"Now, you just wait here. Those pigs ain't gonna be getting you," Bobby said.

"Yeah, they were out earlier, looking for anyone they could get into trouble," Leroy said.

"They was harassing some boy out front of the store earlier. Those pigs be rude. Damn rude, if you ask me," Bobby said.

"Thanks, guys. I can't afford another ticket," I said.

"That white t-shirt is making you stick out back here. Take it off, man," Bobby suggested.

"What?" I said.

"That t-shirt, in this light, is glowing. You best take off your shirt," Bobby said.

"Nah, I'm good," I said.

"Come on now, son. Don't be uptight. Lose that shirt," Bobby said.

"Stop it, Bobby. He don't have to take off that there shirt," Leroy added.

"I'm good," I said.

"All right. I'll go upfront and see what's happening," Bobby said.

Bobby left to check the front gate, while Leroy hung around with me. I felt my heart rate begin to go back to normal. The sweat on my body became cool on my skin. I didn't dare take out my phone. I was hidden in the shadow of the van, the fear still lingering that the cops would come in to investigate. I wasn't sure how bored they were or how much they wanted to catch me. I had the final scene of the movie, "Heat," flash before my eyes. Then I became paranoid for a moment and wondered if Bobby and Leroy were really allies. Would this become like a scene in *Pulp Fiction* instead? I wasn't sure, but I did know one thing; I watched too many movies. I was pissed more than anything that I wouldn't be seeing my lady in Crown Heights. That's how I had wanted my Monday night to end. I didn't want it to end like an episode of "Cops." (I also watched way too much television.)

"You got any smokes on you, brother?" Leroy asked me.

"Nah. I don't have any smokes," I said.

"I could use a smoke right now," he said.

"I got some money, if you wanted to buy a loosie," I said.

"No. I'm good, brother. If you had a cig on you, that'd be good. No worries. Do you want a cig? I'm gonna head to the store."

"No, thanks. I'm straight."

I immediately felt bad about offering money. Was that uncouth? Was it racist? Was it classist? Was it ageist? The guilt of the white male is strong in Brooklyn. I knew Leroy was cool with me and didn't read anything into me offering money. Leroy and Bobby were allies. This time I analyzed the situation as I waited in the shadows. What did they have to gain from turning me in? I also knew the ancient street code: snitches get stitches. So, there was that. They wouldn't snitch on me. We were united in our disdain for authority. I waited and took deep breaths. Leroy came back with a cigarette. He was taking long drags as he rocked back and forth on his heels. He looked out toward the street and stood watch. I didn't see where Bobby had gone. Leroy walked by the front of the van and looked over at me. He took another long drag and adjusted his trucker's hat. I held onto the handle of my bike.

"So, it looks like the coast is clear," Leroy said.

"That's good," I said.

"You're gonna want to hightail it home, ya hear?"

"Yes, that's what I plan to do."

"Be careful on the way back."

"I probably shouldn't take Bedford."

"Nope. I would cut down a few side streets."

"Okay, that's what I'll do."

"Get home safe, young man."

"Thanks. Send my thanks to Bobby, too."

"I got you, son. Now, you better get on your way."

I rode out of the lot and immediately began racing through the side streets. I lost track of where I was going but knew I was heading in the right direction, despite veering off a little. I rode as quickly as I could and didn't encounter red lights. It was quiet out. I rode for about ten minutes or so and came upon a bodega by Grand which I knew was a mellow area. I pulled out my phone and saw some missed texts from the lady, but I didn't text back. I dialed her number.

"Hey," I said.

"Hi," she answered.

"I'm sorry I couldn't make it. I had to run from the cops."

"Oh?"

"I blew through a red. I needed to get out of there. Two black men helped me; they hid me behind a van."

"Wow. That's a story," she said.

"Yeah, well, I won't be able to make it tonight. They'll be looking for me."

"Really? So, you're not coming over now?" she said, revealing her disappointment.

"I just evaded the cops. I can't be there now. I gotta lay low."

"You're kidding, right?"

"No, I'm serious. I'll be in big trouble if they get me."

"All right, whatever."

A moment passed as we both heard each other breathing on the other end of the line.

"Seriously, you're pissed at me?" I asked.

"No, just disappointed."

"Well, I am too. I didn't want to flee from the cops. I had other ideas for this Monday night. I wanted to see you."

"Another time then."

"Yes, maybe tomorrow."

"I have class tomorrow."

"Okay, maybe Wednesday."

"I have plans Wednesday."

"Okay, well, we'll play it by ear then."

"Okay, goodnight."

"Goodnight."

I made my way back to my apartment. I was bummed. I had had a different Monday night planned and intended it to turn into *Boogie Nights,* not *The Fugitive.* I would have even settled for some incarnation of *Say Anything.* Instead, I was back in my dilapidated apartment, smelling my gym bag from the next room. I climbed into bed and searched through Netflix. It was the strangest thing. I searched and searched, but I couldn't find anything to watch.

Gay Pride Represent

O ne of my regulars invited me to a house party for Gay Pride. The party was to be held in a brownstone building. Kay, the man who had invited me, was a party boy. He was usually on some mix of cocaine, booze, and semen. He came from Lebanese oil money and taught at New York University. He dressed as exuberantly as Sarah Jessica Parker on her HBO show. Everyone loved Kay, who was a social butterfly. He felt as comfortable gabbing with Wall Street suits as he did gabbing with Stonewall queens. I had never been to any Gay Pride parties, even after living in the city for years. I agreed, wanting to see what this was all about.

It was brutally hot. NYC was always humid and muggy during the summer season. I wore a teal *guayabera* with a black wife-beater underneath, black shorts and royal blue Vans. I rode my bike into the city and locked it in front of the Sunset Hotel then walked over to meet Kay on the corner of 16th. He was always dressed in some eccentric manner and had pulled out all the stops for this party. His hair was pulled up in a topknot. He was wearing Daisy Dukes, a mesh tank top, a denim vest with metal spikes on the shoulders, and combat boots. He was ready and seemed to have started to party early. His pupils were dilated like a Japanese cartoon character's.

We walked over to a brownstone on 14th. It was nearing 6 PM, but it was still bright out. This part of Manhattan was teeming with packs of gay men, and all the groups and subgroups were present. You had your bears, otters, twinks, Chelsea boys, and leather daddies. It was like being at a gay zoo, with all the species present and in their local habitat. I had never set foot in the apartments on this side of town and was looking forward to seeing the inside of this impressive brownstone. The owner was a famous writer, pundit, and lawyer. He could afford the astronomical price tag connected to this property.

Up the stairs and into the lobby, I panicked. I had spent years in Miami as a college student and was very comfortable with all sorts of people. I had many gay friends and had been to gay bars as the token straight guy before. It had never bothered me. Sometimes I would find the token straight girl, and you can fill in the rest.

But now there were five men in the lobby, every one shirtless and in tight pink jeans. They all looked like body builders. The hall was decorated with grass, flowers, candy canes, dildos, and a popcorn garland. It was a lot of gay all at once. There was also a photographer. Kay and I were asked to stand over to the side for a photo. I panicked; I didn't want my photo taken. I didn't know where these photos were going. Was my face going to be plastered on gay billboards in Chelsea? I really shouldn't have cared, but I did, and I couldn't back out and show I was a big square, so I posed with Kay. They showed me the photo. My mouth formed a smile in the photograph, but my eyes were blank.

We were led to the private backyard. Kay went over to one of three bar stations and grabbed us vodka tonics. I took a heavy gulp. They were blasting house music, and it was so packed that it was hard to move around. Kay introduced me to his cousin. We had some things in common, since he was a painter, but he didn't have to work. I think he came from money and was able to paint full-time, whether he sold any paintings or not. He was also a token straight. We chatted for a while, until he got called away by other friends. Kay introduced me to another one of his acquaintances, only a couple years older than I, who fit more into the otter category.

"So, what's your deal? You here to party?" he inquired.

"Yes, that's why we're all here, right?" I asked.

"Sure, but you're not gay… or are you secretly?" He was playing a game with me that I had played in Miami. If I denied being gay and declared I was straight, he would pick at me until I said I was gay. It was a dynamic I had experienced from angry gays before.

"No, I'm gay. Yep, always gay."

"So, you have a boyfriend?"

"Yes, he's not here though."

"Where is he?"

"He's working."

"Where?"

"Um, he's working at a bar."

"You're not gay."

"Sure I am."

"No, you're not! Why are you here?" He was a little miffed that I, a straight, had crashed this party. This annoyed me. What about the Gay-Straight Alliance, bro?

"I've never seen one of these brownstones before from the inside, and my buddy Kay brought me. Also, my brother and friends are gay, so I was showing support."

"Yeah, okay. Whatever," he sauntered away toward one of the bars for a refill.

I was left alone in a sea of drunkards, but not for long. I moved along to one of the garden walls, and two gentlemen approached me. They were Latinos in their forties, both jovial. One happened to be a spinning instructor and my mom was one, so we talked about workouts. It was like talking to any other bro, only that this bro banged other bros.

We turned our attention to a performance that had begun near one of the three bars. A small, shirtless man started to dance and then blew up a pale pink balloon, big enough to pull over his body. We were watching this guy, who now took on the look of Humpty Dumpty. The top part of his body was an orb, while the bottom part was his skinny, spandex-clad legs.

The otter came back to me with a friend, friendlier now that he had enjoyed a few rounds from the bar. He introduced me to the friend, who was a pale, white grad student from the south.

"Hi, bro. I'm, Dustin," I said.

"Oh, hey. I'm Matt. Isn't this party the absolute best?"

"Sure is. It's quite the scene," I told him.

"Yeah, it's not really my scene. I'm pretty conservative," Matt explained.

"I'm not!" the otter said.

"Well, you know, I grew up in the south. I come from a Baptist church, after all, even if that was ages ago!" Matt said.

"Wow, and you ran away to NYC?" I asked.

"Well, the school I wanted was here. I couldn't stay down yonder."

"That's cool, man. What are you studying?" I inquired.

"I'm studying psychology with a focus on neurons."

"He's an egghead. I'm good at giving head," the otter said.

"Hush, child. Anyway, I have a disorder that sparked my interest. I have seizures, but only when someone touches my back. I've been to many clinicians who can't find exactly what the cause of the problem is."

"That sounds terrible. I'm sorry to hear it."

"No worries. Life is a grand party!"

Kay was calling me over to the raised patio, where he and his cousin had a bottle of tequila. I excused myself and joined Kay, his cousin, and one straight girl. We passed the bottle around, taking big swigs out of it. I had reached the point of drunk where I felt that all was right with the world. I saw the haze of movement from testosterone-riddled men circling each other like sharks around prey. They were each prey and predator. All they wanted was to eat and be devoured. Women were not that difficult to bed in NYC, but a straight man still needed to employ all kinds of tactics in order to close the deal. They were like bison, and we were Native Americans with a bow and arrow who needed a precision shot to land. These men could close the deal as often as they liked.

Kay's cousin and I split off to the side. He showed me some of his paintings—big abstract expressionist works. I saw qualities of Jasper Johns in them. They weren't very good, but he claimed he had sold a few of them.

"It's all about painting for me," he said.

"I hear ya. I love painting, but I have found myself drawing more. I make cartoons, so…"

"Cartoons are great. I love that Japanese stuff. You do that, man?"

"No, I don't do that. I'm more into the Franco-Belgium comix movement."

"So, like street art?"

"No, not really."

"Yo, I love Basquiat. Did you see the movie? It was dope. New York in the eighties was the place to be."

"It sure was. The economy was booming too. We've had a shit economy for over a decade now."

"Yeah, remember when Basquiat was painting those tires, dog? That shit was great. . . so outside the box."

"Yeah, you gotta appreciate innovation."

"Yeah, we all got to take it to the next level. There ain't a do-over. You gotta paint, live, fuck, dope, and screw your way to the top."

"That's what's up."

I didn't understand what he was talking about and had to find the bar. I wanted another vodka soda. I was fairly inebriated and feeling the music. I got my drink and moved back to the garden wall I was at earlier. I saw a flock of straight girls move through the crowd. I had planned to approach them later, but they left before I could. I did lock eyes with one in a red dress. She was pale with dark hair. She looked like she had stepped out of a John Singer Sargent painting.

Matt and the otter came up to me.

"Hi there, straight boy!" the otter said.

"Hi, Dustin. How you liking this lil' ol' shindig?" Matt asked me.

"I'm having a great time. Glad we all got to meet."

I patted Matt on the back. He froze and went pale. His thin-lipped mouth curved downward. His forehead began to perspire. It occurred to me that he had just warned me of his disorder.

"Hold me!" he screamed. The otter froze too.

I held Matt's hand. Our eyes locked, and I could tell he was in sheer panic mode. He began to shake in place. I was terrified of him falling down on the pavement and cracking his head open. The music was loud, and nobody seemed to notice. The ones who did thought he was dancing. I thought for a second that I should join him. I was already holding his hand. I thought that maybe if I did the same it would cancel out. He settled down and let out a long sigh. He excused himself, and the otter took him into the house.

I was too drunk to take in what had just happened. I rejoined Kay and his cousin to polish off the bottle of tequila on the patio and didn't mention it. It was nearing midnight, and I had to go. I wanted to take Dantae's MMA striking class in the morning. I left by the grassy front entrance. The pink jean-clad musclemen were still guarding the gates of Gaydom. I started walking down 14th, heading back to grab my bike that was locked up at the Sunset Hotel. I knew I was in no condition to ride back. I had ridden my bike drunk before, so I decided to take it on the subway with me.

I walked along and saw two girls sitting on the sidewalk in dresses, with their heels off and to the side. They were eating halal cart meat from a shared container, though they looked too attractive to be doing this. The clubs were still in full swing. I knew the Meatpacking District was always a late-night nightmare.

"Hey, girls. What's going on?"

"Hey, we just got out of Tao. We're just trying to sober up for our ride back into Jersey," one of the girls said.

"You know it isn't a good idea to be eating street meat on the sidewalk—and barefoot, no less?"

"I know."

"Do you girls need help?" Do you need to make a phone call?"

"No, thanks. We're gonna make it to the PATH train by one. Our friend is gonna pick us up after."

"Okay, take care of yourselves. I would suggest wearing shoes, though. You don't want to step on a dirty needle or anything."

"You're so sweet."

"No, not really."

"Yes, you are."

"All right, have a good night, ladies."

I grabbed my bike from the hotel and felt sober enough by then to ride. I rode slow and steady. The air was sticky. I pulled off my guayabera and wrapped it around my hand. I went down First Avenue to avoid the drunken NYU crowd, connected to the Williamsburg Bridge and ascended. My ears were buzzing from the house music. I thought about the girls on the way up. I hoped they had made it back to Jersey.

Jones Street Lounge

I started like I started every new job. I showed up ready to embrace an ass-whooping. Scooped up from Nashi as a "fuck you" from one business partner to the other, I was rudderless in a sake-soaked sea. I landed ashore in a past-its-prime lounge made famous by *Sex and the City*. Now, it sat as a relic of New York's past. I quickly met the regulars, whom I dubbed "the entitled." They were rich like royalty. They rarely tipped well and expected more than what was coming to them.

The staff was a collection of burnt-out restaurant folk. Most were in their late twenties, some well into their thirties. What all these grumpy, booze-addled bringers of food and beverage had in common was their dwindling hopes and dreams. Yes, I was among them. I was in my late twenties and felt the existential dread of evaporating purpose. My saving grace was that J.C., our old AGM from Nashi had also been stolen from that rotting establishment, as yet another "fuck you" among rich men.

Jones Street was a three-floor operation. The top floor held a private dining room and service bar. The middle floor housed the main dining room and main service kitchen. The downstairs accommodated a lounge, prep kitchen, office, and stockroom. It had aged well. It had been at the height of interior design back at the millennium. Now it was akin to a 50-year-old man trying to sport an undercut.

I got pulled downstairs to work the lounge. It was a pretty bar. The dark wood bar top was beaten into an old-world relic. The lounge held 80 seats. Small sections had been carved out as private lounging experiences. The music that filled the space harkened back to times before the real estate crash. A cool, unnamable nostalgia hummed softly in the background

I met her on my first day. She was a tall, well-built, faux redhead. I could tell from her turned up nose and posture that she was an aspiring actress. She happened to be pretty and evolving into the typecast of young mother. I hated having to introduce myself, but I knew I wanted to get along right away. I wanted this work experience to be free of the travails of times past.

"Hi, I'm Dustin," I stood in front of her and blurted out.

"Hello, I'm Ana," she replied defensively.

"I'm the new bartender here. I used to work for Jonah in Miami and then here at Nashi. Now, I'm with you guys. I'm happy to be on the team; it seems like a great spot!"

"Yeah, okay. I just need to get back to pick up some plates from the back."

"Okay, good talk. . ."

I could tell I had overdone it. Ana was swamped by my energy. I had tried too hard to get her on my side. I wanted to be liked. It's tough being a herd animal. Do hermit crabs have it any better?

I shared a bar space with sushi chefs. They made sushi at the far end of the bar, and we would trade beer for sushi rolls. We who controlled the product had a bartering system in place. It was our black market. The managers knew to some degree but turned a blind eye. Our servers downstairs in the cocktail bar were all women and kinder than the servers upstairs. We who worked in the lounge still had a semblance of hope. The women and sassy gays who worked upstairs in the main dining room were nasty. They were crushed by harsh reality, but I rarely had to interact with them. I only saw them at the lockers downstairs, when we had to get dressed.

During the first week, when I was throwing on my black garb for my shift, I had parked my bag in front of a waitress's locker. She worked upstairs in the main dining room, and I knew her casually from Nashi and Jones Street joint holiday parties. Apparently, it was her locker I had put my bag in front of.

Ferrara had an unusual name to go with her unusual look—quite severe. She appeared to be average but upon further discovery, seemed less than.

"Looks like you're not the sharpest pencil in the box, but can you get your bag out of my way?" She locked eyes with me.

I was taken aback. I wanted to give her a quick jab to her pale English face but refrained. I had never had a man take this approach with me in this context, because men know that the veil of civilization is only one fighting word away from being torn. Ferrara knew that being a bearer of ovaries would keep her intact and my hands tied. I could not strike her with the much-needed reminder of decorum. I stared at her, facing her squarely.

"So, you don't know how to speak either. That's good to know," she told me.

"You know, you can go about this differently," I appealed to her.

"So, mind moving your bag?" she yelled.

I grabbed my stuff and moved along. I breathed deeply and pushed the anger aside. I rationalized her behavior and understood what I was dealing with. I had before me a failed actress who looked like a beaten English tart. Reality had been like Jack the Ripper to her and left her dreams gutted on the cold city blocks for all to see. She was no different from so many people I knew in the industry.

Every new work path, commute, café, and crappy apartment leant itself to an entirely new vision. Before Jones Street, I would ride my bike into the city on the Manhattan Bridge. It was different from the Williamsburg Bridge. The Manhattan Bridge was frequented by normal core-clad genial folk as opposed to the hipster fixed-gear sycophants. I liked the new path I was taking and loved the city for its refreshment.

Now that I was working at Jones Street, my habits changed. I would grab coffee at Bean by Union Square. I would peruse the independent comics section of Forbidden Planet. I would climb to the second floor of Whole Foods and watch the flow of Union Square below. The West Side pre-work hangout was replaced with the East Side. My mind was refreshed by new possibilities. I knew it could last anywhere from a few months to a couple of years, based on my track record.

Jones Street catered to the six-figure crowd. We had some want-to-be six-figure poseurs too, but more often than not our folks were loaded. At this point, money didn't flow like it once had. But I did right by myself. I stayed on the course. While certain friends in my tax bracket were shopping at A.P.C., I was shopping at the Salvation Army. While these friends were racking up big bar tabs at Employees Only, I was drinking at Rocka Rolla. These friends were being sucked dry by the city, and I was absorbing what I could. I knew the city would start to suck me dry too, but I wasn't going to let it take back what I took from it.

Jones Street felt like a final stand. It was a beautiful spot, and I knew my time was coming to an end. I didn't have it like I used to. Guests annoyed me almost instantaneously. My charm and performance began to wane. I was beginning to transform into the crotchety bartender. I had known this type from my years of sucking down brown juice in loud, lonely rooms. I needed to make a change, and changes typically cost money. Money was what I was working for.

The menu was similar to Nashi's. Asian fusion had been big in the early days of the millennium. It remained big but other food trends had eclipsed it. My old bar buddy Warren claimed Scandinavian was the next big thing. Another drinking buddy swore it was South African. I didn't know or care all that much. I only knew I wanted to be out of it before the next big thing.

We were all clichés. I knew I was, and Ana certainly was. I was the disheveled, drink-slinging artist who fancied himself a toughie. Ana was the cocktailing, black-laced aging beauty who longed to be a star. We were all archetypes moving along the stage of the dinner theatre. We played along with the script and took our places as the curtains lifted. Every night was a show. I performed my mixing, shaking, and pouring liquids from tins like I was a magician: "And for my next trick . . . the Manhattan!"

Ana was bitter. Life had been a constant flow of disappointment. I think she liked me because I had a fighter's mindset. I would keep getting back up from the blood-spattered mat after each rejection. I soon learned to laugh in the face of these knockdowns. I was the matador getting beaten down by Robert Cohn. No matter how many licks I took, I propped myself back up. Ana had a tragic past, but she wouldn't go into detail. Anyway, it ended too soon to go into detail.

As always, the bottom rung of restaurant workers were the best of us. These young, hungry newbies handled their tasks with zeal. I remembered when I was part of the merry band of busboys at the Stan Ward Hotel. Now I was recast as a new character. I played the new role, took my spot on stage, and looked over the new cast. Maybe one day I'd be the director.

I saw some of our guests from Nashi at Jones Street. They knew a few of us had been brought over. Kay swung by a couple of times. He was a West Side mainstay but made the trip on the L for us. Sometimes, Calvin would come in for glasses of sake. We all knew each other in this industry. Anybody who worked in this tier of establishment crossed paths. As big as the city was, we all revolved around the same axis. Winter began to set in, and I was grateful Jonah had scooped me up, since I had quit without a backup plan. Jobs are hard to come by late into winter. Riding my bike became increasingly difficult, so half of the time I opted for the train. How I loathed the late-night trains.

We batched many cocktails. I was thrilled. I had never liked specialty cocktails. I thought they were a sorry attempt to match what the kitchen was doing. I really liked the classic drinks. A clean martini is like a soak in a hot tub; an old fashioned is like candy you stole from mother's cupboard; a Sazerac is like sitting on the grass butt-ass naked. I think we got it right and achieved all there was. I wasn't inspired by muddled cucumber (unless it was in a Pimm's Cup). I wasn't longing for a spin on a Negroni. Mostly, I'll just take the poison straight in a moderately clean glass. The batching helped though. When the lounge was popping, we had gallons of sake martini and lychee martini ready. There wasn't any other easy way of doing it. We needed to turn and burn, as they say.

I worked Tuesday nights with a skeleton crew. Mostly, I went without a barback. They got me ice, and that was about it. Ana and I worked together on Tuesdays, usually with one other girl working alongside Ana. Those two also had a busboy who gladly followed behind them.

Ana was guarded. I was able to crack a joke on our third shift together. I couldn't tell you what it was, but I could tell you how wonderful it was to see her face light up. It was an awful lot of work to get her to even notice me, let alone laugh, but I was happy. And that was what started the chain of events that led to me needing to find a new job.

John popped in during my first week on his way back to our apartment in Brooklyn. I poured him a Sapporo and a shot of whiskey. John had left the restaurant world a year prior to work in art production. He knew all the ins and outs of this line of work though. Nothing got past him. We talked shop, and he took a moment to notice the guests. Only a small part of him missed this line of work, but that part rose to the surface when he laid eyes on Ana. John worked with prop department girls who typically weren't easy on the eye. He missed the looks of cocktail waitresses. Who could blame him? I was surrounded by women whose job it was, in part, to be easy on the eye. John spent some time sipping his whiskey after he sucked down his beer. I saw him turn into "Drunk John." Having known him for six years now, I knew this side all too well. I gave him the boot before he could get me into trouble.

When I was slow at the bar, I watched Ana interact with tables. I would notice how a man would look her up and down while his woman was scanning the menu. I would notice how women would look her up and down, wishing they had her hips or hair. It was like a little science experiment where everyone noticed her and became like the volcano you make in science class: they fizzled.

A few weeks passed until the day she came in with a cookie for me. She assured me it was vegan. She had paid attention to me, and I was old enough to understand that she had to be interested. At least, I thought she was. Was she so naïve and unaware of what a cookie meant?

Every Tuesday she had a new little treat for me—sometimes it was a fresh juice she had made at home, sometimes it was candy. One Tuesday came around, and she didn't bring me anything. She did, however, invite me to meet up with her and some friends at a bar in midtown.

I was nervous. I couldn't make a move on her. I shouldn't make a move on her. I worked with her. I remembered what so many bar brethren had told me, "Don't shit where you eat." Did it still count if they fed you cookies? I arrived at the bar late, after meeting up with my cousin for dinner. The loud, geek-filled bar looked like band class on recess. I didn't see the midtown bros I expected. I saw a bunch of spindly, well-behaved types.

The bar was set up with game areas— a Jenga station, a Boggle station, and all the games that harkened back to a time before social media. Then I saw her. Ana came over to me, her faux red hair trailing behind, as the wind lifted it up and back. She hugged me, and we stood there for a pregnant moment. She kissed me on the cheek and the corner of my lips. Then the kiss on the cheek turned into a passionate kiss, and the board game players faded into oblivion.

"We shouldn't do this," I told her.

"I know," she said.

"We work together. . ."

"I know. It's a bad idea."

I held her tighter and kissed her again. She asked me to step outside with her for some air. She waved back to her friends who were standing over by a raised table. We stepped out to the west side of the building. I pushed her up against the brick wall next to the dumpsters as she shivered in the cold air. We French kissed, and I groped her body. I pressed my hips into her and let her feel my joy. She asked me to go back to Astoria with her, and I couldn't say no.

She ran back in for her coat, and we hailed a cab. We made out all the way uptown and over the Queensboro Bridge. We only took a break when she told the driver to stay straight on 28th Street. We climbed her stairs to the third floor. Her apartment was drafty, and she led me to her room, which was painted black. We stripped down and climbed atop her raised bed. She had a woman's body. She pushed me off of her and went down on me. I looked down at her working on me and felt like I was hallucinating. It had happened. I was here with Ana, and it wasn't a masturbatory fantasy. I was complete. I rolled her off me and entered her. We took out our combined frustrations with the world on each other. We were one unit. I held her close and deeply as I came. We were warm now, and our hearts beat against each other's chests.

Ana and I awoke the next morning. She took me to a bagel spot a few blocks away from her apartment. It was warmer than it had been the night before. And she was warmer than she had been before. During the weeks before, she had been inaccessible, giving me glimpses into her inner self but keeping me from stepping behind the curtain. This morning, over bagels and orange juice, we lived the same moment together. I wondered if this was it. Was she for me? Was I for her?

We kept it quiet at work. Nobody knew. We didn't want to advertise this precious thing to the jungle that was work. It was a sanctuary only we knew about. It was a temple tucked away under overgrown vines hidden from the monkeys swinging by. We would get coffee together two blocks away before our Tuesday shift and hoped we could keep this between us. On off nights, we would see improv or sit for a drink in a bar. I introduced her to my friends. John, Quinn, and Calvin all approved. They had never seen me date a girl before and seemed startled that I was romantic. *I* may have been startled that I was romantic.

I pushed harder on my art. I was cranking out animation at a faster rate, feeling empowered by Ana. She assured me that I was truly meant to do this. She pushed for more auditions, as I assured her that she was the next big thing. She was made for the stage and so much more.

I was a flirt by nature and a flirt by nurture. My job in hospitality made it obligatory, since it's at least 50 percent of what we do. I would watch Ana flirt with her guests from behind the bar. I wasn't jealous. I knew how she was. She had been celibate for eight years after college. She was choosy, and I was honored she had chosen me. It was a turn-on to watch her charm men and women. She had a Medusa's gaze. You couldn't divert your eyes once you had set them upon her. I wouldn't turn to stone when she looked me in the eye, but I would stiffen up.

I pushed along with my routine. I met up to play punch pals with the guys from the gym. I pedaled my ass to all pertinent spots I had to be. Ana was my little vacation. Ana was the levity in an otherwise arduous journey. The lounge was not what I thought it would be—the money was so-so. I remember the money I had racked up at Nashi. I had felt like Rich Uncle Pennybags. Now I felt like an indentured servant. I knew this was the path, though. I had too many outside interests to be stuck in a cubicle nine to five. The bar life gave me precious time to fight, draw, ride, read, and make love. I kept my mindset in check. I felt gratitude and tried to keep that in the forefront, as much as a disgruntled, crotchety bartender could.

Time went by but our relationship didn't grow. Ana took steps away, as if time traveling to when we'd first met. She had let me in but grew to be guarded again. Sometimes the passion was there; other times it was like a legal separation. Was I too much? I felt things I hadn't felt in a long time. I would give her sweet pecks on the cheek when meeting her for pre-work coffee. I would wrap my arm around her and feel proud we were an item. I would play with her hair and realize that I was revealing all of my cards. It was unpredictable, how she would be at any given time; there wasn't a formula. Sometimes we were star-crossed, and other times we were crash and burn. I kept the idea in my mind that we would work through the rough punctuations. We would survive in the jungle together, even if I had to perform a human sacrifice.

Our company party was approaching. This year Nashi and Jones Street wouldn't be united. The two owners were in a blood feud, and the families were split up. We were having our party at a new spot on the LES, a hip little Mexican restaurant with a lounge downstairs. I have always enjoyed the awkward company party. Restaurant folks are party folks. We are surrounded by food, work late nights, and go out after for nightcaps. Company parties are always a debacle. Someone usually ends up vomiting in the decorative plants, and someone usually has dirty sex in the single-serve bathroom. Everybody gets inebriated and lets the wild thing out.

Ana and I decided to show up separately. We didn't want to let on that we were an item. This party had the potential to hack away the vines of our sacred temple. I got there after Ana, made the rounds, and took a tequila drink off a server's tray with every new interaction. By the time I made my way over to the table where Ana was seated, I was three sheets to the wind. We were sitting with one of my barbacks, another cocktail waitress, and a hostess. Everyone appeared to be at the same level of drunk. I looked over and saw the beaten English tart Ferrara chatting with a group of nasty upstairs folks. A server brought us all margaritas, and we drank ourselves into a warm, cozy place.

Toward the 1 a.m. point in the evening, Ana sat on my lap. I was too drunk to care what anybody thought. I also realized that everyone had been drinking for four hours or so, and this was clearly going to go unnoticed. I saw J.C., my friend and manager, looking over at us. He smiled coyly at me. He knew that I knew that he was onto us. I trusted

J.C. more than anybody in the restaurant but wasn't ready to share my sanctuary. Ana and I left the party together. The barback, cocktail waitress, and hostess all had a clue what our joint departure meant. I hailed us a cab to Bed Stuy and led Ana to my godforsaken apartment. She went to use the bathroom, and I waited in the dark living room. I pulled her into my room. The rats were scurrying around the dumpsters outside my window, and the floodlight illuminated my mattress on the floor. We had sloppy, clumsy, disorienting sex, as though we were on a sailboat in a great storm. She froze up. We stopped and lay next to each other with the rats squealing outside only thirty feet away. I couldn't sleep well. I don't know if she slept well.

At 11, we awoke to an empty apartment. My roommates were out, and it was just the two of us. I set the kettle on and made us two cups of green tea. I had no food to pull together for a snack. We were quiet. The rats were quiet. The building was quiet. We sat in the ever-present silence, sipping our tea.

But I couldn't keep quiet, even though we didn't have our lines ready to speak. We just looked at each other in this empty house and froze.

"You know, I feel like there are times when you push me away."

"Yeah, I know."

"I feel like we do well, but then it gets to be too much and. . . it's like you can't be okay in this."

"What are you saying?" she asked, looking at me with deep concern.

"I don't know if you are ready for this."

"Every couple has problems."

"I don't think these problems should be happening now. . . it's so early in what we have."

"I don't know what to do."

"You mentioned your ex said this about you too, right?"

"Yes, he did."

"Well, I don't know how to make it better. I can't do the closed-off thing. I can't do the frozen thing."

"So, what are you saying?"

"Maybe we should take a break for a bit, and you can figure out if you want to really do this."

". . . Okay."

"Yeah?"

"Sure."

"This isn't the end, but I think you need some time to think about if you really want to be in this with me. . ."

"I get it. Okay."

She kissed me on the lips and went back to Astoria. Was I overreacting? Should I have been more supportive? Was it beneficial for us to have some space? Was she never coming back? Had that been the last night we would spend together? Was the last time the memory I should hold onto as a consolation prize for a doomed relationship?

I saw her again on the following Tuesday on our shift. She was in her black lace dress, and I was in my tattered black shirt. It was an unusually busy Tuesday. We handled it well since we were consummate professionals. I thought we were undetectable until my barback came to check on me.

"Yo, Ana seems different. You don't notice that?" he asked me.

"Nah, not really. It was a little busy, I guess. Maybe she's just distracted."

"No, that's not it. She seems a little off."

"What do you mean off?"

"You know off. Like she lacks that usual thing about her."

"Yeah, I guess so. . ."

"I have to run back up to help Daniel with his bar. Holler if you need anything."

"Sure thing, captain."

My barback ran back upstairs, and I watched Ana from behind the barricade of my bar. She did indeed look different. She was still beautiful but different from how she used to be. Now she was tragic and beautiful . . . tragically beautiful. Maybe I was feeling a swell of pity for her. Maybe I pitied myself for feeling so strongly for her while knowing it was destined to be ashes. I saw her bend over a table to pick up a check.

Her faux red hair fell over her shoulder; it was lovely. She was equal parts graceful and strong. She avoided me, but that was normal. She had a way of pushing me aside when in public. There was rarely a wink or a smirk to let me know that we were in on the joke. I was erased like a Jasper Johns drawing. Now, in this moment, I didn't expect any different. This was Ana. This was me.

Later she came up to the bar to pick up a couple of lychee martinis for table 42. She looked up at me to ask for more canned lychees to garnish the drinks. I smiled at her and dropped down to my lowboy. I pulled out a quart container half filled with lychees and poured them into the caddy. She popped one into her mouth and locked eyes with me.

"You know that's the last bit of lychees we have, right?"

"Yes, I know," she said, and smiled coyly.

"Okay, just so you know."

"They're so good," she said, as she chewed up the rest of it.

"I'm glad you enjoyed them. You sure you can't fit one more in there?"

"One lychee is my limit." She spun around with the tray of drinks and went over to the table.

It seemed as though she was fine with me. It seemed like she had forgotten all about our tryst. She buried it, like she buried her past, and went on. The night was winding down. I was amazed we had made it through congenially. I seemed more affected than she was. She got cut before I did, as was the custom in restaurants. I had to stick around to break down my bar. My bar manager was anal, and I needed to make sure everything was done to his liking. It took an extra 30 minutes, because he said so. She passed by me as I was cleaning, on her way out the door. She gave me a dispassionate wave. I knew her route back home; she would take a right out the door on Jones, then she would head over to Broadway and walk three blocks north. At this time of night, she would drop down to the subway to take the Q. I knew how she would sit, and how she would carry herself. I knew she would transform from a beauty into a menace. I knew that she would make herself an herbal tea when she got in the door, and then read a bit of an old play she had read many times before.

I would finish up and pull my stuff together. My bike was parked out front. I would take a right over to Broadway and cut south to the bridge. I would get home and read the *Times,* then pass out, only to awaken once I felt my laptop roll off my stomach.

I hadn't seen her all week. We only had Tuesdays now. I went about my business. I continued my drawing, riding, and grappling. I had the occasional beer with John and talked about the future of the city. I was looking forward to Tuesday. Maybe this break would come to an end. Maybe she was ready to be in it. I hoped I was ready to be in it too. I felt I could be.

I rode into the city for my shift. We would be reunited, in some fashion, on Tuesday. Tuesday was when we would potentially resume our relationship, stronger than before. We would be past this divot in the road.

I came in and started goofing around with my sushi chefs. There were two of them set up behind the bar with me. I knew random phrases of Japanese due to my curiosity about all things Japanese. It was too early in the night to share Sapporo and sushi. The guys were setting up their station, and I was salivating at their sushi rice. I could smell the starch and the white rice vinegar. One of the guys had a long, square blade and cut into some red snapper flesh with precision and ease. The other guy began slicing cucumbers and ginger. I stood over on my end pulling beer off my bar and down into the lowboy. I went up to grab another six-pack of Hitachino. There she was, in her black lace dress with her faux red hair trailing behind her. She appeared, like she always was, remiss.

I was highly caffeinated. I had taken to my old routine of coffee and drawing for an hour before my time at work. Caffeine affected me like an antidepressant; my spirits were high after gulping down a cup of the black stuff. I began goofing around with my sushi bros. We were loud, but it was of no consequence. Guests wouldn't show up for another hour and a half.

I was cranking along, pulling my bar together for service. Ana, the other cocktail server and their busboy wiped down the tables. The sushi guys and I became more boisterous toward the end of their set up. We drew a crowd. The hostess, Ana, the other cocktail waitress, the barback, and a prep kitchen guy all came to see our show. I began reciting the dirty Japanese I had learned.

"*Chinko!* (cock)" I declared proudly.

"Haha, chinko!" the sushi guys repeated.

Our audience behind the bar was enjoying the pregame show, so we continued it with zeal.

"*Manko!* (pussy)" I said with a vague Asian accent.

"Haha, manko!" the sushi guys repeated.

Our audience seemed to be enjoying this performance. Everyone except for Ana seemed pleased, but I wouldn't let her ruin the show for everyone. Nobody had asked her to be in the audience. We continued the show for the rest of the crowd.

"*Yah-re-tai-ee!* (I want to fuck you)" I hooted in a drunken manner.

"Haha, yah-re-tai-ee!" the sushi guys continued with the game.

"*Se-I-shee!* (cum)" I ejaculated.

"Haha, se-I-shee!" the sushi guys were laughing and pointing at me.

Everyone was enjoying this, but then I looked over at Ana. She was bemused but under it all, seething. She was offended on a couple levels—one was that she wasn't the center of attention. Another was that she resented me for implementing a break between us.

"I hate you," she said wryly.

"Yeah okay. . ." I tried to move along with the show without her heckling stopping me.

"I really hate you," she said and smiled.

"Right back at you." I tried to steer the show back on track, but she wouldn't relinquish the attack.

"I hate you," she said with malice.

"Okay, and you're boring!" I said clearly and locked eyes with her.

Everyone was silent. The show was over. She was hurt. It was as though I had plunged a knife into her chest. She froze up and gasped.

She exited stage left, past the corridor to the back. The crowd moved along, and the sushi guys just shrugged at me. I had done it. I had ended it once and for all. There was no coming back from it.

The weeks that followed were a cold war. We wouldn't speak beyond the task at hand. If she needed a drink, she'd let me know. If I needed to know if a drink was up or on the rocks, I'd ask. Other than that, we were not speaking. The budding of our love affair decomposed into a giant pile of shit. Nowhere we were in a toxic work environment. The stench was great. I went to my friend and manager J.C.

"So, I think we both know why I'm here," I told him.

"Really, bro. You're just gonna quit?"

"I have to, J.C. This sucks. I made a terrible miscalculation."

"Dude, people screw at work all the time!"

"This time was different. It wasn't just screwing."

"She'll get over it."

"Maybe I won't."

"I knew you were screwing her."

"Yep. I knew you knew."

"Why didn't you tell me?"

"I guess I just wanted it separate. I wanted to keep it tucked away."

"Bro, you sure you want to quit?"

"Well, it ain't fair to her for me to stay. I don't really have a choice. She hates me."

"All right, if that's what you want."

"It's what needs to happen."

"I hear you, buddy. I'll let the higher-ups know-"

"Let's leave out the Ana part."

"Way ahead of you."

I left Jones without a backup plan. I knew something would turn up, and it did. My buddy Calvin scooped me up. I went to work for a small mom and pop in Gowanus. It was so different from Jones. The pretension and illusion of the metropolis was removed. It was like moving into suburbia, but I didn't mind it. I was at the end of my bar spoon and needed a place to rest my shaker tins.

Ana and I never ran into each other again. We had different routines. Plus, she was in Queens, and I was in Brooklyn. Never the two shall meet. I would have expected to see her in the Village, but it didn't happen. We were separated by time, space, and enlarged egos. I didn't know what she thought of me. I didn't know if she thought of me. I only knew I thought about her. Our dinner theater had finally come to a close. There was no after party. The curtains were drawn shut, and the scripts were never opened again.

Coffee_69

The breakup was harsh. The winter was cold. The city froze under a coating of snow. Women seemed to vanish altogether. The only heat emanating was from my loins. I wanted to share this heat with a lady to take my mind off of Ana but, alas, there were no women to be had, because they had apparently vanished.

Training Jiu-Jitsu was painful in the height of winter. You couldn't get warm fast enough. Your feet would crack and split on the blue mats and injuries seemed to increase. At least ringworm, potential scourge of the sport, seemed to be kept at bay. Jiu-Jitsu was my sanctuary, and the guys who trained there were my family. Nothing brings men closer together than beating each other up. We knew everything about each other. Class didn't matter—white-collar guys rolled with blue-collar guys. A good submission was a good submission. Technique was paramount, as we all strived to achieve the next level. One of our heavyweights was a guy named Gerard. He was a couple of years older than me, grew up on Long Island, moved to Manhattan, and became a bike courier. He saved his pennies and opened his own bike shop. We competed alongside each other in the Amateur Grappler's League.

Gerard got laid all the time. He was a big guy with tattoos, a mustache, and a Tinder account. I partly hated him for it. He had a digital harem of hipster chicks awaiting his text commands. There was never a dry period for Gerard. He was always singing in the rain. I, in contrast, was essentially living in Siberia. My mojo was dried up, and I needed a woman to restore it—a Catch-22, because you needed the mojo in the first place to bed a girl. I buried my frustrations in rear naked chokes.

Monday nights were the long ones. We trained for hours and ended it with punch pals, where we gloved up and went rounds beating the pulp out of each other. After, we would grab falafels at a small shithole by the train. This particular Monday night I limped over to the spot. My right ankle was throbbing, completely my fault. I had kicked out of range and hyperextended my foot.

We arrived at the falafel spot with our damp gym bags and ordered falafels one by one at the register. Marc, Danny, Gerard, Juan, and I sat at a small table by the window. Big Gerard dove into his falafel. He cared not about the tahini caked onto his mustache.

"I wonder when professor is gonna give me a purple belt," Danny pondered aloud.

"Professor doesn't hand out belts. His belts mean something," Marc said.

"I've been a blue belt for three years now," Juan said.

"I've been a blue belt for closer to four, I think," I said.

"He'll promote you when it's time," Gerard said, as he wiped his mouth with a napkin.

"I really want to get that north-south choke. I can never do it," I said.

"You need to set that one up to get it. It takes more finesse," Marc said.

"He just muscles everything. Dustin uses too much strength," Danny blurted out.

"Whatever, Danny! You flail around. Too spastic," I replied.

"It's true, Danny. You flail," Juan agreed.

"What about you, Juan? You're perfect?" Danny asked.

"Nope. I'm a blue belt," Juan answered.

"Me, too!" Gerard said.

"Yeah, but he has a black belt in slaying pussy!" Danny said.

"Gerard is always getting laid," I lamented.

"He gets it, because he has the proper technique. He sets up the position before submission," Marc illuminated us.

"Yeah, and he uses Tinder . . . which is like sandbagging," Danny said.

"It's legal. I think the federation would say it's totally fine in competition," Marc countered.

"You think Tinder is a gamechanger, guys?" I asked.

"Yeah, man. It's the way of the future. Going up to girls in the wild is archaic. This is how it's done in 2014," Juan explained.

"Dammit! Maybe I should get on it. . . Tinder seems too much though.

"OkCupid seems like a viable option. I've used it before," Gerard said.

"Well, that seems more approachable. Okay, I'll give it a shot," I declared.

"There you go. Get with the times, man. We don't fight with swords anymore. We fight with light sabers!" Marc exclaimed.

"It's 2014, dammit! I'm gonna be a full-fledged Jedi, like Gerard Wan Kenobi," I said.

I went online. I built myself a profile. Granted, I wasn't experienced at it. I was better in person. This felt too much like a sales pitch. . . in fact, it was a sales pitch. I was selling myself. My sexual market value was at an all-time high. I had my youth, my wit, and money in the bank. I hoped I could sell myself to a pretty little thing. I looked for a photo on my laptop. I tried the subtle smirk, but I looked sarcastic. I tried the big smile, but I looked like a serial killer. I tried the empty yet reflective face. My face was too angular for that, and I ended up looking like an angry person. I decided the subtle smirk was best. If these ladies couldn't handle a little sarcasm, we were dead in the water anyway. I wrote up a little blurb about myself, disliking this part most of all. I didn't enjoy speaking about myself like a salesman.

I read a few of the ladies' profiles and cringed at most of them. They went something like: "Hi, I'm Debbie. I'm smart but not annoying smart. My sense of humor is out of control, but I know when to turn it off. I love Sylvia Plath, Patti Smith, and Lena Dunham. My perfect date would involve having cocktails and playing Jenga." Puke . . . no wonder these ladies were single.

I could illustrate why I was single as well. My profile read: "Hi, my name's Dustin. I am an artist. I bartend. I like to have fun, ya know, nothing too serious. I'm just going where the wind takes me. I'm that kind of guy who would take you out for a round . . . possibly two, if necessary, then invite you back to my place to watch *The Big Lebowski*. After that, texting between us would become less and less frequent. Eventually we would cease all communication, and you would move on to the next asshole."

I set up my profile and sent word out to almost all the women on the site in a five-mile radius. I included personal messages like "You look like a devious one," and "I think we would have a mediocre amount of fun." Eventually, I became bored. So I sent out stranger messages, like "Help, I'm trapped in the internet. . . release me," and "My mom says I'm a good boy, but I don't believe her."

A couple of days passed. The temperature dropped more than I could have imagined. It was grueling. John, my best friend and roommate, was seeing a mom who lived in Cobble Hill and had two kids. He was set for the month, at least until she got sick of him or vice versa. I was jealous that he had these rations for the cold months. I was starving and would have settled for anything, even scraps.

Then I got a response from a woman—at least I thought she was a woman. The picture was hazy. I saw a sea of black, frizzy hair and a plain face. Her handle was "Coffee_69."

I read the message I had sent her. It was pitiful. It read, "I'm freezing, how 'bout you?"

She responded with an equally sad combination of words, "Yup, cold. You seem nice."

I noticed the green icon above her picture that indicated she was currently online. We were communicating in real time now. We bounced back and forth for a short while and danced around the point. We were both single, lonely, cold, sad, and pathetically testing each other. I finally proposed the idea that we meet up, and she agreed to it. We exchanged numbers and decided to meet up within the hour.

This should have been crazy, but in the modern-day world, it had become normal. New York folk wanted things immediately. They wanted their trains to run on time, their espresso served up speedily, their late-night bagel spot open 24 hours, and their potential romantic interests to appear before them, ready for anything. I didn't know much of anything about Coffee_69. In fact, I hoped she was a bona fide woman.

I wrapped my face in a scarf and put on my sherpa jacket. I rode my bike down Bedford Avenue toward the Williamsburg Bridge. She lived in the LES, so we were to meet up there.

It was dangerous riding through south Williamsburg. I especially kept an eye out for dented Sienna minivans. Their drivers were famously lousy. The white bikes along the way reminded me of my frail mortality and not to get too comfortable peddling. I got warm as I pushed up the bridge. Not many cyclists were on it; as populated as New York was winter took the pep out of the step of the streets.

I descended from the bridge. My hands ached from the cold wind as I rode up to Eldridge Street, our meeting spot. I stood next to my bike with my hand on the handle bar, swiveling my head from side to side. I saw a pretty girl come down the north end of the street, but she passed by me. It wasn't her. I wondered where that girl was going. Was she going out for a drink nearby? Was she single? I began to get cold. The sweat along my back felt unpleasant. A homeless man sauntered by with a brown bag, presumably with a bottle in it. I wondered how he was dealing with the winter. Where did he go to sleep at night? I considered bailing. This was stupid. My contingency plan was simple. I would ride back home and do some drawing. Then I would jump on Redtube, find a nice five-minute "point of view" clip, and masturbate. That sounded like a swell evening.

I saw her coming down the street. She was built like a caveman, her hair a big frizzy mop. I expected that from her photo. She came closer, and I saw the mess I was dealing with. She was not something I would ever look twice at. There was no visibly redeeming quality about her. She was dressed in a brown overcoat, Kelly green t-shirt, and red pants. Her muffin top was precise. If I ever needed a stock image of a muffin top, Coffee_69 would have been the perfect model. I wanted to end the conversation right away—before it began. I wanted out. I was immediately angry and sad. I had gone from Ana, a veritable goddess, to Coffee_69, a veritable muffin top goblin. Woe was me in this space and time.

She approached me and there was no confusing who we were. It was cold and empty on the streets. I could have done an about-face and left the scene without so much as a hello. Instead, I stood in front of her and grimly smiled.

"So, you're Comicboy007," she said to me.

"Yep, that's me . . . and you're Coffee_69. . ." I said demurely.

"Well, don't look so freaked out, kid. Ya want to get a drink or what?"

"Um . . . yeah, sure. Drink."

"Haw, haw!" she laughed.

"What's funny?" I asked.

"You look like a deer with an arrow through its neck. Come on, let's find a spot."

"Okay."

I walked toward the street side and rolled my bike along. She walked clumsily. It was quiet between us. She pointed out spots, and I passed on three of them as we walked. My spirits began to sink. I felt defeated; the cold, desperation, and beastly companionship rendered me a broken man. We cut up by Tompkins Square Park. I saw a small group of homeless, face-tattooed kids hanging by the gates. We walked along, and then I heard my name called out.

"Hi, Dustin!" a small blond girl called out to me.

"Hi, Brooke." I panicked. Coffee_69 was standing right next to me.

I felt a tremendous swell of embarrassment; I thought I'd been found out. Brooke was the ex-girlfriend of a fellow bartender. Nobody really cared what you were up to in the big city, but it felt like a small town at that moment. I imagined everyone would know that Dustin was a disgusting pervert, who was into weird sex partners. My face felt hot, and I imagined it must appear flush. This would prove that I was, in fact, a disgusting pervert who was into weird sex partners.

"What are you up to?" Brooke asked me.

"Um. . . I'm just walking around with my friend. I was running around the city and ran into her. So, we thought we'd find a drink. I mean I thought we'd find a spot to drink. I don't know where I feel like going. It's a weird day, ya know?"

Coffee_69 just stood by and watched the interaction. I spoke quickly to steer the conversation along, so the ladies wouldn't interact.

"Well, my friends and I are meeting up at Meet the Johnsons later, if you're interested," Brooke said.

"Yep! We may swing back around that way. It's on my way home, so that could work."

We parted ways, and I felt the color leave my face. I calmed myself as we got halfway down the block.

"Haw, haw!" Coffee_69 laughed.

"What's so funny?" I asked.

"You are. You were so nervous. What do you think? You think she thinks we were fucking or something? Haw, haw!"

"Nope!"

We continued down the LES. I felt like excusing myself but didn't know how to do it tactfully. I didn't want to hurt her feelings. I was annoyed with her; she misled me with her blurry photo. I barely knew her but didn't want to leave her abruptly. I decided to stay the course. I would end this depressing date with class, even if she had misled me.

We walked a couple of blocks over, and I was apprehensive about stopping into any spots. I didn't want to run into anybody else I knew. Mostly, everyone I knew from my line of work) hung out in the LES. It was a hotbed for disgruntled, bohemian restaurant workers. I needed a safe spot but couldn't figure out where. She proposed a change in destination.

"Hey, I almost forgot. I realize my neighbors in the building are having a party in the basement. Would you want to go?" she asked me.

"Yes, let's do that."

I was elated. We got to avoid the chance of running into anybody else I knew. We got to go to a party, where I assumed there would be booze, and I wouldn't have to spend any money. I could mingle with random folks and then split. This was the proper way out. It was like god had whispered into her ear to tell her what I wanted to hear. I was one of the chosen people, so I figured god had manipulated her for me, obviously one of the perks of being chosen.

We walked down Eldridge Street, then far over east, and came upon a ten-floor building. It was white and looked like it had recently been painted. I locked my bike wheel to the bike. She assured me nobody would mess with it but I kept it close to the elevator and the door to the room that held the party.

We walked into the room just behind the elevators. The party consisted of Dominicans. We were the only non-Dominicans there. Their music was blasting from an old boom box. In the center of the room stood a table. Half the table contained bottles of vodka, rum, sodas, and Dixie cups. The other half contained bowls of food. I saw *mangú,* rice, beans, *platanos maduros,* spaghetti, and a bag of chips. The Dominican partygoers were all friendly. One of the older gentlemen handed me and Coffee_69 drinks almost immediately. I gulped most of it down within a minute. Coffee_69 downed her drink and went back to the table to pour another one. The older ladies were dancing, wearing colorful summer dresses, since they lived in the building and hadn't had to go outside in the cold .

Even though I had never met these people and assumed I would never see them again, I was embarrassed. I thought they knew I was on the internet looking for cheap sex. I had no intention of having sex that night but felt embarrassed all the same. I wanted to explain to them that while I was a sexual compulsive, I had limits, dammit! I wasn't a complete disgusting animal. At least, I hoped not.

We had another drink. I practiced my Spanish. We talked about the city and how cold it was. I explained that I had lived in Miami for five years, and that's why my Spanish was decent. I ate a handful of chips and felt the alcohol in my veins. Now I no longer cared what anybody thought. I was in that 80-proof zone. I felt sexy, and I felt like salsa dancing.

Coffee_69 asked me if I wanted to head up to her apartment. She said she had booze up there and wanted to check on her cats. I should have assumed she had cats. I agreed, scooped up my bike from the lobby, and up the elevator we went.

At about the sixth floor, I felt nauseous; the silence made it the forefront of my moment. I watched the red numbers climb upward. I needed to break the silence.

"You have cool neighbors," I said.

"Haw, haw! You barely know them," she laughed.

"Well, they seem cool," I said.

The elevator doors opened. She got out first, and I followed behind with my bike slung over my shoulder. We took a right down the hallway. She unlocked her door, held it open for me and instructed me to place the bike next to the door. The apartment was ill-kept. We entered the kitchen. Magazines were piled up on the table. The sink was at maximum capacity. The distinct smell of cat piss lingered in the air, as though incense with that smell were burning. I began breathing through my mouth. She gave me a tour of the railroad-style apartment. She lived there alone in that sad, dark place. It was passable as an apartment for someone ten years her senior, but for her it seemed pitiful, a mausoleum haunted by a child of the night. She disappeared into a small room adjacent to the kitchen. She came out with a bottle of moonshine.

"I hope you like moonshine, and if you don't, more for me! Haw, haw!" she laughed.

"Well, I'm already buzzed, so that'll do," I said.

"Of course, it'll do!"

She led me into her room. I saw where the child of the night slept, on a blowup mattress on the floor without a covering. Her comforter was a tangled mess hanging off onto the floor. Her bare room was cleaner than the rest of the apartment. I took off my boots and jacket. She did the same, and I was confronted with her body again. We sat on her blowup mattress with the wall as a support. I understood she was a grown woman and a city girl to boot. I knew where she was taking the evening. I was a grown-ass man: I relied on the *Big Lebowski* play; she relied on the moonshine on a blowup mattress play. We were in the final act of an unholy consummation to a desperate evening. Bottoms up. I took the bottle from her and gulped down a neat pour of the clear fire. She grabbed it back and doubled down.

My body began to relax. I felt as though the air mattress was swallowing me up. I looked at her out of the corner of my eye. She was nowhere near what I would have considered an adequate partner, even for an evening. I needed to go further down the moonshine river, hoping to make it to the rapids, so we could get this over with. I took the bottle and sucked back the sweet burning spirit, then handed it to her. She followed suit. I gave myself no time to decide against it—I leaned in and kissed her. She returned the gesture.

I started groping for her chest. If she had decent breasts, this could work. If not, it was all an unlikely possibility. I groped at her chest. The breasts weren't where I thought they would be, so I searched lower, and there they were. From what I could make out with my hands, she had the body of a 70-year-old Russian fieldworker. My spirits were dropping, but the alcohol was sending a lift to my nether region.

I pulled off her shirt and saw what I had imagined. I took off my shirt and climbed on top of her. I pressed my erection into her through my pants. She was licking my face all over. Either she wasn't experienced at this, or she was half-canine. I sat back on my heels as she undid my pants. I helped pull my penis out. She dropped down on me and began to suck. It felt good, but it only lasted a moment.

"This is moving fast, eh?" she asked.

"No, not really. Pretty standard, I'd say," I responded.

"Yeah, I don't normally do this," she said.

We began to kiss again. I put my hand down her pants. They were tight, and her gut made the angle difficult for my hand. I felt what I thought was her vagina, but I couldn't be certain. She undid her pants, so I could have an easier time. I noticed her legs. They had pimples and red blotches all over them. What was I doing? This was a new kind of low. I had gone from bedding a beautiful, faux-redheaded, real-life Disney cartoon to the polar opposite. I decided that we should push through to the finish line and end this sad exchange.

I sat back on my heels, reached into the back-left pocket of my chinos and pulled out a Durex extra-sensitive. I tore it open and rolled it down on my penis. I climbed back on top of her and was about to enter her.

"What are you doing?" she asked.

"What?" I asked back.

"We're not gonna have sex," she said.

"Oh. Okay then."

"Don't get all rapey on me now!" she said.

"What? Am I pushing this? No! Jesus," I pulled away.

"I didn't mean anything by that," she said.

I pulled the condom off my dick and rolled backward, tucking my penis back into my pants and doing my belt. I looked over at her. Her gut covered her vagina, as she sat back on her elbows. Her legs were alarmingly unattractive, and I looked over toward the window. I felt ill. The alcohol was making my stomach heave a bit. I grabbed for my t-shirt and then for my boots. She grabbed her pants and fought to squeeze back into them. Then she threw on her shirt.

"I better get going. It's late. I need to be up early," I said, deflated.

"Okay, then. Yeah."

"See ya."

I went out into the hallway and opened the door with my bike balanced over my shoulder. I felt the color leave my face. I hoped I wouldn't hurl. I steadied myself in the doorframe and breathed deeply. She stood in the kitchen as I was on my way out.

"You can't just do that. You can't just kiss someone and leave!" she scolded.

"Okay," I said.

"You don't do that. You don't do that to someone," she continued.

"Yes, you're right. I apologize."

"You're a monster."

"Yes, I'm a monster. I apologize. I need to leave now."

I made my way to the elevator and hoped I could disappear. She slammed the door, and I knew I was safe. It was done. I promised myself I would never internet date again. I wouldn't go down this road or go that low again. No longer would I go down into the mausoleum like a monster looking for other monsters. I would resurrect myself as a noble creature.

I rode my bike over to the bridge. It was over. The cold wind was sobering, and I wanted to forget the whole evening. I wanted to delete it like a story written in Word. I wanted to never again ever think about

Coffee_69 and the shame I felt. I had to wait at a red light before I could ascend the bridge back to glorious Brooklyn. I checked my phone and saw three big chunks of texting. It was quite the poetic rant. She called me every name in the book, plus a few I hadn't heard before. I blocked her and rode on.

I deleted my account as soon as I got back to my apartment in Bed Stuy. I took a shower and let the water wash off the faint smell of cat piss I had on me. I was a dirty monster, low-life, but the water removed that identity. I was baptized in my shower a noble child. I climbed into bed and put on Redtube. I watched a clip I had seen at least five times before. I masturbated and began to drift to sleep. I listened to the rats outside call to me with their squealing. Yes, my brothers. We are the same. Yes, my rat brothers, we are the same.

Improv Is for Everyone

I signed up for an improvisation class at Upright Citizens Brigade. It was an intro class, but it was still nerve-racking for me. That might surprise you. As a barman, I could hold court and talk about any subject. Every time I stepped behind the bar, the proverbial curtains withdrew, and showtime it was. I played a part—me, but in disguise. I became whomever the patron desired. But I don't like eyes on me unless I'm perfectly ready. Deep down, I am an introvert. Rod Serling once said something I whole-heartedly agree with: "Every writer is a frustrated actor who recites his lines in the hidden auditorium of his skull."

I was that guy! I was a sort of writer, who sort of sketched, who sort of made art. Creation is what interested me. The giants of creators past plagued me. I thought of Philip Guston, Jack Kerouac, Art Spiegelman, and so many more. I would look at their mark on the world and despair. I always thought it would be bliss to be acknowledged as an artist. I pictured two tables set for a feast. The obscure artist sat at the children's table with the other children. The established juggernauts of art history sat at the adults' table. I wanted to be at the adults' table! I wanted to have a seat there with Hemingway, Goya, and Louise Bourgeois. I yearned to be recognized for my creations. I kept my ambition alive like a small flame bullied by harsh winds.

I signed up for an improv class, because I wanted to conquer the fear. I wanted to move past the embarrassment of being out in the town square with all eyes judging, not because I wanted to be an actor. Theater types tended to annoy me. I hung out with them only because I worked in restaurants, enduring their audition spiels. Theater types never cared if you'd rather not hear about it. They wanted to flap their mouths about the injustice of their cruel industry. Yes, we get it guys: Hollywood, Broadway, and the commercial market are harsh mistresses. You picked it. You have no one else to blame for a horrible career choice but yourselves.

I marked my new class on the calendar. It began in three weeks' time. I felt nauseous thinking about having to stand up in front of strangers and perform. It was unfamiliar ground, but I was dead set on pushing forward.

I showed up to class as scheduled on a Sunday at 10 a.m. There were about 20 students to begin with, but by the second session it had shrunk to 15. By the third week, around 12 remained. Our teacher was a kind woman, probably around my age. She started with an overview of what the course would entail. We would work the fundamentals of this practice.

The teacher had us introduce ourselves with an adjective attached to our name and a hand signal. I don't know why I found this basic exercise embarrassing, but I did. I remember I had had a figure drawing professor in college do this same exercise as an icebreaker. It's a great way to get the class on the same page and familiar right away, but I found the practice of formal introduction embarrassing. I hated it when, coming into a new job, I needed to say some things about myself. In the back of my mind, I guess I'm always assuming nobody wants to hear me speak. I think there must be a childhood incident that made me crumble when needing to present myself formally. It's buried somewhere in my gray, folded matter.

I wanted something zippy. I was halfway along in the circle we had formed. Everyone was taking to it, all seeming totally without fear. I felt my heart begin to beat irregularly, as it got closer to my turn to introduce myself. The young students were gleefully doing it. There was "Majestic Maggie" and "Eager Eric." There was "Polite Paul." I gritted my teeth as the expectation grew. It was my turn. I recycled the one I had used from my figure drawing class close to ten years prior.

"Hi, I'm Dopey Dustin. . ." I waved the index finger around as my hand signal. I felt like a steaming turd in powdery snow.

Could they see my insecurity? Could they tell I regretted signing up? Did they know that I was analyzing what they could be thinking and thinking I'm all the more pitiful for it? We went further around the circle, and got to a young man even more awkward than I. I felt a certain relief in that. The plain, young, blond man introduced himself.

"I'm . . . Joe . . .," he mumbled to the floor.

"Can you do that again? We didn't hear you," the teacher called to Joe.

"I'm . . . Joe . . .," he said, slightly more audibly. His face turned red, and his eyes deadened.

This was beginning to become painful. The energy in the room turned downward. We waited quietly as the teacher instructed Joe.

"Can you add an adjective to your name for us?" she asked.

"I'm . . . I'm. . ." A vein began to bulge from his forehead. It was pale green and stood out against his red skin.

"Any word will do. This is just to get us familiar with each other. Any word will do."

"I'm Jokester Joe," he said and put his hands up, as if asking, "Are you not entertained?"

The class repeated his name and repeated the hand gesture. It would have seemed like we were all teasing him, if it hadn't been part of the exercise. We did a few loops around the circle, where we had to remember everybody's name, adjective, and gesture.

The first exercise involved us getting up three at a time, in front of the remaining class, to tell an anecdote in pieces. The teacher would stop each of us, and the next person in our trio would continue the story. I went up with the second group of three. The pressure I put on myself was burdensome. I couldn't make eye contact. We had to talk about something that annoyed us. My mind immediately went to girls marching around the city with lattes. I had a lot to say on it but realized half the class were women. I didn't want to appear sexist and make the rest of my classes uncomfortable. I thought on the spot about how people dress their dogs in human clothing. This didn't annoy me at all, but it was safe.

I stuttered and stammered through my story. By the end of my spiel, I felt pitiful. It was so strange to be in this position. Had I not grown since high school? I felt like a pimple-faced teen all over again. We moved on to some more theatre games that involved clapping and snapping at each other. I didn't mind, as it was less personal. A few of the students had studied theater in college and were eager to show off their emoting prowess. Jokester Joe became one of my favorites, almost immediately, because of his vulnerability. I thought he was brave and naturally funny.

He had an amazing improvisation scene with one of the actresses in the class. It was funny, because he broke the rules—without realizing it.

What happened was this: we had to do a physical activity, to practice pantomiming action. Joe was sitting in a chair and pantomimed eating. It was convincing enough. The young actress stepped onto the floor with him and assumed the role of wife.

"Honey, honey, you need to fix the sink," she delivered, with nuance befitting an experienced actress.

"Yeah, yeah, I'll get to it. . ." Joe said, as he stared into space and pretended to stuff potatoes in his mouth. His face was already beautifully red.

"But, honey . . . we need to the fix the sink now," she delivered like a woman lost in a domestic malaise.

"Yeah, yeah. . . I'm eating now," Joe muttered. The vein began to bulge from his forehead.

"You always put off what you say you will do . . . there's a reason we sleep in different rooms now," she said with an underlying pain and yearning for her husband to come back.

Joe's face had turned a new shade of red. I hadn't seen it on him before. It looked like the color Chardin used to paint raw meat with. He took a moment to pretend to put down his potato. He looked her square in the eye.

"Well, maybe if you weren't such a stupid bitch… " Joe delivered, without an ounce of real emotion.

The teacher called "cut." The room was silent for a moment. Then the class was in uproar. Joe was genius. Sure, the scene was barely a couple of minutes long, but he was an improv god. It was brilliant. The actress added beautifully studied vulnerability. Joe brought his real-life discomfort and his own vulnerability to the scene. It took time for the class to calm down.

This transformed the class for me. I began to take more of an interest in it. I didn't have a dream of performing improv professionally, but I did have a new appreciation for the exploration of the moment within the confines of the game. Joe inspired me to let it hang out, to pour my guts out for all to see. This was a journey that seemed similar to martial arts. Both brought up fear within me; both required community in which to practice the art; both were practical for a life journey. The class revealed to me the strength I could gain from improv.

During this time, I had been animating shorts. I created a character who was the lead in all of them. He was a humanoid hotdog who suffered from extreme neurosis. I performed all of the voices, wrote the scripts, storyboarded, and animated the shorts. My buddy Bryan edited them.

I first saw *Beavis and Butthead* when I was in elementary school. I felt a deep kinship with Mike Judge, its creator. I studied his background and knew he had hit it big at 30. I was hoping to do the same. My animated hotdog would be the new Beavis and Butthead! My classmates were quick to offer their services.

Another score from the improv class: I realized I had taken it in preparation for being out in the world. I had elements of being painfully shy and needed the formal training to grow past it. Around this time, I had gotten my cartoons into a few small film festivals. I had to present my films in front of an audience. I saw that the class was helping me, and I was getting stronger. It was just like martial arts. After getting choked out multiple times, you learned how to defend yourself. After acting like an asshole in front of an audience, you learn how to not give a damn.

The people in the class grew closer over the weeks. I don't know what people thought about me, but I had opinions on all of them. There were some I liked; some I thought I liked, then didn't like; and some I just plain didn't like. One of my favorites was Eager Eric. Nobody seemed to like Eager Eric much. He was primarily a musician and worked at a pizza spot in Midtown. He was about my age and had grown up in Massachusetts. People thought he stole scenes. I thought he made the scenes. He felt completely at ease playing gay men or women— pretty much anything with a lisp. Eric had a multiple-person scene that involved pantomiming. He was paired up with an Orthodox Jewish kid who wasn't my favorite. The kid was a standup comic, and everything he did involved him putting his rehearsed material into a scene. He saw every scene as a match to win.

Eric saw every scene as a chance to be subversive and weird. He began the scene in his regular fashion. He stepped out onto the floor and strutted around. He stood facing sideways as though he were looking in the mirror. Illusory Isaac, the Jewish standup, accompanied him onto the floor. Illusory Isaac stood behind Eager Eric, not sure of what the scene was. Eric took the lead.

"Oh, my lord . . . I'm having an ugly day. . ." Eric said, and the class chuckled.

"What do you mean? You're beautiful," Isaac said flatly.

"Nope! No. Kevin won't look at me. It's these ugly long skirts they make us wear in Catholic school," Eric said.

"Kevin is so damn hot. Everyone wants Kevin," Isaac said.

The third student took to the floor. It was the actress who had performed with Jokester Joe. She strutted around in an authentically Kevin manner.

"Oh, my god, there's Kevin. He'll come back this way soon. I'm sure of it. I've got to get his attention," Eric said.

"Yes, yes, you do. . ." Isaac responded uncomfortably.

"How's my hair look?" Eric started messing with his hair.

"Good. . ." Isaac answered.

"How're my breasts?"

"Good, too. . ."

"This ugly skirt is too damn long. He'll never notice me. Take these scissors and take off a couple inches."

"The teachers will be mad at you."

"Oh, just do it, Tiffany. He'll be back any minute!"

Isaac started pantomiming cutting Eric's imaginary Catholic schoolgirl skirt. Eric let out a loud shriek, playing that Isaac had slipped with the scissors. Isaac was performing this action with fervor. I glanced over at the teacher, who was sitting on the opposite side of the room. She looked dismayed and then subtly grimaced. Eric held his hand to his face, staring at it.

"This is not my period blood! This is not my period blood!" Eric screamed it loudly. All of the women in the class, including the teacher, were dead-faced. I could feel their annoyance with Eric. I was doubled over laughing; it was too much for me to take in. There were too many emotions in the room for me not to lose my composure. The teacher called a stop to the scene, and three more students went up to perform a new scene. I couldn't stop laughing. A half-hour went by, and it would replay in my mind. This would cause me to laugh like a hyena again. The actress looked over at me, and that triggered it again. I excused myself to go the bathroom, so I could pull it together. It wasn't any use. That class session was almost over, and I couldn't help replaying the moment.

I gained steam as the course continued. I felt more comfortable with improv and enjoyed the challenge. I began sweating bullets over our graduation show. It was just an introductory class, but I still felt the pressure of putting on a great show. It was scary to prepare for the unknown. Wednesday nights were an improv jam at Upright Citizens Brigade East. A few experienced improvisational actors would lead an auditorium full of aspiring players through scenes. Eager Eric and Illusory Isaac took me along with them on a Wednesday. I thought this would get my feet wet and make me feel more comfortable. I thought it would be like sparring; once you get past the first punch in the face, the rest moves along smoothly.

I got there before Eric and Isaac, feeling queasy. The auditorium was filled. I couldn't imagine that this many people showed up to do this. Did anyone feel as I did? I wore dark pants, in case I pissed a little. The energy was raucous. Eric and Isaac came in just when they had us filling out pieces of paper with our names. They were calling up groups of 12 to 15 people to perform seven-minute spots. Every seven minutes, the buzzer would sound. The leaders of the improv jam would move on to the next set of names, and those people would go up to perform. I sat waiting in my chair, like in a cell waiting to be brought before a firing squad. Eager Eric got called up with a group of 15.

The leaders initiated the round, calling out for a word to inspire the improvisation. Someone screamed the word "chicken," and they accepted that. The seven minutes that followed were a calamity. Too many people up on stage wanted to be stars. The sentiment was "It's every man for himself." It was a literal battle of egos. Eric had no fear and didn't seem to notice a crowd was watching him. He ingratiated himself into the scene as a chicken who enjoyed having his feathers plucked. In Eric's classic way, his chicken character was a thinly veiled, lisping gay. He didn't seem to be hearing what anybody was saying but kept insisting people pluck his feathers. He got a few chuckles from the audience. The seven minutes ended, and the next 15 got called up. They called my name along with Illusory Isaac. My heart began to flutter. I also felt like I had to piss; panic was taking over. The expectation shouldn't have been great: I didn't have a theatre background, I didn't take debate in school, but I wanted to be funny. I wanted to be great.

Isaac and I stood together; 13 other random people were up there with us. I looked over at a big, bald guy who had a large beard. I recognized him as a cashier at Trader Joe's. It shouldn't have surprised me that he had interests other than stocking trail mix. He was six feet away from me, and his body odor had no trouble smacking me in the face. He began waving his arms around to participate in the scene, and wafts of B.O. made me breathe out of my mouth.

I stood in the background, only glancing past the lights into the audience. Everyone was loud. I froze. I thought about dashing offstage left but couldn't sneak away. Minutes were flying by, and I resolved to remain standing in the background. Somehow, Illusory Isaac stepped out onto center stage playing a baby. It was strange to see this awkward, hirsute man roll around on stage, speaking like a baby. I imagined he must have turned off every woman in the theatre. He pretended to be playing with a gun. I looked out at the audience, and they seemed confused. I was grabbed by one of the female performers to step out onto stage center. I desperately tried to hang back, but she wouldn't let me escape. I felt the blood leave my face.

"Oh my, honey, that baby has a gun!" she exclaimed.

"Yes, dear, he sure does. . . ." I said, almost squeaking.

One of the experienced improv actors came over to help out. He had a positive energy and was thrilled to deliver lines.

"Well, everybody here better watch out! This baby has a tommy gun!" he declared.

"No, it's a rifle!" I ejaculated.

I immediately felt like a loser. I had broken the number one rule: "Yes, and." "No" immediately stops a scene dead in its tracks. I didn't mean to do that; it just happened. I looked at the leader's face. His eyes were wide, and he had nothing else to do but to agree with me.

"Yes, it's a rifle!" he shouted.

The stage lights went dark, and I felt like I wanted to disappear into the darkness. The house lights came back. The audience cheered, and we gave our bows. We were ushered back to our seats. I felt like vomiting, avoiding eye contact with everyone. Eager Eric patted me on the back, and Illusory Isaac sat down next to us as well. The next set of performers got called up. I sat in my chair for the next three sets and lived inside my head. I relived the humiliating performance. I didn't notice too much of what was happening in the scenes. I just sat in the dark with a hand up to my face.

As soon as the lights came back on and the show was over, we exited to the street. Eric, Isaac, and I were hungry. I took them over to my comfort food spot where they had never been. It was a Punjabi I visited at least three times a week after work. We ate standing at the back counter and discussed the show. I lamented over the complete failure I had suffered. They were supportive and thought I was being too hard on myself. We called it a night, and I rode back into Brooklyn on my bike. I tossed and turned all night, dreading the performance we were sure to give upon graduating from 101.

There were only a few more weeks left until our show. We started working more purposefully. I realized that I was far better without an audience. I seemed to impede myself by questioning what an audience was thinking. I liked working alone without anyone else's expectations. Obviously, once the work was presented, it became a different story. For example, I had one good scene in class. It was with that actress. I played an old Jewish landlord, and she was my tenant. The scene became a seduction, and my character fought it. I went into talking about my eight children, my sweet wife, and the family business. The actress heightened the scene by taking it into a gutsier realm; she became more sensual and moved around as though she were offering herself to me. The class loved it. The teacher cut the scene, as she put her arms around me. Then we discussed the scene as a class. I enjoyed this part. It was just like art school—the critique. We had done well. We had listened to each other, done "yes and" and used the space well.

I felt like maybe I could put on an okay show with the class. We would be performing at UCB East, where I had crashed and burned just weeks before. The space haunted me, and I wondered if I'd have a flashback being there. Would I choke? Well, I had signed up for it. I needed to do it. I thought about something John and I used to repeat to each other: "Dying is easy, because living is hard." Real living is uncomfortable. We need to put ourselves out of our comfort zone. Otherwise, what's the point? I wanted to experience as much as I could in this one life. I could handle a little humiliation. Hell, I could handle a lot of humiliation. I had survived middle school and high school. What's more uncomfortable than that?

I only invited one friend to the show, my friend Quinn, who was a vegan baker. I met her at her bakery. I would go in before work to coffee up and have pastry. We became inseparable platonic friends. It was an unusual relationship, since we were about as close as two hetero friends could get without sex. She also had a theatre background and prepped me the day of. She told me to forgo coffee. She told me to relax and not be concerned too much with the audience. She told me to listen. Quinn left me at the door. We students had an hour with our teacher to warm up, so we played our theatre games on stage. I felt okay in the warm-up. Everything started to calm a bit. I was in the moment with my fellow improv players, and then it was showtime.

The class went back into the greenroom. Our teacher introduced us; w e could hear her speaking to the audience. I began to get sick and looked over at my classmates.

"Guys, I hate this. I'm getting nervous," I said.

"Don't worry about it. It'll be fine," one of the actors said. Sweat was pouring off his face.

"Eric, please punch me in the stomach. I think that will set me right," I asked.

"Nope, I can't punch you. We're going on in a minute or two," Eric said.

"Please, Eric. I think it'll get me into the right mindset. Please sock me in the stoma—"

Eric grabbed me and held me tight. I appreciated the hug, but it was going on for a little too long. I began to feel uncomfortable, but he wouldn't let go. His instincts were perfect, however: his awkwardly long hug put me right back into the present. We went out before the audience. The lights were bright, so I couldn't see too many people. I felt at ease. One of my classmates asked the audience for a word, then another told a quick anecdote.

I knew I couldn't wait too long. I needed to step forward and face the music. This could happen the hard way—or the easy way. I remembered when the girl had pulled me onto the stage. I needed to do that to myself, jump right into the cold water. I didn't want to be dragged in kicking and screaming.

I stepped out in tandem with Jokester Joe! It was brilliant. We, the two most awkward guys in the class, took the leap of faith together. I looked at his beet-red face. His pale teal vein only faintly popped out of his forehead. We performed. I played the part of his father. He took on the role of a teenager with overgrown dreadlocks. The mother was no longer in the picture. The scene went well. I couldn't tell if anybody found it funny, but I enjoyed it. It was just like sparring. Everything else faded away. Jokester Joe and I were in the dark cosmos together saying stupid things. Oddly, it occurred to me in the moment that I possibly liked this. The rest of the show went on, and everybody was present. We all existed in the dim space together and mind-melded. It felt like the afterlife in all its eternal glory.

The houselights came on at the end, and we took our bows. Quinn and I went out for a beer with the cast afterward. I met various family members and friends of the other classmates. Quinn and I sat at a table near the back and sipped on draft beers. I asked Quinn how I had done.

"You did well. It went well," she told me.

"Tell me. Really."

"It was good. You did overact a little bit."

"Okay, I'll take it!"

I looked over at Jokester Joe, sitting a couple of tables over. I caught his attention and held up my glass to him, and he held his glass up to me. I looked over at his coral face and felt a sense of pride. We had both been in our separate battles together. In the weeks of the class, we had suffered embarrassment after embarrassment. It didn't kill us; it made us stronger. I looked into Joe's dead eyes and saw a glimmer of newfound manhood. Jokester Joe and I had done it. We came; we saw; we performed.

Mexican Standoff

"John, I broke my fucking rule," I told my best friend in our two-bedroom apartment.

"Well, that's what happens when you break the rules. You break the rules, and they break you," John said, as he sipped his French press.

"I shouldn't have even started with her. I knew it. I fucking knew it," I said.

"Yep, you sure did, but little Dusty spoke up and made you do it."

"Yeah, he sure did. Now, here I am, jobless yet again."

"You could have stayed there. You didn't need to quit, just because you were banging her."

"We were dating actually, and no, I couldn't have stayed. It was the worst. It wasn't fair to her anyway. She was there first."

"You always find a job. You know there's always a place ready to hire a little charmer like you."

"Yeah, you're right. I know that. I hate doing this. It's like Groundhog Day. You get the girl; you get the job, and then you lose the girl and lose the job. Then you get the new girl, and you get a new job. Inevitably the cycle continues. Nothing changes. You just get a few new hairs on your back."

"Sure, but what's the alternative?"

"I don't know, but I do know one thing."

"Yeah, what's that?" John asked, as he put his mug down on the coffee table.

"Dying is easy, because living is hard."

"Dying is easy, because living is hard? What are you, Yogi Berra?"

"Nope, but I do throw my balls around."

"Well, life throws curve balls. Be ready to swing and miss."

I had to get myself together. I had an interview at a new hot spot in the LES. A friend of mine from the Stan Ward sent me over to them. This new spot was under the same ownership as a very cool spot in the East Village.

Everybody in this city, in our industry, knew each other. If you weren't a complete derelict, you could jump from place to place. I jumped on my bike and rode into the LES. John had the day free, and I planned on meeting up with him later for a beer on DeKalb Avenue. I locked my bike up in front of a Punjabi three blocks away. The LES was a terrible place to lock up a bike. The guys at the Punjabi would keep an eye on it, seeing as I was a frequent patron.

I stumbled into the place and felt the impending doom. I knew this place was not a keeper—it was a six-month stint. It was dark inside. Nobody had turned the main lights up. A young man in the back came down a hallway and up through the main dining room, where I was standing. He had the popular undercut with requisite tattoos, t-shirt, and black jeans. He looked like every other young guy in a five-mile radius.

"So, you must be Dustin," the young man told me, with an accent.

"Yes. My friend Joe, from Acme, sent me over."

"Yes, I know. My name is V."

"V, as in the letter?"

"Yeah, that's what everyone calls me." His accent was apparent. I assumed he was Spanish.

"Is it short for something?"

"Yes, Evangelos."

"Oh . . . cool. Where are you from?"

"Greece."

"Oh, that's cool. I know one Greek thing to say: *Christos Anesti, Alithos Anesti!*"

"That's pretty good, man. Where'd you learn that?"

"I was in love with a girl named Paula Kotzamanis in my middle-school days. She taught me that."

"So, you like Greek girls. I have some Greek girlfriends you should meet."

"I need a job first, and then I can start mingling with some pretty Greek girls."

"Of course. Let's have a seat."

Evangelos sat us down at one of the booths. I handed him my resume. You always kept them to one, easy-to-skim page, and only selected the best of the best spots. I was terribly disorganized and always had to fudge the dates of my work experience. I never lied on these things but couldn't attest to the specifics.

"Yes, the Stan Ward Hotel, good," he read the page aloud.

"Yes, that was quite the spot," I said.

"Oh, just recently at Jones Street. I know that spot. It's very nice. You worked for Jonah at Nashi, too. Nashi was fun. I've been there, too."

"Yes, I worked in various neighborhoods over my years here. It's been fun to experience different spaces."

"Yes, the LES is the best though. This is where the people go to party."

"Right. Where were you before this?"

"I worked at a Greek club in Astoria before this."

"That's cool. I bet it was fun."

"Yes, but I wanted more experience. I wanted to grow as a bartender. You can only make so many vodka Red Bulls before you want to jump off the Queensboro Bridge,"

"Yeah, I worked at a speakeasy in Chinatown. We worked mainly with tequila and mezcal. I love the stuff."

"So, you know the product already."

"I know a fair amount."

"That's good, man. That's very good."

I climbed back on my bike after leaving the restaurant. Once you leave school, you no longer count your years on this planet based on the school year; professionals probably use New Year's Eve to punctuate time passing. Restaurant folk count time by leaving one job and starting a new one. If I spent six months at Jones Street, that was one year. If I then spent two years at Nashi, that was one year. Restaurant folks live in an alternate dimension where time ebbs and flows as if on a spaceship lost in outer space. In-between restaurant gigs, it's as though we've crash-landed back on Earth—only to find it ruled by monkeys.

I met the staff officially on my first day of training. Their collective low IQ underwhelmed me. These were the kids who had had to do extra tutoring sessions on the side or stay behind. I should know. I was one of those kids, so I assumed I would fit right in. I had never been the fastest bartender or the most inventive about creating cocktails.

I was one of the best, though, at talking to a wide array of people. I could mingle with radical feminist NYU students, Goldman Sachs executives, the Chelsea art crowd and everyone in between. I was that kind of bartender.

Mostly, everybody was nice enough. One of our hotshot bartenders was in demand. He had the right look—the same undercut, tattoos and skinny jeans as V—but he didn't have the gab. Or he might have if you could have understood him. He sounded like Benicio Del Toro's character from *The Usual Suspects*. The guy was a masterful mumbler, so I couldn't understand 80 percent of what he had to say but I'm sure it was insightful.

The owner of this establishment was a rich, gay, French man. I didn't like him. It might have been my diehard liberal *Rules for Radicals* leanings. It may have been the little communist tucked away inside me who whispered about the haves and have-nots. Or it may have been that he was French. God love the French, but if you've been to Paris, you know what I'm talking about. Maybe the only thing I liked about him was his gay side. He dressed great. I knew I couldn't afford his threads, but I was impressed. That's how those guys do it—it's called "winning."

V was in constant war with our floor manager. V was technically the bar manager, but because we fancied ourselves a cocktail bar first and foremost, there was a tug of war. Our floor manager was a butch lesbian Filipino. Her name was Jasmine. She dressed well in a masculine manner. V and Jasmine were at each other's throats, while the French owner was hands-off. For example, when V told me to make a jalapeno vodka infusion, I left the bar to do so. Jasmine found me and reprimanded me, because I left my post. V came behind Jasmine, and they started a screaming match. So, Jasmine apologized to me, and I continued on my way. I was forever the pawn on the chessboard, being used as a sacrifice.

I had walked into a job at one of the most tedious bars I'd ever known. All the many specialty cocktails had at least six ingredients apiece. And they all required special measurement. We needed two different jiggers in our hands at a time just to craft a cocktail. (There's a reason I love the classic cocktails of Hemingway's day; drinks were commonly three ingredients, with standard measurements.) Our drinks also involved elaborate garnishes. One drink in particular utilized a long, mandolin-sliced cucumber snaked into the rocks glass. After that, you still needed to add a mint sprig ever so daintily.

The LES kids who came into the bar were my nemeses. They were young, with pa's credit card, and no understanding of tipping. Oh, how I loathed them. Early on, I knew this ship I was sailing would be a short cruise. By this point in my career, I could know what was a stable spot and which spot would deliver imminent death. I decided to go along for the short cruise ride because, after all, I didn't want to deplete hard-earned savings.

My higher-ups however had the idea that this would be the next hot late nightspot. Where else would coked-up kids with disposable incomes go to drink and fornicate other than a spot in the Lower East Side? We had a promoter set up the first late night extravaganza. It went hard from 11 p.m. to 3 a.m. Our star bartender had to be pulled back from an altercation with a rich Saudi. One young lady vomited on a barstool. One of the servers got into a shoving contest when he asked a gay couple to refrain from rounding third base. Police came in to escort the heavy petting duo out.

V ended up getting everybody out the door by 3:30. The place was littered with glasses. The vomit had been cleaned up, but I could still smell the faintest whiff of stomach acid. Servers and bartenders began sweeping up. I felt a buzzing in my brain from pounding tequila shots with coworkers and listening to electronic dance music. My body felt like an object I was wearing. Two of the cocktail waitresses started to pull money aside with V. We still had hundreds of checks to close, and there wasn't any time for taking it slow. We had been rapid-firing cracking beers, pouring tequila and making those obscene cocktails. We made fantastic money at the end. We were doled out fat stacks of greenbacks. It was all worth it—the vomit, the aggression, the EDM, and the police intervention. I thought to myself, God Bless New York City. It's a hell of a town to make money. By 4:30 a.m., I pulled my bike from the basement and rode back up over the Williamsburg Bridge into Brooklyn. I had always liked the journey over the bridge, that surreal time when everything in my tissues rattled, and I was aware of my mortality.

It only took a couple of months before we stopped the late-night parties. The restaurant was getting ripped apart by construction, and it was hurting dinner service. The problem with new spots is that they need to grow. They don't know what they want to be at first, and it's difficult to make decisions on where to take them. Our place was trying different identities, doing that teenager thing—one week it's goth and the next it's punk.

Early on in my time there, I had to work a brunch shift once a month. The late-night parties having been a disaster, we thought brunch could be a problem-solver. It was terribly slow, but they had thrown me the bone of a higher hourly. I mainly deep-cleaned the bar during that brunch, but I didn't mind it. I didn't have to see V, and that took some stress out of my life. Robert, the GM, would swing by every so often to chat. He was also GM of a sister restaurant and stretched thin. Added to that, he was preparing for a marathon—and developing an exit strategy for NYC. He was like a father who had another family, and they came first. We had one particular conversation that whispered of the end of the city as we knew it.

"Hey, man. Things aren't picking up with brunch yet."

"No, Robert. They're slow."

"We're competing with established spots in the area for brunch. It's gonna be hard to carve out business."

"What're you thinking?"

"Maybe we could get a DJ in."

"That's an idea."

"It's a dark space. Nobody wants to come in during the day for eggs and margaritas."

"Yeah, that's a good point. We could build a sundeck!"

"Yeah, I'm sure the investors would go for that."

"New York City is making it harder and harder to make a living."

"Yeah, you're telling me."

"Man, when I was coming up the money was crazy."

"Really?"

"Yeah. My first job was at a spot in Times Square. It was like a Planet Hollywood but for fashion. They hired models mostly. We would walk each night with close to a grand, and then be out after putting most of it up our noses!"

"Damn, really. Well, those were the days. It ain't that way any more. Even Crown Heights is being developed. I don't know how much longer I'll be able to hang in there."

"My wife and I are looking at properties in Brazil. Her family has been looking for us. Have you been to Rio?"

"Nope. . ."

"It's fantastic. I love the food, the weather, and the people. Yes, it's a fantastic place to be. We can live well there."

"How long until you split?"

"Between you and me, Dustin?"

"Yes."

"I think next year I'll be splitting. I've spent most of my life here. It's changed a lot. Now we want a change."

"I hear ya, Robert. That makes perfect sense to me."

Robert took off, and I was left to tend an empty bar. I ate some rice and beans before leaving and rode back over the bridge to Brooklyn.

Shifts grew more tedious. V ordered us around and scolded us on the regular. Jasmine and V kept having huge, explosive fights. English wasn't either one's first language, so I feel a lot got lost in translation. I hated looking for new work and rode the wave of shit; I stayed out of sheer dogged laziness.

Finally, I got scheduled to work a party downstairs. V wanted me out of there, but Jasmine wanted me to stay, because V didn't like me. My base pay for the party wasn't much, but I'd be out early, and I could hit up Rocka Rolla to see my bar buddy Eugene.

I dropped downstairs to begin setting up my bar at four p.m. Naina, a gorgeous Brazilian girl I used to work with at Nashi, was serving the table. She spoke three languages, didn't take bullshit from anybody, and looked sexy while smoking. We were buddies. She was arranging the table set up, and I had to prep my bar for full service. We only expected a party of 16, but I needed the cucumber margarita available, and I needed to be able to bang out a Reposado Manhattan. I didn't know who these people were, but this was a professional establishment; I couldn't tell them I didn't have a tequila old fashioned ready to serve. Everything had to be at the ready. Naina and I would get this party done.

I had brought my sketchbook downstairs. I was doing big, bubbly, drawings, but none of them were particularly good. I knew that once the party were seated, after schmoozing, I would be able to take a step back and draw. These parties were never difficult. The waitress made sure they were watered and fed while I made sure they were liquored and feeling groovy. Hospitality is the art of making a stranger feel at home, and Naina and I were masters.

I waited behind my bar. Naina stood behind the hostess podium and had her phone tucked out of sight. I pushed my stomach out so I could rest my sketchbook on it. I took out my Micron pen and began to draw. Three people came down the stairs before I could finish the sketch I had started. Naina greeted them. They came over to my bar—three androgynous beings. Two seemed more on the female side, while one appeared more male. They all wanted a salted-rim house margarita, so they had that in common too. I used two shaker tins to craft the three cocktails. They immediately started talking about fashion, specifically designers. I assumed they were fashion students. I then saw a small child barrel down the stairs, a little girl in a dress, with her father following behind. He looked familiar. I knew him from serving him at another bar and remembered he was a marginal soap opera actor. Most wouldn't recognize him. All would recognize his wife. She was tremendously famous but not in attendance that night. I began to wonder what kind of party this was.

The rest of the group arrived. I scrambled to bang out drinks as quickly as possible, as Naina brought out bowls of guacamole and chips. Then I saw her in the crowd. It was she. I knew her from my youth. She had been on one of my favorite childhood shows (that I had watched in secret). I had followed her—to this point in time with her looking me in the eye. Yes, I was starstruck. How pathetic was I? Here she was, ordering a glass of wine.

I tried to act like I didn't know her. She was just another Hollywood starlet, and I was just another LES bartender. This was just another New York City night, and we were just passing through time and space. The starlet had brought her daughter too, who looked to be about seven or eight years old. The marginal soap opera actor had brought his daughter of the same age. These Hollywood types lived in the same zip code, went to the same spots, and did the same PTA meetings, as naturally as traces of cocaine on a dollar bill. Naina guided the group to the table in the middle of the room. My portion of the party was basically over.

I sat on the back bar with my sketchbook. The two girls were running around and spinning in circles, competing for best twirl. I was immediately pulled back to looking at my own childhood. I saw myself in my seven-year-old body. I remembered my years absorbing television shows. TV became enmeshed with my own history; the two were indecipherable. I was in a schoolroom set piece alongside this Hollywood actress (and now single mother).

I thought about my birth in Philly and traveled through my youth in LA to my family's move to New England, my exodus to Miami, and my eventual arrival in New York City at this point in time. Then my printer went off.

I pulled the ticket and saw three salt-rimmed house margaritas. I pulled two shaker tins out, set up three rocks glasses and rimmed them halfway. I smashed the ingredients inside the metal tins and strained the contents into the glasses. Naina brought them to the three maybe-FIT students.

Hollywood Mom was calling out to the girls to behave. They listened for a moment and then went back to playing. I sat back sketching.

The girls came over to the bar and sat on the stools. As they called out to me, I was all too aware of Hollywood Mom looking at me. The girls were asking to see my drawings. I wasn't sure exactly what I had in my sketchbook; were all the drawings age-appropriate? I selected one of the Cinco de Mayo women I had drawn. The girls liked it. I ripped out two blank pages from my book and set them up with pens. They became quiet and began competing again, this time for who could make the better drawing. I hadn't realized how competitive girls were.

I heard my printer go off and saw a glass of wine on it, the same glass I had poured for Hollywood Mom. I grabbed a glass, poured it out and waited for Naina to bring it over to the table. Just as I had thought, it went over to her. She looked over from her seat and smiled. I felt an undertone of shame for having craved that attention from her.

I still couldn't make out what the party was about. It seemed work related; more specifically, it seemed like a production meeting. Maybe it was a wrap party—I couldn't pinpoint it.

I ventured back into my mind and started trying to pull up the most significant memories of grade school. I recalled games of Manhunt and a pool party where I was caught nude by a troop of girls. I reminisced about the neighbor girls, Joanna and Lindsey. I abandoned skateboarding for unicycling, which I mastered in three days. I thought about cold winters and hissing radiators cooking my wet socks.

She got up from the table to approach her daughter and her daughter's friend, within a few feet of me. I felt tremendously nervous and tried to pull myself together. I forced myself to exist in a moment separate from youthful hero worship. The girls informed her that I was a good artist. Hollywood Mom seemed grateful, and pleased that I had been kind. I genuinely like kids and enjoyed sharing art; her kid happened to be unbelievably polite. I don't think I had ever heard "please" and "thank you" so often from such a tiny person. The girls insisted I show her my sketches, but I panicked and refused. I knew I drew all over the spectrum and couldn't be sure if I had totally decent drawings for them. I couldn't let them see inappropriate sketches. They insisted again, so I handed the sketchbook over to her. My face felt hot, and I prayed that there wasn't anything torrid in there.

Hollywood Mom looked through my sketchbook. It was surreal. I had spent years watching her, and now she was looking at my drawings. My drawings were me. Being an artist was my identity, my top priority. Bartending, riding, and fighting just went to serve my art. I knew that the identity I held so dear might go unnoticed. It could turn out to be my secret, and I could die alone with it.

Here she was, though, looking at my sketchbook. She wasn't just flipping through. She was analyzing, taking it in, really looking. She wasn't perusing; she was truly seeing what I had done and seemed like she authentically liked it. I felt strong. I felt good. Maybe, just maybe, I could be somebody. Maybe I was a contender.

Hollywood Mom thanked me for keeping an eye on the girls. Then she split with her girl, and soon the rest of the crew followed. Naina smiled at me, having seen my interaction. I began to break down my bar and poured some soda from the gun into a rocks glass and drank it down. A man from the party came over to me. I assumed he wanted to order one more for the road.

"Hey, man," he said.

"Hi, sir. What can I do for you?" I asked.

"She wanted me to get your information," he said.

"Oh." I was shocked.

"I'm in charge of her production team. She wanted me to get your contact."

I immediately pulled out a sketch and wrote my information on the backside of it. Was this it? Was this the moment my life would shift? Had it all been for this encounter? Did she want me? I'd take that too! I tried to bury my thoughts away. I didn't want to get my hopes up. I took disappointment poorly. I didn't want to set myself up for defeat.

Naina came over to me once the last people in the party were gone. She was happy for me. She wasn't like most. Most people would have been envious, but not Naina. Her excitement for me only allowed my buried hopes to resurface. I needed to forget the interaction and keep on going forward. I futilely attempted to erase the memory from my mind. I pulled my bike from the basement and rode home to Brooklyn.

I thought: this might be one of the last times in my life that included mixing drinks.

Weeks went by, and I heard nothing. Maybe I hadn't legibly written my contact information. Maybe I had panicked and written my seventh-grade email. Maybe she had looked me up and found some disturbing artwork. Maybe I had somehow insulted her production head. Maybe they just didn't care or were too busy to reach out. I wallowed in imagined failure. I told myself not to hope. I knew I was setting myself up for disappointment. I had been in similar situations before: I had fallen for the bright lights of Hollywood glamour and dropped down a mineshaft.

I felt stupid, silly, angry, and, most of all, uncertain. One part of me had always imagined success. The other part was not realistic enough to have studied something practical. And now here I was, back at it behind the bar of this Mexican hotspot in the LES. I wasn't making the money I needed, because we had too many students passing through. I needed to hit those spots where the finance people went. It was like I was fishing in a pond but only catching goldfish. I needed to fish in an ocean to pull in the big tuna.

...

V came over to me to let me know that he was writing up tests for everyone to take. I would have to come in on my own time to complete the test. I was irate that this bastard was going to be testing us. I hadn't even had tests at the Stan Ward. That was as corporate as it comes, but they still wouldn't have pulled this.

"What do you mean, a test?" I asked in disbelief.

"Everybody is being tested, not just you," V said.

"You have to be kidding me!" I jested.

"No. We all need to be on the same page. This determines your rate of pay. If you don't do well, we tax you."

"Dude, there's a reason I'm a bartender! I'm not a good student, and I'm not taking any tests."

"You have to take the test."

"I don't have to do anything."

"So, what are you saying?"

"Consider this my two weeks notice."

"Seriously, bro?"

"Yup. I'm good."

"Okay, then."

I stuck around a little after that to help out and was exempt from the test. One of the other bartenders scored low and had a big shouting match with V. It didn't matter though; he still had his pay cut. I started asking around for new spots. I knew it was going to be difficult to find a decent one. I was becoming that curmudgeonly bartender whom nobody likes. My hospitality powers were fading, but I didn't know what other jobs I could do. I felt limited. I abandoned ship just before autumn and had interviews at various spots in lower Manhattan. Hollywood Mom may have unwittingly crushed me with the allure of LaLa Land, but that was no matter. It helped get me out the door from that Mexican shithole. It also humbled me and made me rebuild myself and reminded me never to trust folks from Hollywood. The Big Apple may have been infested with worms, but LaLa Land was gold-plated shit.

I Was an Artist Once

Before I quit the Stan Ward Hotel, I had a friend there who was a smart kid. He was so smart he had two worthless master's degrees from the New School, one hundred grand in debt, no job prospects, yet spent like a girl with her father's credit card. I didn't get along with him right away. I don't think Calvin liked me either from the get-go. He was blond, like me, but better looking. It took me time to warm up to him. All of the guys who worked in the lobby of the hotel were writers, actors, artists, or some form of the three. Many nights behind the bar were spent sneaking old fashioneds and discussing Hemingway or Bukowski. It was a good time to be in New York.

Calvin came from a small town in the Midwest. He suffered from depression and self-medicated with booze. He had an abusive girlfriend who would kick him out at three in the morning. He pined for a cocktail waitress we worked with, but she was dating another bartender (who also suffered from depression). Calvin dressed only in the finest threads—I think I learned most about high-end fashion from him. I mentioned that Calvin was smart. He was so smart he paid an exorbitant amount for Alexander McQueen dress shoes. He may have only been earning $30,000 a year, but he dressed like he worked in finance.

Everyone knew me as "the artist." I was almost never without a sketchbook. Sometimes I would draw sketches of me and a cocktail waitress copulating. This could have been disrespectful, but it was seen with humor. I was always complimentary in the depiction of their bodies. Always. I would even use cocktail bitters to color in vulvas or nipples.

One day, Calvin came up to the service bar and used some bitters to make a design on a service napkin. It was nothing of consequence, but I knew he sought my approval as the artist among us. I encouraged him, and he began drawing more. They were terrible drawings, but he was my friend, and I supported his efforts.

We had this great *salon* here in our service bar nestled in a hotel lobby. It was the center of the world. The beautiful staff would go out after hours to the dingy spots of the Meatpacking District and discuss dreams, projects, and futures. I was not a big drinker at the time and could do with one beer. Calvin drank multiple drinks and would somehow end up home, safe and sound. The hotel crew got closer over time; we spent much of the week together. It felt like college, but we were learning actual things. We learned lessons like, "Your boss doesn't give a shit about you," "You're replaceable," "Money is very difficult to make," and "Try not to fuck your co-workers."

I daresay I learned more in the service industry than I ever learned in college. Our crew was taking these "classes" together in the school of hard knocks. Our after- hours discussions were a time for reflection and action. Sometimes it led to sex, but not for me. I steered clear of screwing the waitresses. . . well, at least the waitresses in our specific department.

Most of us continued working together at different venues. A bunch of us finally left that godforsaken hotel for another godforsaken hotel, only we made a hell of a lot more money after leaving. We were all in our twenties, intellectually curious, hard-working, and hard-drinking. The Stan Ward Hotel had been our undergrad education, and the other spots became our grad school.

During my time at the hotel, I'd been working on a graphic novel. This was my great book . . . that never saw the light of day. It was about 500 pages of full-color World War II mayhem. It was a deeply sad moment when I got my final rejection letter from Topshelf Comics and knew publishing it was ill fated. Calvin supported me, as did the other hotel workers. We were still young—I was only 25 or 26. I knew from then on, I couldn't spend years on one project.

Calvin had only been futzing around with painting for less then a year, but he hoped to have a show. I was partly offended by this. I had spent years making work and felt I had earned the title "artist." I saw him somewhat as a poseur. He was not an actual artist. He merely played the character. I blame the Dadaists. It annoyed me that anyone could play that game in the art world. If you were a comedian, you had to earn it. It would be apparent if you could make a crowd laugh or not. We all listen to music, so as a musician, it was apparent if you were legit or not. Actors were also something young New Yorkers liked to pretend to be. They also happened to be the most annoying.

Calvin asked me if I wanted to do a joint show with him at a bar in

Park Slope. I was offended at the invitation and wondered if he knew that we were not in the same league. Annoyed by his arrogance, I accepted the invite. My work was just sitting around collecting dust in my room. I was terrible at self-promotion and refused to be on social media. This was an opportunity for me to show some ink drawings in a decent space. We agreed to set up the show.

Calvin had been fighting with his girlfriend as usual. She wasn't around to help him bring his paintings to the space, so I dropped my work at the bar and walked about five blocks to his apartment to help bring in his work. When I got up to his third-floor walk-up and saw his work, it was dreadful. I regretted agreeing to the show. My work legitimized his work. I felt like a sellout. He had one piece in particular that I implored him not to bring. It was a mirror with knives and other sharp objects glued to it. It was about as pubescent angst as you could get. He knew his work was lousy. I reassured him anyway. I was his friend, after all.

We hauled his work over by hand. The bar was fairly empty; not many people were hanging around on a cold Tuesday night. I had bought cheap frames at Target, and taped wires to them to hang them. While I was putting my work up on the wall, a drunken young woman and her plain boyfriend examined my work. She did not see me come over, as she commented on it.

"Good wall, bad art," she said.

I was enraged but kept quiet. I stood there, quietly staring at her. She turned around, and I saw her embarrassment. A patron at the bar overheard it and came over. He had complimented my work earlier.

"What's your problem? This work is great, and this guy is putting it out there," he said to her.

"I didn't mean anything," she said.

"I don't care what you meant. Have you ever done anything? Have you? It's so easy, huh?"

Her boyfriend didn't intervene, and she stepped back toward the door and left. I didn't feel bad for her. I was still angry about the comment.

I was putting it out there, so I had to expect possible backlash— I just wasn't expecting a sucker punch. My defender spoke to me.

"Hey, buddy. Don't let that bitch ruin your night. The work looks great," he said to me.

"Thanks, man. Thanks, I really appreciate it."

"No worries, buddy. Let me buy you a beer."

He bought me a beer, and I drank it slowly.

Calvin hadn't seen much of what had happened. He was busy setting up his work on another wall. He hung the knife-mirror. I dreaded it falling and slashing some bargoer. We finished the set-up, and Calvin was arguing with the bar owner over the money for the show. The bar owner was only taking 30% of the work sold. He didn't realize most galleries take 50% or 60%. I pulled Calvin aside and told him to chill out. There was no guarantee we were selling anything anyway.

I walked him back to his apartment and jumped on the G train back to my apartment in Bed Stuy, where I laid in bed in the dark with my eyes open. "Good wall, bad art." I was shaken by it. I was also reliving the rejections I had received in the past few months. What was I doing? Was there anything else for me to do? Should I be a businessman? Should I be an old barkeep? I felt deflated. My mindset was deflated. Doubt was ever-present. I thought about the odds of an artist making a living off of his or her craft and felt despair. I knew I needed something aside from making pictures. I needed a vocation. I couldn't give up making art, but I could take a side step. I could make a living in a fashion more congruent with my proclivities. It would come together . . . or so I hoped.

It was a quiet week in the city. January was a slow month in general, after people blew all their money on New Year's festivities. I continued making my little ink drawings and kept training Brazilian Jiu-Jitsu. I stopped riding my bike. I could get away with it in December, but January was harsher. I began delving into the *New York Times* more deeply and found a growing distaste for it. It made sense. I was getting older, and when one gets older, they typically become more conservative. My discontent with the city began to brew.

Calvin sent out a big Facebook invite to all. We were supposed to have lots of people come through Brooklyn to see our work. I had zero expectations. My brother Jake and my brother Max, along with his boyfriend, were coming out for it. I was happy about that.

A huge blizzard hit the night of the show. I trekked through the winter wonderland, cursing under my breath as harsh winds blew ice into my eyes. I got in the door of the bar and saw people looking at my work. It felt good. For once, I felt like an artist. Calvin was chatting up the waitress he secretly pined for, since her depressive boyfriend hadn't shown up. Calvin's girlfriend was across the room mingling with people I didn't know. The girl from Tuesday night didn't show up. I wanted to see her and shit on her. Alas, she was not there for the opening of my show, "Good Wall, Bad Art."

But Calvin wasn't having a good time. He felt deflated. I think he must have realized his work was far from decent. He was fighting hard to form an identity, and reality has a hand to play in that. I should know. It takes a lot of mental fortitude to lift yourself up when the world crushes you down. It's a balancing act; we need to listen to what the world has to say, but we have to ignore some of it too.

I could not take "good wall, bad art" seriously. That girl was your basic drunken bitch. Her plain boyfriend was a beta male nothing. I knew my work was solid; I knew my intentions were true; I knew, in my gut, one day, things would start lining up for me. A man needs time and vision. Luck is helpful too.

The night was winding down. My brothers and the boyfriend left. I darted my eyes around the room to see if I could find a lady to have the after party with. There was only a lesbian couple by the bar and a few dysfunctional art chicks. I left and took the G train back to my apartment. I slept easy that night and felt good. I felt like I had done what I was supposed to do. I showed up, I did the work. I shook hands, smiled, and told a few anecdotes. I even ended up selling one of my drawings. I don't know who bought it. It was an ink drawing of a group of black altar boys singing, with "Sunday is here to stay" written below.

I still wonder who has that up in their Brooklyn apartment. It was a very good piece.

...

Calvin and I became closer. I quit my job in the basement of the Sunset Hotel in the Meatpacking District. My bar manager was fired wrongfully, so I immediately put in my two weeks. Nobody could say I wasn't loyal. Calvin had quit earlier from the same spot. He had taken a managerial position at a small spot in Gowanus, where he became my boss. It was a bakery and small restaurant, a mom and pop shop. The money was terrible, but it felt good to be seen as a human rather than a racehorse. We didn't have porters; it was all our work. We swept, mopped and even did windows. The crowd was local. Nobody came to Gowanus unless they were local. They had recently dredged the Gowanus canal. It was a toxic dump, but the growth in Brooklyn was unending. It extended into all the boroughs and neighborhoods. The growth was different block by block, but basically it went from slum to expensive slum. Once they put in a Whole Foods, the rest was history.

Calvin had broken up with his abusive girlfriend for the last and final time. He signed up for Tinder and began fucking every girl he swiped "yes" to. He was handsome, and this gave him the tool to thrust his arrow into those deer. He went out with one woman in particular, and she was kinky. She had him bind her in plastic wrap and then photograph her. Afterward or during, I can't recall, they had sex. She did this with many men on Tinder and was calling it "art." I never saw the photos, but they very well could have been art.

She was an Ivy League woman, eight years older than he, with a trust fund, beautiful apartment, and radical feminist views. She saw me as a novelty and tolerated my banter. She wasn't used to conservative types. I was really left of center (socially), but that basically made me Rush Limbaugh in her eyes. She had just directed her first film, and had a career lined up to direct more movies. My friend had lucked out. He was one hundred grand in the hole, with no real future, and a lack of direction. She wanted a baby, a man to order around, and for that man to have good breeding. It was a done deal.

...

During the early spring, Calvin's lady proposed to him in a non-heteronormative fashion, and he accepted. He would have accepted carrying the baby too, if that had been scientifically possible. He sent word to me it was happening, and I encouraged him, because I knew this was his shot. It was a mutually beneficial endeavor. I used to hang out with the two of them, but it had become less frequent over time. In fact, none of Calvin's friends were her cup of tea. Her friends were worthy of their time, but Calvin's were not. He accepted this, and life moved on, with her making all the calls.

Calvin sent me an invitation to the wedding. I knew his invitation list was limited, and I knew it meant my presence would be greatly valued. I thought long and hard about it but decided not to go. I was burning away my savings, and continuing my meager existence right by the projects. I didn't want to go to the Catskills, stay at a large manor, and perform pagan rituals. I had gone to a Halloween party they hosted, and it was mind-numbingly boring. They had bound us all up in plastic wrap (I don't know what their fascination with plastic wrap was), put masks on us, had us dance the waltz for three hours, and barely gave us anything to eat.

Calvin was very upset with me. Our mutual friend Molly had decided not to go as well but was spared the chastising. I think Calvin considered me his best friend. He let me have it, mainly through email. I apologized to him but did not have it in me to go. I had too much to do, and with limited resources. I also didn't want to go to an *Eyes Wide Shut* party where 99% of the ladies were lesbians.

So that was that. Calvin and I were no longer friends. I was sure his bride and baby mama was thrilled. She hadn't liked me much toward the end. She even thought I was a misogynist. I knew better; she had disdain for men. She was part of an all women's collective. Her first major film was about female innocence and the evils of man.

I, on the other hand, was part of no male collective. I even trained Mixed Martial Arts with women—if punching a woman in the face isn't equality, I don't know what is. I was just more conservative than she, and she wasn't having it. She and Calvin would live their life in a non-binary manner, well and good for them.

The End of New York

J ohn and I were set to move into our third and final apartment together. We needed another roommate for the tiny, first-floor, three-bedroom apartment. We scoured John's Facebook to find a solid candidate.

John and I were best friends and shared certain values. We desperately wanted for someone who could fit in with that. We wanted a roommate who was cool with us being in our underwear at all hours when in the apartment, and with the morning ritual of reading the *Times* while eating oatmeal and discussing the stories at hand. We resented New York City for the inflated rents. But we loved it in Brooklyn and didn't know where else to go. Two-bedroom apartments were impossible to obtain, earning what we were earning. It would be the end of New York City. We felt it in our bones. We knew our time was coming to an end.

John found one match for a third roommate, selecting him from a special place called the third level of Hell. This special place was reserved for strange, diminutive line cooks. Jose was, simply put, a creep. John and I had known him at the Stan Ward, but only barely. They had kept him in the back of the kitchen as the morning prep guy. He would slice, dice, and julienne. He stood about five feet five and was mostly skull. He wasn't the Vitruvian man. He was more like a Wolf Baselitz cartoon, but we had no choice. This was our final go at the Big, Harsh, Unloving Bitch of an Apple.

We had to move in February, and it was freezing. The Hasidim who owned our new flophouse had a small office on DeKalb, five blocks away. They had no love for me or my cohabitants. We did a walk through of the dingy, drafty, first-floor rental. It was sad. It was bleak. It was ill-kept. In retrospect, I wish we had spent money on a decent two bedroom, but we were pragmatists and cheapskates. We had nowhere else to go.

Within three days, John and I had our first of many sit-downs with Jose. Jose had moved in with nothing— a couple black garbage bags and a cart. He did have the essentials, though—a full collection of Dragonball Z comics, one towel (stained) and a computer (for porn, I assumed). John and I had brought all of the furniture, pots, pans, cups, and everything else you would need to live in a civilized manner. John had to lend Jose his air mattress, because apparently Jose didn't have one. He smelled funny, like undercooked onions. If I hadn't known he was the origin of the smell, I might have been hungry.

We found him on the couch, curled up fetally, watching cartoons on his phone. The 34-year-old man didn't do much. He would sit in the living room numbing his brain with the flashing colors and poor lip-synching. He would paddle his bare feet on the coffee table we had bought at IKEA. His feet alone were enough to make one want to puke. His lack of grooming translated to all areas; his feet were just one. Jose only drank Coke, forget water: I was like a shaken can of Coca-Cola ready to explode. We needed some changes. One of the first was getting his feet off the coffee table. John and I had nicknamed him Paddle Foot; Paddle Foot would have to be housebroken. So we asked him to have a talk one weekend when he wasn't working. I have always hated confrontation, but John was seemingly okay with it. John had to be around Paddle Foot more, because they shared a more congruent work schedule. I knew he would hammer this sad, diminutive man, and I wanted to make sure he wasn't too brutal. Paddle Foot crept into the living room. It was an interrogation, with John standing and me sitting on a chair. PF sat in the middle of the couch.

"So, I think you know why we're all here, don't ya?" John said.

"I don't know," Jose responded.

"You don't know. You can't tell that it's been uncomfortable?"

"Well, I don't know. I guess so," Jose responded sheepishly.

"Look, I think this move has been stressful for all of us, and we all just want to live comfortably. I think we can make this a solid situation," I threw in.

"Don't you like your space?" John asked.

"Yeah, sure. I do," Jose responded.

"Okay, see. We have that in common. The apartment is tiny. It is barely an apartment for three grown-ass men. We need to give each other a little more space," John said.

"Oh, yeah. That makes sense," Jose responded.

"We're not forcing you to stay in your room. We're not saying that.

I guess it would be nice for all of us, if we gave each other a little more space. That's all," I said.

"Yeah, guys. I hear ya. Is that it?" Jose asked.

"Sure. I guess that's it," John shrugged.

"All right, gentlemen, I need to head into the city. I am working closing shift at the bar tonight," I said and gathered my things to leave. I couldn't help but go from hating this man to feeling awful for him. He was both terribly frustrating and tragic.

John and I were approaching 30. As a younger man, I had thought I would get everything I ever dreamed up. As an older man, I realized life doesn't work that way. Life is a large wave, and you have to go with it. We were in a dark place, a sort of Twilight Zone, where reality was altered with a dark twist: "Dustin Asman, age 29, living at 709 Dekalb Avenue with two grown men, no job prospects and a dismal future of failure. He took the wrong turn down Life Avenue and entered . . . the Twilight Zone."

I worked to change my entitled mindset. Brazilian Jiu-Jitsu and MMA sparring helped me through the bleak parts. It didn't matter whether I was doing the smashing or getting my ass kicked. It was about the moment. In the moment, nothing else was real. Then I would go back home and deal with Paddle Foot. I would resume tending bar. I would get further rejections as an artist. These were the facts, but when I was in the fight, everything faded away. My body informed me that I was a fighter. My brain believed it, and my spirit would grow stronger.

I figured we had worked out the living situation. I was elated we were starting a new chapter, one that didn't include a double homicide or suicide. John had informed me PF was keeping his feet off the coffee table most of the time and went to his room as well. I felt like the heart-to-heart had paid off, but it turned out to have been short-lived.

John had met an Australian girl gallivanting in Spain the year prior. She was visiting the States and wanted to rendezvous with John on a night I was bartending in the city. I wished him luck and told him to use a rubber. John met up early with his Olivia Newton John lookalike.

They had a few happy hour drinks and decided to have one more at the apartment before copulation would ensue.

Unfortunately, PF was already home when John returned, as he usually was, back from work around five or six. He was in the living room doing what he did best, curled up with his phone blasting anime. What better sight if you wanted to get lucky? John introduced PF to Olivia, and the three of them sat for a bit and made small talk. I wish I had heard them, but I was slinging drinks.

PF didn't get the hint John wanted to make a move on this gorgeous Aussie. I presume he was a virgin and didn't understand male-female dynamics. He just sat there and added bits of dialogue. John was confused: why was PF hanging out with them? In his dumbfounded state, he couldn't think of how to get Jose to go to his room. Finally, Olivia noticed a guitar in John's room and asked if he could play her a song. They went into John's room, and he did more than play her a song. He told me the story in full the next morning.

"Yeah, man. He wouldn't leave. So we went to my room, and I played a song or two and then went at it."

"Damn, John. That's great. Did she sing for you?"

"She sure did. I got her to reach those high notes."

"I bet you did, you fucking maestro!"

"But then it was weird."

"What happened?"

"Well, she went out with a towel to clean up after our session. Dude, PF was on the couch the whole time. The whole time I was inside her he was out there on the couch with his phone."

"Are you fucking kidding me? I mean, seriously. That fucking pervert!" I snapped into anger.

"Yep. It was weird, like was this kid for real? Who does that?"

"Did you talk to him?"

"Nope."

"John, that's fucked up . . . a woman has a right to privacy. After she services you, she shouldn't have to take a walk of shame to get cleaned up in the bathroom. I mean what is this place? Iraq? What the fuck?"

"Easy man. It's fine. I just think it was weird is all."

"No, it's more than weird. It ain't fucking right. He ain't fucking right. I'm going to say something."

"Don't. You'll just embarrass him. Let's be reasonable and have a conversation with him but not get too specific. I hope he gets the point.

"Yeah, he better. That sick fuck better get the point!"

John and I planned another talk, covering topics like what two adults like to do when they're alone together, etiquette for getting it on, and why being a creepy pervert ruins a good time. It was frustrating to live with a man who was unaware of so many things. John and I were at least adult-like. Sure, we were short of the mark, but Paddle Foot was on a sub-level. He didn't seem to get basic things. He never cleaned or contributed to buying household items. He would leave pizza boxes on the floor (though we lived right by the dumpsters). He was a catastrophe of a man. I wanted to push forward, but he felt like a pair of concrete shoes. I had daydreams of outfitting him with an actual pair and throwing him off the Brooklyn Bridge.

Paddle Foot was on the couch. I was standing, and John was sitting in a chair, nice and calm. I felt my blood rise. Just looking at PF made my skin crawl. His smell made me angry. I was thinking that diminutive creep needed to pack a bag and crawl back to grandma's.

"So, obviously we need to discuss things again," John started off.

"Yep, sure," PF said, with big eyes.

"Yeah, I mean it's kind of annoying we have to do this, right?" I asked.

"Look, I think there are things that have been irking us. Pizza boxes left out. . . you know we have roaches. Most importantly, dude, we need respect when we have women over," John said.

"I mean seriously . . . a woman can't get cleaned up with privacy. Seriously?" I added.

PF was quiet. His eyes just widened. I felt partly sorry for him, but when I thought back to the woman, I felt angry again.

"Look, this is a small apartment. Are there things you want from us?"

"Nope," PF replied.

"Yeah, well, let's just have some common sense maybe. This will be a long year, if we all don't get with the program," I said.

"Okay, okay. Look, we'll all just try to be more open with our dialog and make this a comfortable place."

That was the end of the conversation. I would love to say that it changed everything, but in effect, it did nothing. It fell on wax-clogged ears. I was upset with my life. I worked hard, but I was running on sand, feeling it was almost impossible to gain traction. John was climbing in art production, and I was happy for him. I had always been in food service and had never seen a way out.

Another weekend was upon us. The weather was pleasant, and John and I planned to get our "swoll" on. We were up fairly early and dressed to work out. Paddle Foot would leave his door open without any shame. I hated this, because it felt like we were living with a patient from *One Flew Over the Cuckoo's Nest*. The boy just wasn't right. That day, after John and I went for our workout and returned home, PF hadn't moved an inch. I thought he must have a bedpan he pissed in.

John mocked him in a brotherly fashion, but PF just remained sunken in his air mattress. John and I got cleaned up and went for a bike ride to Red Hook. We hit up Fairway Market and had lunch overlooking the Statue of Liberty, which really brings home that "God Bless America" feeling. My grandparents first saw the Statue of Liberty as they sailed into New York Harbor, after leaving a displaced persons camp in Germany. To Holocaust survivors, this symbol was a truly awesome spectacle, signaling their arrival in a new land with new opportunity.

John and I returned to the apartment, and there he was, still glued to his phone with his door wide open. I felt my fury rising. Seeing him in this capacity was a reminder of where I was in my life. Maybe I was scared there wasn't a huge difference between PF and me, that I, too, should give up and lie in my bed, watching cartoons and pissing into a metal pan.

Later that night I had a lady coming over, and John was staying in

Greenpoint with a girlfriend. I would have had the apartment to myself, but PF wasn't going anywhere. I panicked. I liked this girl. She was basically a lesbian who had made an exception for me. I felt honored.

I stood in PF's doorframe and engaged him in conversation.

"Hey, buddy."

"Hey."

"So, I have a lady coming over at nine."

"That's cool."

"Yes, it sure is. So, here's the thing. I need you to not be around. I would like to have some privacy. I rarely have a girl over, so this would be nice for me."

"Do you want me to go out?"

"No, I didn't say that. I would just like for you to shut your door and let me have my space."

"Yeah. I can do that."

I was elated. It sounded like the little creeper understood, like he was doing his part. I felt proud of him and what felt like growth. I had visions of the three of us roomies running in a field of sunflowers, John throwing a frisbee and PF running to catch it in his mouth. All was well with the world, and Dustin was going get to have sex with a beautiful lesbian in private. God bless America.

I cooked up some pasta and drank a beer. PF had already left his door open, and this irritated me. I could see him in my periphery. He was on the floor like a slug, illuminated by his computer, also on the floor. It was almost cool, as though he had evolved to not need the use of his legs and could just slither around on his stomach wherever he wanted.

Closer to nine, I heard rustling from PF. I assumed he was getting dressed to go out, but I was nervous he was cutting it close. I didn't want my lesbian to have to interact with him. The rustling stopped, and his door was actually closed. I thought he would sneak out when I brought her to my room.

She texted me, so I knew she was about five minutes away. I sat waiting in my dark room, as the time approached. PF could leave right now, or he could leave after I brought her to my room. This was the agreement, as I understood it. But when she buzzed the door, I knew this was all too tempting for PF. He had to see her. He needed to screw my evening; this was his nature. Lions kill, salmon swim upstream, and koalas get stoned. PF needed to creep girls out and be gross in every conceivable way. I wanted to go into his room and throw a chokehold on him, just to put him to sleep for a little bit, but I didn't have any time to consider more precisely how to get PF to not do what he was meant to do.

I opened my bedroom door, only a few paces from the entrance. I didn't even have to turn around. I saw PF in his leather duster and beaten-to-hell Chucks. He had timed it masterfully. The lady now stood face-to-face with him, as I felt utter rage. All I had wanted was for him to be nowhere around when she was in my space. I should have known better. She obviously didn't care, but I was infuriated. I begrudgingly introduced her to him, led her to my room, and heard PF exit. I was already planning another sit-down, but I wanted it to end with an ax in his head.

I closed the door behind us, and we immediately disrobed. Her nipple rings reflected the ambient light, and she smelled of perfume and tobacco. I sat her on my bed. She started blowing me, as we listened to the rats outside my window. My room was right next to the dumpsters in the courtyard. It sounded like the rats were getting frisky too, reminding me of *The Island of Doctor Moreau*. We were all animals getting freaky in the shadows of the night. Human grunting and screeching provided the soundtrack for this particular pornographic episode. She felt good. She wasn't as comfortable with a penis and had almost broken it when we first hooked up last year. I took the lead, not wanting any mishaps.

It was about midnight; we chatted about New York City and Brooklyn and how it had all changed. I told her that the Hasidim were raising our rent to an amount we deemed cruel. She mentioned that she was living with her sister and still had time to figure out her life. I was a bit older than she. Rents were just going to escalate, jobs wouldn't pay more, and nobody would give me a shot to monetize my art. Yes, it appeared that this was the end of New York.

I spooned with my lesbian lover for a little bit longer. The rats were calming down, I imagined them spooning too. Our little private island was sinking below the crashing waves of a cruel ocean. I wouldn't be able to save myself. I would have to surrender to time.

John and I agreed to minimize our contact with PF. The situation wasn't good for anybody. Nothing ever came out of our little talks. PF would not change, or could not change, but that was of no consequence. We accepted it and detached ourselves.

It was becoming harder to grind out our days in the city. We hated every group, only now our hate was not so much about New York, our hate was a fire that had turned on us, and we were the ones burning. This was a defeatist hate. If we stayed in the city, we would be the crispy critters being scraped up off the charred concrete.

I had seen frequent evidence of this during my time in NYC. The women—and I had dated a few—were convinced they had the same amount of time to figure things out as men. As a result, a man would drag them along until they hit forty, when their fertility was in a state of decay. These women would be without a family, working jobs that demanded all their time. The only solace they would find then was playing mommy for cats. Men would also play around until their forties and deplete any chance of their finding a good woman. Most of these men, like me, lived with roommates and worked shit jobs. I could see the absence of a future. New York City was a party, and you didn't want to be the last one to leave.

...

John and I were planning our final nights of partying in Brooklyn. It was to be an epic celebration and exit. John's older brother Joe was coming into town to load up a U-Haul with all of John's belongings. It was going to be a drunken booze fest, and I had never had the stamina for that sort of thing. I had stopped working only a few days prior and also had to box my belongings. My dad and brother were driving in to take me back to Massachusetts.

I had never met John's brother before. I saw his parents every time they came to the city, as though they were my in-laws. Joe and I got on right away. He was a family man with a wife and kid and a regular nine-to-five job. He was very conservative, the opposite of John but shared the same gregariousness. The moment Joe arrived to party for our three-day bender, we were family. Paddle Foot knew at this point not to ingratiate himself in the collective. It was done. It had been a tough year, and that fucker had made it even tougher. I was elated that our escape from New York was here. John was so excited to leave it that he was running all the way to Australia. I didn't completely understand the logic of it, but John was an adventurer. He wouldn't be content in Chicago or any other city. He wanted out, for a while anyway.

John and I didn't dress like the city people at first. It wasn't bad, but we stuck out. If you wanted to be taken seriously and be included, you needed to play ball. It wasn't necessary to spend a lot of money. You could do all your shopping at Goodwill, but you needed to look like you gave a shit. Even the kids who dressed like they didn't give a shit were purposeful about it.

So, John and I had grown fashionable over our time in New York. There were rules. If you were out and about, you needed to heed them. Joe broke all of them. He was a dad from Chicago. John and I dressed Joe to be ready for the evening. We gave him an army coat, slim-fitted slacks and beaten-up boots. Joe commented that he looked like a Travis Bickle, and we said, "Yes, that's the point."

We took Joe to a little spot in Greenpoint first. This was mainly for us. John and I thought the girls of Greenpoint were the prettiest. Many of them had decent jobs and put themselves together well. And they were athletic. The girls of Williamsburg seemed to abuse alcohol more, and their bodies showed it. It was freezing in February, which was to be expected. John picked up a round of IPAs for us. It slowed my drinking down, because I never could stomach IPA. A table behind us was having a retirement party. Most of the crowd was older. They were singing Polish folk songs, remnants from when Greenpoint was a Polish neighborhood.

At the bar, as expected, were a couple of girls who were gorgeous. We had no intention of speaking to them, only to admire them from afar.

We left the bar to get dinner and found a Thai restaurant three blocks away. Joe had never had Thai. I was always shocked when someone hadn't tried some kind of ethnic cuisine. I didn't mean to make a value judgment about it; I realized that I had worked in the food and beverage industry since I was seventeen. We ordered some curry dishes and noodles. Obviously, we were getting Americanized Thai food, not the kind that Bourdain ate on his show. It would suffice.

The three of us started talking politics loudly at the table. Joe and I were discussing the positive things in our minds about Trump—not to say we had voted for the guy. The liberal diners at the Thai restaurant looked over at us in disgust, but we didn't care. John enjoyed confrontation; Joe did as well, and I didn't mind a healthy debate. Nobody would have approached us anyway. If they had, I doubt they'd have had any objective facts to present, or ground game.

The three of us split from the restaurant and jumped on the G train south to Bed-Stuy. We figured it would be good to show Joe the difference between those two distinct districts of Brooklyn. We took him to our favorite spot, Pedro's, a small bar with a backyard. The yard was closed because it was 30 degrees out. We ordered tacos and tequila. After our second round, John transformed into "drunk John." He started dancing. Three girls joined him, so I jumped in to even out the ratio. The bartender was admiring John . She was pretty—black, with tattoos and a nose ring. I was jealous that John was getting her attention. Joe was talking sports with a guy at the bar. They were discussing the Bears. The bartender poured us three shots of whiskey, and I was feeling groovy. The brown juice was warming me, and I felt like Burt Reynolds on a shag carpet. It was getting late. John exchanged numbers with the bartender and assumed he would be sleeping with her that nigh but ended up falling asleep and getting her text message the next morning.

We got back to the apartment. Paddle Foot's door was closed. We knew we had to be quiet. We didn't want to wake the beast and have him infringe on our fun. This three-day bender was to be our time.

We had a few bottles of low-end alcohol on a bureau, so we poured out three vodkas and sucked them back. Joe and John both had rose-colored cheeks. We started laughing, and PF's door creaked open. He slithered out but didn't say anything. I nodded to him and turned away. It was uncomfortable, and I started looking for the packing tape. Our apartment was a chaotic packed maze of brown boxes. PF walked to the fridge and pulled out a two-liter of Coke and drank the last of what was left in the bottle. He set the empty bottle on the floor and slithered back to his room. He left his door open and went to lay down on his bed with the lights out. John and I looked at each other without saying anything. It was only a couple more days until we were free of him.

We awoke the next morning with only mild hangovers, so we threw on our clothes from the night prior and went out for breakfast. We played a game with Joe: "Guess Who Comes from Money." John and I liked pointing out people's backstories. It was fun to guess at their socio-economic backgrounds and professions. After several years of living in the city, I felt like we were pretty good at this. It was positively tribal how people dressed and carried themselves, all of us presenting ourselves according to our specific groupings. John and I pointed out to Joe how the tribes interacted. He was in awe of the machinery of the city. We were used to it. As a bartender, I constantly sized people up. Were they going to be trouble? Could I sell them the more expensive whiskey? Should I give them a free drink in hopes of obtaining a regular? John had also had this kind of experience. I know I was likewise sized up.

The three of us went into Manhattan later that night. We were visiting our friend Jim who worked at Acme. Acme catered to the upper class of New York City. It wasn't exactly ungodly expensive, but it wasn't a place to go unless you were doing well. We were getting hooked up with some drinks, so we got to enjoy this side of the city. John and I had never done this in all the time we had lived in the city. Only at the end were we making an effort to go to this kind of spot. As expected, the women in the establishment were gorgeous. The staff was attractive as well. New York wasn't as shallow as Miami or LA, but let's not fool ourselves—looks are a commodity in the city.

We decided to take a walk over to Washington Square Park. The walk from Acme wasn't far, and it wasn't as cold as the night prior. We had parkas on, as well as hats, gloves, and boots. I always walked around with a backpack so I could carry my sketchbook and supplies. It was midweek and late, and not too many people enjoyed walking around in shitty weather. We took Joe to the giant arch in Washington Square Park. It was lit from below and filled me with a sense of pride. It was a reminder for me of all I had learned and experienced, thanks to the city.

I saw a man and a woman in front of the arch. He dropped to his knee, and we were witnessing a proposal. I looked more carefully at the woman's face to realize I knew her well. We had gone to college together in Miami. I hid behind a bush and watched from there. I didn't want to ruin the moment by being seen. Joe and John didn't know what was going on. They were confused, but I explained it after we were about 50 feet away. It had been a truly beautiful moment. I felt sad but happy at the same time. I was happy for them but couldn't help but reflect on myself. I felt like I wanted these things too, like it was time. That was an opportune moment to see right before I was to leave the city. I was changing; the city was changing, and I couldn't go back.

We took Joe over to the Stan Ward Hotel. John and I still knew some of the staff, so we were greeted like celebrities. We were given three old fashioneds and stood up near the front grill. It felt different being on the other side of the bar. I had changed a lot since first moving to the city. I had been a young, naive busboy. I grew into an older, cynical barman. The only thing that didn't seem to change was that I was an artist. I knew that in my gut. I realized it was constant and I needed to rework my life to accommodate it.

The three of us went over to Rocka Rolla. Our old hotel co-worker Eugene was tending bar. Eugene had made a small fortune cracking Miller High Lifes and pouring pickle backs. John had some cousins, work friends, and a quasi-girlfriend meet us there. He was drunk but carrying it well.

I noticed the response he was getting from the women in the bar. I had never seen John get that much attention. It was as though his complete lack of attachment was an aphrodisiac. His quasi-girlfriend Lauren was visibly upset. John didn't notice, he was too inebriated. He was also intoxicated by the female attention. I pulled him aside.

"Hey, what are you doing?" I asked.

"What do you mean?" he responded.

"You know what I fucking mean."

"I don't get what you are saying."

"You are talking to all these girls and not to Lauren. She's a good girl, and she loves you. You are going to give her some attention. You may never see her again. This is it. Be a good guy. Buy her a drink and then go back to her apartment in Greenpoint."

"You're right. Okay. Is she pissed?"

"Yes, but you can fix that."

John did as I said. He bought her a drink and started talking to her. I could see her mood change quickly. He left with her, but Joe and I stuck around for a little longer before we left for the G train, only three stops away from the apartment.

. Joe lit a joint for us, and we smoked it in the living room. Paddle Foot made an entrance and sat on a stool looking at us. We all sat there quietly, like a group mediation on finality. I got into bed and listened to the radiator hiss. I stared up at the ceiling and felt my brain swirl. My thoughts went from work, to women, to art, and to fighting. Somewhere in the waves of memories, I fell asleep.

I awoke to our final day. John brought bagels on his way back from Lauren's. Paddle Foot was at work. The three of us sat around the apartment. We wouldn't go out until the evening, when we planned to have a big finale. We were going to bring Joe to the Mecca of hipsterdom: Union Pool, but we needed food before drinking to our limit.

We went over to our favorite Mexican spot on Skillman, in the middle of a Hasidic neighborhood. The place was authentic. Mexicans ate there. They would drink several Coronas apiece, and some of the guys would spit on the floor. It was like being in Puebla. John ordered a chicken burrito, Joe ordered a beef burrito, and I ordered a vegetable burrito. We ordered up some beers as well, as we waited for our burritos to arrive. When we first started hitting up this burrito spot, almost no whites ever showed up. Now, the restaurant was filled by at least a third of them. The demographics were changing every day. It wasn't about race; it was about class. The landowners could rake it in when mommy and daddy were paying the tab. The suburbs supported the city. Plenty of Chinese moms and dads were a part of this rent bubble too.

The burritos arrived, and I devoured mine. We didn't speak much during the meal. John had always been a slower eater than me, but he seemed to be eating even more slowly than usual. Joe raved about the food. If Mexicans ate here, it must have been good. I made sure to coat the burrito in homemade chipotle salsa. The smokiness of the salsa added the finishing touch to this perfect burrito. That burrito chased with cheap Mexican beer was a godly marriage.

John couldn't finish his burrito and decided to leave it. We threw down cash for the bill and braved the cold winter night. We walked down Nostrand Avenue and cut down DeKalb. John made a run for the bathroom as soon as we got home. Joe and I heard him hurl. It was unpleasant for him and unpleasant to hear. You could hear the toilet water splash around with the chunks of beans, chicken, and tortilla. Then we heard a spray, which I assumed was the beer. John held his stomach as he came into the living room. He told us he thought the burrito was bad. I took a bucket from the kitchen and brought it to his room. We decided not to go to Union Pool. And that was it. This was the finale, this was our final stand in New York City. We all turned in and called it a night.

John and Joe woke up early, and I heard them moving boxes. I threw on my clothes and put my boots on. They had propped our front door open with a box. The building door was held open by a copy of *Satanic Verses* wedged into the corner. We started filling their U-Haul with some furniture, his boxes, guitars, and a keyboard. Paddle Foot stayed in his room with the door closed. We went in and out of the void that had become our apartment. The gravity of the moment began to sink in. My best friend and I were splitting. I had never thought I would be this close to John when I first met him at the bistro in SoHo. We had been through the brunt of our twenties together, and most of my memories included him. He wasn't actually my family, but it felt similar to when I had left for college, a hollowness I couldn't name.

I picked up the last box and handed it off to John. We looked at each other as the U-Haul was packed up. This was it. There was nothing more to say. Our twenties were almost over, and it was the end of New York. Joe came up to me and hugged me. Paddle Foot came outside, and I was irritated that he was there. I had wanted a perfect moment, and it didn't involve him. John shook PF's hand.

Joe started the U-Haul. John stood by the passenger door. PF was on the sidewalk staring at us.

"So, this is it," John said.

"Yep, sure is," I said.

"It's crazy, man."

"I know."

"I don't like it."

"Me neither."

"Let me know when you get to Chicago."

"I will."

"You better write me when you get to Australia."

"You know I will."

"Get one of those Australian beauties to make sweet music with your didgeridoo."

"I hope I can."

"Good."

I hugged John and felt numbness, a quiet lull in mourning. I watched as they took off down Dekalb. Paddle Foot went back into the empty apartment. I couldn't take going right back inside, so I walked down the street and grabbed a coffee at a cafe. I watched the people at the various tables in conversations with their friends. I reflected on our friendship and remembered our fights. We had had numerous flights, but we always were able to go forward. We pushed each other to read more, work out more, live more, and be more. My New York adventure wouldn't have been the same without him.

I'd had a group of friends I had grown up with who had faded away. I never thought I'd have another friendship like those childhood friendships. We had experienced so many things together that each of us was inextricable from the other. I comforted myself with the fact that we had email and phones. It wouldn't be like the old days, and that was fine; he would always be my family.

A week later, my brother and father drove into Brooklyn to take me back to Massachusetts. It felt like I was down for a ten count; I had taken one too many punches to the head, and I was seeing stars. God was referee, and the spectators were the city people. I looked over to the far side of the ring and saw old managers. I looked over to the other side and saw past girlfriends. I looked up toward the stadium lights and saw countless faces of bar patrons. I got to my knee. It wasn't over. This was a new round, and I was ready to swing. It may have been the end of New York, but it was also the start of something new.

Life on the Wharf

S alem, Massachusetts was in stark contrast to New York. It felt like I had been taken out of the adult pool and placed in the kiddy pool. As bitter as I was about NYC and about life, I wasn't ready for the change. My high school friends who had stuck around Salem barely talked to me. The girls in town were mostly nothing to behold. The bars . . . oh hell, the bars were sorry places to drink. I had no job lined up, and the weather was harsh.

My brother was the only consolation. He lived in the second bedroom of my apartment, and he was my only friend. The culture shock was almost the same as being bushwhacked in Bushwick. Obviously, I didn't have to worry about my safety. The town was decently safe.

My parents were in the next town, and I saw them a bit at the beginning, but less as time went on. I popped into every bar in the area. Bartending was all I knew to make money, and I was going to need it.

No bars were hiring. The town came to life in the spring, but this was the end of winter. It was dead. I felt dead.

I got a callback to a restaurant on the Wharf, a seafood spot that sat at the edge of the water. When I met with the GM and bar manager, I did my best to not let on how defeated I was. I felt empty but knew how to contort my face into a smile to feign confidence. If there was one thing I had learned from NYC, it was that.

John was in Australia working construction. He was my best friend, now he was on the other side of the world. He felt as I did. We had spent so much time there struggling to achieve. We achieved—but not the things we had seen for ourselves as young men.

The interview went well. They gave me an application, which was demoralizing. I was used to giving employers my resume. I hadn't had to fill out an application since I was 19. Now, as a 30-year-old man, I had to fill out the packet. It was enough to make me want to run away to Australia too.

They gave me five training shifts. It was excessive, but we weren't in the city anymore. I couldn't hold on to the same bullshit anymore; I needed to move forward. I wasn't in my twenties anymore. I wasn't in New York City anymore either, and I sure wasn't going back.

People from Massachusetts are referred to as Massholes. This is a clever name, and I have found it to be accurate. It was rough when I moved there from the West Coast as a six-year-old. I went up to a group of kids and asked them if I could play with them. They responded, "No, fag." I did an about-face and cried. This was, in essence, the heart of Massachusetts. It's not very friendly, so you just have to be tougher. I never thought I would be going back when I left for Miami all those years ago.

As an artist who worked in the service industry, I knew a lot of gays. I knew gays of all sizes, colors and creeds. But the gays of Massachusetts were a new thing altogether. Miami gays were thrilled to be gay. We had some sassy NYC gays, but they were far from aggressive. Mass gays were aggressive. I don't mean sexually charged or forward; I mean physically aggressive. Or at least they wanted to give that impression. It was strange to encounter it but if I thought back to my own memories, it made sense. I had heard the word "faggot" all the time growing up. To be fair, I don't think too many people ever thought of gay people when using it. I am not saying the word was good, but it was kind of like the word "ass." There are two separate meanings for the word "ass." I feel like "faggot," back in the nineties anyway, was a different word.

One of my superiors at the seafood restaurant was a gay man. He was only five years older than I and quite sassy. One day he came in with scraped-up knuckles. I asked him how he had hurt his hand.

"You should see the other guy," he said.

This took me aback. I had never experienced gays fighting like this in NYC or Miami. It was weird to hear those words with a lisp. The Massachusetts gays were a warrior lot. They had more in common with Alexander the Great than Liberace.

I was fairly straight-edge in my teens and early twenties, but life makes one turn to the bottle. There's a reason old people have red wine every night with dinner, and it ain't for their heart. This particular bar was strange. Nobody cared about inventory. The owner was a millionaire, and the money kept pouring in during season. We were able to drink whatever we wanted. The waitresses would descend on the bar at closing like locusts. They would pull bottles of white and suck down the wine. I didn't go for white wine myself; I drank all things brown. I had learned the joys of Dewar's from my father. I began hitting it every shift. Everyone I worked with had some kind of substance abuse issue. If you didn't, you were the abnormal one. I would try to abstain on my nights off, except for the occasional beer.

I was lonely at the beginning. My whole life had been obliterated. Now I was just a man existing. I had no friends, woman, or career I liked. I felt like a zero. This, obviously, colored the way I saw Salem. It may not have been fair, but I was hurting.

Within the first week of working, I had met all the regulars. They had a few things in common: they were over 40, drank partly for free (as was the policy of the establishment), and were alcoholics. Most of them were nice enough. I enjoyed them, but they would sit for hours at a time. Most of them drank six or seven drinks in a few hours. The city was so big that regulars would pop into different bars. They spread their drinking out. It saddened me to see these drunks on a daily basis. It was bleak and turned me off to the idea of opening up a bar for myself. I didn't want to be around that. Caffeine is a far more positive drug, and I saw myself running a cafe more than a bar.

One night, I was finishing my shift and had done all the cleaning. I threw back a Dewar's and felt it relieve the tension in my shoulders. I decided I would go home and sketch. I was ready; it was a Tuesday, and I had to be back the next day to do the whole thing all over again. A few of the waitresses had taken a liking to me and invited me to the late-night bar across the street. I wasn't interested but knew I needed to go. It would offend them if I refused the invitation. I could just sit for one beer and leave.

The place was filled with what looked like extras from *The Town*. It felt like a high school party that had gone on 15 years too long. The girls grabbed a table, and I remained standing. I ordered a bottle of Budweiser. A few of the girls ordered Jello shots, the specialty of the house.

I noticed the bartender immediately. She was attractive, in a rave-girl sort of way. We had been in middle school together, but I hadn't seen her since then until this moment. She wouldn't let on that we knew each other. I didn't mind. There were many people I knew from my youth around town, and many times we would pretend not to know one another. I didn't want to explain my present life and cared even less to know about theirs. My sixth-grade girlfriend came up to me to say hello. I recalled that we had broken up because she used to punch me in the arm. She was sweet but unrecognizable as the girl she once was. I felt like I had to squint when looking at a lot of these old faces. Some had partied their 20's away and were paying the consequences. She offered to buy me a Jello shot, but I declined. The girls were chugging their beers and talking about the shift we had all just worked.

We heard a scuffle on the other end of the bar. I couldn't make out who was fighting. I saw a tall man with a buzz cut making the most commotion. One of the girls let me know he was the brother of the bar owner. Some people stood between the guy and two other men. It looked like it was a standoff, and it would blow over. I knew it was normal; this was Massachusetts. In Massachusetts, after a couple of drinks, fights ensued. It had been that way with the colonial fishermen, and it had carried over to the present. I had left at 18 and come back 12 years later. The place hadn't changed a bit.

The girls got up to see what was going on. The bartender rang a bell to indicate last call and told everybody to "Get the fuck out of here. The bar is closed!" Everyone started piling out of the bar. Half the bar exited to one side, and my group exited toward the harbor side. I formed a semicircle with the waitresses who all pulled cigarettes out and started puffing.

We heard metal banging and shouting from the other entrance. I knew there would be more fighting. This time, it would be a full-blown pugilistic beat-down. I ran to the other side of the building, where a circle had formed around two young men. The smaller guy had the bigger one by his jacket. He was landing punches to the top of his head. The punches were short and rapid. The sound of bones colliding punctuated the screams of the crowd. I thought it might end up being a fight to the death. I threw myself between them and pushed them apart. I hated seeing people fight—without a ring and a ref. I heard my Jewish father in my head, telling me I was a schmuck for jumping in. He might have been right.

The bigger guy rolled back over a car. His eyes darted in opposite directions. We heard a police siren in the distance. Everybody was yelling and started to scramble. It was a haze of moving bodies. I looked around me to see if anybody was going to jump me, but nobody was paying me any mind. Everybody started running off in different directions. The commotion died down. I focused on the sirens blaring in the distance and breathed the cold air.

I leaned up against a light post and saw my sixth-grade girlfriend approach. She had a lit cigarette and was puffing away. She was joyous.

"Life on the wharf! Life on the wharf!" she said and chuckled.

"Yes, it sure is," I said.

"Aren't you glad you're back?"

"Sure . . . sure, I am," I said. She gave me a kiss on the cheek, and I walked across the grass field next to the harbor. The old sailboat that sat in the water was hidden in shadow. It was a large, menacing monolith that swayed ever so slightly. At the sidewalk, I hung a right to my apartment. I cleaned up and got into bed. No rats, thugs or ambulances. White noise reverberated in my ears. I knew tomorrow was another day, and I would have to live it as it was, my life on the wharf.

Another night was winding down at my seafood bar and restaurant on the harbor. I wasn't closing, and I was grateful. Chelsea was going to close. I got out and saw the activity on the streets. It was the season Salem got mobbed with tourists. It was a Saturday night, but it didn't excite me.

There were perks to my move from New York City to Salem. One was money. I was loaded. I owned my condo, and my cost of living had dropped drastically. My brother occupied the other room, and while I didn't profit off of him, it helped. I also made lots of cash behind the bar.

I had nowhere to spend it. I was at that weird age—for living in a small town. 30 is young in New York; 30 in Salem is old. All the girls of marrying age in Salem were married. In NYC, they were single. All of the young girls were cute but fairly dumb. The older women, if divorced, were sad. So, I was sad as well. I was used to anonymity when I went out. I enjoyed playing the part of the stranger. Everyone knew me in Salem. I had grown up in the area, and I bartended at a popular spot. There was no mystery. It was like watching a television show from your youth that you knew all too well.

Leaving my bar still dressed in my work clothes, I heard my name being called. I turned around and saw David. David was a fuck-up. At least, that's what I had heard. I hadn't seen him in many years. I knew he had been in and out of rehab. I remembered him from my high school art class as the jock. He was a mess then, too, but not an unpleasant guy. We couldn't have been more opposite. I was an artist, anti-social, and a prude. Simply put, I was a nerd. David played multiple sports, banged cheerleaders, drank, partied, and got into trouble. Simply put, he was popular. He was nice to me and thought my artwork was good.

He came up to me. It may have been 12 years later, but he looked about the same, even with the habitual drug use.

"Hey, Dustin! What's up, man? I heard you were back in town."

"Yeah, man. I moved back."

"Oh, that's great. What are you up to?" David asked, his eyes a bit glazed over.

"I'm not sure. I just got out of work. . ."

Two girls were passing us on the street. They looked as though they were around twenty-two or so. They were pretty, but I had zero interest in getting to know them. David engaged them, and they responded.

"Hey, ladies. Where are you going?" David asked.

"Probably home, why?" one of the girls responded.

"Lame! What are you girls, nerds?" David chuckled.

"No!" the other one answered.

"We're going to Churchill's!" David commanded.

We climbed into their Honda, parked only a few feet away. There was a baby seat we shifted to the middle. I couldn't imagine these girls were moms yet, but I couldn't be certain. We drove four blocks up and over, and the ladies parked right across the street from the establishment.

Churchill's was packed. There was a crowd outside, mainly young people in their early twenties. They said they would meet us inside, but they were going to get some rolling papers across the street first.

I was open to being in the moment. I had been very bored in town. NYC was too hard to compare to for a good time. I likened it to fucking a ten with perfect tits. The ten is gorgeous. The ten will take you for the ride of your life, but you have to pay for it. The ten can get whomever she wants, and there's always another dope ready to bleed for her. Salem was like fucking a six. A six is cute enough, but the body is homely. The sex is fine, but when compared to the ten that got away, it hurts. The six is not all that exciting, but there is security in the six not leaving you. I wanted to be open to reimagining the six as a ten. After a moment, I also wanted to be open to being less misogynistic. I wanted to believe there was hope for both of those things.

David had me follow him to the front of the line. Most of the kids standing in line looked like townies. The girls were all so regular, but attractive. The men looked like Matt Damon's crew in *Good Will Hunting*. I had always felt attractive in New York. I would get eyes on a daily basis. I hadn't realized what that did for my self-esteem. None of these girls were paying me any mind. I was thirty, which might well have been retirement age to these youngsters. David had us flash our wrists to the bouncer, pretending we had been in the club previously. We got right in without waiting in the line. David had me pay the cover charge at the podium and told me he would buy the drinks. He flirted with the bartender as he got us two Svedka Red Bulls. This was a drink that made us NYC bartenders cringe just to hear ordered.

David pulled us onto the dance floor with a gaggle of basic bitches. I hung back; David worked them. His charm was operative for a moment. Then two of their boyfriends came over and gave David the brush-off. We went back to the bar, and he got us another round.

David and I stood by the wall and caught up. He talked a little about his substance abuse, then brought up my art. He talked about how he thought it was great, but I needed to push it in a different direction. I considered what he said and couldn't deny it was worth a shot. He told me that he had admired my skill set, even back in high school.

David got happier the more he drank. I was getting a little drunk at this point but felt blue. I was already wallowing in self-pity, and the alcohol brought me down lower. I felt a regression. Being in town had kicked me back ten years or so. It felt like a strange nonlinear dream. David went to engage a pair of girls, and I stayed behind. I wanted to go home and go over my life choices. The DJ played the song "Closing Time," and the corniness of it all made me cringe. A bouncer called out that it was over; the night was coming to a close. They put the lights up, and we were told to settle our tabs. David went to close out his tab but couldn't. His card was declined. It was up to me. I was annoyed that I had to pay the tab; I had left New York but forgotten that I could still get hustled. David was obviously a fuck-up, as I would soon see in closer detail.

We left the bar, only just then realizing that the girls who dropped us off had never shown up. They were smarter than I had thought. Girls in heels were stumbling around outside, and meatheads were preventing them from busting their butts on the cobblestones. David eyed one only a few paces away. She was plain but had her breasts bunched up as though they were honey baked hams. David went over, but she wasn't giving in to his charm. I went over to try to get David to leave them be. A guy in a button-down shirt came over. It was obvious he was her boyfriend, a meathead with steroidal biceps bulging out of his tacky dress shirt, buttoned up as though he were a member of the Bee Gees.

"Hey, is there a problem here?" he asked confidently.

"No, is there a problem?" David responded.

"All right, so I guess you'll be on your way then," the boyfriend retorted.

"Why don't you lose one more button, faggot?" David blurted out.

"Okay, that's enough, David," I said.

"Seriously, fucker?" The boyfriend's blood was up.

David wanted to fight. I had heard about David a little bit, and it was coming back to me. He had been in and out of court for fighting and substance abuse. I had forgotten til now that he had been stabbed once. I realized I was dealing with a deeply conflicted man. I had been training martial arts for years but never one to street fight.

I was one to break up fights. I had never understood the idea of squaring off with a stranger. Defending yourself was one thing, but starting shit was something else. David was acting out, and I wanted to protect him. I was confident that he could handle himself with this meathead, but I didn't want him getting arrested. The last thing he needed was more time in court. I stood between them, and other guys came over to hold the boyfriend back.

"Please, David. Stop it. You don't need to do this!" I was pushing him back, and he kept moving forward.

"You think I'm scared of that faggot?" David asked rhetorically.

"Let's go, bitch!" the boyfriend said.

"That's enough. Nobody is fighting," I said to the boyfriend.

"You want to fight?" the boyfriend asked me.

"Nobody is fighting," I said, and smiled.

I would defend myself if need be. This young man had no idea I sparred in striking and grappled three to four times a week. Not to say he couldn't get some shots in, but I wasn't a stranger to getting punched. I just did not want to go through litigation. My goal was to focus on my art, save money, and try to figure out the next step of my life. Court would have been a setback, even though part of me welcomed a fight, because I, too, was miserable. I was friendless, stunted, rudderless, and in need of a high. But I would not cave in to my reptile brain. I exercised my prefrontal lobe by dragging David down the street.

We were only a block away, when I heard someone call out. Brandon was with a group of friends. A few mildly attractive girls and a few bland men were following him. Brandon was the son of our art teacher. He had a plain, long, face with duck lips and a cowlick. He was dressed in an ill-fitting suit and was noticeably the same character I had known 12 years prior. It was an impromptu reunion. As we were walking down the same road, Brandon invited us to come to his house, which was a five-minute drive away. David and I packed into the back seat, and Brandon drove us to his house. During the ride, David became noticeably aggressive.

"You think you're a hotshot now?" David asked Brandon.

"What's your problem, kid? Too much drinking?" Brandon retorted.

"Why don't you get a suit that fits. . . Where'd you get that shit, Men's Warehouse?"

"Okay, David. Let's take 'er easy," I said to David.

"What do you wear to work, eh, a pair of overalls?" Brandon turned over his shoulder at a red light.

"Yeah, beats a suit like that," David said.

Brandon turned up the music, as we continued on down the street and into his parking spot. He had bought this house around the time I had bought my condo. Salem was still affordable for young people to buy into then but had been steadily climbing. Boston was prohibitively expensive, and Salem was becoming the equivalent of a Brooklyn hub.

We entered the house that looked like a 30-year-old with no taste lived there. Shitty posters were up on the walls, lacquered furniture from dead grandparents littered the rooms, and bottles of alcohol were hanging out like wallflowers. We continued down to the basement, which was carpeted and had couches. We were handed two Heinekens, and I noticed two girls chatting across from us. David engaged me as I hunkered down in a La-Z-Boy. He was at the end of the couch closest to me.

"That faggot thinks he's so cool," he said.

"Yeah, I don't know. I haven't seen him in 12 years," I said.

"He was always a tool. His house sucks, too."

"Well, it's a big deal to be able to buy property now, what with student debt and the housing market."

"Seriously, you see that ugly suit? Loser thinks he's James Bond."

"Okay, David."

David turned his attention to the girl across from us. She was by herself at the moment. He started engaging her, but she wasn't having it, so he was becoming more agitated and aggressive.

"Oh, so you're too good for us?" David asked the girl.

"No, you think that. How high are you going to roll your pant legs?" she asked.

"This is normal. This is how people dress."

"Why are you being a dick?"

"I'm not being a dick. You just think you're better then everyone, and the fact is, I'm hotter than you!" David declared.

I couldn't let this continue. I got up off my recliner and moved over to them.

"David, stop it. We're guests here," I said.

"She is the one being ridiculous," David said.

"David. . ."

"Listen to your friend," she said.

"She's not even hot. How can a girl put that on when she ain't even hot?"

"David, that's enough. She is very attractive. Don't be a dick."

"Thanks," the girl said.

Brandon approached us to tell us we needed to leave. I immediately apologized and just wanted the night to be over. I was at a low. My life used to be exciting, and I had hung out with the best of the best. Now, I was a townie. Transformation was taking place; my previous identity was dulling to gray. This place was too small for me and running into the faces of Christmas past was truly dreadful.

"David, you got to go," Brandon commanded.

"Come on, David. Let's go," I said.

"I'm not going anywhere," David exclaimed.

Brandon grabbed David by the arm and started to drag him, but he refused to budge. I told Brandon to let him go and coaxed David to calm down. We walked upstairs together. Two muscle-bound men were upstairs hanging out. David knew them a little, and they seemed to have a mutual respect. Brandon was up in the kitchen with us. I apologized to him again and told him I would get David back home. David was docile for a moment.

"Jesus, kid. You're a mess. Get it together," Brandon said to David.

"Your house looks like a crack den," he replied.

I was angry, feeling like the only adult in the room. I knew there was no stopping the vitriol. I could only help clean up the mess laid out before me. Brandon shoved David back. Then David shoved Brandon. They were going to maul each other. I went to step in the middle, but the muscle-bound men held David back. I went to collect him from the men restraining him and get him out of the house. Brandon threw a punch, as he was held in place. It was a lousy punch and merely slid off David's cheek. The two men helped me get him outside, and I apologized yet again to them. They assured me it was all good.

I pushed David along the desolate, tree-lined street, toward the center of town. It was quiet, and no cars were driving by. I couldn't have guessed I'd be taking a midnight stroll with a junkie.

"David, you need to stop doing that," I said, breaking the silence.

"Brandon is a loser. He's always been a chinless loser. You see that limp wrist punch?"

"Yep . . . you need to get your shit together. You can't be getting into fights with everybody. You're 30 years old now, for Christ's sake."

"Yeah, whatever. He started it."

"I saw you start all the fights tonight. Man, you can't do that."

"Where are we going?"

"We're getting you back to your place."

"I have my car. . . ."

"You're not driving. We'll get you a cab."

David and I walked in silence, as we saw two boys in their late teens smoking. He stopped to bum a cigarette.

"How old are you guys?" David asked.

"19," one of them responded.

"Make sure you bang plenty of chicks. That's all they're good for anyway."

We continued on down the street until I could hail a cab. David asked me to get in too. I tried to say no, but he wouldn't let me leave. He insisted he drop me off, before he went back to his apartment. We got in the cab, and David directed it down Lafayette.

"Where do you live?" David asked me.

"Just drop me off near the park, and I'll walk the rest of the way."

"Let's just go all the way there."

"Fine."

I told the driver my address. David had the cab driver stop at a bank, so he could pull some money from the ATM. We continued across town to my place. I counted down the seconds until I would be free of him. I looked out the window at the emptied streets until we finally made it to the end of my street. We pulled over, and David handed over some cash. I got out of the cab, and he followed.

"What are you doing? Your cab is going away!" I said, frustrated.

"I lost my house key. I have to stay over."

"No!"

"Come on."

"What the fuck?"

"Am I supposed to sleep in the park?"

"All right then. . ."

I was livid. Never trust a junkie, I remembered from my D.A.R.E. days. I told him he had to be quiet. My brother was working early in the morning, and I didn't want to wake him. We went up a flight of stairs into my two-bedroom condo. We entered my room, and I began to put a pillow on the floor for him.

"What's this?" David asked.

"I'm setting up a space for you to sleep."

"Let me get into the bed with you."

"No."

"Why not? Are you gay?"

"No, but I don't want you in the bed with me."

"If you're not gay, then it doesn't matter."

"Listen, man, take it or leave it. You're not getting into the bed with me."

"Fine."

He made himself at home on the floor. I couldn't sleep that well. I also thought of the thousand dollars in cash in my sock drawer and prayed David wouldn't snoop around if I passed out before him. I finally got to sleep for a bit. David awoke at 5 a.m.

"All right, Dustin. Thanks, man. I'm heading out now…"

I pretended to sleep and heard him exit through the kitchen. I got up to make sure he was gone. I climbed back into bed and dreamt of blackness. I awoke to an empty apartment. My brother had taken off for work. I stood in my kitchen and futilely tried to forget the dismal night. The sun shined brightly, and I let it wash the sorrow from my worn body. I made a cup of tea and popped some bread into the toaster. I looked out the window and onto the garden below. I saw a squirrel skip through the tulips and onto an adjacent bush. It was a pretty town, at least.

…

I found my brothers: I was blessed to find a Brazilian Jiu-Jitsu gym near my place. I had gone without classes for months and was teaching a small group at a Crossfit gym but was getting bored and knew I wanted to learn more myself. I felt like I was halfway through a road trip: I needed to continue down the path that had been set out before me. I knew of this particular gym but wasn't sure about it. I had only really known my initial professor, and I had learned a lot from him. I was hoping to find the same camaraderie I had experienced at my old gym I finally scheduled a time to come in and met the head instructor in the parking lot. I was at ease. He had a calm energy and openness of spirit. I quietly hoped that this spot would indeed be my sanctuary, because going without Jiu-Jitsu was rotting me from the inside. When I joined the gym, it was like a heavy rain over browning crops. Things started coming back to life, and it was abundant and good.

The level there was impressive. The gym was filled with purple, brown, and black belts, but it wasn't an MMA gym. I had come from an MMA gym and was used to striking being a big part of the curriculum. This gym was centered on Gracie Brazilian Jiu-Jitsu. I was a decent grappler from my training in Brooklyn, where I had mainly trained no gi. I wasn't as proficient with my gi on. It slowed me down, so that I couldn't slip out of things. Once one of these big Massachusetts men caught me, it was over.

These guys were specialists in submission grappling. There weren't many distractions. God, family, and Brazilian Jiu-Jitsu reigned supreme in this land. I got choked out and ripped apart without mercy. In Brooklyn I was a bigger guy. Here I was a medium-sized guy. The uniform revealed some deeply held secrets. Early on, I kept getting caught in collar chokes, since these guys were masters at sneaking their worker hands into deadly positions. One moment I thought I was safe from the choke, and the next I thought my head was going to explode. I wasn't used to it and knew I had a lot to learn. The gi slowed things down, so technique became paramount. I couldn't pull off explosive escapes. I also wasn't as comfortable being on my back. If I got paired up with the big guys, I would be flattened out until submission. I had to go back to basics, work my shrimping and hip movement. Yes, school was back in session, and I was going to be a star pupil.

I went to the dads' class on Wednesday morning. I call it a dads' class because most of the men were fathers. The ones who weren't fathers were old enough to be. A lot of the guys were big, old-school Massachusetts men. They had Mass accents and worshipped all things Mass. They were blue-collar salt of the earth. I admired them.

It took a little time to be part of the crew. I had abandoned ship for about 12 years, but now I climbed aboard the U.S.S. Mass. Everyone here loathed folks from Marblehead. Headers, as we are called, are generally a rich and WASP-y bunch, but many Jews live there too. Some working-class folk, government housing folk, and a slowly changing racial demographic complete the town.

Mostly, though, people outside Marblehead had the wrong idea. Yes, some Headers are dicks. But I was not a dick—well, not a major dick. I hadn't known that Salem, Gloucester, Manchester by the Sea, and the other North Shore towns viewed Headers as dicks. I had to keep my origins under wraps at least for a bit. I would try to change my speech. I subtly dropped my *r*s and talked about my blue-collar work. I knew nothing of sports, so couldn't really proclaim my love for the New England Patriots.

One day, the guys started to ask about my past. Jack, the eldest, started the questioning. He reminded me of Batman from *Return of the Dark Knight*. A brute of a man, at 63 he wasn't slowing down. On the mat, he was impossible to move or to get to submit. He would have done well as a Roman soldier fighting on the front lines of Gaul.

"So, you lived in New York. Why did you move to Salem?" Jack asked in front of the other dads.

"Well, I grew up in the area."

"Oh, so you left for New York and then came back."

"Yeah, well, first I lived in Miami. Then I lived in New York. Then I came back."

"Oh, so you lived there. Now you're living here again. You were born in Salem?"

"No, not really. I was born in Philly. I grew up partly in LA and then mainly here."

"In Salem. . ."

"Not exactly. . ."

"Danvers, Swampscott, Beverly?"

". . . Marblehead."

"Ah, I see. You're a rich kid. I thought so. You talk funny."

"Yep, I'm a rich kid."

I was outed in front of the dads. It lingered there in silence. I would have to work doubly hard now to earn the respect of the old Mass men. I was up to the challenge, though, and knew I could ingratiate myself. I had crossed the racial, socio-economic line in Bed Stuy; I could certainly break down the Marblehead-Salem barrier. It took two weeks before they had all but forgotten about my association with Marblehead. I was accepted as one of the Salem guys.

It felt good. I had earned my place among them. I was still getting my ass kicked but was happy I was slowly improving. I took a few of the younger white belts under my wing. We didn't do too much standup work, including wrestling. Mainly, we kept the battle on the ground. I was a decent wrestler and was a good enough striker. I had even been part of an Ultimate Fighting Championship fight camp in Brooklyn. This responsibility pretty much boiled down to me getting smashed while trying not to tap too quickly. I passed on what I had learned to the new team. I called the young white belts the wolf pack. They were great students. They learned from everyone, happy to absorb all they could.

My old professor in Brooklyn had kept a strict distance. He did this to instill a sense of order, and it also aided in creating discipline. We weren't friends per se; ours was a classic master-student relationship. He was there to show me the skills and occasionally choke me out. Moving to a village from the big city is a strange switch—a new dynamic with no anonymity and no secrets. There is very little separation between a person and his business. Business in a village is very much about the personal connection. Here I befriended the black belt instructors—Danny, Keith, and Travis.

Maybe it was turning 30 or maybe it was just boredom, but I was craving competition. I had never earned a gold medal, and it irked me; I had always wanted it. I saw this as the best possible time to go for it. The bracket for my division thins out by 30, and I knew I had the drive.

I was afraid to fail at something I had given my all to, but I knew that I needed to do it. I needed to see if I could handle myself in a stressful situation. I wanted to prove I could keep my composure and let my skills dominate all the other competitors. I got online and entered the Grudge Grappling Tournament Boston 2017 event. Now I had to polish up my skills, lay off the booze and broads, and push my strength and conditioning. I had my sights set on victory. I would give it my all.

Danny, my black belt instructor, was excited for me. This wasn't a competition school. Danny was about the long game—teaching real skills and pushing self-defense, the original intention of Jiu-Jitsu. Jiu-Jitsu was designed for unarmed samurai. Punches and kicks didn't work well on the battlefield, and armor protected against strikes. Samurai needed to get past the armor in order to kill. Chokes and breaking of limbs were the way to destroy the enemy if they were unarmed. My skill set had grown dramatically under Danny, Keith, and Travis's tutelage.

I wasn't sure if that would translate to sport BJJ, but I was going to give it my best shot.

I forced myself into the abundance mindset. I was miserable at my job but wouldn't let myself wallow. I thought instead of the good points and kept positive. I had money coming in and was building a small fortune. I owned my condo and my car, had a nest egg, and was building it up. Most of my friends had zip, zilch, nada. The economy was a bust. College had ruined many of us in more than one way.

I was sticking to my path, though. I nurtured my positive attitude like a candle in a storm. Some of the bar folks would wear on me. They lived in a loser, alcoholic mindset, their minds softened by abuse of the brown juice. My job was more like being a daycare provider. I had to push through my mental malaise. I couldn't let them rule me. I would become the king, and I wouldn't stay in this role forever.

As the weeks passed by, I kept to my schedule of cartooning, grappling, slinging booze, and avoiding women. I wanted gold. There was no point in competing to try for the silver; I had one of those already. I was doing this for the gold.

I continued to get my ass kicked. Old man Jack beat me up during training sessions and then passed me over to Travis. Old-school punk Travis would crush me and then pass me to old teamster Lenny. Old teamster Lenny would twist me into a pretzel and then throw me over to caveman lawyer Louis. Caveman lawyer Louis would demolish me and then the bell would sound. I would pick up details from why I had gotten my ass kicked and then try to apply them to the next training session. The wolf pups worked hard too. They were competing in the white belt division. White belt fights are hard, because they don't know what prior experience the opponent has. They could have been high school wrestlers, which would make them dangerous adversaries. As you go up the ranks, everybody has seen it before. You adapt to the Judo guy, the wrestler and the footballer.

Only a couple of days were left before the tournament, and my nerves were up. I wanted to back out. The fear of the unknown was heavy. It gave me an appreciation for professional fighters, who live in that anxiety. This is their world; I was just visiting.

I was happy to be a tourist. It takes rare breeds to subject themselves to the world of combat sport. So many men think they are expert fighters, having never stepped foot into the ring. Men are just wired that way. I knew many of my old bar alcoholics who thought they were tough guys. You'd have to nod your head to placate them. I knew what it was to get punched in the face. I knew what it was to have a much smaller man choke me to near death. It's a sobering endeavor, an endeavor the non-sober couldn't truly grasp.

The night before the tournament was sleepless. I was drowning in thoughts of my demise. I listened to the wind whiz by the bare trees. I thought about my motivation and wondered why I had decided to do this. I had to remind myself that I had no choice. I needed to see this through. It wasn't as scary as an MMA fight, but I had not competed in years. I wasn't used to the nerves. My folks were going to be there and my brother too. Two of my black belt coaches would be in my corner, and the wolf pups would join me in the battle.

I awoke early in the morning. I ate some oatmeal and had some tea. I practiced my Wim Hof breathing and took a shower. I got in my car and ventured out towards Quincy, an hour drive. I had the radio on but couldn't focus on what was playing. I drove and focused on my breath. I checked in with my body. I was rested; I had gone easy for a week; my muscles felt fresh; I had no injuries. I put gold in my mind and pushed the negative thoughts aside.

I approached the school where the event was being held. There was seemingly no parking. I looked down the road and saw a kid approaching. I opened my window, and the cold air hit me instantly.

"Hey, brother. Where did you find parking?" I asked him. I could tell he was a competitor. Who else would be out on this day?

"There's parking back down that street."

"Damn, I hope I find a spot. I got to weigh in!"

"The fight begins now, man. Spots are hard to come by."

"All right, thanks."

I drove around. I cut back closer to the school, and then down a side street. I found a spot behind a tree and parked. It was terribly cold. I practiced my Wim Hof breaths again as I made my way down the block and into the gymnasium. I already saw the other warriors moving along the same path. I entered the gym and checked in with the makeshift front desk. I gave them my name. They marked my hand with a Sharpie, and I entered into the main hall. Fights had already started. My eyes darted around, taking in the whole scene. The center of the gym had mats laid out. Men of all shapes and sizes were running around in Japanese gis, some in rash guards and shorts. I saw a few female competitors and some children competing. I saw a wave of bodies colliding into each other and crashing like ocean hitting rocky shore. My heart began to race. I looked around, trying to spot my opponents. I couldn't tell who they might be.

I went over to the far-left corner of the room and weighed in. I stepped on the scale; I was in the middle of my weight bracket at 180. I felt good there. I waited for my call time. I went over to the right side of the gymnasium and sat on the bleachers. I pulled food out from the bag I had put together early in the morning—a peanut butter and jelly sandwich, banana, and plum. I had a water bottle with me but decided not to drink. I had an urge to pee that I knew was just from nerves. I ate and looked out onto the mats. I saw the fury of combat. It wasn't like sparring—the ferocity was something I wasn't used to. Normally, there is more give and take. These matches were all for the taking. Everyone here was hoping for a gold medal. They wanted victory. I wanted victory as well and went back to visualizing that. I was alone there on the bleachers. The sounds of yelling, bodies being beaten into the mat, and bells sounding off muted my internal monologue. I sat transfixed by the fights.

Keith and Travis arrived and walked over to me. I felt relief. I had two black belts with me; I was no longer alone. They got my mind away from the tournament. We chatted about girls and how lousy the weather was. The time was approaching for me to battle. I looked at my watch and knew my call time was coming up.

My parents and brother showed up. I felt more dread now. I didn't want to lose immediately in front of them. This added even more pressure on me. I needed to get my head on straight and remove them from my moment. This was about my mind, my body, and me. My mom, dad, and brother took a seat on the bleachers, and I excused myself to change into my gi. I went downstairs into the basement with my bag where was a line for the bathroom. Everybody was changing into their uniforms and tying their belts. The energy was palpable. The deepest parts of our reptilian brains were awakening, and we were reborn as primal beasts.

I gathered my gear and pulled myself together. I looked myself over in the bathroom mirror. I rinsed my hands in the sink and splashed water on my face. I looked deep into myself and knew I was here for a reason. I would give it all of my focus. Nothing would prevent me from being in the moment. Fear needed to take a back seat. I couldn't falter at this final moment.

I walked back upstairs to the gymnasium and went off to a corner. A few other competitors were going about their warm-ups. I stretched out and practiced my sprawls. I held a handstand, then took thirty Wim Hof breaths. I cleared my mind of thought for a moment. My body felt strong. I had timed my training regime perfectly: I had built up strength but had enough time to heal and be perfectly ready. I knew where I was strong and where I was weak. The speakers called out my name along with five other competitors. My nerves began to act up; I calmed myself.

I stood in the gated-off section with the other guys. Middleweight, lightweight, and heavyweight purple belts were grouped together. The fights were divvied up, going back and forth between the weight classes. My heart began to race again. I looked over to my black belts, Keith and Travis. They nodded to me. I practiced my breathing. Suddenly, my name was called, and it was go time. I walked onto the mat. My opponent looked tough. He had a buzzed head and visible tattoos. I knew he must have been feeling a similar anxiety. He wouldn't look me in the eye. The ref had us shake, and the bell sounded.

He walked up to me and grabbed hold of my collar. I matched his grips. We circled around, still locked onto each other. I could feel his anxiety. He realized that he wasn't going to be able to goon me and use his strength to dominate the match. I wanted to take him down. I began to test him and grab at his front leg. He cut his losses and pulled guard. He landed on his back with his legs catching my thighs. I was still standing. I wouldn't let him get the sweep.

I pushed my knee behind his and stuffed his hip movement. I got to side control, secured the position and was up in points. He was active on the bottom and kept moving around. It was like wrestling a wet fish; I couldn't keep him in a spot for too long. I looked up at the clock and knew if I prevented sweeps I would win. I wanted to dominate the whole match, and end it with a submission, but I knew not to get greedy. I wanted to go to my basics—position before submission. I didn't feel his submission game was strong, but I wouldn't get too confident. I tried to pry his arm away, so I could tap him. He rolled around frantically. I couldn't secure the position long enough to set up my grips on his arm. I stayed on top for the duration of the match, periodically looking at the clock. It sounded. The ref held my hand up, and I looked over at my mom. She was proud. She didn't understand the sport but understood what my hand raised up meant.

I watched another middleweight match commence. The first guy who stepped out onto the mat was older; he must have been at the top of the age cutoff. He looked strong. He had a face like stone and a gray crew cut. He went against a younger guy, who looked like a wrestler. The older man muscled the younger guy. I paid attention. He was strong. I knew if I went up against him, it was going to be difficult but not impossible. Keith pulled me aside and told me not to fight this guy like a bull but like a bullfighter. I knew what he meant, as I watched this older man demolish his opponent. There was skill involved, but it seemed like he had overwhelming physical prowess. He won the match, and two lightweights went on to fight their match.

I looked at the timer and practiced my breathing. A couple of matches ensued before I was called back up. I was paired with the wrestler, who wouldn't look me in the eye. I realized I wasn't as nervous as I had been at first. The mere realization that everyone had nerves relaxed me. I wasn't unusual. I felt like I was actually ahead, because I chose to look my opponent in the eye. The ref had us shake, and the bell sounded. He got low to the ground and extended his right hand to my forehead. I was grateful for the notice. He told me with his posture that he was a wrestler. I knew I couldn't shoot on someone that low, but my sprawl was solid. He swiped at my forehead again. He then took a crisp, clean, shot at my legs. I sprawled. He had my left ankle. My arms were around his waist, and my chest was heavy on his back. I popped my leg out from his grip and spun around. I got my legs wrapped around his legs and pushed his thighs away from his body. It flattened him out.

I looked at the timer. I was ahead on points but still had time to go. I had a shot of submitting him, so I took it. I took my right hand up toward his neck. I grabbed his collar and leaned to my left side. It was enough pressure to get a blood choke. He tapped. I had won my second match. Only the old man now stood in the way of a gold medal, and I wouldn't let him stop me. This medal was for me. This was my purpose.

Keith and Travis prepared me again and reminded me not to fight the last opponent with strength: to be a bullfighter, not a bull. It was 20 minutes until my last match, and I was getting antsy. He wouldn't look over at me. I observed his posture, and he seemed perfectly at ease. What did he know that I didn't?

They finally called us up. He looked me in the eye. The ref had us shake, and the bell sounded. He grabbed for my collar. I matched, but I was overpowered. I lacked the knowledge of how to disengage. It felt like a battle between Superman and Doomsday. We moved around the mat. My body was beginning to break. I got to my knees, still locked in a battle of grips. I let go with my right hand to swipe at his leg. He moved back, and I got back to standing. I half-heartedly tried to move in with a judo sweep. He blocked it.

He threw his hips in, trying to sweep me. I leapt over his leg to regain the standstill. I looked over at the clock and saw we were half way through the match, and I was stuck. I couldn't risk a shot and have him stuff it. I couldn't goon him either; he was too strong. His hands felt like vise grips; I couldn't break them. His belt came off during our circling, so the ref pulled him off of me to retie it, and I had a moment to regain my breath. I looked over at Keith and Travis, who again reminded me that I needed to be the bullfighter. We began the match again. He came at me, and I wouldn't engage in grips. I wouldn't play that game. I batted his hand out of the way and saw that he was more conservative in his movements.

I began my movement. I started faking high-low to put him on the defensive. He began to move back, so I waited for him to take a step back in and then shot for the single leg. He spun around to try to leap out, but I held on with everything I had. He tripped and landed with his arms extended and hips ups in the air. I had this chance to finish the take down. I knew, judging by time, that this would be my shot to secure gold. I dropped to my knee on his left side and hoisted him to his back. I pushed through his shrimping and defense to secure side control.

I was up on points for takedown and securing position. I just needed to prevent any kind of submission. I stayed on top, and he was able to get me in his guard. The bell sounded. The match ended. My day of battle was over. The ref called it and stood us back up. My arm was raised for all to see. I was the victor. It had taken everything I had, and then some. My opponent patted me on the back. Our personal war was over, and now we were gentlemen again. The veil of civilization blanketed us, and it was a warm feeling.

We walked over to the far side of the room and stood on the three-tier podium. I climbed up to the top tier, a place I had never been before. It was a dream I had had forever, me with the gold medal around my neck, standing tall for all to see. My competitors were gentlemen and warriors, and I felt a deep kinship with them. I knew what it took to get here. I knew that they wanted it just as bad.

We stood together and shared this awesome moment. We put the immediate past behind us to exchange compliments and good wishes with sincerity. I changed out of my uniform and stuffed my medal into my bag. I stayed to watch my young teammates competing in their white belt matches. I saw them fight valiantly. I looked upon them and marveled at their determination. I, too, was once a white belt. I became reflective. It seemed like forever ago that I had been there.

I had been away from New York for less than a year, but it felt like ages had passed. I was once a kid in his early twenties, and now I was 30. Where had all of the time gone? I watched as Kyle battled his opponent to the ground; he was just beginning his journey. I had ended mine, only to begin a new one.

I had journeyed through the concrete jungle. I had battled through the hardships of adulthood. I had grappled with inner demons and shameful acts. I had fought hard and lived to see another day. The bell had just sounded the end of the fight, and now a bell sounded for the new one ahead. I buried the boy I was in Brooklyn and emerged as the man I saw in the mirror. I was confronted with the present, peering into the future There would be countless battles yet to come, whether I wanted to fight them or not. You have to fight; at least I learned that much.

It was calm and quiet. In that moment I realized that it was over. Yes, I lived in the void, and I confronted the unknown. There was nothing else to do but to say "hello" to the present and stand before it with humility. So, I said, "Goodbye, New York City. It was a pleasure knowing you."

Zach Danesh was born in 1986 in Philadelphia, Pennsylvania. He grew up in Los Angeles until age six and then he and his family moved to a small town north of Boston. He studied art at New World School of the Arts in Miami, receiving his BFA through University of Florida with a major in printmaking and minor in art history. Upon graduation, he moved to New York City, enrolling at the School of Visual Arts' Continuing Education program with a focus in animation. He currently lives and works on the North Shore of Massachusetts.

photo by Max Danesh

Printed in the United States
By Bookmasters